AD VANCE PRAISE FOR *NOTHING THAT IS OURS*

"In his visionary and completely original debut, D.J. Palladino shows us how the California of Raymond Chandler turned into the land of Huxley and Pynchon and blew the mind (while transforming the consciousness) of the world as a whole. This is a light-filled, haunting, entirely essential work whose afterglow grows steadily more and more intense."

—**Pico Iyer**, *author of Video Night in Kathmandu and The Lady and the Monk*

"*Nothing That Is Ours* is vivid, rich, and poignant. D.J. Palladino's novel is full of heartbreak and insight, a noirish glimpse into the Santa Barbara of the fifties. Unforgettable."

—**Meg Gardiner**, *Edgar Award–winning author of China Lake and The Memory Collector*

"D.J. Palladino has crafted an impressive debut novel that's a real page-turner. Gripping and atmospheric; part noir, part mystery, all engrossing. It's a fascinating read that leaves you wanting more."

—**Tab Hunter**, *actor in Damn Yankees, The Pleasure of His Company, and Ride the Wild Surf*

"Move aside Carey McWilliams and Nathanael West. D.J. Palladino fuses luridly delicious details of neo-revisionist California history with the narrative flow one might expect if Raymond Chandler ever bumped into Thomas Pynchon at a drunken party. In the process, Palladino manages to save Santa Barbara from the burden of its obviousness, giving readers a rare glimpse of the town—during the late 1950s—when it was just becoming what it eventually would be."

—**Nick Welsh**, *senior news editor, Santa Barbara Independent*

NOTHING THAT IS OURS

D. J. PALLADINO

*For Shery Denbo
In hopes it takes
you on a strange trip
through old Santa
Barbara.
With best wishes*

Asahina & Wallace
Los Angeles
2016

D J Pallad

10/18

Copyright © 2016 by David John Palladino

Published in the United States by Asahina & Wallace, Inc.

(www.ashainaandwallace.com)

ISBN: 978-1-940412-20-7

Library of Congress Control Number: 2016941817

There is no absolute up or down, as Aristotle taught; no absolute position in space; but the position of a body is relative to that of other bodies. Everywhere there is incessant relative change throughout the universe and the observer is always at the center of things.

—Giordano Bruno, from *De la causa principio et uno*, 1584

Chapter 1

YOU LIVE HERE NOW. Call it home. Times, tides, and straying roads have brought you back. Maybe not by choice, and likely not for long, but isn't it pretty just the same? A quaint little beach town often shrouded in fog, though vibrant when the sun burns through, wedged between foothills and breakers. It's a rich man's playground but mild and kind to the poor as well. History makes itself at home here too. There are painted caves of tribal art, a colonial mission fastidiously rebuilt after a terrible earthquake, a Mission Revival movie palace, and an aged and massive Moreton Bay fig tree near the old depot. A mosaic mural on the downtown grocery store chronicles the eras passing from earthbound Indians to future folk heading out into the cosmos. You live somewhere in between. You come down Castillo Street past Victorians and lath-and-plaster bungalows, drawn by death and water. The road is hilled, uneven, and guttered, lined with oak and then eucalyptus and then palms as you near the highway and the ghost of the old highway. After the park and public pool comes this water. The kids out playing on the beach there are the last of the long California season, warm days spilling into the still warm winter but today the weather seems ready to turn. The children have slung down an inverted metal bucket full of wet sand. They pull away the pail, leaving its contents behind. The column of sand, its form rounded by time and ordinary erosion, stands in the zone between the ocean proper and where the edge of strand lays as yet untouched by foam. The air is sullen and the children crane their heads to see their parents, chatting and smoking up on the rocks, suddenly erupt into waves of laughter. Then the cold water rushes in unexpectedly with its acrid salt smell, and the children run screaming as their little monument melts into the sea.

I hurried by barely noticing, the short hike to the breakwater wall still ahead. By the time I got there, the fog was draining away slowly like needles and pins fading from a sleeping limb awakened, and the poor sap had been dead at least three hours. As I entered, with the dusk scrawling overhead, a squadron of ants crawled over a flailing hermit crab. Tiny, flat leaves of seaweed stuck to the dead man's open mouth like waste paper. The crescents of green and maroon on his blue lips stood stark against the off-white cement where he lay, drawn up from rust-colored rocks piled against the seawall. All his life's stories lost, leaving only the descriptions of his settings behind, soon to follow on an outward tide.

Some guy from the *News-Suppress* was already snapping photos with what looked like a giant Brownie. I only went down to the break-water because I had been listening to the police channel on my big wooden Silvertone back home and knew that 10-32 meant a possible drowning; and I only got inside the crime scene because some cop who knew my dad remembered I was indeed a stringer for the big city paper south. Many of Santa Barbara's finest loitered on the seawall that dreary evening. They didn't know nothing, they all said.

The person unknown was apparently shot once in each hand and foot and once in the side with a small-caliber weapon: five wounds. But there wasn't any blood to speak of, or bullets, so maybe the harbor patrol guy wasn't negligent, or drunk on the job, when he called it in as a drowning, as June suggested later that night. That is to say, maybe the harbor guy didn't hear any gunshots because the dead man was killed somewhere else and brought here to make some kind of point. Which is what I heard somebody suggest as I walked up. A meaningful death, the young detective who sometimes had a drink with me at Jimmy's mumbled. The other fellas looked askance at him and right through me.

"Is that the theory you are working with?" I asked the one cop who looked like he knew what was going to happen next, like he might be the chief. He also couldn't see or hear me.

"This guy's from the *Los Angeles Times*," said my erstwhile drinking buddy, and for some reason that straightened a lot of posture.

"It's much too early for a theory," said the detective. "We don't even have a name for the deceased. Nothing in his pockets. Maybe it was just a bizarre robbery. Though the lack of blood is puzzling." Suddenly the blank-eyed guy can't shut up. He gave me his name and rank very clearly too. I flapped my notebook closed and stared out at the iron-blue ocean under what light remained in the mists.

I wasn't shocked. Perhaps because I never saw the whole body, and the face for only a second—or was it described to me? The body had been pulled onto the breakwater sidewalk, covered with what looked like a sailboat canvas. The lieutenant kept flipping over corners deftly revealing particulars but never the whole. I never saw the whole man, nor his whole death, never lost any sleep, at least at first. I remember the sleek body solely as an object of meaning, a gray thing engendered by the overcast skies. I thought about a seal breathing air but living in the ocean, or maybe I heard one bark and sing from the nearby buoys. Days later Gin Chow said it felt like a Tong murder, maybe the Elementals gang, but then he never believed in chance or accidents. Things happen for reasons here.

I wandered back alone through rich seaside smells—greasy distant

foods, fermenting nearby kelp, and the salt-heavy air off roaring winter waves drifting our way. And I made my way back to the cordon line
after speaking to a few police and what passed for a forensic scientist
chewing down a butt of old cigar, laughing and whatnot in the face of
finality. He told me the guy was dead, in his regarded opinion.

Back where the breakwater sidewalk meets the harbor parking lot
was a fat policeman I also knew from around town standing with a
group of gawkers. He had one of those old double-breasted coats the
cops used to wear and it looked good on him. His name was Dooley, I
recalled from my father's stale quips, a duly sworn officer of the law.
Anyway he had both hands up in the air like a football ref declaring a
touchdown.

"This is exactly where it used to be. Two stories high," he said,
then spread his arms out to describe a mass. "And think of it, so huge.
Tourists came in their flivvers just to see the plinth, the megalith that
stood right here, until the city said, let's get rid of it and build our-
selves a harbor. They blew it to bits thirty years ago. But maybe it left
its spirit behind; maybe we can still sense its atoms and molecules
floating through the air, even today, year of Our Lord 1958, almost
1959. You had to see it. It was so beautiful."

The others laughed as if mocking some stumblebum, but he wasn't
drunk. "You mean Castle Rock, don't you, friend?" I asked out of the
night and into his reverie.

He smiled as he closed his eyes and turned around, his arms still
stretching straight out but then slowly coming up to mime the natural
wonder that was gone. "Indeed I do," he said, popping open his eyes.
The others laughed and one made a screwball sign with index finger around an ear; crossed his eyes and stuck out his tongue. Dooley
flipped them all off in a beautiful sweeping counter-spin. "But you're
too young to remember when they tore it down just to shelter some

rich man's boat," he said, addressing me.

"Maybe, sort of, but my uncle Frankie used to tell me about it all the time. He wrote the poem about it."

"Frankie? As in Francis? Of course, Francis Dal Bello, of the tire fortune," laughed the policeman, referring to mine nuncle's former store. Firestone tires on the corner of some street and another way downtown near the wharf. "He wrote that poem made it in the news-paper and all the teachers, the nuns, used to read it to us, nuh?"

I smiled. I liked that poem and I liked my uncle Frankie. He was one reason I moved back up here after college, besides escaping awful L.A. smog. Besides all the other stuff I don't discuss.

"He dreamed there was a real castle on Castle Rock, alive to the fairy world," said my smiling policeman.

This drew a resolute hoot from his blue-clad comrades. "Well, why not. I wouldn't say this world we know is always so great," he said.

"Like what happened to that guy on the breakwater," I said.

"Oh no," he said, "I know your wily reporter ways. I'm not sayin' nothin' about Snake Jake's final resting place or the curious way he was drummed out of the brotherhood, neither," said the big policeman, thus obliging me twice.

"You're a solid example of police discretion," I said.

"That I am," he said, returning to his dance with the invisible past.

Chapter 2

MY PACKARD WAS IN the shop, la-la-lee-lee, the same old song. I crossed the misty side of Cabrillo to Sunseri's to eat a burger, but nobody was there. I needed company, I guess. So I took the stinky number three bus up to Jimmy's Oriental Gardens where I could get a drink and maybe ask around and make some sense of my little clues and cop slippages. And, oh yes, eventually file. By phone. From the booth where I used to call June and talk for drunken hours. Then I might even find a ride home sometime before the world ended.

I found the man I wanted. Fortunately he was ensconced in a booth across from a woman I wanted too. The steamy heat of the bar mixed with chop suey smells and lots of tobacco hit my face and glazed the old specs. The laughter was plummy and thick too.

A lot of greetings and all returned. "Mister Newton Knowsitall, I presume." Newt did not look happy to see me, though sweet Mary Annie did; she slid her warm self over and bade me join the party. Again, Newt looked slightly sore.

"And to what glorious twist of fate do we owe thanks for your company, Mr. Trevor Gindrinker?" he asked.

This stupid name game started at UCLA where Newt and I served baccalaureate time in lit classes enhanced on many an evening with heated discussions of applied Eros at the Westwood Rathskellar. Against the grain, I had traveled south to go to college, (considered déclassé back then), arriving in Los Angeles in the midst of the Hollywood wave of Red Scare and the annunciation of American poets. Eliot and Pound ruled the classes I took, and every discussion seemed to end on a couch or a silly golden bough; you were either Freudian or a member of the Golden Dawn. I went to classes riding on my wunderkind celebrity, which broke apart when called upon in class to perform profound. I read *Four Quartets* for a week on visits to the beach, days ending with my eyes twitching black colors at the horizon from the glare and nights lulled by hallucinations of breaking waves. I read Eliot, but I dreamed like a Time Machine, of Baker Street and Mysterious Islands.

One day a TV executive asked me out to lunch; he had vaguely promised a writing job, based on my infamous oeuvre, but it turned out over consommé at Musso and Frank that he and his station wanted me to invest in a new underwater ride beneath the pier at Pacific Ocean Park and a smaller version of the same idea in Santa Barbara: the Undersea Gardens, they called it. He didn't want the writer to write; he wanted my ridiculous bank account, and the name below the title, my name—the one Hollywood helped make so preposterously large.

On another day at the watery terminus of Wilshire Boulevard, though, I stood up on a hillock of sand and saw something hump out of the water and suddenly everything made immense and perfect sense, a six-dimensioned ghost geometry you completely know as one knows things when beginning to doze, lost abruptly when jerked awake. I lost it; it's gone, traceless. I was near tears for a month. I'm still waiting for it to return.

"You hear about the dead guy in the harbor?" I asked Newton, calm.

"No. Yes. No. I don't know his name."

"Cop let it slip it was some fella name of Snake Jake."

"You guys are so sweet," said Mary Annie.

"Thanks," Newt said. "And thanks to you for the news. He owed me money."

"Okay, then, that's why I killed him, Newt Coverspread," I said, warming to my old classmate who was known to make book even in college dorms. "So who is this Snake Jake?" I asked. "And from which brotherhood would he be curiously drummed out? Cop said, and I quote, 'He was curiously drummed out of the brotherhood.'"

"His name is Jacques: as in, our famously exotic State Street Santa Barbara Continental Restaurant."

"Oh, I like snails," said pert Mary Annie, regarding her crimson nails.

"That's *his* crappy food?"

"He doesn't own it anymore. The partners bought him out months ago. As to any brotherhood, he wasn't a cop. I'll guess Knights of Columbus, or an Elk, but who isn't? Or maybe he was a naked communist."

"Or a Mousketeer," said *la femme* in a fake innocent falsetto.

"Hey, did someone say he was crucified?" asked Newt, reaching for his bucket drink of booze with clinking ice. "Your photographer said 'harbor guy crucified.' It all makes a kind of eerie sense, K of C on a cross, Christ on a crutch."

"We didn't send any photographer. The local paper had a guy out there."

"Well, he knew you were there, this guy I had words with."

"Impossible," I said. "But you're sure about this Jacques? Whose last name is … ?"

"Brown."

"Oh, one of the Brown boys, then. Oh, okay, then."

"No, I'm not bullshitting, pardon the French." He chuckled miserably. "I mean it. Jacques Brown, though his father's name was probably

Bruno something and his mother's most likely Day-Lah-Kwah."

"I still like snails," Mary Annie said, "but frogs' legs will do."

"If he keeps ignoring you like this, I'll take you out for all the French food you can eat," I said. "You want a drink?"

She shook her head and pointed to her dainty gimlet. "Besides," she added, "we ought not be celebrating. Jacques Brown's body lies a-rotting in the morgue."

Even tough guy Newt gave a grimace. I thought about forever gone in a split-second, the Red Sea closes in on Pharaoh and his men. At least she didn't ask about my girlfriend this time. She usually does.

Sun Lee the bartender appeared at the table. "You want a Pabst or a Schlitz this time, big spender?" said Newt.

I said yes. "The Schlitz in a long-necked bottle is creamy and delicious."

"You see, darling?" said Newt. "Beer on a champagne budget."

"Lee, this is the first time I've ever seen you this side of the bar," I said. "I always just imagined your legs."

"Pretty shapely, huh?" he said looking down and laughing that nicotine-stained cackle he patented. "I came out to tell you that Gin Chow was in here looking for you," he whispered without moving his lips. He smiled and winked.

"Gin Chow was in here?" I mouthed, incredulous.

"Yeah," he said, then aloud, "what's wrong with that, you think this place not nice enough? I'll go tell Jimmy you think so highly of him."

I said out loud too, "I love this dim room. And I'd love a Schlitz." I thought, I've just never imagined Gin Chow this far from places where I usually see him.

"You mean Ching Chong Chinatown," said Lee, returning to psychic communication as he stalked lightly back to the bar.

Newt smirked though Mary Annie looked puzzled. I was busy

jotting in my notebook. I had enough to call. "I've gotta file," I said. "And you're sure about Jacques Brown?"

"I'm sure he's the only guy around town named Snake Jake. Why he is named like this I think has nothing to do with herpetology. But that falls under a broader category of speculation," he said, smiling. "Happy New Year, by the way. And all that muttering to yourself cannot be healthy."

"Well thanks anyway. I mean thanks a lot." I nodded to Mary Annie who was distracted signaling Sun Lee over her pretty shoulder.

The phone booth was outside near the dreary parking lot, around the corner from the Art Deco pseudo-Oriental neon, which was glowing in the cold fog like a dream in a movie. I put a nickel in; the receiver felt like it was made of cold, hard lead, one of the old phones built for distance over time. The operator let me reverse the charges. Editor G. Gawkhaven Dooley picked it up and made some gruff noise. "What do you got?" he asked.

I gave him a general idea, which he said sounds intriguing without much conviction but transferred me over to Rewrite, a guy named Gus Grass, who also told me to give. Instead I launched.

"Santa Barbara. Police here are puzzled by the body of a man found late Thursday afternoon on the breakwater rocks near the pleasure boat harbor. The unidentified victim had been shot in both hands and feet and once in the side. Lieutenant Skip Handy admitted that the corpse provided more mysteries than clues, particularly since a lack of blood at the scene suggested that the victim had been murdered elsewhere. 'It's much too early for a theory,' said Handy when questioned about what appeared to be a ritualistic arrangement of the wounds. Harbor authorities said they had heard no shots.

"Sources close to the police claimed that the victim was widely known as 'Snake Jake' but either could not or would not elaborate further on his identity, beyond the suggestion that he was familiar in Santa Barbara restaurant circles.

"'We will take this challenge seriously,' said Lieutenant Handy, former head of the team assigned to investigate delinquent Mexican and Anglo gangs that, police believe, are responsible for narcotic sales in pinball and pool parlors lining the lower end of the city's main thoroughfare, State Street, below Highway 101. South Coast authorities claim such gang activity has spread to Santa Barbara from the Los Angeles area.

"'This is an unusual murder, though I do not want to speculate on any significance behind its admittedly bizarre circumstances. We will find the guilty party without doubt or delay,' Handy added."

"That's pretty good stuff, he's cute. Don't know if the Snake Jake or pachuco stuff will stay in though," said Grass.

"Well don't *you* take it out," I said, then yelped. A face pushed up against the glass, a beautiful face. "Jesus, June," I said.

"What?" asked Grass.

"Nothing, there's a woman trying to get into the booth with me," I answered. There was a cool smile on her face. She turned around like a dancer and ended her spin looking directly in the phone booth door, which she opened to the cold air.

"God, you reporters have all the luck," said Grass.

"Don't bet on it," says I, hanging up.

"That's not writing," she said, the lost dream of my life. She had a big scarf, more like a cowl, wrapped around her hair, hair that filled the tiny booth with a lush fragrance. And thus lush memories. She smiled as if she was seeing into them.

"I make money at it, and I'm rarely bored," I said in a low voice.

"You're wasting your talents, my darling friend, and you know it. You have so many."

"According to you. What are you doing here?"

"Oh, I'm out on a date, but *I'm* bored. It is New Year's, or almost. What did you do this night last year?" she asked, as if she cared. Maybe she did not, but I know she remembered. I saw the bedroom and the empty bottles and her scarf smelling of her and her perfume. In my mind's eye. And now she knew what I was remembering.

"Bored? Even with him?" I changed the subject away from all that pain.

"What's the story about?" she asked, re-changing the subject and standing too close to me. Her gloved hand ran over the edge of the black telephone.

I told her the gist of it.

"What do we even have a harbor patrol for, if they don't respond to gunshots?" she muttered.

"I said, *even with him*?" I said.

"Yeah, even with the son of the Italian businessman and liquor distributor," she sighed. "He's right there, want to wave?"

She backed out of the booth and her furred shoulders were momentarily silhouetted in bright Chrysler Town Car headlamps. He was standing tall by the door in a sharp-brimmed hat in the pool of dark behind the auto lights. I waved; he waved a gloved hand back. It wasn't much. We knew each other from Our Lady of Sorrows. I used to like him, though I was as fearful of his family's mythology as everyone else was, gleefully assuming the worst. Nobody I know ever witnessed any overt criminality. Of course, that just fueled the whisperings.

"Go home and write something good," she said. "Like you did when you were fourteen. Tell me again, was I your Muse?"

"Was," I said.

Alone, I caught a ride up to Mitch and Castillo from the older Echeverria brother, who seemed more than a little bit lit; I think he stayed on the road by closing one eye. I thanked him profusely and walked three blocks from Micheltorena to Islay, safe blocks not in a drunk-driver's car, to my digs. My place was new and had streamlined sconces, like it was going to take off into outer space with Buck and Flash. Crash Corrigan's Undersea Kingdom. I had a bathtub and stove and a bed. I'd glugged down my Schlitz before I left and the glow was nestled now around my nerves. I couldn't stop thinking about Mary Annie. Home: a brand new television, a Philco, my Christmas present to me, its big cardboard box still in the corner of the room. I turned it on. My apartment came with a working antenna so I got three channels, sometimes five. Click and the window unto the darkness fills with black-and-white images. I looked nervously at the typewriter, the old Underwood with its frowsy ribbon hanging. I used to like the radio shows, but now they're on TV: *Amos 'n' Andy* and *Dragnet* and I liked the way George watches Gracie from his study on his television and I liked boxing; all on TV. The talk shows I watched late at June's one lovely sinful night. Click, and there's no end of the road—your black-reflected living room emptying into *their* rooms, mirror worlds, you see yourself black-and-white on the dead screen, turn it on to quips and thoughts transmitted by a wave, electronic telepathy. TVSP. I wonder if its episodes will change the way we dream. Click. Don't touch that dial, we'll be right back. Say the Magic Word and Mission Pack is on its Merry Way.

The holiday season was waning away from us. Christmas soon would be New Year's Eve, that night when everybody got kissing drunk and then cried on each other's shoulders. I never understood the artificiality of it—the year ends and there's a boozy inventory due that finds each life wanting. Personally, I never really understood people celebrating change.

Chapter 3

This old man told him they would meet at the bean field up by the Navy dump. It once had stored waiting equipment, the remnants of a war never joined. They also serve who only sit and rot. The grass weeds grew in between the diamond patterns of the link fence. The young man got there as the sun was just coloring the eastern sky over the mountains, a parfait of sickly yellows reaching up into the midnight blue.

He was on time but the old man said he'd been waiting there for eons. The young man asked what was going down, what was happening. The old man always laughed at American slang, as if he were hearing weird music for the first time, with fresh ears, repeating it the way you might mouth the lines of a tricky melodic phrase.

The old man had a gunnysack and a bucket, and made the young man carry both as they slid and crawled down the sea cliff where there was a rough-blazed path, changed by every person who used it. That is the science of erosion.

On the wide, empty beach at low tide they walked below cliffs and away from town. The old man began describing Tide Pool Johnnies, eyeless fish that lived under the underwater rocks. The fish had de-evolved, moved backwards from what one might call progress, he said. Their once-functioning orbs had become useless bumps grown over—scales had not fallen from their eyes, the old man laughed. A soothsayer, he was well versed in natural selection. But this, he said, was the science of natural deselection.

The young man asked him what he knew about Darwin. The old man said they'd met. One never knew when he was kidding. Darwin's error lay in maintaining a one-sided paradigm, said the old man. The great theory of natural selection is far too limited compared to the interactive process that actually fills nature with life. In a mirror world, the animal selects the environment as nature returns the favor. I'm a part of it's a part of me, he hummed. When the young man asked if that was an ancient proverb the old man laughed and said it would be a popular song in the future, like "How Much Is That Doggie in the Window?" though not as cute.

Then the old man said: I have no explanation for seahorses though. Do you? They seem like pure poetry, whatever that is.

The two men came to a wide cove below the Meigs's grove of eucalyptus trees.

I like seahorses, the old man said. I wish we had them here. He started poking through a tide pool, overturning rocks and touching florid anemones with a stick he found, giggling when they contracted. He grabbed a limpet quickly off a rock and then scooped its flesh out of the shell and popped the shellfish flesh into his mouth and said yum, watching the young man for a reaction.

When he tried to take a limpet it stuck like cement. His friend laughed triumphantly.

Out of the cold pool the old man pulled an octopus curling about in slow motion. Ah, yes, he said, and reached deeper into the pool as if into the womb of ocean itself, delivering up a blue-gray black fish swimming in the cold brine cupped in his hands. See? He asked. And then grinning, he put the fish into a metal pail. It's too small to eat, he said. He pointed at its eyes. Tide Pool Johnnie, he said.

He had been looking at the sun and holding up a finger, the way an artist measures a distant object with his thumbs. What are we doing out here? asked the young man.

Wait and see, the old man said, stooping over a stand of eelgrass.

Then suddenly he stood straight. Out of his big bag he pulled a flute made from those worm shells you see on the beach, white like perfect cigar ash. He blew into it. The young man felt a strange tickle on the back of his neck. The old man pointed beyond the tide pool, where suddenly the rocks and flat places formed into a stepping-stone trail out and over the flat sea. The angle of the sun made silver contrasts between the ocean and the stones. There was a clear path now between small lapping waves.

The two men walked out, but about halfway the young man hesitated and tried to turn back. The old man pushed him from behind, and he started forward again. When he got to the large final step he stopped to let the old man take the lead.

What is it? The young man asked, as they stood crowded together on the last flat rock. The old man gestured down and his companion could see there was something hovering just below the water's surface in front of them. He put his white whistle up to his thin lips and blew. The thing lurched up out of the waters. The young man almost fell over but the old man grabbed him by his madras shirt and steadied him.

A globed steel-and-glass vehicle bobbed to the surface with water running off in cold rivulets. A hatch near the craft's roof flapped open, air expressed out. Two empty seats beckoned. A trapdoor, the young man thought, conveyance into unknown space.

Chapter 4

AFTER JUNE I CAN'T think straight, and even in my dreams I sail through choppy waters. Maybe … maybe I need to leave this town before I'm pulled into some slough of despond forever. Sometimes I have to remind myself I came back here, after all the calamities befell, for what the GIs call rest and recuperation. It's not like I didn't know she would be here, right? It's not like I was unaware of my own secret hopes, those things I keep secret from myself but know. Who am I to say anything at all about her running around with that Italian clown, when, after all, I wanted Newt to leave the bar to Mary Annie and me alone? Kettle, pot, frying pan, fire, I thought. But all lingering June disturbances got splintered apart that morning by the phone.

"H'lo," I managed.

"Where did you get that Jacques the restaurateur stuff?" said a deep anxious voice.

"What?" I asked, noticing my face puffy in the dismal mirror of the TV screen. I had fallen asleep in the armchair, leaning back from the Underwood, precarious on a TV tray. Every time I hit a key it rocked. Shake, rattle, and roll.

"Listen, Mr. Westin, this is your goddamned editor demanding to know where you got that crap about Jacques for the piece you wrote featuring an unnamed victim in a highly suspicious shooting?"

"Hell, Grass told me he thought you wouldn't even use it."

"Well that's no excuse now, is it? Because the night desk let it through. We got Russians with H-bombs shooting rockets at the sun, that story was killed. But yours went over the transom, and a certain Mrs. Jacques Brown, whose husband has been missing for three weeks, wants to know where we got it and wondering aloud can she sue us for something called desecration of character. So where'd we fuggin' get it?"

"A cop, for Christ's sake, Dooley, I got it from a cop. And I sort of confirmed it with a guy who grew up here."

"You sort of confirmed it. Great. We can take this to the Supreme Fugging Court on a sort-of-confirmed waiver. You know this cop's name?"

"No, I … I mean I've just seen him around forever. Dooley. I don't know why I suddenly remember that, but his name is Dooley, same as yours," I said, genuinely perplexed. "He actually gave me the nickname, Jake Snake, but it was Newt Nesselrode, the bookie, he's the one told me the real name. You want me to check it out with him?"

"Listen to yourself, Trevor Westin. You got it from a cop you hardly know oddly enough with my same name, and confirmed by a man who makes book. I think I'll find someone else to check it out, if you don't mind."

"Course not. Listen, I'm not apologizing, though. I've never been wrong. I've never been sued before."

"That's because you usually write about books and thee-uh-ter. Forget it. She can't sue us, and you're doing a fine job. How's our competitor Mr. Thomas Storke doing?"

"The same. His big dam is still full of rain."

"Shit, I hate that fugger."

"Storke's Folly," I said. "It's still full and you owe me twenty bucks. A month's rent where I live. Such language."

The editor of the local daily, a Roosevelt crony, built Cachuma Lake, dammed a dinky river and made our postwar development possible, including the neighborhood around the new university. The idea was born doomed, according to everybody. But after six years of drought ended, rain runoff filled the man-made lake, and his muddy hole became the future, creating Artificial Paradise. An oasis of horror in a desert of boredom—and I won the bet Dooley and I made months ago after I filed that piece about the Sherry brothers, Norm and Larry, the Jewish battery, who came up from the Santa Barbara farm team Dodgers.

Dooley had worked up here when Hollywood tried to infiltrate the city; he wrote publicity at Flying A Studios, then later for Famous Players back when Chaplin and Arbuckle threw parties at the Montecito Inn. He cursed me roundly renewing his displeasure and I wondered if the phone lines might catch fire.

"But enough about you," he said. "I really called to find if you know who Aldous Huxley is? Huh, college boy?"

"Sure. *Brave New World* ... "

"Yeah, yeah, that's the one. He lives in the Hollywood Hills, but he's going to give some lectures up there. Staying in some place called the Upham. Why don't you see if you can set up an interview? I'll pay ya. But you have to make it so we don't get sued afterwards. He has this theory about intelligence makes me laugh."

"Which is?"

"Geniuses are breeding themselves out of existence by not breeding themselves."

"Imagine that. In Eisenhower's America? How does that work?"

"Christ, it isn't Ike's fault. It's not Ike's fault. But it makes sense. Listen: Your average bowling league Joe has four kids of equal or less IQ. But smart people, they have only one-point-five children of smart down to average brainpans. The point-five kid might explain you. Sooner of later, mathematically, morons inherit the earth."

"One-point-five doctors recommend Pepsodent. You'll wonder where the yellow went, when you brush your teeth with Pepsodent."

"Get me an interview and stop chasing cop calls on the radio. They've got their own newspaper up there last time I checked. Oh yeah, Mr. Storke's *Mudrake*. I don't even know why I let you string for me."

"'Cause you're too cheap to make me staff. I could cover the booming development of the American Riviera. How's this for a feature, 'The Nuclear Family in the Atomic Age'?"

"Get Huxley and we'll talk. Hear he had a deal with Disney."

"Honest to God? You and I, we'll talk?"

"Get me Huxley, and stop angering widows."

Hung up. It didn't matter how diverting the chat, I kept returning to her. She has a laugh that made strangers join her, because they automatically assumed the joke must be wonderful. After all, she liked it. I wanted to call, tell her about Huxley, an assignment. I couldn't bring myself to do it, though we used to share everything. I had her in this room, without interruption, for a day and a half. Even driving down to Jordano's for milk, champagne, and food seemed like a sad separation. Her parents never guessed. She was mine and now she isn't. The moment wasn't here anymore, just a memory printed in my brain cells or whatever it was, real but impossible to touch—there but un-enter-able. I ought to leave town. Sometimes just remembering, though, I could smell her: Hypnotique. Hell. I could smell her at any department store, so what's the point moving?

The phone rang, and, surprise of surprises, it was Gin Chow.

"I didn't know you even used the phone. And you went to Jimmy's last night."

"Never mind that. Meet me for dinner at Frank's Rice Bowl."

"You don't like that place either."

"Don't be absurd," he said. "I like it fine. It's Frank I hate. My old office used to be upstairs. He smelled it up with his Horse Shit cigarettes. You just be there. I have something to say before the New Year, the one you celebrate."

"That's how many days away? Okay. I'll be there. No previews?"

"You talk funny."

"Oh *I* do."

I thought I should call my mother, but I didn't. I held the phone to my ear, and it was cold and the sound droned on into some endless void.

Which still didn't stop me thinking about June. Kettle, pot, frying pan, fire.

Chapter 5

WALKED DOWNTOWN AT MY peril. I walked because A1 Motors hadn't fixed my car's voltage regulator and had ordered a new one from the big city. I assumed this meant waves of electricity ran through the engine now without restraint, assaulting reason. I suggested to Tom Castano that I could crawl to Los Angeles and fetch back the thing in less time than their delivery boy takes. I was then given an invitation to contort my flesh into an uncomfortable mode of self-satisfaction. We live in a vulgar age.

But back to risk: Chiefly it's my Aunt Pearl I feared, the apotheosis of nag. She made this town, and on the Seventh Day she did not rest. Not actually my aunt, but Miss Pearl Chase, as she is known, used to dandle me on her spinster knee and cluck like a soothing hen. Now that I think of it, she likely wasn't wizened then, maybe only thirty. There are many tales about Auntie Pearl's inconsolable beaus: the man who invented discount brokerage, the playwright who wrote *Death Takes a Holiday*, and the man inside Martha Graham. But she never married. She stayed home after her mother's death and tended to her father's broken yet lengthy life. It's said she tossed a suitor's diamond into the surf as many watched; threw passion to the wind.

When I asked her once about a sad life alone, she pinched me and clucked. "I thought you would be the smart one, Trevor," she said.

"The Westin with a brain of his own."

Her father came home one afternoon with her mother in the car but could not brake. She passed halfway through the back wall of the garage and entered that other dimension, the world beyond the world. She died. He never came all the way back. I always wondered if papa was drunk. Maybe that's how he survived.

Pearl wanted me to come work for her. But I am the Westin with a brain of his own and I was not going to become some kind of creeping factotum for civic improvement. I hate all the simpering that goes on around her even now; grown men begging me to ask her to see reason. That word again. And I was not even on her payroll. I didn't have any official tie, so I could pretend to ignore them. What I really feared, though, was consigning myself to perpetual adolescent-hood in her sight, all that stand up straight, when are you going to get a haircut, and, worse, whatever will you do with your life, young man. She sprayed me with her guilt Gatling gun, and never cared who was there when she fired. She clearly loved me.

On the other hand, in the plus column, maybe I'd see June. She worked downtown (over Aunt Pearlie's dead body) with the state senator and his young South American wife. June was window dressing; people liked to duck into the office just to behold her willowy grace and those unbelievable curves. She used to laugh at the people who wanted to look. The sublime June, even the quiet, head-shaking aged sighed before her.

But I saw neither Pearl nor June before I made the Copper Coffee Pot and picked up an off-lime plastic tray and set it down across the chromium guides and slid it past watery scrambled eggs and heaped bacon and bore it through throngs of the decrepit gathered there in shy troupes. I drank two cups of coffee sitting near the patio where the cigarette smoke lifted and blew back in from time to time carried by the breeze off bulky city buses whooshing by—swirling past my face inside to mingle with cabbage and mentholated liniments.

I found an abandoned copy of the *News-Press,* flipped through, and found the murder downplayed, now termed "suspicious death." Concentration camps will hitherto be known as temporary housing for Semitic citizens. I felt a vile taste in the back of my mouth. The city was in the middle of some change. The place was surely destined to become a tourist trap, no longer a wintering watering hole for the rich. It needed a public image, so the barons, industrialists, and even a few Gentile movie stars, our version of immortals, would stay. God forbid the next wave, visiting hordes of middle-class sun-worshippers come to make this into Pleasure Island? If Storke wanted to maintain a false dignity, who could blame him? Even if it's what they call conflict of interest. Storke's name was already on a major thoroughfare and will probably crown some futuristic tower someday, so why wouldn't he want to protect the land of his legacy from defamations, even though his putative job was to expose the city's tawdry sins?

You can't allow our scenic ocean to become a spewer of corpses, or let on that something like murder might happen in lovely old tea cozy Santa Barbara By-the-Sea. God knows the major metropolitan newspaper I worked for down south wouldn't shed light on urban dangers if it meant casting shadows on the real estate section. But at least my article named detective and victim. Storke's paper obfuscated the sordid affair into the world of sad happenstance. My story, meanwhile, would be read in a million little palaces south of here. That was satisfying. I was smug.

I hadn't seen it yet, by the way. And then I found the *Times* tucked into a Naugahyde throne over by the wall, and unfolded it.

Jim Murray foursquare for sports, big sissy Jack Anderson on pets and vacationing woes, Part Two: the city and its environs. Nothing yet. I found it on the second sweep: page three, column one below the fold, with the tiniest byline. Shit. Well, most young reporters don't even get *that,* and I'll get paid, and they hadn't changed a word I could remember. It would be gone tomorrow, said another voice.

Nothing to do till I meet Gin Chow, might as well play reporter, I thought. Walk over to the police station, see if I can dig up anything else on this Snake Jake. Just want to. That's all. Not reading about it in the local paper bothered me more than I first admitted. Keep busy. Idle minds might risk going a little you-know-what again. Not again.

Didn't meet Pearlie, didn't meet June. Arched over the street was a blustery blue, though a bruised sky threatened with clouds over the ocean and the eastern mountains too. Mary Contreras walked by; I spent time watching the line curve down her red wool skirt as she passed out of sight down State.

Two blocks east on Figueroa, past what they call a health food restaurant for Jack LaLanne people who eat honey and vinegar and never touch meat, trees towered over everything; then the stalwart police station, blinding white, and inside, officers standing hunched amid a sickly tobacco residue emanating from the furniture, walls, and ceiling.

"May I speak to the desk officer?" I asked, a bit hazy, with vocabulary drawn from the movies.

The balding man who slid toward me on the other side of a low cabinet barricade between the halves of the room smoothly said, "What do you need? Maybe I can help."

"Thanks. I'm looking for information about the shooting yesterday."

"Shooting?"

"On the breakwater."

"Are you related to the victim?"

"No, I've never met Mr. Brown."

"Oh, so now you know his name now?" he said, drawing attention from other officers palely loitering.

"Excuse me," I said, "I'm from the *L.A. Times*. I wrote about the murder, uh, shooting in today's paper." I don't know why but I suddenly saw myself from outside myself standing before the law, and it was a stilted performance.

"It *was* a murder," said one of the other cops, also balding, with a ridiculously long paunch rolling over his black belt. "And, hey fellas, *this* is the guy. We just solved the case." He seemed angry.

"Captain says not," contradicted another rotund officer in the corner. "He says accident, like the paper."

I felt rubbery. "I'm *what* guy?" I asked, fearful. What's the point of following hunches if they betray?

"Naw, he don't look like the guy to me," said first baldy. "You know, given your sterling press credentials, I think we oughta usher you past any *desk* sergeant," he said, pronouncing the phrase daintily. "Yep. Right past and into the homicide department. On wings of a dove."

"Flutter off," said a third policeman, jabbing air with his coffee cup.

The second cop exited left, entering a chamber beyond. Now I wished I hadn't come. I was not a cool customer after all. In their jaundiced eyes, I probably looked like the *Dragnet* crook that always tripped himself up. The officers fell back into mute discussions.

"Come right back," said policeman number two, reemerging. "The homicide chaps are desirous of your acquaintance."

I passed reluctantly through the heavy door he held open, down a hall past a painting of a sailboat dead in the water. "I don't know anything. I came here for your info."

"Sometimes one surprises oneself with unexpected wisdom," he said. We walked into darker zones, down a medium-lit hall, and half-way down that we entered a room with pebbled-glass, gray light, and two desks pushed together. "Lieutenant, this is the L.A. guy."

"The hell he is," he said, indicating a wooden chair. "Please sit down. I have to finish this last word." It looked like a crossword puzzle on which he had written upside down and backward, though his hunched carcass cast shadows over the pad, this Chip Hilton, All-American Boy. His neck was muscled, adamantine cords cloaked in cement. Yet he was very short and his manner radiated surprising sunniness, at least in these dismal quarters. I decided to like him.

"The hell he is?" I asked.

"So what's your story?" he asked with a smile stretched almost straight across his freckled face.

"Pardon me?"

"*In nomine Patris, et Filii, et Spiritus Sancti,*" he said, making three crosses in the air.

"Catholic schoolboy," I said. "You're a Petrini, aren't you?"

He laughed. "The hell he is an L.A. guy," he said. "I'm worried about you, man."

"What do you mean?"

"Who told you about Jake the Snake? I heard it was a department source."

"Who I'm going to call an unidentified-close-to-the-investigation-type person."

"Fine, but let's play a little guessing game, and I want you to flush red if I get the answer right, okay? He always used to blush in school," said the officer I called Petrini to his invisible partner in an empty chair across from him. "Let's just say for the sake of argument, this officer's initials are Francis Xavier Dooley, and you and I used to see him coming out of six o'clock mass as we were going in to serve the eight. I see blush creep on thy fair brow."

"I never served mass with you," I said.

"Jesus Christ, your memory's poor. I mean, we didn't work the same shift all the time, but it was a long summer out at Holy Cross, right after they built it. I gave you a ride on the back of my bike at least twice. All right, you knew my little brother."

A fog cleared. "Baby Bird Bennett."

"Hey now. Haven't heard that disrespectful moniker in a while. Guess I'm just glad I'm not wop Petrini."

"Okay, so maybe it was Dooley. But why are you worried about me?"

"Because Dooley's disappeared after giving you insider information, according to the rookies he was with. His wife of twenty-five years calls this morning. He never came home. We found his car parked near an orchard up on the Mesa."

"He's drunk. He has a woman."

"Nope. Strictly TT. Teetotaler. Boy Scout pack leader, sterling. And you got a look at him. A woman?"

"All right. Still I don't see what that has to do with me."

"Well, first place, we didn't think much about you until you came in. The rookies were talking about you last night, but it didn't seem important, because of or despite the illustrious family name: your father, the detective legend and you, the illustrious artiste, and even when your name came up again on another missing-person, last-seen-with conversation kind of thing. I know your magical anonymous source for the same reason, friend. Namely a suspected bookie named Nesselrode."

"Jesus. How the hell you know that? You guys are pretty good for a small town."

"Hah, like bloodhounds. Okay. Actually your editor tied up

everything when he was double-checking and asking after the fact. Seems like a nice boss. Anyway, now he's gone and disappeared."

"My editor has disappeared?"

"No. Nesselrode. His wife and kids are still waiting three days for him to come home from the store. We found his car over by the oil derricks. On the Mesa too. We found his car near the building sites, the new tracts. Now, I also remembered that's where your uncle lives. Somebody else remembered he's the contractor. See how many times your family name can come up in one day? Still, a small town, I don't think there's anything there, like the oil they used to pump by Schoolhouse Road. Gone and ain't it the way. Nothing's where you remember it being, the well runs dry, the old ways change. And no one knows where Nesselrode can be found since last night at Jimmy's. I think you saw him, right? There yourself?

"Yeah, he was at Jimmy's last night."

"With a doll, I know. He left her to go to the bathroom. Didn't come back. To anyone. See why I'm worried?"

"Maybe a little," I said feeling numb and underwater.

Chapter 6

DIDN'T STAY LONG. THEY didn't know what to ask me, and I didn't know what to think.

In fact, the police palace had become a dim memory by dinner. I had no story, unless I was the story—which seemed absurd the more Bennett and I talked. He knew I wasn't a murdering psycho, even considering my checkered past. And there was my father, who was obviously no stranger to these men, even if his legend was already dimmed by his long-ago departure into the Navy. Inside there, where he used to work, he always seemed more indistinct than he did on the streets. Now he was not here to help me, and I was not there to make problems for those men. I just was pretending to be a reporter, like I had pretended to be a student. I just wanted something to do, somewhere to go besides down.

I did feel things: sorry for Dooley, who seemed all right, he liked the old town; and for my old college chum, the bookie—well that was more like ambivalence. I avoided him normally and had a hard time thinking of him now, thinking of him missing. And then the dead guy I sort of saw? Snake Jake was missing person the first, according to my new friends the police. His wife had reported him gone weeks ago. His car, for those keeping count, was found way up by the Friendship Circle cult houses on the old part of the Mesa, above the new homes being built by my uncle Dick down below on the milked-out oil fields. All three cars on the Mesa, for those counting.

You know, I do have some experience with the missing. Besides, I went to Catholic school where nuns reminded us every day about mortality, God's thief-in-the-night plans for us, warning us against strangers who'd sweep you into cars, into horrors they were too delicate to describe, kids old enough to remember atom bombs, concentration camps, and closer-to-home soldier and sailor fathers who wouldn't talk about it making the imagination a terrible place to wander. Postwar America was a fine time to be alive. Especially if you were interested in death.

Snake Jake knew no wrongdoers, according to his hysterical, outraged wife, who refused to identify his body. More than a few guys at the station knew Jake, so it was no problem. It was him, though him no more. Mrs. Brown was trying to sue everybody, according to Bennett. Maybe even you, he said. After that our conversation went dead too.

"You don't need me, and I can't think how to help," I said, still feeling a peculiar numbness where my mind was. Bennett stared for a moment, got up, left the room and then came back quietly. "No, you can go," he almost whispered. "But when leaving you should say, 'Good to see you, man.'"

I said, "Listen, I didn't come in to make you mad."

"Who's mad?" he asked. "I'm stuck with a bizarre death, two disappearances, and my wife just had a baby. I'm sleepy, not mad. I'm a man of many changing moods."

"Congratulations," I said. "I mean the baby."

"Baby Baby Bird," he said, exactly what I was thinking; short waves of thought had passed between skulls. He nodded politely, indicating the door. As I walked down the dark hall I felt presences there, voices whispering in my ears.

But the incident was soon washed from my mind by the blue of the breezy day outside. An edge of cold on the land, finally come into this warm winter; I wandered over Anapumu, through the courthouse yards, their sunken gardens, and looked up at the windowed jail, imagining faces of the temporarily damned hovering there in the dark, looking back at my restless freedom. The wind blew harder. I walked into the downtown library through the children's section with the empty deep-sea diver suit standing there, a portal and a portent of my dreams for life beneath life. I liked the kids' librarian, but she wasn't on duty in her cardigan and tight skirt.

Poring through card catalogues, I found a book or two by Huxley and browsed them up and then wandered across Anapumu to the Book Den for gossip. Nobody was there, except the old man who ran the register. I meant to ask him something about Huxley at the Upham, but lost my will as I looked down on him bent over a volume in the wan light leaking back from the big front pane and the hooded green lamp. His skin was pale, like paper, wetted then dried over and over through a series of years, going yellow along edges and almost translucent where a vein swept through, an interstate on a map of times gone by. I kept my peace and never entered his.

But then a cloud turned the front window dark. He looked up, surprised. He didn't speak, his hand trembling minutely. I smiled and walked back to the poetry section. I looked behind the Yeats volume always there: *The Tower*. Upon a woman won or a woman lost? Immune to the pains love brings. And there it was, the Poe; he had put it there, up behind the Yeats, worked and wedged up inside the bookcase corner. I pulled it out and there the page circled on the table of contents, circled by my brother. And then I opened it to the page, 163, which I knew by heart and never needed to see, just wanted to: the circle and the underlines he made with his mischievous pen.

There shrines and palaces and towers
(Time-eaten towers that tremble not)
Resemble nothing that is ours.

I just wanted to look again. Outside, the wind's noise distracted me, blowing the season that had come late toward us, making up for lost time. I could hear a whistle from the old man at his desk, too, breathing and rebreathing. My favorite lines were next, underlined by me.

Resignedly beneath the sky
The melancholy waters lie. ...
So blend the turrets and shadows there
That all seem pendulous in air,
While from a proud tower in the town
Death looks gigantically down.

* * * *

There was a Hitchcock movie at the long, narrow State Theater, a second run house that used to be a ten-pin alley in our city's Golden Age. I must have walked three store-lengths beyond before I decided why not, and then, I'm entitled. Walked up to the ticket window, and the little white card said the movie had begun twenty minutes ago. It was playing with a monster movie about atomic crabs, which was blessedly short, so I decided to sit through the whole thing until I caught up with the story. I'd be out in perfect time to meet Gin Chow.

I ended up liking them both. I came out into the lobby for popcorn during the B movie and wished I smoked cigarettes, everybody else does. I went back. Jimmy Stewart was an ex-cop and he got dizzy climbing up the stairs to a not so proud church tower, where bad things happened. It was good, but I couldn't make any sense of it until I saw the beginning, after the giant crabs. A race across the roofs that ended in a fall. Things like that effect us. That was what I missed going in late. But maybe Stewart deserved all the trouble because he was so easily fooled. The whole thing was a mystery in reverse, since Stewart himself was the question mark, even shaped like one. He was looking for a woman he couldn't have, always looking, the detective was the crime. I wish I could believe that I could get the past back, the rainy windows of Edgewater Way. What I really liked, though, was a pale blonde in a funny Hitchcock preview for a movie starring Eva Marie Saint. A breathy thing like Marilyn Monroe, but more seductive, she had a voice like a ghost. Saint or ghost? So beautiful that I came out into twilight in love with Eva Marie, a saint with blue eyes. Resignedly beneath the sky the melancholy waters lie.

Words built around us become moods.

The wind moved newsprint-gray clouds over the street sky. A few lights on inside stores spread warmth out onto the cold sidewalk and into the four-lane road over which smoking cars lumbered, and the wind and the winds from the automobile beasts swept tiny elm leaves forward as if to lead the way. Come on, hurry up, they said. Then the hopping yellow leaves fell still, wind-abandoned, turned to litter.

At Carrillo Street the bus station exhaled odors of fuel, exhaustion sweat, and cigars. At De La Guerra the Penny's promised sanctuary, comfort with popcorn and peanuts. Outside Ott's Hardware came bitter smells of hard rubber wheels and oiled steel; I could navigate the streets without eyes or ears. Past Ortega Drugs I started rubbing elbows with drunks. Everybody drank always it seemed. I decided to join them for a beer before I hit Frank's, ducking into the cleverly misspelled Ofice (I stayed late at the Ofice, says the technically truthful spouse), where the onyx-covered bar reflected our dingy world back with a false nobility. It was quick and it was delicious, the beer, and it made me feel angry, angry at nothing. The sky bruises had turned black and I saw an unencumbered evening star there in the west without one wish dangling from it.

Most people ate Chinese at the Nanking Gardens, a big room with oak tables and high windows across the street from Frank's. Your ears would ring a half hour later from all the monosodium glutamate they used, though we didn't even know what that was then. I thought the tingling sensation might be the work of an invisible vortex of timespace.

Frank's was smaller, with a winding stair as you walked in. There were also secluded and secluding booths, popular, since the opportunities for privacy in a small town were few. I slid into one with impunity. I figured Gin Chow would figure where I was and lo!, he was there.

"What do you think about the Dodgers?" he asked. "Be funny if they won it in L.A. this year. I predict they won't." Their second year in Los Angeles after leaving Brooklyn, the Dodgers were it now, augmented by the lost history of the Brooklyn club's farm team that played in a park on Laguna Street in the Italian neighborhood. The field was empty now, but everybody hoped the team would come back. Gin Chow looked at me looking at the menu.

"Why do you bother? You always get the paper chicken and the chow mein and the sweet-and-sour crap. You should let me order for you."

"No, thanks. Don't fancy eating brain and coxcombs again."

"Admit you liked it."

"I will not and I did not."

He did his squinty grimace. He told me more about the old days, how the city had changed. He leaned back and went totally silent when the time came to order. I switched from beer to a pot of pretty-scented jasmine tea, and ate both the fortune cookie and the almond cookie. He touched nothing. Despite being Chinese, he drew no interest from waiter or busboy. I listened. I liked his stories, even though I knew most of them.

He told me about a pirate who visited the pueblo of Santa Barbara in the eighteenth century. Instead of fighting, the whole town went into hiding in the hills north, except for a squadron of soldiers that rode around on display for the pirates. The soldiers would stop behind a tree to change clothes, thereby convincing the scurvy salts that their numbers were huge and accessories lavish. The pirates left through heavy surf on longboats by Castle Rock. This was long before even Stearns pier was built.

I liked the story, though I'd heard it before—it had pirates for Crissake, and it felt Greek, like the *Odyssey* without Odysseus in it, as if it ought to have a point. It didn't.

"Why did you make me come here?" I asked. I was curious. I was pretty sure I knew what he wanted, though.

"Only because you are in a lot of danger," he said, playing with the glass pepper shaker, rolling it in his delicate fingers. "That's all."

"You don't sound too worried about it," I said.

"Well, I didn't say you were doomed. What have your dreams been like?"

"Well, I dreamed about you," I said.

"I knew it," spake the True Seer. "What were the circumstances, where were we?"

"Who said I was there?"

"The dreamer is always there. Where?"

"I don't know. Maybe it was on a beach or something."

"Up on the Mesa, below the new housing tracts, but down on the beach. In *my* dream it was back a few years ago when the Navy dump was still there. When did you dream all of this?"

"I didn't say I did. I said the beach—could've been Butterfly or

Thousand Steps—hell, it could've been the Pit."

"Shut up," he said. "You are in danger."

"Up on the Mesa … "

"What?" He looked happy.

"Nothing. It doesn't matter."

"What do you know? Everything matters. In my dreams I saw a man trying to make you disappear."

Now I did feel a chill, as if underwater again, the same as when I was with the police, whom I did not mention. "You saw it, your own dream?" He shook his head and nodded, confusing me.

"So what should I do?" I asked, knowing again what he would say.

"You have to go there. I would say the sooner the better."

"And, of course, you won't go with me."

"Why even ask? I'm an old man, I can't help you." The place had been getting noisier because a large drinking party had entered and the door kept opening, changing the atmosphere inside—cold air in and hot air out. I could hear people gassing to each other about cabbages and naked communists and was Elvis the King?

"So I guess I'll go out there in the morning. Except my car's not running."

"Yes it is. They got the part today and popped it in. Don't let them overcharge you."

"What am I going to learn from this?"

"How should I know? Do I look like a college professor? Uh oh," he said, and began to look shifty.

"Hey, look who's here, everybody." It was sweet Mary Annie, again. I looked around the bend of the bench and waved at everybody, but except for a guy from the Dolores choir back when, I didn't know any of her friends.

"Hey honey," she said, pushing me over to make room in the

narrow booth. "Who were you talking to?" Gin Chow had evanesced into the night.

"Nobody," I answered, pointing to the empty bench across from me.

"No really, I heard voices coming from over here," she said, furrowing her pretty brow.

"Just me talking to myself. You know how weird writers are."

"Do I ever. Come to think of it, how would I? Buy me a drink?"

She had me pushed up against the cold wall and her muscled nyloned legs were pressed against the thin stuff of my slacks. Of course I said yes. "But they only have beer."

"That's okay," she said and pulled from her purse a whole pint of nice Scotch, barely touched. She popped off the cork and took a long swig and then passed it to me. A tiny silver thread of saliva stretched out in the distance between her lips and the bottle and then it was gone. I took a drink too, making a point of not wiping off the rim.

This was not a good girl. The way she mashed and leaned into me, as we chatted aimlessly, I was soon painfully excited. My lungs were blowing like a racehorse. But I tried to keep cool. I decided not to mention Newt's disappearance. It would be more interesting if she told *me*; and a cold shower if *I* brought it up. I never said I was noble.

But we talked and talked. Mary Annie kept up the banter, asked what I was working on, Clark Kent. I told her about Aldous Huxley. She said she knew where to find him tonight. Did I want to go there? You're kidding, I said. She said something a little suggestive with her lips very close to mine and she made a biting snap at me. I jerked back a little too hard.

"What's wrong? I won't hurt you," she laughed huskily.

"Even if I ask you to?"

"You flirt funny," she said, and no doubt I blushed. Bennett was right. I often blush.

She decided to break the spell. "You know Newt disappeared last night?"

"Cops told me," I said, feeling a little puffed up, though she didn't notice.

"We weren't dating. He just bought me a nice gimlet. Then scooted. Said he had to tinkle. Cops didn't seem to care much. They called this morning. I'm worried his wife, well, she might think bad about me and, then worse. Where the hell did he go? What do you think? I think it had something to do with your snake man conversation. What's the matter, big writer? Cat got your tongue? Not so easy talking to someone real? I'm not going to make trouble. I know you're still in love, and I respect that. But for one thing, it's still wrong."

"Why?" I said, knowing the answer.

"Here's your headline, scoop. You're in love with your cousin. I saw her at Jimmy's with the businessman's son last night. June and the Juvenile Crime Lord."

"She's not my cousin," I sighed.

"Oh, right. She's just your aunt and uncle's daughter."

"Adopted. She was adopted."

"You know, I wouldn't be so sure about that," said Mary Annie slowly, singsong.

"What's more sure? Everybody fantasizes about being found in an orphanage. She knows she was."

"You know, she and I were talking a few weeks ago, like girls do. I mentioned that Walt Disney and his wife were both adopted. Eleanor Roosevelt too. Did you know that?" she said putting her finger on my nose and moving closer.

"No," I said, feeling the rush return.

"And I asked her, I always wondered how it would feel to know your parents were somebody different than your parents, not really yours. And you know what she said to me, your adopted cousin, June?"

I regarded her blankly.

"She said, 'Why are you staring at me, how would I know?'"

Chapter 7

WOKE FROM DEEP UNCONSCIOUSNESS feeling great. The sun bashed into the room looking for me, elbowing the place rudely awake, and there I was, waiting. And no, I didn't get any, though it was close. I drank some but it mercifully spared my morning head and my accidental sinlessness technically kept the June torch burning.

But it wasn't because I didn't try.

We drank a bit, like I said. So my memories were figures lurching, spasming forward through time in a spotlight on a dark stage. A slide show if you will. She has a car and maybe we shouldn't have been driving. Mary Annie wanted to go to a livelier spot, and I wanted her to take me to Huxley as promised. I would've settled for her place, or better, her coming to mine.

Flash first: We were with a smart-mouthed crowd at the El Paseo. Journalists, most of them; few seemed to think much of me. One of them knew my father, he kept saying. Another knew my uncle; in fact, this guy was on assignment up on the Mesa interviewing Uncle Dick about GI Bill housing. I told him to say Hi, Uncle Dick and then remembered I was going up there tomorrow, so never mind. I'll tell him you're coming, he said with a weird sneer. But all I kept wondering was, what did June mean? I can grill Dick tomorrow, if I see him, but even then I knew that was booze thinking. I wouldn't dare ask.

Maybe she was pretending. It's all pretense.

There was a band playing big band music and a crooner who looked Italian. The reporter asked if Dick already had a house on the Mesa. He knew the fugging answer, pretending like it was a trap he was laying for me. Dick's family lived on the north side of the Mesa, past Meigs's farm, on Edgewater Way, my favorite place. In a house built for luxury seaside life, but built just before the oil came gushing up. The derricks and pumps had already come and gone, but still nobody wanted to live there. June lived there with Dick and Helen, who adopted her. I didn't care what anybody said.

Coincidence he got to build the Mesa houses? asked the reporter. Your uncle makes some general improvements to the neighborhood, drives his own property values up. Was it Westin influence on city fathers? Some young guy worked at the *News-Press* wanted to know who were these fugging guys they kept calling the City Fathers? Were they rich people, the kind from Montecito, with duplex names like Bellwether Knapp Hoyt or Lockwood De Forrest, or just the obvious scions memorialized in our Spanish street names: your Carrillo, De La Guerra, and Cota, families that bred with the Yankee rich ranchers to produce offspring with indomitable nerve in midday heat and swollen appetites for scrubland? Did the term infer a pack of City Mothers and, thus, City Siblings, as well? he drunkenly asked.

I don't know, I said. My father once was police chief—a city father to me.

Your father? he said. He laughed, then clammed up, and then lurched. Joe Westin is your fugging father? He ran the fugging city, he laughed wickedly, before he got run out of it. He laughed. I was about to punch when Mary Annie intervened.

"You're asking who runs this place?" she intoned, brandishing a martini glass with waves of gin rolling around at the rim. Then she threw it back neatly. "I'll tell you who runs this town. It's a little old couple that bought a house on Park Lane in Montecito. They're very quiet. They throw one party every year. New Year's Eve."

"I think that's tonight," I said. She looked at me like I was drunk. "What does he mean about my father?"

"He's drunk."

She returned to her speech. "If you're invited, you're in the cabal, the secret society. The City Fathers sit after dinner cracking walnuts, drinking port, and deciding how the year will go. The place they sit in is like a burnished throne room, in a tower, and outside on the fake turret you can hear the waves break on Butterfly Beach, even though it's many miles away. Plus, the coyotes wail."

"I could listen to you all night," said the *News-Press* scum, leaning over me.

"Sit on it and rotate," I said, Mr. Charming, as I led Mary Annie to the teeming dance floor. Her hair smelled like dust and tangerines. She leaned into me, not resisting an ounce, providing counterweight.

Flash the second: The big canopy was off the roof for some reason, so it was cold in the Paseo courtyard. The band played popular songs and kept breaking into fake rock and roll the way parents might envisage it. Shake, rattle, and roll, splish splash I was taking a bath. She bent over and shook, showing off the shoulders. Someone else would ask her to shimmy with him, but she would say, I've got to ask my boyfriend. One of the *News-Press* reporters came over while she was out powdering her nose and asked me if I felt like a man who had kicked a nest of hornets by mistake. I said, I guess so. Then asked him what the fug was he talking about?

He barked out a laugh, oh you innocent kid. This was not a killing, it was an abomination, a message sent to us from underwater, beneath the source of things, like all life, forecasting the future.

I laughed and asked again, what the fug? He said, Snake Jake died for our sins. He laughed and said that the Storke family has information, the Hollisters have land, the Moshers own the oil. But this secret is hidden in the heart of the waters, the network that makes a wave. He laughed again, and I told him he was cuckoo. Maybe, he said, but he knew that his newspaper wasn't crazy. It will never print anything about Jacques Brown's crucifixion.

Then Mary Annie said, it's a good time to go, leading to flash three. I was ready to drop the whole Huxley thing, there will always be another day. And then she said, he's over there. We're walking over to Howard's house a few blocks. We're at the door and she said, go on in while I freshen up. She waved at Howard, the big famous painter. I looked at the work he had on his walls, this Mr. Howard Warshaw, who asked me if I was a student. He was suddenly a teacher, he said, and he couldn't keep his students' faces straight. I complimented the paintings, which looked like objects sprouting ghost shadows. He handed me a drink. Aldous Huxley was here earlier but he left with Vincent and Dewey or Douwe or however you pronounce it, he said. Howard was a little drunk or something. He said, let's go over to the library, it was only seven blocks. Mary Annie, who had come back, said, go ahead, she'd catch up. I can't remember now if it was sunny outside or dark. Seems it should have been dark. And the wind was blowing down from La Cumbre Peak's pine-tipped ranger station. We walked up to the library window and saw the janitor inside. He beat on the window with the flat of his hand, this Mr. Warshaw, who talked to me about goat men and maenads. He pointed to the wall inside, my mural, he said. Inside, the janitor gave us the finger. Whoa was us. A car honked behind us: Mary Annie. We got in and she handed us a bottle of bonded.

We whooped across town and up Montecito Street and up

Eucalyptus Road and up Barker Pass, and the night was getting colder but the windows were up and we whooped. And you could say this was flash four but it all seemed tied together by a string now.

Wait, there's a gap: we were standing on the back porch of a house and it turned out that the servants lived here and they called the big house and Mary Annie was draped all over me and holding hands with Howard, until I asked, what's all this? And he started to push me on the chest, and it became apparent to him, I mean to me, that a fight was in order. So I fugging punched the big fool and suddenly Mary Annie was on the floor laughing.

She whispered in my ear, he's a sissy.

Later, we were standing around a fireplace, and somebody had opened a bottle of California retsina. It's lovely at this time of night and there was this guy in a tee shirt with big bulging muscles and a pompadour haircut like Steve Reeves, shit, maybe it was Steve Reeves, and then Howard came out of a bedroom. This is a place where a lot of guys are sissies, someone said. But what's that Rock Hudson-looking guy doing over there? I realized it was Hudson, transfigured by the mountain starlight.

Howard introduced me to some people from a think tank in Montecito. One guy's name was Tugwell and the other (I'm not kidding you) called himself Stringfellow. I was out of my league, but everybody was sizzling on the sauce, which equalized me with frick and frack from the brain emporium. Frick said he was rewriting the United States Constitution. I said, that must be nice for him, what does something like that pay? Somebody knew I was a writer too. That book. And right behind him suddenly is the *Sea Hunt* guy, Mike Nelson, Lloyd something in a satin shirt. Ha! It *was* Mike Nelson, and he and frack are talking about the League of the World, which sounds like a comic book villain, and I asked Lloyd Nelson what it was like to breathe underwater, and he just looked uncomfortable. Bridges was his name.

Then I thought I saw Huxley. He was holding down the large bar. I walked over to him and thought I ought to be nervous; he wrote *Brave New World*, he knew the future. Al's not here said the stately man whose name turned out to be Bob, an official American intellectual, he said. Al's at a better party, for poets, with Vincent and Douwe or Dewey or whatever his name was. Mountain Drive near Banana Road. "He'll be the one who doesn't drink."

I was in the car with Mary Annie again, she said we were heading for a better party, and Howard wanted to go there to see Vincent, who collected him. Vincent Price collected Howard Warshaw? But we started giggling because when we looked around there was no Howard in the car and we were down the road too far to turn back. Flash five, if you're counting: I thought I ought to stop drinking. Good, then you can drive, she said. I can't really see right now. One lumbering submarine ride later we arrived, surfacing and hand in hand.

We walked in over an uneven path that seemed to be paved with shards of ancient pottery, the stars above were shards of cracked light, and there was some young guy named Marvin or something like that and he was laughing in a wicked way and he asked me if I knew who Dylan Thomas was.

"Old age should rage, rage against the dying of the light," I said.

"*Pas mal, monsieur*," said Vincent Price in his unmistakable semiprecious Southern Gothic tone, and I was wondering about how many sissies in one night, and Douwe, the Proustian, for he was there too, laughed, so maybe I had said it out loud and thought, where there is smoke.

"You know he was here," said Marvin. "Thomas, I mean, drinking, much like yourself, visiting the charming houses of charming Montecito, then in short order began christening the garden chambers of the charming with his alcohol vomit."

"Oh. It's you that's charming," said a sonorous voice behind him. The tall, gaunt novelist with abstracted eyes; Huxley, this time for real, but I was too anesthetized to be nervous about it.

"Anyway," continued Marvin, last name Mudrick, explained Mary Annie later. "The poet, after ending his ruminations," he laughed, eyes askance at Huxley, "takes up with a waspish yet lovely faculty wife named Wilson. They head off into the corner and share thoughts no doubt about the Alexandrine line or some other voluptuous scansion." Here even Huxley smiled. "All this is much to the chagrin of husband Larry, an esteemed professor of something called American Lit-er-ah-choor."

"Gesundheit," said Huxley.

"Shut up, Mudman," said one of the bohemian gents with Luciferian facial hair ensemble and a Greek sailor cap jauntily employed on his pate, "that's your game too if I'm not mistaken."

"Touché, Mr. Poet," he laughed. "Then, next thing you know, they're gone."

"Gone?" asked Douwe Stuurman.

"Yeah, Larry goes crazy, right from the start. He's askin' everybody, then he goes into the bedrooms. Apparently the jealous type. But she's not there. They're not there. Goes outside starts kicking at cars. Nothing, not a trace of them."

Jesus Christ, I think. Is there some kind of epidemic? "When did this happen?" I asked.

The Mudman looked at me. "1949, why?"

"Did they find him? Did they find them?" I asked.

He was still looking at me. "Yeah, of course," he said. "Larry's wife called three days later from a cheap hotel in Oxnard. She was contrite. Had a black eye next day. Larry's mute and Dylan Thomas returned to New York, where, they say, he asked somebody if he was going to tour Southern California soon. Didn't remember a thing. He died then. After the first death there is no other."

"That's bullshit," I said.

"Excuse me? Who are you?"

"People are disappearing all over again," I said. "It never stops."

"Who is this?"

A man I didn't know leaned over and whispered my name. "Trevor Westin, the author, the prodigy?" he said. I think it was Tab Hunter.

"I knew your father," said Marvin Mudrick. "But the important part is that he was here. Dylan Thomas in this room, and now he's here, Aldous Huxley. Here. Now."

"He drinks a lot," said Huxley, jabbing a thumb all over the room, but first at Marvin. Then Huxley began talking to me as if we had been interrupted in a lifelong chat. He was a fount, it turned out. I said I had a question for him after hearing him descant too long on Malthus and the cedars of Lebanon: He asked me what question? I said they ought to make a movie out of *Brave New World*. This produced richly phlegmed laughter. Do you know that I wrote a screenplay for Disney? *Alice in Wonderland*, he said. Disney told me he understood every third word. Besides, that's not a question, he added.

"More like a query," I said, drifting on a seabed of dozy notions borne on movie dreams.

"That's why I love America," he said.

"They want me to write a profile of you," I says.

"Who does?" he shuddered, staring at the end of a friend's cigarette.

"*L.A. Times*."

"Why, I lived there for a decade and they never wrote about me. Who are you, really?" he asked, shuddering, yawning, and producing a crooked smile.

I introduced myself. He has very poor eyesight, his pupils were huge but he seemed to see me okay. "The author of *The Neverknown Chronicles*?" he asked in a soft voice, the kind we reserve for children.

"I'm flattered," I said.

He said, "I can't picture you as anything but a crew cut fourteen-year-old blond boy in *Life* magazine. They asked you if you knew what a prodigy was and you said ... "

"I said, 'My grandfather always said that pretty is as pretty does.'"

"I thought you were a Zen master."

"Obviously, I thought so too," I said

"Have you ever taken psilocybin?" asked an actor named Dennis who was joined at the hip to some director named Curtis, who kept asking people what they thought about mermaids. They didn't seem like sissies though.

Huxley looked flummoxed by the brazen interruption. The actor Dennis said he was friends with Vincent and Aldous, and it was a shame that the L.A. papers never wrote about *him*, since *he* was king of the L.A. underground, that he had read my book, and that he had seen the race of mermaids singing each to each named Mora who must kill by the light of the full moon. He acted as if he might be a beatnik poet, but I don't think he was that either. He reached elaborately into a pocket for a medicine jar, shook something out, and gave me five little pills. "This is the pharmaceutical stuff, my fellow mystic. All very legal if the police stop you tonight. Take them all at once. Or at least three of them."

"Now?"

He laughed. "I like your spirit. No captain. Take them sometime maybe this week, give yourself twelve hours alone, and safe. Then call me and we'll do your profile."

"We?" I said.

"I'm managing Al's time when he comes to Santa Barbara."

"You mean it."

"Every word. The author of *Neverknown*." He raised a glass, but I had nothing except five pills of psilocybin. I raised them in my palm and he laughed, and doing so, did look like a beatnik poet, a crazed light in his starry eyes. I thanked him. He gave me the cellophane off a neighbor's pack of Lucky's to keep the pills safe.

"Bon voyage," he said.

By this time Huxley had wandered off and like everybody else, disappeared into some haze of holiday lights. I went to the bar in the rec room of the pine-paneled house; it had big windows that allowed night shadows to leak into the corners from outdoors. There was a black woman there—in this town a sight so rare—who looked like Lena Horne in a cowl in the growing dark. I thought what it must be like to see a mermaid in green waters. Vincent Price came into the room and I asked him if he knew the Poe poem *The City in the Sea*. He didn't know it all, he said, leaning towards me, but he just had been cast in a movie, *Under the Sea*. Then fireplace smoke started to fill the room.

I felt ecstatic coming away from the party and out into the night air, filled with the smell of outdoors, wet wood mixing with the smell of fireplace burning wood. Without even trying I had connected with the man. Only connect, the poet said. On cue, Isherwood and Auden walked out of the party too. Then some young kid approached me there on Park Lane and said he was a truth detective. I said that was redundant and then hiccupped. He laughed and said, shit yeah, you're right.

His name was David Van Cortlandt, and he *was* a real beatnik. His dad was in the movies, made them. David fished sometimes, caught barrels of red snapper, which the natives devoured all winter long. He claimed that the Russians had enough nuclear bombs to annihilate the world several times. Crazy, man, he said. Somehow, he said, we have to get together, man. I want to know about the Hidden Harbor Murder Mystery. I asked him what he was talking about and he laughed again. He must have been sixteen but he was drinking a giant Rainier Ale and asked me if I wanted any reefer. I laughed.

"Come and see me, cool daddy. I play music at the Noctambulist. It's, like, gone," he said. "You'll meet the highbrows and the hipsters; something something and the phony tipsters. I'll even help you with your mystery, man, if you come."

"*My* mystery?"

"Yeah, man. You're the only one, beside us harbor rats, brave enough to talk about Snake Jake in this town, man," he said. I tried to ask what he meant, but words just billowed out from him, wind from a cartoon cloud. He told me that he lived on a Chinese junk, abandoned in the harbor, when he was running away from his parents, which was all the time. He looked around. "Am I talking too loud?" he said, leaning toward me and cupping his hand over his mouth. I shook my head. "Good!" he roared into my ears and laughed and laughed. "I don't want them to hear me. Be cool and stay that way, daddy. You're on to it, I can tell."

I was congratulating myself for escaping when it occurred to me I had not the faintest idea how to contact either Dennis or Curtis, my liaisons to Huxley. All I really knew about them was that they were making a movie about mermaids, and drugs were oddly involved. I tried to walk back to the bar but it was very dark inside, like a sea grotto, I thought.

There was another memory. Some time passed without leaving any trace, but Mary Annie was on my arm. I was less happy, perturbed by some slight I won't remember. I can't remember who took us up the path to the cottage, Queen Anne it was. After we stopped in the cottage for sherry of all things, there was a bigger house. The crenellated top of the roof was like a cross between a medieval fortress and a Moorish tourist trap. The door had a sign made of sea pebbles that just read "Heaven." My Blue, I thought. The old couple there took us up some funny stairs into the tower, and I felt a strange brand of déjà vu for something that had been described to me. Like the living memory of a scene from a book, physical but made of words. A new kind of vu. "We never meant for the oil people to push into this neighborhood," murmured the sandy-haired woman with dancer's tights underneath a starchy peasant blouse, holding my hand and reciting some French verse about being weary of the ancient world. She handed me off to an older gent who looked like a well-manicured bulldog.

"They hold the ocean itself hostage," he said, pointing out the window and down a long canyon to where the platform, the famous platform Hazel, stood in the dark. A tower in the waves, I think he said. "It feels like they are raping it. Are they, darling?"

"Long as it isn't those Hollywood people, I don't care. Don't want them ruining the neighborhood. But here we are, and what can you do?" she answered. "Someday soon we will both be gone. And, as far as that's concerned, from our perspective, the universe will cease completely. Who needs to care about the neighborhood and whether or not the Jews get in," she said.

The fire was brighter in one corner than the other. "My better half believes in Plato's Cave. Like it was a religion, the Sermon on the Mount," he said. A gong, a muted song like Big Ben's, rang in the distance.

"On the mouth, darling. Kiss us on the mouth," she said. I thought she meant me, and both of them started to laugh at my backwards jerk.

"Hell," he said. "He might be Jewish from Hollywood too."

It was exactly midnight, time for another day and celebrating change. There were port and walnuts on an old rough-hewn table.

Suddenly we were outside, transported by a wind of farewells whispered. Mary Annie was on my arm and at the corner of the driveway and the trimmed hedge, we stopped near her big blue Mopar, and when I turned into her she came forward in the cold breeze, her lips warm and her mouth smelling like rum and Juicy Fruit. I took both of her arms and pulled her close and my heart was beating a fast dance.

On the mouth she said, and laughed. And then she said, what took you so long?

"Did you want me to kiss you inside the El Paseo, or in Howard's house? Because now I'm sorry I didn't."

"No, I mean, I've known you since high school. You had too many other girls. Or one." She looked a bit pouty. When I leaned over, though, she kissed me with her tongue and then laughed a tiny bit and sweetly.

"I was gone for four years," I said. "Living in Los Angeles. When I came back for visits I thought about calling you."

I thought that was mostly true. June only saw me when the house on Edgewater Way was empty—parents gone to Palm Springs or off to the city for shopping. A lot of time not seeing me. And then a lot of other things happened, I thought, and I might remember them now in the cooling wash of all these drinks. The city of Camarillo outside my steel-reinforced window glowed and twinkled like the indifferent stars. Glowing; it was a big little place. And you didn't need to share a room like a dorm. Not with all my money and my father's pull. "And you didn't seem interested then when I first came back. Then June moved in with you."

"Men never know anything," she said. And kissed me even harder. Her hand wrapped up around my neck.

The kiss broke and she looked into my eyes. I thought about electricity and she read my mind. "A lot of people have trouble in college, Trevor. Nobody thought bad of you. We were rooting for you to get better and look, you did." Like it was a war, I thought. I must be pathetic. "We should have visited," she said.

But you were afraid of the changed boy, or the charged boy, I thought. The merman in the tubs where they made you soak.

"Where to now, St. Peter?" she asked.

"Anywhere, but how about my apartment?"

"Mmmm," she laughed, and pulled away, walking toward her car and swinging her arms. I followed, curious, and pulled open the heavy passenger door. She demurred; despite her earlier blindness she wanted to drive. I got in and sat on the cold vinyl of her front seat. The engine rumbled up and then purred. When she pulled on the chromium post that turned on the lights, it lit the radio green, but up here in the cold air, it looked like the neon at Jimmy's, spreading out through fog. I reached across the bench seat and softly enclosed her hand that was gripping the jet metal of the steering wheel. She swung her head around, and the look was a pure brand of hunger, at bottom a predatory darkness. "*Nel blu dipinto di blu*," sang the green fog radio.

June was not like this. I could hardly remember what June was like.

"Aren't you ever going to kiss me ever again?" I asked.

I leaned forward awkwardly, but that tiny insecure feeling disappeared when she wrapped her arm across my neck. "It has to warm up," she said after a long while. "The old engine, I mean."

"Let's give it time, then."

She made that mumbling hum again when she leaned forward. It's safe to say I was lost. She laughed at the way I looked at her. She reached over and gave me a wet kiss inside my ear. I almost exploded.

My apartment was far away, but she pulled up in front of the place in no time. Flash six, letting the idle run. I kissed her and she moved into it. When I broke away, though, the moment fell. I could feel it. "Turn off the car," I said. "Please. A few minutes."

"I don't think so, honey," she said. "What kind of girl do you think I am?" she sang.

"My kind? The kind for me?"

She laughed. "You are good aren't you?" I leaned toward her again, she did not resist. "I mean, good-hearted," she laughed.

"You'll see if you come up," I said.

"You probably ran with a fast crowd in L.A. But I don't ever go to a boy's room on a first date. And we haven't even had a first date."

I knew she meant it now. "Take you to dinner and a movie tomorrow night?"

"Not tomorrow. But call me tomorrow night. You know my number by heart."

"I do?"

"Think. I was June's roommate. She moved out."

"I haven't called that number in over a year," I said, and went to open the car door.

"Hey, I'm sorry," she said. "I guess I should be doing whatever I can to make you not think about her."

"You were doing fine."

"Aren't you ever going to kiss me?"

I did. Then I got out and walked backward, clowning a bit, until I bumped against the wrought iron of the apartment house stairway. She held her hand over her mouth as if to repress a giggle, a mime of a mime. I might have been a little drunk. Alone, I knew I'd think about June and be sad as well as be a little disappointed and yet elated about Mary Annie. I hit the bed and fell asleep dressed, but woke up

Chapter 8

I T WAS A NEW dawn and a new day. Putting away my sports jacket, I felt a crinkle of plastic in the pocket. The pills, I thought, Al Huxley's dope. I wasn't a complete stranger to drugs; there was this beatnik place in Westwood Village we used to go and hear jazz, and, of course, there was the Noctambulist. I sometimes drank and took a couple Nembutals to forget. Did June just forget? I wasn't so sure about taking these pills by the light of day, though. Suppose they made me sick or something. I would take them, I guess. I found Dennis's number in the same pocket. Hopper. Interview Huxley, call Dennis. I guess I did know how to get in touch with him. Wild-eyed mermen remember to leave numbers. My editor would be happy. I would get a job. I would date Mary Annie. Maybe I would forget June. But I still wanted June and a road back to Edgewater Way. Meanwhile, what to do with the drugs?

I called about my car, and, of course, Gin Chow was right. It was fixed. The mechanic quoted me a price; I said fine. I have nothing but money. People think it's so great. He said, you know, I'm gonna knock ten percent off. I didn't say anything. It's weird how people who know I'm rich are always floating me discounts.

I put a cardigan on over my knit golf shirt. I brushed back the pompadour and shined the specs and walked out into the light of morning on Islay Street. There were bacon smells and diesel bus smells. I turned left on Garden and bumped into Pearl.

"Good afternoon, young Trevor," she said, emerging from an old war-era Chrysler, the kind with a visor over the front window.

"Oh, Auntie Pearl. You can't fool me. The banks aren't even open."

"Is that any way to greet me, boy? Give me a proper kiss. Thank you," she sniffed with pleasure. "I talked to your parents. They're coming to town to see your uncle Dickory and Aunt Helen. A cookout is planned, I believe. Maybe that little ne'er-do-well daughter of theirs will show up, too."

"Why are you so mean to her?" I said, and then remembered who June was working for. "It's political work and it's what she always wanted. Everybody needs a job, Aunt Pearlie. Why didn't you hire her?"

"Like you, she refused me."

"Well, you are legendary among the slave drivers."

"Nonsense. It never hurts to work hard. It's the secret of life, long, happy life."

"Then why are you always so blue?"

She smiled that scowl of hers, which was meant to seem human. Who knows? Maybe she was, once. "You know, you are the only one who ever spoke to me that way. You and your father and, well … "

"And Patrick."

She ignored me pointedly. "Where are you going? What are you coming from? I thought you had a car?"

I told her my plans included retrieving my car from Castano's and going out to the Mesa to investigate a story. I was vague. She stared at me, then pronounced. "That was bad business the other day."

"What was?"

"The piece you wrote for the *Times*. Brown's death a murder, all open-ended. What's the use of speculating? That job, I believe, is reserved for the police."

"Not in a republic such as ours, where we have this little-known amendment … "

"Don't start with me. I'm just saying it's bad business, and you should be careful."

I was about to argue when I realized I was speaking to Miss Pearl Chase now, not Auntie Pearl. You could observe her sea change between the two personae even on the street, where the sunlight and the official light tended to blend.

"Okay, tell."

"You know that Jacques's Continental restaurant is where the city fathers like to carve up the body politic."

"I do? How would you know what goes on in that déclassé diner? He sold the place."

"It's hardly a speakeasy, Trevor, and I'm hardly a nun. I actually like the snails."

"Oh, come on."

"Trevor, all I'm saying is that the men who bought that place spent a lot of money securing Jacques Brown a line of work far elsewhere, so he wouldn't darken lower State Street with his big hulking insinuations."

"What other job?"

"I'm not at all sure. I believe it was deep-sea something. Diving? Fishing? Somewhere he could not be heard."

"He was a talker was he?"

"He had his theories. He enjoyed expounding on certain themes when in his cups. Some of them were about me, Trevor."

"I didn't know names could ever hurt you."

"Oh, Trevor, don't be venal. Or naïve. Nobody has that thick a skin. I practically live for this community and it smarts to have people say, um, cynical things."

"What cynical things? That you're a bully?"

"Nobody says that."

"To your face. But what nasty things do *you* hear?"

"That my father and my brother are real estate people who practically invented Santa Barbara. They literally invented Hope Ranch," she said, referring to a plot of land the Chase family developed as horsey estate land for the New Rich. "And everything I do helps my family business." She was a well-known backdoor dealer, and late-night phone call terrorist for civic prettification.

"So far, I'd have to say that these are not entirely false or even newsy items—but what have you to do with Chase Realty today?"

"Don't you see, Trevor? All this civic improvement? I've made Santa Barbara even better than my father imagined. That's all I ever wanted."

"You've been living with gossip since I was a toddler."

"But it's happening again. Father bought the Mesa a long time ago, you know. But oil made it undevelopable. He sold it—or did he? Even I've lost track. Today it's being covered with houses of ticky-tack being thrown together by plunderers like your uncle who ought to know better, who grew up here. The GI Bill is buying the Mesa from my dead father and handing it to the bowling alley set. It will be the slum of our city before you die."

I was getting dizzy. Aunt Pearlie seemed to be actually stating something. "Why are you telling me this? I do write for newspapers, you know."

She stared at the cement, cracked and shivered. "You should write about this new group of actors, they're making fun of me too. Call themselves Sound and Fury or Play's the Thing, I don't know."

"Why would anybody crucify and drown a man who howled out in the wilderness about land crimes?" I asked, changing her favorite subject from her to Brown. "Beheading seems more appropriate."

"You know, you really should try another novel, a purple one."

"You're the only one who ever speaks to *me* like that," I said.

She sniffed and seemed ready to laugh, in a matronly way. "I think he just got tied up in his lines and hooks and ended up looking like Our Savior, or a parody thereof. You didn't see the *News-Press* writing about it, did you?"

"The *News-Suppress*."

"Oh, Trevor, you know I'm no fan of Storke but he covers things that matter."

"I'm sorry, hearing's bad, did you say covers up things? I'm going to the Mesa. You know a lot of stuff turns up near there."

"Child. What are you talking about?"

"A cop disappeared and a friend of mine too: people who knew about Jacques and told me things. Maybe it's a coincidence their cars ended up there. They didn't write about that either." I was babbling because suddenly she was twitching. I was convinced she was about to have a seizure when a rapping sound came from the upstairs window of her big house behind me and she turned white like a ghost. "Father," I thought she said. It might have been "bother," though.

"Wait," I said, but she was clearly shaken and heading across the lawn. "Is that any way to say good-bye to me?" I asked. She smiled, stopped, and turned a heavily powdered cheek for me to kiss. I walked over and planted one. Maybe she had seen a ghost. As I looked up at her window, I was pretty sure I was going to see one.

"You're a good writer."

"I thought you said it was bad business I was about," I said.

"I said, be careful what you write."

"Auntie Pearl, is that some kind of threat?" I asked, and she turned to me sharp.

"Careful because you're in danger of shrinking from good writer into mere reporter," she said, and galumphed herself to and through her big wood door.

I ought to have felt miffed. Like most reporters, you could say I had a novel in me. Except I already wrote it; a famous one too. People never forgive me for that. "I'm happy," I whispered to myself—but the word had no meaning. I knew I was never happy.

When they made the *Neverknown* movie I was happier than anybody in the world. That kid from *Father Knows Best* who played Bud always wanted to hang out with me. My father was so embarrassed when the publicity people made "dates" for me with big starlets like Debby Reynolds and Ann Francis and I once saw the goddess herself, Elizabeth Taylor with her indigo eyes, across the lot at MGM, *Rhapsody*. She waved and smiled, I don't know why, at me. Bette Davis came on the set, she lived in Maine, she said, came all this way to meet me. Why didn't I write a part for her? Back then I wasn't even sure what that meant, but I laughed heartily with all the studio folk. I liked the starlets kissing me for cameras, my heart pounding.

Then nothing. The wave of popularity broke and I was left alone in that big, quiet house that got so much quieter. Believe me, writing another book might have killed me.

I moved on down the street at a clip. The Castanos had my car parked with one wheel up on the curb. I paid, the car went vroom, and off I went. I drove down State, turned right at Mission, and headed west toward Castillo. From there, under the highway to Cliff Drive. I began to feel self-conscious. I was acting because somebody else was pulling strings. Gin Chow had declared the visit vital, but what or whom was I seeking? The radio after warming up produced "Melodie D'Amour."

Serenade from your window. Tweet tweet little birdie. Tell her of my love. A bird could fly from the din at this end of the Mesa to her quiet window on Edgewater. It made my pulse rush until I remembered she would not be there. She had an apartment downtown now, probably had the gangster son there.

The construction site, vast acres of frame and plywood sheets, buzzed with simultaneities of sound. Who would ever live here in boxes so crowded so close to the beach? I turned down La Marina and drove as far as I could to park. With constant fogs of early summer, the old-timers called this asthma gulch. Today the clear morning air was especially sound-conductive, though; catcalls and even muttered conversations from scaffoldings carried clearly. I heard a snap that sounded nasty, and a bunch of heavy boards fell followed by deft imprecations, waves of insulting diction wounding the ear.

I walked the edge of a fine, powdery dust slopping on to crabgrass growing on the path. "Hey," I heard somebody say, but ignored it. It's not likely meant for me. "Hey," I heard again nearer. "Where you think you going?"

Wincing at the inevitable, I turned my head around. It was Petey Pepitone, whose uncle owned a gym.

"Hey Petey," I said. "You got a job."

"Not for long if I let the boss see me dallying with riffraff."

"Don't let me keep you," I said.

"Whither hence, pale wanderer?" he asked.

"Long walk off a short pier, I guess." He looked confused. "Beach walk," I said.

"You got a rough life. Is this an investigative reporter job?"

"You know, in a way it is, Petey," I said. I thought I might as well become backwards bait, the hook rising to the fish. "I'm following what you might call a hunch."

"Hey I had one of those with my wife last night," he laughed.

"Poor girl."

"Better than starching the socks, polishing the rocket, whacking the whippet. You ought to get hitched, instead of chasing … " He swallowed the rest of it, and I'm sure he suddenly remembered about my cousin. My God, I'm an incestuous pervert in the eyes of this town. "Hey if you see Perkoe down there?" he changed the subject nervously. "Mr. America? Look and see if he's got a surfboard, yet. Tell him I want to try one before I die. Okay?"

"Why would I see Bob Perkoe, Peter?"

"Because I just saw him and a bunch of the Regular Guys heading down there with beer. I figured you were meeting them?"

"It's a little early for me, man. You mean the Normal Guys." Then I thought, why be coy? "Tell you what, I'm actually looking into this guy got killed in the harbor."

"Brown," he said. "Except he didn't get killed. He reaped just what he sowed."

"Meaning what?"

"Didn't you know about him? He asked for it, my friend. I know all about this guy, I do. In fact, your uncle introduced me to him."

Now he had my attention. It was the second time I heard my uncle mentioned with respect to all of this, the universe was stuttering neatly. But it does that in a small town.

"He asked to be crucified?"

"I don't think he was. He was a fisherman going after shark, what did he expect? Fishing for livers."

"What does that even mean?"

"Oh, my. Trevor Westin doesn't know some fact about the Santa Barbra Channel, this *is* a red letter day." My obsession with the sea, shared with my late brother, was a widespread joke. As a kid, I used to bore grown-ups to death with books of odd creatures from the bottom of the sea.

"During the war, the Navy grounded our illustrious fishing fleet, most of them sons of Italy," he said. "This caused not only hue and cry but also a sharp spike in criminal adventures around the harbor and the lower east side."

"Careful. Some of my favorite uncles are fake guinea bastards," I said.

"And your father was on those beats."

"Why does everybody know so goddamned much about my father? You were saying about the livers."

"Somehow Army doctors learned that soldiers who took their vitamins fought harder, and lasted longer. Like me, va-voom. The Army needed a source of vitamin A, I think it was, found in abundance in said inner organs. They paid a fortune for the livers and let the men go back out in the water, to catch a fish the old wops used to throw way. Some of them made five-hundred scoots a day from the Army, more than they made in a month of mackerel before the war."

"They don't get vitamins from shark livers anymore, do they?"

"Of course not, scientists make them in a lab-or-a-tory." Suddenly, he's Boris Karloff.

"Then why was Brown fishing for livers?"

"Everybody assumes he was crazy. I assume everybody's crazy. The sharks were nearly wiped out during the war, but bounced back. Brown had some crazy idea about selling to the Chinese. Even got some government agency to buy him a boat. They're easy to catch—sharks—claimed they were edible too."

"Eat shark? That does seem crazy."

"See, it was justice. It wasn't any coincidence those holes in his hands and his feet."

"Sharks made the holes in his hands and feet?"

"I know, foot-ti-lah. Weird, man. Huh?"

"What do you mean weird?'"

"Well, don't *you* think it's weird?"

"Of course I fugging—oh, never mind. I gotta go, Petey. You're an original, you know that? You'll go far in this town. See you at Jimmy's if you ever break away from all that hunching." It's the town, I'm sure of it, an impervious keep, a safe harbor, for bewildered idiots holed up against waves of reality. People flock here to not make sense.

"My wife, she's a carpenter's dream," he sang like an Italian opera singer. "Flat as a board, easy to screw. I'll say hi to your uncle when he comes over checkin' up on his taco benders."

"What?"

"You know, the greasers?" Another crash came from behind us, the sounds echoing in waves. "I gotta go," said Petey, waving.

The blue was barely visible until I was on the edge of the cliff. This was where my uncle Frankie, the poet, liked to take me and my brother when we were little kids, walk down the back way, the old path people used to take walking to Castle Rock, like my father and his brothers, when *they* were little kids. It was a destination then, like the missing policeman Dooley said. Everything disappears, though, even places. I had to watch my step on the nearly vertical trail. I used to ski down the dust in my high-tops, dirt and little rocks always invading my shoes.

The cliffs stood in sandstone solemnity, subject to erosion, said Sister Mary Alphonse: a thousand centuries to wear it down. One hundred percent of nuns agree; everything disappears. I walked out to the rim of the world where the foam hissed and, on whim and hunch, headed toward Thousand Steps where houses beetle o'er the cliff. The government commandeered this land during our recent skirmish with the Japanese. Now it would be tract homes for the soldiers.

I felt the sea lion's presence before I saw him in the shining inter-tidal mud, lifting and dropping his head. He didn't seem right. Waves came, deep sheets of water, which the sea lion ignored, bobbing his head. Death was near. He would not drift out again, he would end in the sand. I watched for a long time, torn between wanting to help and fearing the teeth, the unpredictable animal behavior desperate to survive, the death that might rub off on me. The reliquary beach was dotted with baby abalone shells, mother-of-pearled, swollen green soda- bottle shards and shatters, sea glass, and two red glass balls, Japanese net floaters come from half a world away.

I saw the two guys minutes later. Tan specks, without features or clothes from that distance, walking unhurriedly toward me as I drew toward them. Soon there would be pleasantries: the three of us alone in the world between land and sea. But what if not? What if Gin Chow was right? If I was going to be taken, if it was trouble, I would know what to do. My father, that famed detective, taught me things. I could hear him say that two guys were always too many, despite what you see in the cowboy movies.

They stopped way up ahead and disappeared behind an outcropping of rock. Meanwhile I heard barking. Perhaps it was the sea lion. But when I looked back, way back, back almost where Castle Rock would have been visible once upon a time, I saw a man hulking forward with a scampering dog off leash. He was dressed in white like kitchen help or hospital staff. He was huge. If this was a trap, I was dead. The sea lion and I would both end in the sand. I felt tired in advance of all that was to come.

I looked out at the Channel Islands. I'd been out to Santa Cruz twice, both times with the Sea Scout troop, though after that summer of tragedy parents didn't let us go anymore.

Patrick had the fiercest eyes. He brought us around the island's point into the cave where the Chumash painted their hands and pictographs long ago. He brought us around in that skiff with the flabby-looking oars that barely fit in the locks. We were screaming, and I don't know if it was sheer joy but it was pure fear too. And then we glided into the cave, the rocks hanging pendulously above, and when I was scared Patrick would always reassure me with a word. He never let his friends make fun of me.

We tied the skiff up on a protruding rock and Patrick climbed out and helped me. Hold the rope, he said, and then he dove. Cold seawater enclosed him. My father never forgave God. Or me, for that matter, even though I was a child. And Patrick was never found. That's what happens when you drown. The worst thing was never having him back, not knowing where he is, I heard my mother say. And I walked back to my room when she said it, and I was numb, lying across my made bed, like everybody else in that house for many, many months. I never call it home. I willed my slurping feet out of the new footprint. I loved that island, though. In the middle of the sea, it stands solid against the lives that change around it, it stands against the cold sea.

I came around the cove and there they were, unexpected. One was leaning his arm across a large rock. The other was crouched. I thought of a greyhound. They were wearing the uniform: a Sir Guy shirt buttoned all the way up and khaki pants and shiny black shoes. Hair slicked back with pomade, thick and odiferous, sickly sweet. The one crouching had a pencil mustache; the other wore a hairnet like it was perfectly okay.

The standing man narrowed his eyes at me. "Got a cigarette?" he asked. I don't know why I patted my pants-leg pocket. I never smoked, not even in college.

"No," I said, but it was already too late. The other had exploded out at my back and I lurched forward, now adrenaline was my edge. I tried to think, as my father said, but an arm wrapped around my face and the bony side clipped my nose. A tang of pain coursed down, adding to my confusion. Think, my father yelled at me. You have to think, and breathe. The next blow almost took care of that. But I remembered the safe posture, rolled up like a sow bug. Two people are too many, he said. Get rid of one, and, for God's sake, find a weapon. They started kicking my ass, making towards my kidney while I tried to breathe.

"Hey, what's goin' on down there," said a voice from the cliff. I looked up and saw a young man standing there. It sounded like Petey Pepitone, but it didn't look like him. My glance gave the hairnet guy a chance to club at my face, but he missed and hit my neck. I felt clear now. I made a fake whimper, a semi-plea and he derided me just before he delivered the kick that would cause me trouble later. In reflex, I turned and it hit the kidney I was trying to protect earlier. It shocked something inside of me but something else was standing aloof, and the time was right. I hurled myself at his feet, grabbed and yanked, he went over and his head cracked against a sand-nestled rock. I don't know if it was luck, but his was bad.

"Motherfugging *pinche gavacho*," said the other as he came at me, but then the dog tore into him. He first said, "Uh," as one does when gut hit. A girlish scream escaped his mouth next. The dog, a German Shepherd, was arabesquing around the body shaking his head back and forth with lightning snaps, his teeth bared, and a low growl sometimes breaking either to a yip or bark. The man mustered his considerable strength and threw the big dog across three feet of sand but it just rebounded back on him, and I saw blood now running near his wrists and a cut across this cheek was sheeting red blood too.

It was horrible and frightening to watch, even if the snapping monster was saving me. My body was starting to hurt and my breath came fast. Behind me the ground resounded as the dog's owner came

Chapter 9

ABSURDLY, I KEPT WORRYING what Aunt Pearlie would say. I'd been up on my elbows and hands, but a sharp pain caught me halfway down my back. I've never cracked a rib, but that's what I supposed it was.

I tried to stand but lost my breath. "Ahh," I said and dropped down.

"My friend?" asked my giant savior.

"Something weird hurts. And by the way, thanks." I was gasping.

"King did all the work. Or you did," he said approaching the twitching assailant with a surprisingly ginger step. "What did you do to this fugging guy?" he asked. The accent was maybe Russian, I thought, a commie come to save me. He hulked over the Mexican.

"I tripped him," I said. Then the thug went still. "Did I kill him?"

"No such luck," said the hulking man. "But what did you say that made them so mad?"

"Say?" I winced at the sharp pain that met every effort to straighten. "What did I say? I asked them what they thought about the Marshall Plan so far, whether it was winning allies or creating dependent states. I think these guys just wanted to kick my ass because I'm a gringo." It made me a bit uncomfortable talking race with this swarthy guy.

"Naw," he said. "These guys are pachucos. They lean toward knives," he said, his voice calmly resonating, as if accustomed to airy halls of the philosopher's forum. "If they wanted to jump you they would've stuck you, and I don't think you'd be making wisecracks now. They seem high?"

"This was not a meaningless beating?" I asked.

He smiled at me and outstretched an oar-like hand to help me up. I stood and the pain came forward, filling me. I draped myself over a large boulder, looking at the prone man. "My name is Trevor."

"Then it *is* you. The writer. I wasn't sure," he said, and announced that his name was Figaro, at least that's how I heard it.

"I'm sorry," I stammered.

"You know, the man who flew too close to the sun, his father was Daedalus."

"Icarus," I said.

"Yes," he said, "Icaro in modern Greek. Eee-kah-row. My father was Greek, a fisherman," he said, answering my unraised questions. "My mother was a Mexican cook on the boat belongs to Larco, the Italian. I grew up here but went back to Greece, fighting German Nazis and then Russian communists. Heinz 57 varieties." His face knit together and a darkness gathered. He kept looking at the cliff. I decided to let the rest rest.

"Is he breathing?" I asked.

"We need to get you to a doctor. But we need to take care of him too. *Malakia*, I can drop a heavy rock over his head, or roll him out into the water and hold him under."

I laughed, then, and it hurt, but it was not clear if he was kidding. Icaro had a long, wide face with a coil of greasy black hair, his eyes were half in shadows but were pale, not quite blue or green. He had a Boy Scout canteen and offered me water. I drank a tiny bit, and then took some in my hand to splash my face. The canteen had a metallic medicine smell; maybe they all do. He seemed displeased with something, like I was wasting his water. He suggested helping me up the cliff. The workers could call the doctor. It was no good to leave me alone with the criminal, he could wake up and then he'd just be mad. As we walked I felt winded.

"You can lean on me," he laughed low. "Are you thirsty still? Why does a novelist get himself mixed up with such people? Are you doing research?"

"I'm not mixed up. I was just walking."

"Oh, I see," he said, in such a way that implied he did not.

"Hey," shouted the big man toward the top of the cliff. I was feeling vaguely nauseous at this point. "We need police," he yelled, up to where stood young Pepitone.

"Is Trevor drunk?" he yelled down.

I waved but the arm motion brought the pain on; maybe I shouldn't be walking. I felt a string of fire run deep through me and almost fainted.

"Here my friend, drink," said Icaro, holding me up. He had the canteen in his hand and it seemed to be coming toward me too fast. All went black.

* * * *

The back of my neck hurt when I came to, but my side felt worse. I was lying on my back inside an ambulance with the flap doors open wide and an ocean view. "Hey, here he is," said some voice. "How many fingers am I holding up?"

I raised my middle finger. "Aw, man, he's a fuggin' drunk. Are you a drunk, man?" the attendant shouted, as if I was deaf. There were two of them, one at my feet standing outside, the other inside by my head.

"Where's the other guy?" I said, having a hard time remembering my savior's mythological moniker.

"You mean Petey Pepitone or that big guy who took off when the cops showed?" he said. "He didn't like cops. Probably had a good reason. Fighting you over a bottle of Thunderbird," he added, as though he thought I couldn't hear him.

"The cops are here?" I asked.

"Never mind that, you're going to the hospital."

I began to protest, but lifting my head made me feel sick. I asked the ambulance attendant sitting at my feet if he had a bucket. He said, "Aw," but reached me a stiff paper container big as a cereal bowl. When I lay back down I felt better. I might have even dozed because when I looked up, we were at the hospital. The ambulance was backed up to the Junipero Street entrance, Emergency, and they were rolling my gurney out and the day was a sparkling blue and the air was perfect between hot and cold and the light wind felt like a caress over my forehead and my bare arms.

Inside was that alcohol scent that made my skin retract, poised for the needle prick. They set me in the hall and the doctor came over with one of those reflector things on the forehead and a cigarette dangling from his mouth. The ambulance driver told him that the cops were coming and that I needed to be checked out, I had been beaten. The doc looked over at me and held open my eyes and flashed a small penlight in my eyes and didn't look happy. "What happened?" he said.

I told the story in a monotone but for some reason left out that the Greek had hit me. Why? I wasn't at all clear if that's what did happen or why. He asked if I could sit up. I did, and his fingers walked down my back and he asked me to say where it hurt. I said "there" when he touched it, but it wasn't unbearable. "I think he cracked my rib."

"Interesting theory," he said as he snubbed out the Pall Mall in a sandbag ashtray. "Tell me, Trevor, right? Have you had anything to drink today?"

"What're you talking about, it's not even noon."

"It's beer-thirty somewhere."

"Not where I live, doctor."

"Okay," he said. "Okay." He mumbled to a nurse. "I'm gonna ask you to fill a cup." He caught my angered expression quickly. "No, it's not about booze. Fill 'er up with ethyl, then we're going to settle you in a room for a little of what we like to call observation. Okay?" I was feeling tired, again oddly tired. I nodded.

They helped me up off the gurney and showed me to a little toilet smelling of disinfectant, but not unpleasant. I unzipped, held the cup down, and then yelped at the blood-red liquid that filled the thin-walled glass beaker. It made me stop and then start and then stop. Cup finally filled, I turned the rest into the bone-white toilet bowl. The stream whirled and diluted, made a pink sheen in the standing pool.

I was distressed. I poked my head out and called the nurse. Presented with the news, Dr. Whatever said, "Umm," the way they do.

"What're you talking about, 'umm'?" I said.

"Well, that was *my* theory," he said. "Your assailant bruised your kidney. And I want to schedule you for a test, especially if the next cup's still red in an hour or two. Meanwhile, seeing as you didn't bring pajamas, we'll loan you some of ours and put you up till the morning. I know your dad by the way," he said. "And I know you, famous novelist. So I guess we don't need to worry about insurance, umm?"

I fell deeply asleep and felt deeply stupid waking up. I hadn't dreamed except for the fiends in red-hot skins pricking me with goads of lasting pain. I felt confused and was drowning in sweat when the nurse came around at lunch. It had only been an hour and a half. She took my temperature and left a plate of meatloaf, industrial mashed potatoes, and succotash on bone china under an inverted and angular chromium bowl. I ate some of it and felt my head list to the side. When

I woke up *She* was there. I couldn't believe it.

"What in Jesus's name?"

"Hush. You are such a sinner," said June, with narrowed eyes.

"No, really, how did you know?"

"A friend."

"The liquor distributor's son? This was probably his idea—funny that I should see him so soon after the murder. And all that followed."

"What're you talking about? Honestly Trevor, you sound like you are doing a bad Peter Gunn impression. Can you do Cagney?" I was staring stupidly, so she continued. "Jeanie Whitefoot's a candy striper here. She called. She thought you were sleeping something off, though."

"And you rushed down here to watch my angelic face. Like old times. Admit it."

She blushed. "Stop. We spoke about all this."

"No. You spoke, but you wouldn't listen to me, so it doesn't really count as speaking."

"I came to see you, and now you're ruining it."

"Okay. Know how much it means to me? Just to see you?"

"Oh, slush, where's my rubbers? Besides, if you get better fast, I'll see you again at the cookout at my parents' house Saturday. I haven't seen your mom and dad for ages."

"I'll get better. I'd better get better or I'll lose a lot of blood." For some reason that struck me as funny. I know I was acting weird. I wasn't sure exactly how to stop, though. I tried quiet.

"Okay," she said. "What happened?"

"I don't know exactly. I was walking on the beach."

"Does this have anything to do with the harbor murder?"

"Shut up if you already know everything, know-it-all."

"Shut up's a bad word."

"No." I said. "It's two bad words."

We grew up seeing each other on holidays. I looked up at her now and remembered the little girl looking up at me until the summer of her fifteenth year when I noticed how much I looked forward to seeing her and how she kept running back to me with some trivial news and how much I enjoyed the breathless, invisible meaning of her prattle.

"The beach?" she said, nervously looking around the hospital room.

I told her most of it, leaving out the bloody pee, which might've wrecked the delicate mood. The young, pretty nurse entered, scanned my love June, swiftly regarded me, and muttered she was glad I had awakened because they wanted to run some test. He's so stalwart, don't you think? she said. June, uncharacteristically demonstrative, bent over, and pecked my cheek and her lips left moist traces.

"I have to go, my one and only," she said. "I'll call you before Saturday."

My face burned like it always does. I waved awkwardly as she retreated into the white-and-gray hall.

"Your girlfriend's cute," said the nurse.

If only, I thought, but smiled at the starched whites and the pink flesh that filled them.

"Think you could move over to the gurney when it comes?"

"I could leap there," I said.

"Whoa, Lone Ranger. Let's first see how you do with the bedpan." She handed it to me. I held it like it was infected with vile effluvia. Perhaps it was.

"Am I supposed to do this in front of you?"

"I'm a nurse. I've seen some surprising things. Entertain me. In fact if you need it, I could even help," she said, drawing the curtain around the bed closed.

It was a contortionist's trick and I still felt weary. The stream was still red, but not nearly so bad. Sheepish, I handed it out. She waited a second, pulled the curtains open, and said she had to draw some blood. She tied my arm; blood rose into a tube. I was cool, surprising myself. She smiled at me with considerable kindness.

"I'm sorry I scared your girlfriend away," she said.

"She's not my girlfriend."

"Good," she said.

"Pardon me?"

She gazed back into my face. "I just mean, if she was your girlfriend she shouldn't go running off in your hour of need. Do you want to know my name?"

"My hour of need," I said. I looked down at the cool ice on her gold band on her left hand. "Say, is it okay with him if we flirt like this?"

She laughed sweetly musical, like a bird leaving for a pool of water. "He'd probably just ask his mother first. It's Marie. My name, don't forget. There's a test. Get over on this," she said, sliding the gurney over parallel to my bed.

"Yes, ma'am. Marie."

"I'm going off to get the attendant."

"I'll miss you," I said. Marie stared back, shooting me a quizzical look. She bustled out, and I returned instantly to slumberous reveries, Morpheus curling around me: a harbor mist. I woke up rolling through dim halls. The attendant had a blond flattop and pop-up ears. He smiled as I nodded.

"Don't worry," he said. "It's the o-o-only way to fly." We slid into a large ward, bouncing swinging doors back, and a nurse asked if I could walk. I said, of course. She said she knew my father.

A bulging X-ray camera covered in futuristic plastic hovered over another hospital bed. A few seconds later, a doctor entered. He hoisted me gently up and suggested I relax. A metal cart with metal sheeting around it and the international radiation sign was pushed into the room. Again the doctor bade me relax as he swathed my arm with icy alcohol.

"Try very hard not to move."

"Okay, why?" I asked.

"I'm going to inject you with some dye. This machine will be able to detect it gathering in your kidney."

"Oh that's reassuring," I said.

He smiled. "I don't recommend you make regular use of the technology. X-Rays. But that's not the scary part."

"Again, I feel so relieved."

"Yeah. It's the shot. I've got to get it right in the vein or else it burns like hell. We don't want that."

Done swathing, he took my arm, cradled it, and shoved in the spike. I grunted, he mumbled some conciliatory phrase and then laid my arm down. "Now stay staying still," he said. The liquid was rushing into my vein; I could feel that. But so far no burn. And now the big machine was over me. I've become one with the atomic age, I thought.

Chapter 10

The old man gestured. The young man complied, and stepped inside the craft with its damp floor, and swung into one of two woven hanging seats. The old man moved into the other just as the door closed and the ship suddenly dropped backward. The young man gasped in surprise.

The old man urged him not to worry. They sank slowly, and streams of fine bubbles flowed past the windows on opposite sides of the craft. Great strands of kelp appeared, but these were just the tops of a hundred thousand "trees" that formed an immense forest they had entered, traveling now in a diagonal downward trajectory. Their seats were comfortable, and since they were suspended from a single point, remained on gravity's perpendicular as the men traveled back and down. Away from the shore now, they rode and plunged far below the ocean's ever-moving surface.

Chapter 11

SOMEWHERE THE EVERLY BROTHERS were singing, "I can make you mine, taste your lips of wine, anytime, night or day." Back in the room, I slept a lot. People came and went, though nobody talked of Michelangelo. Tests revealed what everybody expected: the kidney was bruised but normal. The healing had begun. Dinner came and went, too, frozen vegetables and chopped steak. I wanted to go home.

By the way, I lied about the shot. I had felt a kind of wave, if not of heat, then of an illuminating flush. The needle opened me to a way of seeing. Where it punctured my skin it met sunlight through Venetian blinds, the hair on the back of the attendant's hand, and all the little ideas floating above us. This is right now, everything in that room screamed.

But the crooning from a newfangled transistor radio brought me back to the world of dreams and regrets. I was breathing in and out. I saw Icaro framed by the door. I squirmed. What was I supposed to say?

"I am sorry, my friend," he said, eyes cast down. Indoors, his accent thickened. "I fear you are angry. I think I hit you with the canteen when we were waving at the friend of yours, the man on the cleeff."

"You think?" I said.

"See. Of course you are mad. I am so clumsy, but I still do not understand how you went down so hard. Do you have, please pardon me, my friend, what the boxers call a glass jaw?"

"What're you talking about? You hit me."

"Of course," he said with such utter guilelessness that I began to wonder about wondering about him. I realized I ought to be grateful. "But you must believe it was an accident. So much so, I don't even know when it happened. Suddenly you were on the ground. At first I thought you fainted. I still think maybe you fainted." He looked honestly bewildered.

After a pause, I said. "I should thank you. What about the guy who jumped me?"

He straightened up, but still looked a little shamefaced. "When the policeman came I went to look, he was gone—your assailant. Maybe his friend, the other pachuco *pustiko*, came back and dragged him off."

"Maybe," I said, because I couldn't think of anything else to say. It was not even evening and this day was wearing me out. The Greek seemed, I don't know, like a savior, though. He glowed.

He spoke in a voice just above muttering. "I'm not sure why you say, 'I should thank you.' I didn't do anything you wouldn't have done for me," said this thick, large Icaro, staring down at his big wingtip-shod feet.

"It's basic politeness, and I forgot it," I said. "What's a *pustiko*?"

He looked up at me and grinned. Then he looked suddenly cognizant, privy to some new information. I would swear he sniffed the air, gigantic Icaro, and said "Fee-fi-fo," though he might have just said his name slow. Then, as quick as a bird leap, his face went sheepish. "I'll tell you later. I just remembered I have a job I go to sometimes." He smiled and disappeared from the frame.

A sound from the hall came and two policemen and a man flowed into the room, slow like octopi in a tank. The detective looked familiar.

He hadn't been at the station, but I knew him from somewhere.

"How you doin'?" he said. "We hear you sustained internal injuries."

"It's weird when you say those words applied to me. I guess so. Did you find the jerks that did this? Are you here to give me a ride home?"

"That's not a service we tend to provide," he said, and I recognized the officious tone: the chief investigator from the breakwater. "We're here to investigate a beachside assault. Yours."

"This was connected to Brown, that's why *you're* here. You think this was connected?" I asked, floundering.

"Anything's possible." He hemmed a haw. "But more pertinent, we want to know if you had any contact with Officer Bennett in the last twenty-four hours."

"Baby Bird?" I said. "In his office. He told me about Newt and Dooley, the duly sworn officer of the court."

"What?" he said. "Was that a joke?"

"No," I said. "Not if you have to ask. What about Bennett?"

"It seems he's disappeared too."

"What the fug," I said.

"We're beginning to see this as a situation developing. We are, of course, worried."

"When it is one of your own," I said, numb again, but picturing a world devoid of all people. One by one they leave.

"Two—Dooley, now Bennett. Men trained to deal with the criminal element," he said.

"Where did Officer Bennett disappear from or to?"

He looked at me then shook his head. "I don't know. His car was in Isla Vista."

"You mean those apartment houses out by the Goleta orchards?"

They were moving north, these disappearances. This was near the spanking new university.

"His car was just past Sands Beach, over the dunes—that's all I know. We're not sure what took him out there. But he didn't return. We're also disturbed about *this*, obviously," he said, gesturing at me in bed.

"Don't worry," I said. "The food was okay."

Gin Chow predicted I would find something, make sense of things. This is where I stood, amid the un-disappeared, at least so far. "What is the brotherhood?" I asked. "Dooley said Snake Jake was drummed out of a brotherhood. You know what he was talking about?"

"Who knows what he meant?" said the officer, too quick. Another cop poked his head into the room, whispered to the cop nearest the door, who then walked over to my reddening detective, who stiffened. "If anything more occurs to you, please call me," he said, wrote a number on a card, and handed it to me. Occurs to me? I had enough occurrences, but that's not what he meant. "Maybe he was a Shriner," he said.

"Maybe the Knights of Columbus," I said. "He was a mackerel snapper, you know."

"So am I. So's your dad. Who isn't?"

"What did the autopsy reveal?" I asked.

"Ha, like the movies," he said. "Mr. Brown's remains will be cremated in accordance with his will. The ashes will be sprinkled in the ocean in accordance with his wife. There was no official need to determine any cause of death beyond contusions and exposure."

I feel a bit weird. Exposure. "How long was he exposed?" I asked.

"Long enough to die," said the cop, who picked up some speck off the floor and began heading out. "Gotta go."

"You investigated?" I said, incredulous to his retreating back. The crucified shark fisherman was about to be cremated and fed to the waves. I'm in a bed and the police are about to be gone with the wind.

He walked back in; he was angry now. "Sure we investigated. You were there. He was wet. He lost a lot of blood. There were holes in his hands and feet. Turns out there were hundreds of little holes, like he was shot with a BB gun or eaten by fish. Who knows? He's a puzzle without witnesses, fingerprints, or clues. His wife says everybody loved him. Had an accident, officially speaking."

"I don't understand," I said.

"Neither do we, but apparently it's beyond understanding. His death has been classified an accident, though maybe it's an unsolvable mystery, like the Holy Trinity."

"Nothing is an accident."

"It would be nice to live in that world," he said. "So long."

They split. One guy stayed, the guy who wasn't a cop. "Are you my bodyguard?" I asked.

He laughed and pulled down his spit curl. "You don't recognize me?"

I couldn't endure any more banter. "No, I guess not."

"Huh," he said.

"Okay, I'll bite. Who are you?"

"Hint: Who saved your life this morning calling the cops?"

I looked at him, "Petey." It didn't look like Pepitone, but it sounded like him.

"Who else? Man, did you get clobbered out there?"

"Uh, yeah, I did." This guy was changing before my eyes, evolving into his own image. "You get a haircut?"

"No," he said. "This Brown thing is what's weird. I'm gonna ask around about it."

"Petey don't. Didn't you hear about people disappearing?

Everybody vanishes. Some into thin air."

"I'll be discreet. Cop ya later!" And then *he* vanished. I called his name, but I had no more strength. I fell back into dark.

I slept all night. I pondered my intricate fate when awakened by the watery morning light. My car was left at a construction site. My new girlfriend didn't come to see me, but the old one who broke my heart did. There was a man who died under suspicious circumstances, but the police stopped thinking about him because it was too crazy. Breakfast came under the same chromium lid. Marie was off duty, and the distant radio played "Love Letters in the Sand." Attendants brought in a television and I watched kids' shows, some guy who drew cartoons, until Marie returned, reborn. "Not your girlfriend, huh?" she asked.

"What?" I blinked in the light reflected from her starch whites. "You're funny, but I'm glad to see you."

"I bet you say that to all your not-my-girlfriends."

"Please elucidate. I understand only American idiomatic English, though I'm learning to curse in Greek."

"How are you getting home?" she asked. "We're releasing you, you know."

"Are you offering?" I asked, but she wasn't. "I guess I'll bite the bullet and call a cab."

She looked at her paperwork. "The doctor made no such arrangement. There is a Miss June Blah-di-blah waiting in the lobby. Apparently she made your arrangements. Says she's your cousin? Kissing cousin?"

I was confused and elated, happiness returning in waves.

"Kissing cousins?" she repeated, her face screwed up sour.

I nodded.

Chapter 12

ROLLING THROUGH HEATED HALLWAYS, back in clothes, I could see bay windows at the end of the tunnel, and I could see June.

The lobby was long and, though sparsely inhabited, my entourage and I crossed paths with a man I knew. His eyes were wet with tears and he held a woman's coat in his arms. He was a friend of my father's—a detective, I think, long retired. Choate, or Plussed, I couldn't quite remember the name. His wife was nice, and now gone, apparently.

Before I got to where June was standing, a man in white gowns, my resident, came loping up holding a clipboard.

"Afraid I'd miss you," he said, breathing hard. The pack of Pall Malls in his pocket and the brown-yellow fingers holding my chart explained the huff and puff. He had an English accent. His eyebrows were tufts, and his breath smelled like sulfur. He looked closely at me. "Looks like you're in good hands."

"Thanks," I said, not knowing what else to say.

"I just wanted to ask you a question if I may?" he said, chest heaving. "About your book?"

"Shoot."

"Are you aware that the problem with living underwater would not be getting oxygen as much as getting rid of carbon dioxide?"

"Of course not," I said, half distracted by my angel, treading polished-floor-reflected sunlight toward me. "I'm not even sure what that is."

"Quite so?" he asked. "It's the by-product of breathing, poison for us, but here we have plants that need it and can change it, and give it back to us as oxygen—rebreathing. It's rather problematic, your book."

"You're kidding," I said, distracted by June's sweet eyes, her high cheekbones and smiling lips. I had initially assumed it was Camarillo calling, psychiatric doctors to kidney doctors, as if I was on probation for the time I spent misunderstanding things. I was relieved on many levels at once. "You know, I wrote it when I was barely a teenager, half a lifetime ago from my perspective. It's hard to imagine that the science of a children's book might make you worry."

"I'm afraid not," he said. "It does matter, if people read it and get the wrong idea."

"It's fiction," I said. "It has to look like the real world, but just enough for people to keep reading it. They don't have to live by it."

Behind him a woman on two canes plodded along the shiny floor with a ridiculous broad smile on her gray face. It was Choate's wife.

He looked angry, the resident, made me sign a form. I tried to joke about giving him my autograph, but that seemed to turn his whole life force against me. It should have bothered me but I had forgotten the whole encounter as we pushed out the front door and I smelled car exhaust and faint sea air and freedom.

Chapter 13

"YOU CAME TO PICK me up."

"Don't be so smug. You look like a puppy."

"In other words, irresistible."

"Hmm," she said.

"At last you admit it," I smiled. Cold wind blew in the open window of her spotless Ford. She was impeccable, this June. Dressed smartly with hair that neatly feathered around her neck and brow, she made her clothes feather too over her slender frame. Somehow casually French and coordinated in blue and ice tones. The vehicle itself looked like a jewel case, everything perfectly placed and sparkling. As she drove, her fingers held the pale azure steering wheel as if she were delicately adjusting space rising toward her, precisely conforming it. Her soft hair held a mother-of-pearl comb, a mother-of-pearl comb held her soft hair.

"Hope your apartment isn't a mess," she said.

"If I knew you were coming, I'd have baked a cake."

She looked over at me. "Who said I was?"

This is *the* woman, I thought. I must be cool, distant, gone, daddy, gone.

"I haven't been there for two days, and when I left I thought I was going for a walk on the beach."

She sighed. "Again. Why did you go for said walk?"

"I cannot tell a lie. I don't know why. Part of it was to follow up a lead, but I didn't really understand the informant much, either."

She looked at me and stopped at the stop sign on the corner of Constance and Bath. "An informant, Trevor, not a voice?"

"I won't continue talking if you always assume crazy."

She was quiet. A sadness deeper than the roots of a kelp forest spread between us. I did not believe the darkness could return. Those days were over.

"It better be clean," she said, peeling time back. "You better have clean sheets."

Now was the winter of my discontent about to scram, I thought.

When we got to Islay and the apartment house I tried being cool going up the stairs. But my side and my back ached and I winced. She winced back like it was a game. The light shone in moving spangles through the giant eucalyptus, and June was pushing gently on my sore-spot back as I fit key in lock and turned its lumbering mechanism. The door swung in and so did we. The place was neat though a bit stiff in the air department. She swung around me and caught my eyes in hers, heading off for the bathroom with a sweet smile, a wicked smile. I stretched into a yawn of pure pleasure. Mine again. The phone rang. I was willing to let it go.

"Aren't you going to get it?" she asked from behind the door. "What if it was me?"

It suddenly occurred it might be my editor. It could be my parents. Soon as I picked it up I felt in my bones it was something bad.

"Hello?"

"God, Trevor, you're alive. I guess I should be mad that you didn't call."

"Mary Annie," I said softly, hoping present company might be excepted from hearing this. "How are you? I was in the hospital." My face was glowing hot.

"Good one," she said.

"No really, I got jumped down on the beach that day after we … I guess it was day before yesterday." Shit, it was yesterday.

"This is your story?"

"Listen, I can get you a doctor's note if you want. I'm sorry I didn't call you, but I had a bruised kidney and a battered ego. Turns out I'm not tough enough for two pachucos."

"Don't get mad, lover. I was kidding, though it did disappoint me when I waited all evening for you. Thought you might want to come over. You could come over now. I'm bored. We could have fun together."

It never rains, does it? "I'd love to … "

"But?"

"I have a deadline. Can it be tomorrow?" Please, I thought, please get off the phone.

"Sure, sugar snap. Are you sure you don't have somebody else there?"

Just then the bathroom door opened. Sweet June put a finger over her full lips, shook back her hair, and retreated into my room.

"Uh, no, I'm not sure."

"Good, a man of mystery. You call me tomorrow morning, he-man who doesn't need anybody. And I mean call. I want to know everything you do from now on." She laughed, hung up, but I wondered at her sudden interest in me. A bird in the hand, I thought, laughed at my shameless self, and headed for my room.

Playing nurse, as she put it, June poked me down the back with her long index finger. "Does it hurt there? There? There?"

"I howl in pain," I said. "How does this game we play get won?"

June laughed. She covered my lips with hers. The light of day changed and a gloom came over the sky, but it just made my unlit room more sheltering. I can't remember many moments when I was happier. Sometimes my back hurt, and I grunted, worried, and she kissed my neck. Always I had to begin slowly with her and if my hand strayed too quickly, she gasped and sent me back to square one. But it was just a matter of time and I had no better way to spend mine. When the hesitant woman at last entered the spell, she changed into the creature June. She had my clothes off and she traveled down the length of my chest and stomach and took me into her mouth, as if I needed the encouragement. I did not object, though, and much as it changed me it also made me worry. A sweet worry I would not last. And there was something that she always did that meant the end was nigh, and end happily. But we both moved on this time, we ended and we couldn't end, I stayed in her. The phone rang twice and she moaned. It stopped and eventually we did as well. I rolled out of bed to use the bathroom. She pulled up covers around her face and smiled at me.

Later she wanted to go eat. We went to the Mesa and got my car and dropped hers at her place. We drove out to Bray's in Goleta because she didn't want to see anybody we knew. We drove through the orchards of upper State Street and the farms outside Goleta. The town itself was swaddled in strange light, and a few drops hit my windshield as we pulled across the highway and into the dirt lot.

By the time we were eating dinner, the rain was coming down. June shivered a bit and pulled the thin sweater over her smallness as if it would help. I took her hand and she didn't pull away, though I saw her look around the room. She smiled, though her eyes were starting to get that furtive look I knew. I was sore and the pain protection was beginning to roll back.

"It's not unlike food," she said.

"I told you to stick to the cheeseburger or the French dip, but no, you had to have the pheasant under glass."

She smiled again and picked up her dry chicken sandwich on toasted Wonder bread. I had a beer, twinkling bubbles rising up through an old soda fountain glass, and it tasted exquisite.

"So why did she call you?"

"Who?" I asked, realizing how acute my darling is.

"My old roommate. Are you," she paused, blinking prettily, "seeing her?"

"I ran into her at Frank's last whenever night. I drove her home; she was pretty drunk. And stuff."

"Oh."

"It wasn't like that."

"I don't want you to sleep with her, Trevor," she said, with a steely reserve that put me off.

"Okay, I won't. Since we're so happy, and all."

"I guess that means the thought crossed your mind," she said with an even, cold, and distant voice. As I began gruff protests, she changed her tact, the nimble one. "I know it isn't fair. It's not like we can … not like I have a claim on you.'

"The claim is there," I said. "You just have to acknowledge it. Shit. I was going to try to keep this light. Try not to scare you off again."

"I know you were, darling, and I appreciate it. It's just that I don't trust that girl."

"Why? I always thought you two got along."

"She won't leave me alone," she said. "She asks such personal questions, but I feel like she's working for some secret organization, like she's spying on me."

"Whoa," I said, remembering inquisitor Mary Annie on the June adoption ruse. And what June replied. And me wondering why and afraid to ask.

"Enough. I'll stay away if it makes you happy. But I do want to know one thing, one thing about her."

"What?"

"Didn't she have a thing with Baby Bird?"

"Who? Oh you mean that Bennett boy who became a cop. I think so. But that was in high school. Isn't he married now?"

"So, what kind of questions does she ask you?"

"That's two things you want to know about her," she said, whirling her paper straw around a vanilla milkshake. I let it ride. The truth seemed oddly unimportant at Bray's 101.

We drove home and the rain became bad. We stopped near State and Modoc, where the Falls bar sign looked double drenched. It was an old-fashioned neon masterpiece that mimed the action of a real waterfall, endlessly sliding into nothing, but producing a calming effect, nostalgic, sweet. Between its own aqueous neon art and nature bending down over in heavy downpour, it made you shiver to be happily inside the car.

We stopped because I saw a big something wash down the gutter like a load of laundry, and when I looked over at June her pale face said she saw it too. People were disappearing, I thought. I stopped the car ahead of where the something should have rolled, got out in the torrent, and saw nothing. Even the dead leave no trace. When I got back in, she put her light hand on my soaked sleeve.

"Take me home, okay?" she asked.

I started up the clunker and we trundled down Modoc to the edge of town.

"Trevor?"

"Yes, baby?"

"When you wrote your book, your mother told me you wouldn't come out of your room for days."

"She exaggerates. I had to pee, didn't I? Besides all she ever did was tell me to go outside and play. She regrets that now."

She was quiet for a second. "I don't think she does. Do you think you will ever do that again, sweetheart?"

"I don't know," I said. "I don't know anything."

"Don't forget to take me to my place not yours. I know your old tricks."

"Crap," I said, smiling into the dashboard light.

Credit me with not mentioning the liquor distributor. Credit me with driving her home without complaining once, though I bit my lip twice. I think she credited me. She kissed me and said she would come over and get me on Saturday before the barbecue.

"Maybe you will do it again," she said. "Write. I could help you."

I smiled. Help me write? Or disappear? I thought. There were still Christmas decorations around town after the holiday had left itself broken on the sidewalks with scattered ribbons and festive bits of paper. The rain let up when she turned around and ran toward her front door. She waved and ducked in away from the bright light of the streetlamp. By the time I got home the rain didn't exist anymore. There were stars and the cold-tipped winds whooshing around them.

Chapter 14

Outside the craft was a blue space fraught with surprises. The young man saw vague shapes: shadows in the distance that he assumed were either large fish or sea lions. But as the dark forms danced through the undulating forest they seemed more and more human. The young man turned to his companion and asked him to please explain.

"This is a world much older than yours," he said. "The people here once believed in eating jimsonweed, though it made them half blind and half mad. You'd fit right in," he cackled. "They left the jimson behind. These are sea people."

"They have engines to breathe underwater?" the young man asked.

"You aren't listening to me," said the old man. "They started with us, as us, but living along the edge of the water and inhaling its salt air and eating its rich bounty, they chose this different world in which to live, which then chose them."

The young man thought about a time before he was born; it might as well have been an age of legends. He sometimes wondered why it didn't bother him that there were lives before his life, and rich times filled with laughter, triumphs, and sorrows. And yet he feared the future because it was time without him in it.

Outside, the sea people were swaying in unison with the kelp. He pressed his face closer to the cold glass and jumped back as one of them glided by not three feet away. Through thick glass and deep blue sea, he saw its pasty-white face and arms, with hair that was like a gray bristle of thin fins. Its body tapered to a point. Beneath the craft whispered the sound of carbon dioxide escaping in silver bubble cascades.

Chapter 15

PHONE CALLS BEGAN PRECISELY at 10:00 a.m. and never stopped. I left the fugging house in disgust just before noon.

First the editor suddenly wanted a follow-up. When I told him about the number of disappearances, he wondered if a more experienced reporter ought to handle it. I said fine, just hope the more experienced reporter doesn't disappear too. I told him about the guys who jumped me at the beach; he said to be careful. I said too late, never mind.

He wanted to know how the Huxley thing was going, and I said I hadn't had time to take the drugs yet, but maybe tonight. After silence, he asked what I meant and don't say never mind, he said. I tried to explain and then *he* said never mind.

Somebody was trying to talk to him behind a receiver-clapped hand. He asked me to write up everything we talked about so he'd remember. He said, poke around if you can.

After all that, I was exactly where I was before he called. At least I hadn't lost ground. I looked at the time. I wondered about Gin Chow. Wouldn't you know? Soon as I did, he called.

"Something bad happened at the beach," he said.

"No wonder everybody says you're psychic."

He was quiet.

"I want you to come visit me in my home," said Gin Chow.

This was a first. "When?" I asked.

"No," he said, changing his mind. "It's too messy."

"I'll be over later today."

"No," he said. He said he had to go. He went.

The next call was from my parents, unexpected. My mother spun my head with details and run-on stories that featured "your father" as chief protagonist and antagonist simultaneously. Several times she shouted, "Isn't that right, hon?" or "What was that French barber's name?" to which my father barely gave articulate reply from behind the muffling screen of a newspaper, through teeth clenched the better to hold his cherrywood pipe. I meant to tell her about the hospital but soon as there was a gap she was off and running. She mentioned this weekend's barbecue and added a breathless, of course, you will be there. Since it wasn't really a question, and since I had already told June I would go, I mumbled an assurance and asked if I should bring something. She was about to answer when her doorbell rang and the teakettle shrieked and she begged herself off from further discussion, seeing as we would be merrily reunited at Aunt Helen and Uncle Dick's. Do you want to say good-bye? She piped up, high-pitched. My father asked whom she was talking to and she said, your son. He said, oh. Do you want to speak to him? Surprisingly, he said, yes. Where are you? he asked. Home, I said. Oh, he said. I was in the hospital, I said. Jumped, but escaped. I won't tell your mother. Are you all right? he asked, though not in surprise. Bruised kidney. They told me we were insured. He was silent. I was jumped, near the Mesa. Near Uncle Dick's office. Did he see you? he asked in a soft voice. I don't think so, I said. Oh, he said. But you're all right? Never better, I said. He said he was glad.

The next call was from me to June. She didn't pick up because, like most people who live in this world, she had a job away from home. I whispered into the receiver as the dial tone rolled unceasingly.

As I sat there sunk and glum, the phone sparked into jangling rills again. "Hello."

"You've got fugging nerve," said a raw female voice on the line.

"Pardon me?" I asked. God knows why I didn't hang up.

"You even know my husband?" the woman asked in a slurred voice.

"Ma'am, I don't even know who you are."

"Who I am? Well, sonny, I am Anita Ramona Sitterly, Mrs. Jacques Brown. How you like those apples?"

I was silent.

"Snake Jake's Veronica Lake," she said with a course laugh, which, I think, ended in a sob. Or maybe it was a dull expulsion of morning phlegm. Jesus, it was an hour to lunch and she sounded drunk.

"Mrs. Brown, I'm so sorry."

"Why? You didn't kill him." She laughed like a rasp on a board. "Or did you?"

After an awkward silence I said, "Mrs. Brown? I wrote the story any reporter would have. God. I don't know what I'm trying to say."

"Of course you don't. The fugging press, all about stories. People aren't stories, they're flesh and blood. A lot of blood actually," she said, and began her indeterminate sob-laugh again.

"But I didn't say anything offensive about Jake, I mean Jacques."

"You really don't know what you mean, do you? But you probably want to know, don't you? You want to know the Jacques Brown story, all the way to its electrifying end. That's what they say in the movies: electrifying. That make you happy, honey boy?" She didn't really sound like she was teasing.

My heart was pounding. "Of course," I said. "I can come over, if you like."

"Honey boy, sonny boy, you just have to wait. I have to keep low or else they'll come after me."

"Who?" I asked, grasping at straws. "The brotherhood?"

"What?" she answered with a question, then started laughing. "No dickless boys would bother themselves with me," she said, but sounded shaky. "Talk of honor and of truth, my friend. Do you know what the motto of the sea is?"

"What did you say?" I said.

"Women and children first. Ha. Maybe Jacques ought to have paid attention to his woman at least. I have to go," she said.

"I thought you wanted to talk," I said, trying to figure how to get her here, or me there. "Who is coming after you? At least tell me that."

"My children come after me, but maybe you're father is coming after all of us. Hey, I don't have to talk to you. But maybe I will when the time is right. Bye honey sonny." She hung up, laughing and sad.

I turned away from the phone to get a glass of tap water from the kitchen. My father? Everybody talks about my father, who was a policeman and then a war hero, though nobody seems to remember what it was he did. A pillar of the community, he rode in the Fiesta Parade every year he wasn't overseas. Probably he will ride in it this year, even though he made an abrupt about-face a few months ago. Quit the Naval Reserves and moved from his longtime home here to Pasadena.

There was talk about his sea change too; some say he was thrown out of the Reserves. His only enemy was Mr. Santa Barbara and nobody knows why they fought. Mister Mystery, my father. He always said Storke wanted the Navy out of the harbor. Now my father was out of Navy and hometown. Why would my father care about Brown's sea witch wife? The little window looked out on a street where morning light fell around the blue shadows on the off-white sidewalks. Snails roamed wet leaves. Just as my glass filled with water, the phone rang yet again.

It was Gin Chow. "Come over," he said.

Santa Barbara water comes down from T. M. Storke's man-made lake or collects in various old reservoirs and tastes terrible most of the time. It reeks of old pipes. I gulped the awful stuff and went back into the parlor. I fingered the little packet of pills out of its hiding place and put them in my sweater. I decided to go out to lunch and started imagining where: Mexican, maybe, the Rose, hamburgers at Petersen's. I was hungry, riled inside, in need of something.

I called her before I left. I imagined she watched the phone as it rang over and over, knowing she couldn't answer because it might be me, crying because she was helpless, afraid of the power, the feelings that were always there, her palms wanting to pick up the receiver, crying because I might prove to be the one for her, after all. Before I knew it, *I* felt like crying, and the phone kept ringing into daylight falling in her rooms.

I got in the Packard and sat. I turned on the radio.

News: The US launched a satellite to enable radio signals to circle the globe; communist insurgents in Cuba were gaining.

Entertainment: "We've been good, but we can't last, Hurry Christmas, hurry fast," sang electronic chipmunks.

I started the engine and headed over to State Street. There, on the way, I spied him lumbering up Mitch, undeniably Icaro. I was about to pretend I *didn't* see him when he began waving at me furiously. This is too convenient, I thought.

"My friend," he said huffing a bit, "should you be out of the hospital bed so soon?"

"Icaro," I answered. "I got out yesterday and it doesn't hurt at all."

"Only when you laugh, ha," he said, imitating some television act. I laughed and then mimed an ouch, which tickled him, still breathing hard.

"You've been running, Icaro?"

"No, my friend. Well, yes." He looked a little shamefaced. "I am, what you call, *in flagrante delicto*." It took time to figure out the Latin. "The woman's husband came home earlier than anticipated, and, well, I went out the back door. Over that fence," he said, pointing way down Micheltorena, "and then I put a little distance between me and the house of my indiscretions."

I looked at him, nodded. "Indiscretions," I said. "That's the state senator's house, my friend." I was impressed. Mrs. State Senator was a brick cathedral. "The wife or the maid?" I asked.

"Do you know the husband?" he asked darkly.

"Yeah."

"Then it was the maid," he smiled, showing golden choppers. "May I sit in the car for a second?" He hoisted in and the seat sagged. He was still puffing and motioned me to drive down the road. I guess he was going my way.

"I would say our friendship is based on serendipities," he said as his breath returned. "Is that not the case?"

"Our destinies seem to be twined," I said.

"Twinned," he said. "But there is one more coincidence I feel I must burden you with." He looked over quickly.

"Burden away."

"You are the same Mr. Westin who wrote about Jacques Brown's murder in the L.A. *Times*, I would say, I would guess. And I have information about Snake Jake for you."

I pulled over to the curb. "What is going on here? Exactly, I mean."

"See, I told you it would be a burden. An annoyance? I am acquainted with Mrs. Brown. She's about to call you, you should know."

I decided not to admit anything, and see if this comradely man was on the level. The car seat wasn't. He raised hand to brow and, with an embroidered white handkerchief, mopped away a swath of silver perspiration. I could watch more sweat pour out onto the surface as he spoke. "The situation is serious, she believes."

"I'm sorry," I said, breathing deeply. "How did you say you know her and all of this?"

"From Mrs. Brown, she is what you call a big loudmouth. She showed me the newspaper story, and before I realized the implications, I told her I knew you. When she said she meant to call you I felt I should ... "

"But how do you know her?"

"I am the chef at Jacques's. I thought you knew this. I'm the only man in town who ... *skata*, it's hot today ... I'm the only chef in town who's ever been to Europe. If it was Filipino food people wanted, well, then, the other chefs in town would be fine. I know the difference between beef stock and a consommé, and look how handsomely I dress and the stylish way I can move around town." His eyes bulged like a lizard's and blinked in slow motion. "The woman is a drunk but a stupid drunk. In their hearts, most heavy drinkers are obsessed with survival. They must be free tomorrow, to drink again. Drunks are the best planners I've ever met. They believe in time."

I pulled the car back onto Garden Street. "I say this with all due appreciation for the fact that you saved my life: Why is it, my friend, your business is so close to mine?"

His looks changed. His eyes narrowed. "If my attentiveness offends you, I am sorry. I thought it would be helpful for your newspaper story."

"Who says I'm doing one?"

"You already covered his death. And you went to the police to follow up."

"It was an accident."

"Like the police, you don't think he was murdered?"

"No, I mean, my story about Brown was an accident. I happened to be listening to the radio, the police band. I was thinking about my ex-girlfriend. And there was a report. So I went down to the harbor to forget my woes. And I didn't see anybody else reporting it. So I did. It was just a thing that happened, you know, inevitable. Like losing a hat in the rain, catching a cold, and then dying. You travel one way or another. I actually ran into my girlfriend that night."

"Your ex-girlfriend," he reminded. "Our meetings, the same thing, an accident." He motioned me over to the curb with a now-unexpected imperiousness, like a rich man in a two-bit cab.

I stopped the car near the corner of De La Guerra and Garden. The highway was booming today, you could hear it four blocks away. Traffic had apparently gotten over a Christmas idle idyll and was revving up for the New Year.

"Really? Seems more like a planned coincidence."

"An accident I saw you at the beach," he said. "An accident I saw you today after my lovely dalliance and near-tragic aftermath. But Aristotle says that accidents are the perceptible qualities of an object. This car is accidentally blue. So am I for that matter," he laughed. He trundled out of the car and onto the pavement. He left without a thank-you. Probably he felt I was an ingrate. He was right.

But he came back to the window. "If you wish, this accident will never happen again."

"All I'm saying is, stop following me," I said.

"*Ay gamisou*," he said, considering the pavement below his brow. "That's Greek. It means go fug yourself."

I was down at the bottom of Garden Street waiting at the freeway lights, when it occurred to me that he had no way to know that I had visited the police, to follow up on Brown's death. I felt too tired to chase him, though. On the plus side, my language lessons continued, which is important. Now I knew how to fug myself in a classical language.

I went for lunch uptown at the Blue Onion, crisscrossing town, ate a fishwich and had a cherry Coke. I like the arty girl Ondine I always see there. I went back downtown, more determined, less antsy. It was my intention to find Gin Chow in Chinatown. I found an alley and came around a corner and a door opened and the air that rushed out of it smelled like a deep concentration of sea life. I glimpsed booths inside manned by spectral clerks who wore concerns on their faces, secrets in their peering eyes. It felt like a confederation of visitant species. And, in the course of the still warm day, I found him alone.

As I expected he seemed unsurprised about the pachucos who took after me—though it was not something he foresaw, he admitted. The future is offered only in glimpses even to seers. After a long debate about accidents, Gin Chow speculated that Brown's murder and my altercation were unrelated. I reminded him how often he denied Chance, and he replied that it all fit a theory he formed after his dream of me in danger. Chinese gangs were responsible for Brown's gunshot crucifixion. They killed in ritual ways; they made death a message. The message is unclear to me, I said. It's clear to someone, he said. A point of view is all that really matters, he said. Dogs think God is a dog, he said.

The day was turning chill as I left Gin Chow. I fished around the backseat and found my heavy cardigan and heard the plastic package crinkle in it. The kids at UCLA used to take pills. Booze is for squares, they used to say.

I drove down State Street and onto the pier. Winter's early sunsets were often orange-hued, but on Thursdays it's a deeper shade of rust. That's incinerator day. All over the city the husbands take their trash to burn and set it on fire like their parents did. The coast is surrounded in trash-fire haze that rims the horizons like a bathtub ring.

I parked the jalop, and swung my feet out onto the wooden planks. The fish cannery at the end of the pier stank, but occasional winds swept in with the nobler smell of kelp. There was a gap in the railing, and I sat myself down, looked out past the Montecito Country Club and into the swerve of shore toward Ventura's point. I liked the way the waves moved under me and moved the pier too. Sometimes the wind would swing the smoke smell around. It wasn't wood from a fireplace. It was newspapers full of odd-shaped words like Che, Viet Minh, and Nkrumah. It was paper bags from supermarts filled with ads and maggoty garbage. Orange flames lodged in our soft tissues as dead ash. Civilization itself burns on incinerator day.

An old bum with a malodorous cigar between black, dirty fingers tried to cadge a dime. I glared over my shoulder. He got the message and shuffled away. Then I felt hollow.

I was looking at things you can't see. That hill across from the bird refuge pond is the city cemetery. It's where the memorial to my brother stands. Ronald Colman was buried there last year, a lot of famous Santa Barbarans too. All those with streets named after them: De La Guerra, Carrillo, and Cota, all that cow-herding fellowship, soldiers of Spain. All the Indians are in a different graveyard at the mission. My brother isn't buried at all. He disappeared.

As my eyes drifted down the coast, something sparkled over the water. Its glow would increase as night grew towards smoke, a castle built to poke the ocean floor for oil. Platform Hazel is the name they gave it, and one night when I was eating at the country club's Marine Room, I overheard a prim woman say it sparkled like a fairy ship. From here pretty, but I bet onboard it was painful cold. Does it move like this pier with the combing waves? I imagined a tidal wave and someone a few yards away said, "Look," pointing out at sea, and my heart thudded in my chest and I looked: a bird bigger than a gull, with a screaking cry coming from its throat, blue like the waves.

I don't want to die. It seems so stupid, some arbitrary rule that becomes more preposterous and cruel the longer I endure. Some part of me wonders if someday I might want to pass away, as the old people put it; all this might be too much to take forever. When I'm tired, maybe, or sad. But what a price to pay. Give up everything for the mere relief of nothing. And don't call it peace because it can't be experienced. Look, this is the part that's bothered me since I lost Patrick and then God. I'm heading towards the empty end of all thoughts. We all are. My living brain won't survive. All gone and with it all that fluffy-cloud eternity the nuns promised. It will be to me as if I never was. And it's not just me that ends, everything will with me. I am the alpha and the omega, said Jesus. But if I hadn't been born, the universe would never exist. From my perspective, which is all there is. Huddled over oblivion is all there is. I'm already dead. You are already dead. He, she, and it, well, you get the picture even if you don't.

On board that platform they bring oil up for a world that's already dead. Atomic power will someday save us, teachers say. Save and destroy.

I got up stiffly and walked toward the Lobster House. It was just opening. The maître d' knew my dad. Lots of questions, ending in the incredulous one: Dining alone? Aren't we all ultimately, I wanted to say.

I had some sole in a meunière sauce, with a big lemon pasted on top. Rice, wild rice I believe it was, and some boiled vegetables draped with butter. The bread was white and sliced, the fancy side of Wonder Bread, with lots more butter. I drank a lot. I had a martini while I waited, dry and astringent, then I had some white wine that curled my tongue and hung vaporously in my nose. I had three glasses to see if it would get any better. A gourmet I am not, though I like to eat in grown-up places. I had coffee on top of the wine. When I hit the cold outdoors it took me a few seconds to remember where I parked the car. When I got there, I took the packet out of my pocket. This is my body, I said to myself, the waves rolling up against the pier slowly rocking it. I swallowed three of the psilocybin tablets like a good little boy.

Chapter 16

"**I**F YOU COULD WIPE that cat-shit-eating grin off your face, I'd appreciate it deeply," said the frail remainder of my uncle, sunk back in an overstuffed chair his parents once owned.

"You see," I said, "this is why my mother does not approve of me visiting you. The language is appalling."

This was the usual pretty banter. Inside, though, I was still negotiating elations: the kind a hero feels recrossing his original threshold, home at last. I was back and I had her; and I had his ear, and I had something to say to him. Maybe it sounds melodramatic, but the mojo medicine was all I was thinking about and it had moved some set stone within me. I never liked or trusted in lessons to be learned, but all was right now, things seemed settled inside me. It was June's idea we pick up our poet uncle Francis and bring him to the barbecue. His late wife's trust maintained him at the Samarkand, a retirement home he occupied like a billowing ghost, probably grateful for a roost after a colorful life. Yet it allowed him little mobility, which made him grind his two teeth. A palm tree–dotted place where the scions of industrialist Midwest America once went to dry out, it was not within walking distance of Santa Barbara's early-to-bed nightlife. Now that the Methodists maintained the husks of that same generation here, the few divertissements the nearly dead had were bus trips to the symphony or visitations by schoolchildren, which would probably not suit my uncle. He was profound of both bark and of bite. But it was my recent psilocybin excursion of which I wanted to speak.

"You getting any?" he asked, hooking his thumb toward the back of his apartment where June had gone to powder her nose.

She had come that day as promised, but hours early, while I was still staring at my typewriter, rocking in a transport that seemed incapable of translation into typed-out sense. She walked in; she swayed in. I forgot she had a key. And from first impressions I could tell she was in an odd mood. She asked was she interrupting. She turned away, crossed the floor, and took a look into the bedroom. Her hand fell slowly off the knob as she entered, swinging the door open for me. Obviously I followed. Later, when we were dressing, she was even more mysterious, wary, and watchful. She came out of my room and walked towards the Underwood on its unsure stand and started to pick up my sheets full of type. I said, what? She raised an eyebrow. She was silent in the car.

Frankie was leering and restless, there in silken Samarkand pajamas before the barbecue. June was out of earshot. "Getting any? Can you tell me why superannuation and sordid sexual curiosity have such a strong correlation?" I asked, trying out uncle's own tone. "That's the oddest remark you've made in a long series of odd remarks, Uncle."

"Oh come on. You light up every time she comes into view, son, it's obvious. But it's not right, I think."

"And what makes it wrong?" I whispered.

"She's your cousin," he hissed, lowering his hand as if to soften all noises.

"Uncle Frankie, you know she's adopted and that technically ... "

"Technically adopted?" he said, sounding utterly serious now. "It's true then, you two? I was joking. You had better be careful.

I love that girl." He shook his head solemnly.

I was careful, I thought. What I should have said was I love her too. "I'm not grinning because of June, Uncle, and you know it. This Huxley interview was transfiguring. Do you remember the holy mystery of the transfiguration?"

"I don't know anything except the worthlessness of your ridiculous Catholic schoolbook learning. You know that Huxley is a nonbeliever who thinks he needs a spiritual life, and that's the worst kind."

"Worst kind of what?"

"I'm tired of you, boy. Already. Now spill the beans. What was it?"

"A hallucinogen they call it—it's called psilocybin and it's made from … "

"Good Christ, I know what it's made from. Mushrooms you can buy on any corner in Oaxaca. Chuy and I were eating peyote buttons in Arizona back when horsepower was applied to horses. Ate mushrooms twice. You act like that Mountain Drive gang, Bobby Hyde and his friends, all high and mighty, so to speak." He smiled into the distance. "So what's the big deal?"

I felt abashed at that. Since the pier and the park and the Noctambulist, I had been burning with a sense of secret membership into some club I was sure precious few could join—entrée into a circle of necromancers, shamans of a cracked sensuality. More to the point, I woke the next day without a hangover and with the strangest sense of freedom—my death dreads of the night before, the morbid strain that ran through my family, if not my race, seemed departed, gone. Dearly departed. I'd been obsessed with dying for months. Now I could think about it with some measure of calm. When I was a child in the linoleum classroom of Sister Maris Stella, I had to struggle against this idea of inevitability, which she would not stop drumming into our childish heads. We all die. Save, maybe, and this was a large maybe, those present at the Second Coming of Christ. This was never to be counted on, she said. Of course after death would be judgment and reward. But the painful act of passing was guaranteed. If there is Original Sin, this is Original Trauma. All other shocks to the system are second place to the moment your young heart admits its own impermanence. You can't work around it. Beneath the linoleum, the dust of everything and everyone mixes down to dust always. But I watched it shine—radiate—once. And I changed.

"I think I saw the real world beneath ours," I said, and here I faltered. "Our this," I finished, gesturing around the crowded apartment with its mildew smell and southwestern bric-a-brac.

Uncle Frankie didn't laugh. "A hellish fire of celestial coal, the grain of the world wavering and breaking down, it is the golden womb."

"Jesus, Uncle Frankie, I thought I was the only one who babbled."

"You have potential, but I guess I understand. The wellspring patterns was what Chuy said they called it. I bet Huxley lives to rue the day he gave the pills to you though. Bet he'll be sorry."

"He didn't do it. His manager did."

"Stuurman?" said Frankie. "He's a scary kid. Another one of those Ojai mystics—Krishnamurti, Madame Blavatsky, Christian Rosenkreuz, Amen. You know the type. Likes Proust too. Weird."

"But it wasn't him either, it was some beatnik kid. No, some actor named Hopper."

Just for punctuation, June walked in the room. "You two making the world safe for windbags?" she asked.

"Together we shall break that wind," said my dauntless uncle.

"Come on, we've got to go," said June. "My mother will blame Frankie if we're late—like she always does."

"I love her like a sister anyway," he said. "Who's going to be at this festival of *pinche gringos*?"

"My parents." I could only hope to continue this frustrating exchange on Helen and Dick's back porch, though Frankie didn't seem as keen as I thought he might be to discuss my low-end enlightenment. The truth I thought I found.

"Good, I can ask your father, the detective, what is up with you," he said, which made June laugh merrily.

"Retired," I said. "Like you, he's retired now, put away all opinions. What about my mother?"

"The ever-vivacious Mrs. Westin. I pray to be seated somewhere far away. She compensates for your father's feigned ineloquence."

"That's my mother you impugn, sir."

"And Pearl," said June, "the goddamned phony crackpot do-gooder."

We both looked at her, surprised. She had uttered blasphemy on top of imprecation. Everybody did, but not out loud. I couldn't tell if Frankie was impressed or worried.

"Here, child," said Francis. "Do I detect bile? Pearl will tell you herself she was vitally important in this town, and I always agree."

"Again with the earthquake," June said, gathering purse and jacket as exit prelude. The 1925 temblor killed thirteen and left the city shambled and isolated. From such devastation, Auntie Pearl and an architect named Hoffmann refashioned a cow town into a Moorish dream through legislation and bullying. Only Storke, my father's enemy, tried to prevent her from prettifying the city by caveat.

"Here, here," Frankie said. "I was in that earthquake. That is, I was in an outhouse in that earthquake. And I can safely say it left a mark on me."

Now I groaned. "Please, not this."

"What Pearl really did was ten years before that, though." Francis was lost to us now, his eyes looking toward the window but gathering only light. "It was when the Potter Hotel and the Arlington still bookended a little wooden-sidewalk town, when *I* went to Our Lady of Sorrows. And one day Sister Mary Hatchetface said, 'You may have noticed Susan Loosebrock absent, children. Our prayers fly to her parents and siblings,' said Sister Nugatory. 'Susan died suddenly last night.' We gasped and she shushed us with a rosary. Only her friend Mary Joy had the details. After dinner Susan began throwing up and wouldn't stop, and they took her to Cottage Hospital, but she died before early morning sun. The next day two more were missing from the school, and the next day there were four. They were my schoolmates. Tom Jovanavic and I used to clap erasers. I asked him the best place to dig clams near the Rincon. Next day he wasn't there anymore forever. He was the ninth. A number of people disappeared before their lives had even opened, never mind becoming Mozart or Dickens. What's that poem?"

"Some mute inglorious Milton," I said.

"Parents began disappearing too. This city was never much for looking you in the eye. On the streets, it's always the rich man too proud to nod at the kid who cleans his house, who hates him for his miserly wages. Now it was a lot worse. Nobody dared to say hello, a smile could kill a passerby. It was medieval, a plague year. The toll reached twenty-five, and remember, in those days everyone knew everyone, and the deaths spread into Montecito rich and Italian immigrants alike.

"A doctor named Winchester stopped an earlier outbreak of typhus, but had no clues about this. He knew it wasn't cholera. It would have to run its course. I know what you're thinking, but no. The influenza epidemic came a few years later, and by that time I was in the Army so I missed that one. Besides, the flu had a whole world to kill, but this was just here. I remember: 'I had a little bird, its name was Enza. I opened the window and influenza.' But this was a curse surrounded by embarrassed silence. The preachers were smug. I hated the praying, but the worst part was the absences all over town. Nobody was on the street. People stormed Winchester's office daily now and demanded he telegraph the state to send disease specialists. He was offended.

"Miss Pearl Chase already had her coterie even then. Pearl's Girls. She knew about men and pride. But she knew something else too. Like other doctor boyos, Winchester had discovered the joys of a morphine jolt self-ministered. Don't look so surprised, today the doctors take pills, don't need fancy dope like your boyfriend here."

June looked up. My stomach fell.

"Anyway, like I said, it's an odd thing in your life when people begin to disappear. After a bit you don't grieve, but end up feeling maybe there's more room now. Inside yourself: relief after grief."

June was looking around.

"Don't we have to go?" I said.

"What do you mean, my 'boyfriend'?" said June to Uncle Frankie.

He laughed and shook his head. "We can go in a second. I just want you to know about Miss Pearl. She got her girls together and went to Winchester's office in the Park Theater building at quarter to noon, and they made like Gandhi there, a sit-down strike in his office, so he couldn't sneak out for his needle full of poppy juice. He seethed, he steamed, and as the urge outweighed his pride, he relented. A telegram to Sacramento and the women left. Turned out it was a well on the lower East side, full of amoebas that rich and poor drew up alike. Pearl saved a lot of children. But Winchester has a canyon and a park named after him and lived a long time for an old junkie, too."

Chapter 17

A FTER I SWALLOWED THE tiny pills on the swaying pier that night, I had a little panic. I didn't know what I was thinking. Maybe I thought that my journalism career would end if I didn't get the interview and therefore needed the drug-taking done right now. I don't think I *was* thinking. Soon as I swallowed, though, I stepped over to the edge by the pilings and tried to make myself vomit. I stopped after the first gag, feeling girlish, stupid.

I walked to the end of the pier, past the abalone cannery, which smelled sharp but not unpleasant. I looked out at the empty junction of water and sky for a while, and a transistor radio walked by me with youth attached. Reached for my darling, held her to me, stole her away from the angry sea.

Then back toward the purplish Packard, the alcohol in my system from the Lobster Trap dinner warring with the adrenaline fear had summoned. Maybe fear summoned adrenaline. What do I know about anything? The sea was empurpled, laced with whitecaps. The wind had an ice edge, and suddenly I had goose bumps.

Then I ran into my third-grade teacher, Mrs. Nose.

This was choice surreality. At first I was effusive—it seemed perfect. You were always such a fine and sensitive boy, she said. The goose bumps on my neck were organizing into waves though, and my stomach tightened, and I could barely stop from yawning over and over. She chatted brainlessly but seemed perturbed that my answers to her dullard questions were a-ramble. Truth be told, I felt intimidated by the quotidian. I told her I wrote for a newspaper: black-and-white and read all over, also a nun rolling down a staircase. I barked a laugh. She smiled worriedly. I yawned deeply. She started in on a story about the Mexican children and what a problem they always are. I thought she would never stop, and it made me uncomfortable knowing that Mrs. Nose had only pretended to like the Saragosa twins. She went on and on, the vile old hypocrite; I thought about cartoon thermometers rising to the blowup point. I almost laughed out loud and then, brusque, I begged her to let me go. I needed to be free. She said certainly in a clipped and distant voice.

I smiled getting into my car. I searched my pockets for a full minute for the keys that were in my fingers. I wasn't ready to drive. It seemed funny somehow so I threw the keys down in a heap. I thought how embarrassing it would be to see her ever again, and then started giggling. Now I really didn't know what I was thinking. But it wasn't disturbing. It was ghastly and funny.

Strange the world seemed, and precariously mobile at its peripheries. When I stopped to concentrate inside the car, the most mundane objects suddenly seemed fraught with beauty. I felt tragic love for the chrome grill over my radio. It was more magnificent than any cathedral I'd ever entered, and it didn't seem odd or inappropriate to think so; this seemed how the world always ought to be viewed. The grill smiled. I started the car and the radio sent out jarring splinters of sound. I felt as if I could see these splinters, an idea that made me nervous.

In a tremendous act of will, I turned the dial to KDB, a classical music station with spidery hosts. I was met instantly with a rush of splendor and terror, though it took me some time to realize it was Prokofiev's *Troika*. By then, *I* was rushing along, raw, and the wintry sawing of violins brought tears to my eyes. They hurt and I laughed. I looked in the mirror and noticed my pupils seemed chasms wide. I was frightened but then the music gathered in my stomach and sent soothing waves throughout my muscles and bones. I sank back. I felt I was becoming the car seat and then more as my integration spread backwards into the whole world. I thought maybe I should wait a few moments before I drove. Meanwhile I beheld the sea. I remembered saying that. I beheld the sea. KDB. These things are happening to me.

I did not hallucinate, you understand. There were no objects floating in front of my eyes that weren't there. Odd and clear, my eyes; if anything the world presented itself with uncustomary clarity, vision was augmented by significances that I had missed my entire life. I rocked in teeter-totter balance. One moment felt horrifying, calm washed over me like liquid balms next.

But really I *did* hallucinate. A filmy design ran through everything, as if the wharf world around me was part of a patterned rug. I closed my eyes and it remained. It wasn't annoying, or even distracting; the design felt like an organizing principle. I tried laughing that off and couldn't. It was true. That grain ran in me.

For a long time I sat. The comfort of dusk grew out of the sky.

I looked in the rearview mirror, peering backward, and watched people walk by, often feeling diminished by their departures. I was drawn into their travels. I'm a part of it's a part of me. Moving became imperative; I should be moving, though looking at my watch made little sense to me. Time was the colors of spreading night. The watch dial was just numbers, absurd points of reference. Meanwhile, city lights began to grow and glow, making me feel wonderful. I decided to start the car. It was already running, the starter screamed a protest.

That shook me for a few.

I took off the parking brake. I pushed down on the clutch and shifted the stick on the column into reverse. Careful, I must not go forward into the sea, I thought. Looking in my mirror, I saw back-up lights come on, reassuring as a child's night-light. I looked around. The pier was empty all the way to Cabrillo Boulevard. I smelled exhaust and the city's infernal trash furnaces, but also the sea and its blossoming spray.

I was everything and nothing, and my mind stalked the roads ahead for more significances, each of which made me laugh. A stop sign and a hotel neon flashing vacancy were equally hilarious, though when I looked in the mirror my own eyes looked haunted and sad. I could easily negotiate the road. I smiled broadly which made my skin pulse out and flare into the night. But when I stopped driving, my body, an envelope, recontracted. My stomach was knotted but it wasn't unpleasant. I was driving like a champ. And then my mind drifted, and the symphony swelled from the speaker, and everything bent across a spectrum to violet. Next thing I know my tire hit the high State Street curb, and I saw a panhandler look at me in terror. A block past the worst part of town I parked, and stuff just washed over me again. I smiled and cringed against the seat. The stuff just washed over me. I became lost in some blind alley of lost time.

The car clock had its beautiful face lit a pale green like the waters in the neon Falls sign. I stood on a glacier for a moment for a time for an age, but when I looked at the clock again only seconds had passed. I turned off the lights and the outside world began to sway and recede from the windows of my car.

I thought about the clear metallic-tasting springs of the real world and drank from a bowl full of those waters, with seahorses playing in rays of light. I buried my head in my hands. There were now sweeping hoops of patterned colors running my emotions. Then I thought about June. I started to feel very good and let out a long breath.

Chapter 18

AS AFTERNOON DRAINED INTO overcast and evening, June, Frankie, and I pulled up to Aunt Helen and Uncle Dick's place. The sprinkler played over perfect dichondra. I was feeling something drift away from me, though it wasn't clear what. Apparently the club I joined wasn't at all exclusive, and I struggled with my disappointment. I wasn't happy with Frankie's smug knowledge of something that had seemed mine alone. Was I really that selfish? The drugs' aftereffects, insights, and blisses were wearing off. I wanted to talk about it, but Frankie wanted out of the car and into the bosom of the family he pretended to loathe.

The door burst open on another world. First there was Helen, my real aunt and June's mother, always clad in pedal pushers and thin cotton blouses of limes and other soft citrus colors that managed to hug her frame without being either attractive or demure. She seemed ready to keen.

"You poor, poor boy, why didn't you call us?" she asked, with the storm warning of imminent tears. She grabbed me by both arms and crushed me to her. If I had been truly hurt, this would've finished me.

"But just what made me so pitiable?" I wondered, then asked, looking blankly at her.

"Listen Mr. Rushmore Mountain, next time you go to the hospital, you call me first."

"Yes, ma'am," I said. "And then my mother will kill me." I had all but forgotten my laying-up adventure, save the odd twinge.

"Oh, hush you black-hearted boy. As if you *even* called your mother."

"As if you called me," said the first voice of my life, emerging from behind her sister-in-law with real tears in her eyes. The trap was both set and sprung.

"It was nothing, mother," I protested as she strangled me in embrace. This did summon hurt. "Besides I was too close to a coma to use the phone." She grappled me then and planted her teary cheek on mine. Her kiss was light but singed a bit, like the sting of a tiny jellyfish.

"If you were that sick then you were sick enough … Oh, listen to me, I've let another heartless Westin boy take advantage of my better nature."

"They'll do it every time," said June, whirling around to catch me with a brash, secret wink. "It's Hatlo's History."

"Speaking of the funny papers, your father says he wants you to do some detecting for him, so go talk to him out back when you get a chance."

"Mu-mah, I don't see what sleuthing has to do with comic pages—Sunday in color."

Nobody was surprised at *her* odd leaps by now. She was always on to something else—badgering Uncle Frankie about his out-at-the-cuffs pants or reciting stories about the tides at Mont Saint-Michel. No one loved her any less for her sparkplug mind.

"No kiss on the cheeks for a family's prodigal senior citizen?" said Francis to Aunt Helen, who smiled at him with sad eyes. And then to my mother: "I still have the same flame burning in me when first I spied your pompoms cheering at Catholic High. Remember how you used to favor me, the older Westin? Too bad he got ya," he said, meaning my not present father.

"Like the black sheep of old," sang Uncle Dick from around the corner at his wet bar, "I'll come back to the fold. Little town in the old county Down." He regarded me with studied blandness.

"Thank God there are no children here to hear your vulgar talk," said Helen to her wayward brother.

"Suffer the little children unto me," said Frankie in a croaking evil voice.

"Thirteen seconds in the door and everybody's exasperated with you," said Uncle Dick, his tray of martinis jingling toward the gaggle in the pine-paneled foyer. "I'd say it was a record, but I remember they were mad at you before you even arrived on Christmas."

"It's a gift," Frankie said, grasping a cocktail. The shared thought was: Here we go again, the coming juggernaut.

Sun was arrowing sharply through the sliding plate-glass door, the one that led to backyard, the barbecue, and my father. The smell of cooking flesh was tickling my nose like crooked fingers from a cartoon houri. My mother grabbed my elbow, though, and led me to a moderne couch-table set, Danish, and like the rest of the house's decorations, kidney-shaped. A flock of fish made of bent wire swam on the flag-stone wall near the rarely used California fireplace.

"You said it was nothing," she said, breathing sherry into my face.

"And I stand by the assessment. Or sit."

"Some criminals beat you up, they bruised your kidney."

"Wow. How do you know these things?" I asked, impressed.

"Don't change the subject. You know how much we worry about you. Is it stupid to suggest Dr. Hake again? You liked him, I thought."

"There's a stench of death around that office, Mother."

She looked at me, and then down at the table with its fan of *Look*s,

*Life*s, and *Saturday Evening Post*s. Her lips were trembling. Tears again.

"Oh, Mom," I said. "I'm better. I hardly ever talk to myself anymore," I said, crossing my eyes comically.

"A good joke *is* a sign of mental hygiene," she said, "according to something I read. The worst part is when we think it isn't funny anymore."

"It?"

"All of it, you know, every itty bit," she said, showing signs of sherry marination.

"Since that was nothing like a good joke, therefore, the patient is hereby declared cuckoo by reason of insanity," I said, putting my arm around her shoulders.

"Oh," she said, reaching for and then tapping out a Kool from her padded cigarette box. "A stench of death. I'll have to remember that."

"I wish I could say I'll behave better in the future, but I'm sorry."

She gestured toward the door, and nodded. "Your father awaits."

"Okay," I said. "But first I need to make myself a nuisance in the kitchen. I brought some avocados from my backyard for Auntie," I said, holding up the brown Jordano's bag I'd plunked down on the floor between us.

"You don't have a backyard," she said.

"Don't tell the avocados that."

"Oh, there's a surprise waiting out there for you, I almost forgot."

The doors were something between French and Old West barroom; I loved swinging into them when I was a kid. I pushed in now and beheld a steaming chaos of pots and pans, brimming with bags of frozen vegetables, and a salad heaped high in a wooden bowl, and no aunt. But across from me, bent slightly at the waist, was my surprise. I put the bag down and gawked.

"I knew you wouldn't call me," said Mary Annie. "Didn't I tell you?"

"That's where you're wrong. I called you twice. I called for help." I wondered why my mother thought this was *my* surprise.

She turned around fast, drying her hands on a white towel. She hastened across the room and put those hands, warmed by soapsuds and domestic laboring, on my face. "My sweet boy, why would you need help? Remember? You're the strong self-reliant type." Her breasts were pushed up against me in a dizzy-making fashion. She knew it as she smiled at my happy discomfort.

"It's a long story, but I got around the problem. Me being a he-man and all. Tell me, though, what are you doing here? And please don't take that the wrong way."

"It's hard to imagine what the right way might be. Let's just assume, though, you are expressing unexpected pleasure and the right words haven't found your tart mouth."

"Who's the tart?" I asked. Outside the window, in the blue evening, a lone man stood. I leaned against the sink and saw my face mirrored. The outside was a watery dusk clinging around the corners gone all the way dark. The man, whoever he was, floated in the liquid evening. Maybe he was Brown's ghost; maybe he was hallucinated, though I had an entirely different notion of that word now.

"Hmm," she said. "Here, try this, it's called an artichoke: it's a thistle. You know how to thistle, don't you? Put your lips together and chew. What'll they think of next?"

Mary Annie went to the window and looked at the same sight, the man in the aquarium of outdoor evening light. "The reason I'm here is simple, but I'll make it complex. You wash and I'll dry. I simply answered the phone at my humble abode and, lo!, it was your auntie calling her daughter, who, I had the unhappy task of reminding her, no longer resides at that address, and, hence, answers a different telephone too. To mitigate her discomfort I readily supplied her with the number of June's new domestic circumstances. Pleased with my ready reply, your sweet aunt condescended to deign to invite me to attend this soirée. Dress simply, she said."

"You should be a writer," I said, admiring her apron's starch.

"So should you," said a voice behind me.

Of course it was June. I watched the man outside disappear into dark and I got lost wondering how this would all turn out.

Chapter 19

"This is where the legend of the mermaids originates," said the young man, gasping in fright at the face outside the window, which gazed back with such indifference, white tendrils hanging from its beard and fingers. "And the mermen."

The old man spat back: "Not legend. These are the mermen and mermaids; the sea people who chose not to leave the sea." He pointed at a huge shape that was beginning to cohere into an impressive mass of dark water below them, their apparent destination. "That became the sea people's legacy, though only some moved toward it. They fell out of the sea. Traveling over nature like snails after rain, they entered the fog bank, they moved west on a rainbow bridge. The merpeople, on the other hand, stayed behind."

"I don't know what you're talking about," the young man said. "Beings other than the merpeople?"

"Those people," he said, pointing down to the dark mass they were approaching, "call themselves Elayawun. It was the Indian word for swordfish, but it was their word for themselves too. Your father said he taught it to them. I don't know, even after all the trips I made with him here. But you'll soon see for yourself."

Chapter 20

I N THE BUBBLING GLOOM, I was trying hard to leave the car. I'd parked it safely at an angle on State Street below De La Guerra, where the streets
were sparsely inhabited. All life seemed distributed around emptiness
here, monuments and vacancies contrasting like a De Chirico painting. Or was it Dali? Time melting over the branches, common objects
glowing like phenomena. The streetlamp was glowing warm. That's
how I realized night had fallen. I laughed and spoke my own name out
loud. I came so far it seemed wrong not to get out and see.

Then another cascade of involvement, a sense that the car was part
of me and should not be left behind. Then I thought about June again.
I felt that only she could save me. Only problem, I couldn't let her see
me in this state. So I thought about Mary Annie, and I was suddenly
overcome by hunger. I needed her. I loved June. Goddamn it.

I looked out at the dark shape of a man in a wool suit with a tri-
angularly peaked hat and a pipe sticking out of his mouth, crossing
the pavement in front of my car. None of the stores were open except
Thrifty's, glowing in the distance. Every day's a special day at Thrifty
Mart. Every day's a special day for you.

I could smell the incinerator smoke and then it all went rolling over
me again. The dark man moved away and patterned light followed
him. When I brushed my hands over my eyes, trailed images of my

hands followed them. This was pleasant enough and quite entertaining. Sometimes my absorption was complete, though I worried that a policeman driving along would interrupt my perfect immersion in the phenomena. Whatever you put in your shopping cart, you save and save at Thrifty Mart. There was mist and there was fog.

But lo! A stir in the air!
The wave, there is a movement there!
As if the towers had thrust aside,
In slightly sinking, the dull tide—
As if their tops had feebly given
A void within the filmy Heaven.

These were the words my brother loved; a class assignment to memorize a poem. It scared his teacher and there were words with my parents. It was the way he recited it. Scary like. Words, each one was a wavelength crashing into the fortress of smoke. I smelled the city burning. Looked out and wondered if I'd spoken the words aloud. Now I was considering how to leave the Packard with the stuff rolling over me and these words became symphonic. I was a radio. I yawned and threw my head back. I didn't know whether to walk or stay. But lo!, a stir in the filmy Heaven.

There was a phone booth around the corner near the plaza. I thought maybe I could call Mary Annie. And then I did it; got out, swung reluctant legs to pavement, walked around the corner toward the phone booth in the evening air, feeling like I was a puppet of my own will. I plunked in the coin, but the sound inside the receiver was too weird and I gave up. My throat was huge and I had trouble swallowing. As I walked away, these feelings diminished.

It seemed sensible now to experience my hometown. I circled around the block, considering a stop at the bar across from the KIST building, tall, pink, and topped with the radio antenna—I am the radio. Mel's, a dark place full of men born to drink as an avocation. Smoke and pissy beer fumes licked out. I retreated. I fell back to the darkened plaza. There were streetlights and the mist rolling in, and many plain things still making me sputter. Phenomena. I chuckled and burst into laughter. I couldn't stop and my eyes flashed terrible. I thought I heard myself sobbing. What if I could never stop? I found the bench on the edge of the small ragged lawn—city hall across from me, the giant newspaper offices to the right. Be calm now, please.

"And now I just might disappear," I said to the park. The *News-Press* building was mostly dark, though lights were coming from the tower office of T. M. Storke. The presses hummed from the bowels of the basement and I hummed, too, in reply. "Disappear. Annihilation and oblivion. Into myself and into the night like a period, full stop, end of sentence."

I wondered if going forth from here the city would be like something Dante dreamed; past its own natural refraction, radiant on this new spectrum, this radio of ideas into light. I thought I might find the whole place renewed. Or maybe it would just be fresh to my blazing eyes. I had no idea whether it would ever go back to what it was. And I saw the darkness better now too. Something shaded and multihued, different kinds of dark available. And then I saw something very dark and cold to the touch, if it could be touched. Period, end of sentence, and incinerator smoke provided incense for it.

Red-topped buildings, I could see inside them. The neighborhood's unseen girders became arteries of raw illumination, poisonous radioactivity running through its veins. More so because this part of town, where I hummed in tune to the newspaper presses, was so fake and faked. Across the street, the famous El Paseo, a mock street in Spain, Moorish bulges fashioned from chicken wire and flock. Its builder's

Chapter 21

"**H**AVE YOU TWO MET?" I asked, backing away from Mary Annie, who had loosened her grip. I was still a little flushed, though. I put an artichoke leaf in my hand and offered it to June whose eyes went wide. "Try it, I think you'll like it."

"Hi, honeybunch," said Mary Annie to June. "Are you gonna ask me what the hell I'm doing here too? Can't say I'm flattered by Mister Man here."

"Okay, I'll bite. Who invited you here?" said June, pushing by me to give her former roomie a little hug. They giggled. "But first, guess who's taking me to the islands 'cause he's sad I've never been there?"

"Oh, God, no. I'll bet he just happens to be flying over there that week. Coinkydinky." Mary Annie was giggling louder. "Did you say no?"

"Who's flying you to what islands?" I said, knowing it was probably Hawaii, feeling I had suddenly shrunk.

June, the love of my life, was leaning against the kitchen counter and hugging her cardigan around her. She looked at Mary Annie and then at me. "It's not like I could just say no. I mean we're going to fly, so sweet."

"He's rolling in the stuff, and you are his sweet tooth's sweetmeat." Mary Annie said. "Two tickets to our Pacific paradise for him are like two bags of popcorn for other boys." She looked at me, perhaps remembering I have a dime or two tucked away in the old Schnitzelbank too. "Well, he seems to enjoy spending his."

"Who is going to fly you?" I asked again, trying to sound casual. They ran on as if I were not in the room.

"I'll go if you don't," said Mary Annie. "By the way, did you see Betty Fregati in the paper looking like Liz Taylor? Eddie Fisher says, 'I like-a spaghetti, but you haven't lived till you had Liz on ya.' Get it? Lasagna?"

"Shame, Sister Mary Aloysius can hear. So, by the way, what *are* you doing here?"

"The same thing Betty was doing in the newspaper. Getting attention for nothing. Your auntie called for you, and then, sweetly, insisted I … Oh, wait, now my feelings *are* hurt again."

"I'm sure she didn't ask you over here to do the dishes. Come out in the rec room and tell me again what girls wear on island flights. Trevor, I almost forgot, your father wants to see you. That's really why I came in here."

They left. I wondered at a girl who could lie across my sheets and never mention tickets to Honolulu. I washed the last dish. I wondered if Mary Annie and June together was a good thing. I'm glad, I guess, she and I hadn't. What was I talking about? She kissed me for half an hour that night. She had nice lips. But June, who won't vacate my mind, was running off to Hawaii. I knew who it was, the wop king of liquor sales. God, what if it was someone else? I know I have no claim, but what did this morning mean? No faith or hope or love and everything subject to change.

I poured myself a thick one from the bottle of Scotch that Dick keeps under the kitchen counter. I swallowed. I wandered outside to the world of men.

"Here's my son and heir," said my lanky and dapper dad. His grin was a bit lopsided, and there was a martini glass, containing a tiny sword sucked free of olive, on a picnic table next to his hand. He waved an uncharacteristically sloppy wave.

"Dad," I said, experiencing a pang. "Heard you've got a scoop for me." I nodded toward my other uncle, Dick's brother Dale, who was scrubbing the BBQ with a wire brush, sending an acrid, beautiful smell out into the chill air. Christmas lights still clung to the house; large pieces of beef filled a platter.

"Here's the news flash, dateline Dick's backyard. Ever have tri-tip before, neighbor?" my father asked. "You're gonna like it. Yep. They call it Santa Maria Barbecue at the country club, according to Dale here."

"Didn't know you were a duffer, Dale," I said. "Much less a member."

"I'm a dentist, Christ," said Dale. That was supposed to be an explanation; we were all used to my uncle's elliptical school of communication. I used to let him look in my mouth for cavities. Open wide, hey, how about those Koreans, huh? He talked while he scraped you with the pointed hook thing. I hated him.

"How are you, boy?" my father asked.

"Not good, according to Mom."

"I wish she had never found out, son. I admire your Spartan spirit."

"How did she?" We looked at the dentist.

"Aw Jesus, here we go," said Dale. "You can't blame me for everything." He looked up at us, one eye shut against the billowing, aromatic smoke. "I know that nurse. She told me. I told the wife. You know how these sisters are."

"I'm sorry, what nurse?" I asked, getting a little testy.

"The one that liked you. The one that disappeared."

"Listen brother-in-law, you're being obtuse even for you," said Dad, the inquisitor.

"Hah!" laughed Dale. "Lothario here knows who I'm talking about."

"No, Uncle Dale, though I appreciate the tepid literary reference, I do not know what you mean. Who is missing?" *Now*, I thought, who is missing *now*?

He looked at me. "You mean the cops haven't come over to your house?" He must have seen the puzzle in my eyes. "And you haven't read the paper? Aw, cripes, a dentist is always a bearer of bad news. The nurse who took care of you in the hospital, she's the one that the big manhunt is on about. What was her name?"

I suddenly saw her. She asked: Don't you want to know my name? "Marie," I said.

"That's the one." He and my father were watching me, scrutinizing me. I drank a gulp and coughed. Suddenly there was a noise inside, a furor, and a few screechy greetings. A little dog barked down the street.

"That'll be Pearl," said my father, who drew me aside to the low wall with the view across the neighbor's dense citrus forest. "Listen, I want to talk to you but not in front of him, Dale the mouth, and nothing gets repeated in Pearl's presence."

"Okay," I said. Brown's murder woes were back and my crazy family's meaningless conspiracies would soon deliver me back to them. Back to dull earth, too, and my visions and their aftermath left in the wake.

"Never in front of Miss Pearl Chase," he repeated softly. A surprising cloud of booze fumes emanated from my father, who looked at me, and then tightened his grip around my shoulders. "I'm very glad you weren't hurt," he said.

"And how are you?"

"I've been a lot better. I never used to drink so much."

The glass door slid open and roistering sounds spilled forth, as did my little cousin, Freddy, Dale's darling bud. "When did you get here?" he asked. "You didn't come and see my monsters."

"You mean the ones I gave you?"

"Be like that," he said. "Come on in, Auntie Pearl is here too. She wants oblations to be made." We laughed; it was an old remark June made, when she was younger than Freddy. Pearl used it always now, without irony. June the obscure. No, June the prodigal, going off to Waikiki without consulting me.

Mary Annie put her head out the door. "Hey, handsome," she smiled, and then withdrew.

"My son, is there something you want to tell me?" my father asked.

"I thought you were supposed to explain that stuff to me," I said, then wished I hadn't, as my father blushed. "Which newspaper has the story about Marie?"

"There's a little bit of follow-up today," said Dale. "The cops called me about it last night. Four days after Christmas and I have cops. They wanted your address, then they realized they already had it."

"You seem pretty cozy with the cops," said Daddy dear. "Did you call the newspapers with my son's whereabouts too?"

"Easy, friends. I said they already knew the address. There have been a number of disappearances around the boy. Seems nursey wrote a note about your Prince Charming in her diary, which they read. Besides, I don't know where my nephew hangs his head since he came back from, um, college life and stuff." That last part was sadistic Dale the dentist.

The kid and I left the backyard and were squeezing through the narrowly opened glass door into warmth only to confront Pearl. My stomach was still tight over Dale's "number of disappearances" pronouncement. I tried to be cool, though I knew I was losing ground—the sordid aspect of my life was displacing the short-lived victory I'd claimed over death itself. My miracle was faded. Brown was officially a ghost. I was afraid.

Freddy was jumping up and down and had my hand. "Finally," he said. "Let's go." Pearl said she also wanted to talk later. I was obliged to peck her on the cheek as Freddy yanked me back into the playroom that Helen and Dick kept for him. It used to be for us. For June and me. And Patrick.

"This one's Dracula, the mother sucker," said Freddy.

"The vampire, the bloodsucker. Who told you the other?" I asked.

"Uncle Frankie," he said. "He explained them all."

"Oh did he?" I said. "And haven't you ever seen the movies?"

"Oh, no. Mom said I'd be up all night with nightmares. But I'll tell you a secret. Cross your heart and swear to die, stick a needle in your eye."

"Duly sworn," I said, feeling a déjà vu. Dooley.

"I saw *The Invisible Man*."

"The movie."

"Yeah, well part of it. On television. You know with bandages and sunglasses."

"And then he takes them off."

"Nobody's there," he said solemnly. "Is he a ghost?"

"No. He's invisible."

"Yeah, well, so are ghosts. I don't get the difference."

"Ghosts are dead," I said. "Then they come back to haunt you. Invisible men are just scientists who go crazy."

He looked at me. "Your brother is dead. Is he a ghost?"

"No Freddy. He's never coming back."

"Don't you want him to?"

"Not as a ghost."

"Nobody knows where he is, my dad said."

"Sometimes your dad talks too much."

"What if Patrick came back as the Invisible Man?"

"That would be okay."

"I talk too much too. I made you sad."

"Don't be sorry," I said, looking around the room where we used to play. "Like you said, he's in this very place, Freddy." I picked up the mummy model.

He looked at me with a fearful look.

"No, don't be scared. Look inside the closet."

"There's some writing on the wall," he said as he poked his head inside. "Is that him?"

"Patrick wrote that when he was a little older than you."

"Is it a secret? What does it say? 'Death looks gigantic, something, something'… This is creepy. Does Aunt Helen know?"

"Best part about being the Invisible Man," I said, "is that you can be anywhere. Anywhere and everywhere."

"And nowhere," said my brilliant coz.

Chapter 22

How LOVELY IT WOULD be to disappear, I thought. The man across the plaza kept walking towards me, shifting directions a little, looking, walking towards me, and then obviously staring. I muffled my mind and pulled myself together into a ball and hunkered down on the damp, cold bench. The man looked over, wary, started to walk—this was too much. I felt a chasm between us open and close like a breathing mouth. I prayed he would not talk to me. He could never understand me.

"Trevor," he said.

Fugging small town. I looked up and almost fell apart with gratitude. The gap between the living and me closed.

"Are you all right? What are you doing in the cold?" said Marty Bohawk, another of June's former suitors, going back to Sea Scout days and bonfire nights. He was a grad student, some liberal art or other.

"I'm not really sure," I answered, laughing. "How are you, Cap'n?" Now I was laughing hard and relieved.

"You're not drunk, are you." It wasn't a question. "Want to tell me about it?"

His concern was touching. Even though it probably had more to do with my concerning past than with the idea of unspecified intoxication, it came across as a nice, human thing to say.

I waved my hands in absurd, large gestures of dismissal, but began confessing anyway.

"You know Huxley?" I asked, motioning him to sit down on the uncomfortable wooden bench. He did so gingerly.

"Aldous Huxley. I'm taking that class next month. I saw him lecture in Ojai," he said. It was the university seminar, the first-ever guest lecturer, which brought the man here in the first place. "So I guess you can say I know him. He makes me dizzy sometimes with all he knows, and he's goddamned blind too." Bohawk looked very tentative as I straightened out from my gut-hugging embryonic posture.

"He gave me some pills. Well, his friend did," I said.

"Mojo medicine," whispered Bohawk.

"Psilocybin," I said, giggling.

"How much did you take?" he asked.

"Three, that's what he said. His friend said."

"Wow, do you like it? I ate some cactus buttons once. I just threw up and felt weird."

"I'm not sure what 'like it' means anymore."

"Wow," he said. He asked some very good questions, first about my disposition. I told him about the bargain: drugs for the interview. He seemed okay with the concept. Then he asked about how long I had been back, and if I liked being down on the farm after I'd seen Paree. He never mentioned my mandatory holiday, the stay at Camarillo State, and the shock therapy I endured. Could be he didn't know, but I doubt it—fuggin' small town.

"I can see this kind of magma running through the courthouse, a kind of serpent's blood phenomenon." I said to my friend, leaving out many of my recent travails. I felt better with somebody to listen, someone to watch over me.

"Aw, that's just the drugs," said Bohawk, fishing out and drinking from a flask and smoking a Camel after offering me both. He would be glad to stick around until I felt like going home, he said.

"You have a bit of a glow outside you," I said, sipping whiskey.

"Serpent's sweat," he said. "I just rode my bike up from the wharf."

"Look at that," I said.

"Sure," he said. "What?"

I began laughing again but not insane this time. A cavalcade of European art treasures rushed through my mind. Honest. It was spectacular and I knew it was a trick but you know, my pal wasn't acting much differently than me. He laughed, yawned, said weird things, and then laughed again. Like he was commenting. Turn right at the Renaissance—here comes chiaroscuro. I really did know he couldn't see this stuff. As I grew calmer, engrossed, Bohawk seemed relieved, and started suggesting brilliant ideas.

"Let's go to the Noctambulist," he said. "This kid David Van Something-land is playing there. He's so young, he just got kicked out of high school, and he sings, well, he sings folk songs. Cool, huh? And songs he wrote."

"He's a beatnik. I met him maybe it was last night before last. I think."

He looked at me. We both started laughing. "Beatnik," he said. "Don't bug me daddy-o, like squaresville. You dig? Oh, and I have another idea, and this one's good too."

"This is becoming a delightful mélange of ideas," I said. "What?"

"Let's call Huxley, get him to come talk to you."

My stomach knotted hard. "Oh come on, I'm in no shape," I said, aghast, and then reconsidered. Ten minutes ago I was too scared to see June and balked at calling Mary Annie. Look at me chatting now. Both girls seemed distant, unreal right now.

"Why not? I think you're in rare shape for entertaining a genius. Besides, this was his influence, his idea, sort of. This was a test and you passed."

It frightened but intrigued me. I did want to talk about the visions, the paintings, while I was still seeing them. Were they in my mind or from some source outside? So I thought, well, maybe.

"He'll know what's good for your, uh, condition and you can strike while the iron's hot. Interview him, or at least get him to commit to an interview. Besides, I want to meet him outside class. Maybe drink a beer or smoke some reefer with him, maybe?"

"That sounds delicious," I said, just as the first French Romantic paintings appeared.

Chapter 23

SMELLS OF GRILLING BEEF drifted down the plush-carpeted halls of Helen and Dick's cozy home. The boy held up a drawing, executed with smudgy finesse, and asked what I thought of it. There were turreted towers and a brick geometric pattern around the structure's roof, which was also flying erect, randy-looking pennants. But as eyes traveled down the shaft of the thing, its texture turned to a bouldered chunk and ended in a child's version of stylized waves—half-moons that denote ripples on the watery main—with starfish cast out of their aqueous home and thrown on rocks below the central tower.

"It's bold work," I said, "not unlike the heraldic art of medieval crests."

"No," he said. "Wrong again. It's Castle Rock."

"Oh, do I detect the influence of one Uncle Frank here?"

"He let me read the poem he wrote about it, Uncle Frank."

"What a surprise. He's not usually inclined to show that poem to just anyone, you know, except humans with functioning eyeballs and minimal levels of literacy."

"Did you ever see it?" Freddy asked, Junior Wiseass. "My mother told me something about your friend Gin Chow." He looked at me funny, as if trying to delve deeper truths than were apparent on the surface.

"He could predict weather so well, the local farmers subscribed to his opinions and didn't buy almanacs," I said defensively. "His reports for the newspaper, that is."

"Clouds hang out like Chinaman's laundly," said the boy, pulling his eyes back in an Asian caricature.

"Don't be crass."

"Tell me about the earthquake again."

"What do you want to know?"

"You know, about Mr. Chow."

I sighed. "One day, Gin Chow walked up to a downtown blackboard and wrote that the city would be destroyed in an earthquake on that day."

"And?"

"Two years later it happened. On that day."

The boy looked at me. "He predicted his own death too. He's dead. Tell me how he died," he said, with the bitter cruelty reserved for children.

Before I could answer, we heard our names hailed. Freddy dropped what he was doing and bolted toward the voices glistening in the other room. I stayed behind a second or two, shaking my head, staring out the window into gray skies and listening for any distant echo of my brother patiently explaining why the bowie knife could not have been made from the point of a shooting star that fell to earth. The room, aslant with light, was glowing with ghosts.

"Hey, you are cute, and I don't care what anybody says," said June, so close to me I jumped.

"I like hearing it," I said. She did care what they say, though.

"I thought you were mad at me."

"I am allowed to have moods," I said.

"Me too. Some kind of mood. Right now you are bringing out the

Junior Miss Trollop mood in me."

I moved in close and said, "Oh yeah?"

After about forty seconds of torrid exchange, she moved away and whispered, "Not here, you brute."

I laughed and she winked.

"Coming?" she asked in her best sultry voice.

"No, but I'm sure gonna wait a few seconds before I leave this room."

"Hurry, I want you to sit next to me."

"Aw, I was hoping for Aunt Pearlie," I said. But June was already gone.

In the twilight, bats make for food, moths for light, and the sun goes to ground. I felt drawn by stars like a sailor lost. I longed to smell some air moving in here. Salt air blown in from the waves full of that particular nothing that plumes up over the long, white-capped areas no human has ever poisoned with contact; wood, steel, or canvas. Imagined all the fallen rising into that mist, brooding over the wellsprings of hopeless surrenders. Drowned and drowning, listen to me: I want that empty place now. Who's afraid of dying? I imagined the cold sea as a poet's grave, and I imagined my brother, either living in secret there or shrouded in his own personal nothing, going down the empty restless waves raising themselves to no one's advantage.

I pulled the coats away and looked at the prayer card nailed neatly at the back of the closet and the words he wrote over Our Savior's face:

So blend the turrets and shadows there
That all seem pendulous in air
While from a proud tower in the town
Death looks gigantically down.

"Trevor, come," said a voice down the hall, and I marveled at my own flight from myself. I had no idea who spoke so urgently, or whether the voice belonged to a living relative or one long dead. I turned out into the hall, looked back once, and headed for the other voices, most of them real.

Chapter 24

THE NOCTAMBULIST GUTTERED LIGHT out in pulsing waves from a failing-bulb sign. It sat inert between the Lobero Theatre and a weedy parking lot where the fog spread in thickening wisps. We had hustled along the two blocks uptown. Sometimes I would stop to observe minutiae while Bohawk practiced patience.

I brushed dew from my lashes and my hair and from the wool of my cardigan. My glasses made pretty prisms in any chance light, such as car beams that swept down Santa Barbara Street. But my light was guttering too, and I was growing cold. Something from the stone-and-wood bench, the dark I almost touched, from where I sat came forward and stayed with me.

The club, almost always packed, seemed lit for nothing that night, through windows you could see unpeopled tables, and that also sent me into a shiver. But the door opened and warm air met the travelers. Inside it smelled like apples, and cinnamon, and cigarettes.

The Noctambulist's owner, mopping a table inside the door, nodded his head my way but leaned his whole bulk into Bohawk. "You came on a good night. The Normal Guys are here and something sweet from Mexico too. Hey, Trevor," he said. We lived across the street from each other once. "Didn't recognize you at first."

"I'm not myself," I said. "Then again, I've never been better, thanks."

He looked at me and I almost could recite his silent review of my public history. I was doomed to repeat it, he thought. I can't. I won't. I made it this far tonight.

"Mr. Westin here has entered into a dimension of sight and sound, of shadow and substance," said Bohawk in a lyrical bass voice.

"Do tell. Hope he enjoys himself. I said, I hope he enjoys himself," the owner said, repeating the words in a booming tone, pretending to address the hard of hearing.

"I need to sit down," I said.

"Stay right here," Bohawk said. He pulled out a worn chair from a wooden table decorated with one of those Italian Swiss Colony wine bottles with wicker, into which dozens of different-tinted candles had been allowed to melt, creating something accidentally beautiful.

"Yes, I won't move. I wonder if I might have a drink," I asked, suddenly craving the stuff. But just as quickly forgetting it as I became absorbed in the meaning of overlapping wax. Sudden warmth poured out of me; I exhaled a cloud of billowing heat. I'm a part of it's a part of me. I looked around.

Bohawk plunked down a mug of tea in front of me, and an art book about a guy named Bosch.

"Tea? I didn't mean tea."

The book was full of images of distorted humanity, subjects and objects of some weird religious zeal—heaven and hell stuff, profusely illustrated but not nearly as good as my own slide show.

"Here's what the nuns didn't want you to know," Bohawk said, and went away again.

I leaned back in my chair. "Wow, I don't know if I can take this," I said out loud to no one. Sure seemed like a lot of crazy assumptions had constructed this moment. A crappy PA squealed as it was plugged into a giant boxed speaker. The sound was as one with the harsh quality of tonight's Santa Barbara nightlife.

"Hi, everybody, sorry," said the performer on the barely raised stage. He looked about seventeen. He didn't look sorry, and at that moment I *was* everybody, at least in the room. I recognized Van Cortlandt, but barely. With his face cut by orange and blue Xmas lights, he didn't really resemble himself. Turning, he gave me a sharp military salute.

A curtain directly across from me parted, briefly revealing a busboy tray heaped with coffee cups and water tumblers, and then an arm, and then a shaggy-looking man emerged.

"Hey are you really Trevor Westin?" he asked, scraping out the other chair of my table and swinging down low to speak, his arms on the table the way my mother always used to tell me not to do at the dinner table. I giggled, confused. "The kid, the guy who wrote the novel about the other world, *Neverknown*?"

I couldn't help but laugh at him; it was absurd that he would know me and not at the same time.

"You're laughing. At me not with, I guess. I must have the wrong guy," he said.

"No, I am he of whom you seek. But … but the way you said it makes me self-self-conscious. And you have the advantage of me, on me, over me," I said, thrusting out an unsteady hand.

"Oh man, I'm sorry," he said. "I'm just excited. My name's Sid Pimpleren and that book changed my life."

Now I was dumbfounded. A glowing nebula spread between us. "You're one, one of the Normal Guys, right?"

"Yeah," he said, leaning closer while folk singer boy began to strum in a minor key to suggest that Barbara Allen might be dead. "I'm one."

"Well it's me who's honored then. I can't believe the stuff you guys get away with. That riff on Alger Hiss was brilliant. Hissing the Villain."

"Close enough," he said.

Close enough for what? I wondered. That was the title on the LP I had at home. Was I mumbling? Fumbled the name? No. There must be some automatic strangeness built into words, I thought. He thinks of me and I think of him but not quite right either of us. Whatever I say is a loose translation. Maybe always. Maybe each word is a Trojan Horse, carrying deceptive cargo, meanings, the same way sneezes carry germs. Words were germ-carriers, more like hosts than signals.

"I can't believe HUAC hasn't rounded you up," I said. Another stream of crashing signals hit my mind, and I shivered. "How did I change *your* life?" I asked.

"You kidding? A kid of, how old were you?"

"Fourteen when I finished."

"Ladies and gentlemen, here's the typical American teenager's bedroom," said Sid, onstage pretend. "Note the manuscript. Like most kids his age, Trevor is nearing completion on a sensitively rendered allegorical fantasy with an almost archetypal feeling for the rhythms of the sea. Mortality's insistent force on each page, told from the point of view of a child."

"That's pretty," I said. "Maybe I'll use it myself."

"You can't. It's a pretty faithful echo of Lionel Trilling's review."

"He's a nice man," I said.

"Listen to you, Lionel Trilling's a nice man."

"I can't help it. He bought me a Fifty-Fifty Bar in Greenwich Village when I did the book tour thing. Everybody else treated me like a freak." I was waving my hand back and forth in front of my eye. Hands were trailing behind my hands.

"No. A freak? The Dickens, you say. And now you're having tea with Aldous Huxley," he said. "Oh, by the way, that's what Bohawk told me to tell you. He went out to pick up Huxley at the Upham. Took my car. Apparently Huxley loves this place. He's nearly blind after all."

"I forgot about Huxley." I must have looked nervous.

"Small potatoes for a kid who had ice cream with the Trillings."

"Just Lionel," I said. He laughed and turned serious. I wondered whether I could ever say anything with real accuracy again. Looking around, he bought a brandy flask out from his gabardine coat and unscrewed the delicate silvery top, presenting it to me. "This will help the tea go down. Is it true about the drugs? Can you get me any?"

"Bohawk talks a lot," I said, purring as brandy hit the celestial fire of my core. "I don't know how that would work. I could ask the actor if I see him. Is he coming?"

"Which actor?" said Sid. "Why would an actor come?"

"Some guy named Hopper, nervous guy. Told me he managed Huxley. He gave me the psilocybin. I wonder why Huxley is coming."

"He wants to look in on you. I think he's afraid your caboose might slip loose. Is this a potential danger?"

"It happened once before," I said, feeling frank in the brandy warmth and reaching for more flask. "When I was finished with the book and the tour and the movie, and went off to college. It was hard being alone. I broke down. It had something to do with reading T. S. Eliot."

"You're kidding."

I was about to say no when two other guys walked up, the other Normals. Perfunctory introductions made: Goldberg and Wagner.

"Aren't you a communist?" the scrawny guy asked.

"Communist? That's the secret word!" said his pal.

"No. I'm a columnist," I said.

"Hey, did you read the one about the commie newspaper. It was black-and-white and Red all over." He looked at me and waggled his eyebrows. "Think about it."

"Don't pay any attention to that man in the corner," the other guy said. "Harpo and Chico were on TV tonight, and now he thinks he's Groucho the Marxist."

"You bet your life, *tovarich*," he said. "First let's go down to Cuba for a fine cigar. The rebels take Havana by tomorrow."

"You know what I think?" asked the second guy. "Know what I think?"

"No, what do you think?"

"I think this country was sold down the river by that commie Jew bastard Roosevelt, whose real name is Franklin Delano Rosenfeld. That's what I think."

"I hate Jews, all Jews," said Wagner. "Orange juice, tomato juice, grapefruit juice."

"You like to smoke some boo?" the other guy asked. I had the profound insight that I was the audience now, as if that ought to explain my life to me. Till human voices wake us. One of the kids got up and closed the door. I guess it was late. The guy handed me a lit marijuana cigarette and nodded and shook his head when I tried to refuse. I took a puff and then coughed it out. I wasn't much of a smoker; I'd had hashish, but I ate it. Up in Hollywood. In college. Not good memories.

Just then I got hit by a rippling series of notes that the kid Dave was playing, over and over, with high notes plucked against the vibration, glowing like the Christmas lights hung in the room to ward off the occluding dark. The song was polluted with human misery, the nighttime he sang about, but with the kind of pain that was brought upon our heads by our own pointless cruelties. No. It was the human situation: imperfection. Followed by the human condition: dissatisfaction. I saw light glisten off his guitar, and the world began to crack open. I held up my hand to delay Sid's inquiries, whatever they were. I sat and listened to the teenager's voice, tender but scarred-over too. No. I saw stories in my head that might not play out as illustrations of anything. I was listening to the sound of human erosion. I had three more draws on the marijuana cigarette. I opened the book and the people in it were writhing. I closed the book. Then it caught up with me, the darkness haunting the park. I had blocked it out. But it found me, attached to the music as host. It was of me falling into the complete well of darkness, and as I fell, parts of me disappeared. Fingers, arms, heart, and then the face, all of which I said good-bye to. They say if you die in your dreams, you die. But what about this?

I came back when he was strumming down hard and insisting that we should lay the bent to the bonnie broom. I was breathing, but I wasn't sure if I had been a few seconds back. I gasped and my heart raced hard. I was sweating, but nobody seemed to even notice I had been gone.

I breathed myself down in gulps. The table around me seemed ready to flap off into the air. I laughed a few times, testing the waters. A large glass of brandy appeared before me. I drank a lot of it. It had no effect, other than to sharpen my fears and joys. I remembered being absorbed in the table, an ecstatic moment. The boy sang over and over about two sisters destroyed by the will of each other, and the lover, the father, the people who won't stop fighting for love's unsparing demands. I felt a hard strangeness ebbing from me as he strummed. I turned around; the table was empty. From the curtain across the room, Aldous Huxley beckoned.

Chapter 25

I CAME RIGHT AWAY WHEN you called."

"I didn't," said June.

"That's weird. I heard your voice down the hall."

"Maybe it was Little Miss Missy," she said, handing me a platter full of relish dishes dotted with shrimp in horseradish-y ketchup, pink-white shrimp that turned out to be extraordinarily sweet.

"I know the difference between your voices."

"Especially when we're calling your name?" she said.

I looked back, almost dropping the tray. I swung through the kitchen door and almost caught my mother at the neck.

"Aack," she said. "Looks delicious."

"This dish you call 'aack' is known as 'shrimp' in our country's tongue. Say after me: 'shrimp.'"

"Your tongue's only responsibility is to remain respectful to your mother."

"Your mother's tongue?" said Uncle Francis. "Is that the appetizer?" He was immediately hushed by those gathered near the table, where he sat with the impatience of an elder tribesman.

Little place cards sat gilt-edged on the gilt-edged plates. I stood bearing the burden whilst Aunt Helen put little glass plates at each white expanse. I was seated between June and Pearl, with Mary Annie right across the table, careful what you wish. This would be delicate, but I had swallowed another gargle of me uncle's whiskey before entering the kitchen, and my social graces were put into comfortable mode, at least temporarily.

"Will you pour wine and water for the kid?" Helen asked Mary Annie, who was just coming into the dining room from some mysterious remote corner of the house.

Meanwhile the back door opened; it had become grayer outside, and the air that rolled in mixed sea smell, barbecue smoke, and an old lady's extravagance of lavender. There also was the smell of the forlorn Christmas tree, unlit and dropping needles, as a faint reminder of more hopeful dreams lost not long ago.

"You know I can't be purchased, but I can be swayed," said Pearl, over her ample puff-sleeved shoulder, to Dale outside still grilling.

"Oh, Miss Chase, you know what an honor it would be, and you know you deserve it above anybody," he said, the only one of us who used her formal name as did the rest of the world.

"Are you stroking my vanity?" Pearl asked Dale, who stuck his head inside the door and sputtered denials as she spread her arms, as if displaying what she must daily endure. "I'm not interested in honors. Well, who knows?" She turned my way and added, "Ask Trevor. I am a package of vain something something. Correct, Trevor?"

"No, pride is not your vice, and yes, you don't have the quote right. Unusual for you. Your vice is something else—the opposite of sloth."

"'I am a parcel of vain strivings tied by a chance bond together,' Henry David Thoreau," said Francis Westin, aka Dal Bello.

"Indeed, my sin is an excess of industry. But this reward is a temptation just between us sinners," she sniffed, marching to table. "They want to give me the first honorary degree bestowed by the new educational institution known hereabouts as UCSB."

"What a feather in your cap, dear," said my mother, indicating the chair Miss Chase should occupy. "We may now address you as Professor Pearl."

"It's the kind of cultured response I expected, and only this dear, dear family could afford me. Pride, then," she said. "I'll stick with pride."

"It cometh before the fall," said Helen, hiccupping.

"I only hope lunch cometh before Christmas," said Uncle Frankie. "Next Christmas."

"But why do you seem skeptical?" asked my father, swishing his martini glass around, gazing at the silvered glass rim.

"Because it's Storke, and he arranged it in order to reward me for keeping my mouth shut about all the new creative zoning he's planned for the tract of land known as Isla Vista. They don't want to build dormitories, you know. Let the Burgermeisters build apartments. Student residential, they want to call it, SR. It's a license to throw up a ready-made ghetto, like the Mesa where Trevor dear was assaulted, another future slum. Apartment houses, for college men and women. Cash cows, and ugly ones. As if I care about it."

"Nonsense, Pearl. Storke doesn't care," said my father. "It's Mosher who started digging there during the Depression and never made a dime off that land. Since he lives a few miles away it's galling the old plutocrat. Now he's going to sell a useless piece of land to build apartments for a bunch of college kids, an assured clientele. It's the glory of the system."

"That's the kind of communist talk that the Navy hated about you," said Dick, returned from some far reach of the ranch house.

The room went dead. He must be drunk, we all thought. Of course, no one elaborated.

"Anyway," said Dick, trying to recover. "All that land is owned by codgers from the Midwest, who bought it for the mineral rights eons before the war. The real money's in development, talking those hicks into building big apartments on their worthless tracts, a path I hope to soon pursue."

The room was still still. My father's own story was not for telling, like so much other stuff spinning in the murky waters of my family.

"By the way, what's the story with Uncle Dale?" I asked, to break the new-formed ice. "Who told him to call you Miss Chase?"

"What are you trying to say, Trevor?" Pearl said. "Isn't that my name? Only the men of this family feel it's their prerogative to overfamiliarize themselves with my Christian name."

"Where are those steaks?" said Dick, who missed the exchange. "And Dale. I better go bring them in before Frankie here starts eating the table legs." He left and the dining room went quiet again, uncomfortably for me. I felt the attention gathering around my head, even though I had bent down to look into the glass bowl with its few sweet shrimp and the tawdry ketchup-red of the sauce. ESP attuned to the unliving invisible ones? Who am I hearing?

"So, tell us," said Pearlie, loud enough for the group, "what you have been doing with yourself, young Trevor."

"He told me some more stories about Gin Chow," said the rat-faced child of Uncle Dale and his mousey wife. The room began to spin for me, and muttering raised itself a pitch. I didn't dare look at my mother. The boy was oblivious. "Did you know, Aunt Pearl, that he predicted the big earthquake."

"Of course I do, child. I was the one they all ridiculed for disbelieving. In fact, I daresay, I'm the only one in this room who actually knew Mr. Chow."

"Trevor," said my mother, defying all family rules. "You aren't seeing Mr. Chow anymore, are you?"

"Of course he isn't," said Uncle Frankie. "How could he?"

My father changed the subject, asked about the cut of meat, what was it called? My mother, when I dared look up at her, managed to look both angry and sympathetic. I looked down at my plate. Suddenly a foot brushed the top of mine. It was an oddly erotic moment, considering that I didn't know if it was June, Mary Annie, or Auntie Pearl. I desperately wanted to laugh.

"I'll tell you one thing Mr. Gin Chow failed to predict," said Uncle Frankie.

I looked up, surprised.

"That's right, the famed prognosticator, who nailed the big earthquake, which helped Pearl so much, so inadvertently." He raised his hand against her gurgling protestations. "Here, here. You know the truth. He failed to predict how the courts would rule against him and for that old kingmaker Storke and his goddamned pretty lake."

"Frankie," said Helen, "there is a child present now," pointing at Dale's young charge, who was smirking at the imprecation. "It is a pretty lake, isn't it? Now that it has water, that is."

"He built that lake and dammed the upstream of the Santa Ynez River, which used to swarm with trout. Downstream in Lompoc, where Gin Chow had a farm, the water came no more, not to mention the trout failing to turn into salmon."

"That lake means water for all of us," said Dick, coming into the room with a heaping plate of tri-tip.

"Not for poor Chow," said Uncle Frankie.

"Gin Chow," said Pearl, as if she was chanting.

"What are you talking about?" said Freddy. "Aunt Pearl, what is he talking about?"

"Ask him," she said, turning to me. "Your uncle who seems to know the will of God in these matters."

"God," said Frankie, with a scorn I'd never heard before. "I'll tell you what God wants, Miss Pearl Chase."

"There is no God," said my father with a slight slur, "and Mary is His mother." He turned to my mother and raised the palm of his hand in a conciliatory fashion. She wasn't even looking at him.

"God wants the rich to leave behind rubble so that when the meek inherit the earth, the joke will be on them again," said Frankie, the bibulous versifier. "When Gin Chow sued Storke over his dam, the court refused to let a yellow man assert any right to ancient American waters." He looked at me. "Storke damned your, um, friend. God helped Storke and his friends, helped them with his sweet rain, just when it looked like the devil was going to have his due. Storke's Folly is full and this city can grow. You know the Bible, speaking of God? It's got at least one whopper in it."

"You mean the miracle in Jerusalem?"

"Trevor," said my father in a quasi-warning voice, barely able to stop laughing.

Frankie looked at my father and then at me and said, "And they say I'm bad."

Auntie Pearl asked, "What is the miracle in Jerusalem?" You could tell she was sorry soon as she asked.

"Jesus tied his ass to a tree and then walked into Jerusalem," I said, matter-of-fact.

"The child, Dick," said Aunt Helen.

"I didn't say it," said Dick. "They're your blasphemous brood, you know."

"He ties his ass to a tree," laughed the child. "His ass."

"He *rode* an ass into Jerusalem," said Pearl, smiling with pursed lips. "I think you have it wrong."

"Of course you do," said Frankie. "Because the worst part of the

Bible is Genesis, chapter one, verse 26: 'And let him have dominion over the fishes of the sea, and the birds in the air and the beasts of the earth.' The Bible always had it exactly wrong; these things have dominion over us. Those fish are dead and Gin Chow's farm died too. Though I suppose it doesn't say anything about the corn in the field. Or did the Chinaman grow rice up there in Lompoc?" He looked at me.

I didn't say anything. My mother looked small and white. My father was gazing around for the bottle of wine. In the room stilted manners took over, politely. Please pass the salt and pepper, my the salad is delicious, please I couldn't possibly eat any more of the mashed potatoes. The salt and the pepper are always passed together. The napkin stays in your lap, though some older people remember when it could be tucked into the collar. We are not those people.

During this period of time, Mary Annie caught my eye and deftly winked. I don't need this, I thought, though a kind of brutal pleasure was welling down at the bottom of my spine. I had to stretch. When I looked over, June was smiling at me too.

"You did not answer my question, young man," said Pearl Chase, the woman who through sheer hectoring manipulation took this town from Cowboy Victorian to Deco Mediterranean.

"You mean me?"

"Of course I do. Has your memory been affected by your visit to the hospital too?"

"No, ma'am. Please rephrase the question so that I can answer it without tending to incriminate myself before this distinguished tribunal."

"I simply asked what you have been doing with yourself."

"Well, I don't know. Oh, I interviewed Aldous Huxley for the *Times*."

That turned the tide of the room at long last to my advantage.

Chapter 26

FIRST THING YOU NOTICE about Aldous Huxley is his towering height. In my state, he seemed almost freakish. He stood round-shouldered just inside the curtain, in a narrow hallway leading to the back room. He looked bewildered or maybe speculative.

The second thing you notice is how blind he is, the glassy stare into the middle distance. When the beacon turns in your direction, though, that first perception seems false.

"How are you, dear man," he asked, with a tender sadness and a first-class accent. "How many tablets did you take?"

"Three, like your friend said," I said, trying out a lighthearted response. Now nervous, the room jittered with dancing atoms. "And I have crossed the Rubicon."

"The die is cast," he said. He was standing next to an intense man with a sharp face and graying hair, dressed like a janitor, in khaki shirt and pants, but with a French scarf knotted neatly at his neck. "Do you know Douwe Stuurman?"

"I don't understand my new destiny," I continued, I'm afraid, rudely. "I'm hoping you can help."

"Me?" he said, laughing. "I suppose I can try. Douwe Stuurman?" He repeated, laughing like dust.

I offered my hand, but I felt like a chimp pretending to be human.

The whole social ritual seemed absurd, outdated in this new universe. Something had shifted. That change might be another form of infection, I realized. The pills were so small, yet they packed such a wallop. Wallop. I would never be the same.

"Has everything changed?" I asked, in a croaking, small voice. "I think I actually died a few minutes ago."

Huxley stared at me and said, "I've heard of this happening. The ego dissolves, like *moksha*, I believe."

"What do you mean? Do you think somebody might have warned me? It changed me. Maybe forever."

"I think, rather, everything was always like this, and now you can see it," he said. "Don't be afraid, don't be afraid. The Chinese believe things are what they are and act as they act simply because of their position in a cosmic pattern. Oh, this was never meant to hurt you. You know. I was a little oblivious the night we met; a little high on my own voice. I'm afraid it's been happening a lot more lately. I'm not always a wise man, though I mean well. I wasn't paying attention to what that actor told people. He's a bit of a zealot to this new mysticism."

"He did this to others?" I asked, disappointed I was not alone.

"I fear Dennis spread the word and the access to many an unprepared acolyte that night, particularly those he found beautiful."

I wondered that he thought a man might find me attractive.

He looked through cloudy, envisioning blue-gray eyes. The milk of human blindness. "You'll be all right, won't you?" he asked. "The important thing is a sense of humor." He made room for me at a big wooden table. Then he began to speak about symbolic death and rebirth and mystic Christians like Saint John of the Cross and Padre Pio. He was staring into the grain of the wood, and I guessed he might be high too. Stuurman looked away carefully when I smiled. Bohawk, returned now, put a bottle of something called ouzo in front of me.

Unprepared acolytes, I thought. All of us.

The infection burrows into the cells and begins to reproduce it-self. It is very small and spreads through the system. The little pills are words, I thought. It stems from sensation, then involves, evolves, and revolves us. I was being poisoned by thoughts, and I shivered. At this point I returned to the conversation, and Huxley was quoting Wordsworth.

"The glory and the freshness of a dream," I said, and felt that thing well up in me.

"Indeed," he said.

"Well, what about our interview?" I blurted, to cover up sudden tears sprung from thoughts, words, and other infections. "Have I not earned the right to ask you certain questions that may or may not lead to material I might publish? Goddamn it, I don't have a notebook or a pen though."

He laughed at my sudden audacity, and some kind of cathartic chuckle spread through the room, beginning with the dour Stuurman, then to the Normal Guys.

"This is probably why he's my hero," said Sid Pimpleren.

"That's okay, I probably couldn't write anyway." The thought of taking notes seemed more Herculean than the achievement of this tête-à-tête.

And then Sid slapped his forehead. "Eureka," he said. "Wait here."

Huxley wanted to know if I had ever read the *Tibetan Book of the Dead* or consulted oracular books like the *I Ching*. I just stared at him for a while, and murmured No. No. And No. Would that help me get the interview too? I asked. I took the pills that took me here. I poured a tumbler full of ouzo, and Bohawk swirled some water into it. I watched it turn to milk, a domestic miracle. Then I felt ill and needed the bathroom. A moment of panic bloomed—the infection of emotion duplicates itself in a crowd of humans. This was my theory. I excused myself and went but just felt odd sitting on a toilet concentrating my life into one uncertain activity. I began to laugh but stopped. It was germinating. I might build an antibody. When I stepped forward to the mirror, I locked eyes with myself, absurdly huge pupils fixed on a reflection. I was one with me. The room was webbed in germinating patterns.

There was a light tap on the red-painted door. It was Bohawk. "They want to know if you're okay," he said from that magic trick called life outside.

"Why wouldn't I be?" I asked, still looking at my face in the still mirror. Not yet infected, I thought. Again I looked into my own eyes, and again the world dropped away. I shivered something away, off my mind forever.

"Yeah?" said Sid's voice. "I've got something you're gonna like out here."

"What is it?" I asked, singsong, stepping gingerly out of the bathroom into a room that indeed seemed better. The large white-faced Gruen clock said 8:45 p.m. I stared at it. I was sure it was after midnight. "Early," I bleated, sheepish.

"What do you mean?" said Pettibon the innkeep. "It's after eight o'clock and everyone knows that the streets in this town roll up automatically. Here it's very late."

He wasn't joking. My stomach felt oddly hollow and my eyes were winding down. On the table was a gray contraption with flywheels and tape.

"It's called a reel-to-reel, Trevor."

"I've seen one," I said. "But what's it for?"

"We have an idea," said Bohawk and two of the Normal Guys, no shit, talking at the same time like Huey, Dewey, and Louie.

Chapter 27

"IT JUST SORT OF happened," I said, trying for a balance between pride and nonchalance. My psilocybin-inspired skepticism about social grace had worn off—the give-and-take seemed real now, grounded in traditions. Which view was better, I wondered. "The interview intervened," I said, playing an old family word game.

"An excellent accident?" said Uncle Frankie.

"Indubitably fortuitous," I replied. "I met him at the Noctambulist, and these comedian guys set us up with a tape recorder. I did the interview and they transcribed it for me."

"Why would you trust a comedian?" my mother said, leaning over for the salt. "You should have taken the tape."

"They already sent it. Hand delivered, transcribed. I finished the piece in half an hour. It wrote itself."

"Well, what did he say?" asked Dale. "Didn't he write that obscene book about the old man with the teenage girl?"

"He said that the world is in a lot of trouble."

"Communists," said Uncle Dick. "Now the Cubans, too, you'll see," he said, speaking more to my father than anyone else in the room.

"Jesus Christ, Dick," said my dad.

"They're in outer space now," he said.

"So are you, brother-in-law."

"Honey," said my mother, though whom she was addressing was not at all clear. "I believe our son was talking. Aren't you proud of him?" A flush of wine crept into her cheek. Proud of me. "Go on, Trevor, how is the world in trouble, according to your Mr. Huxley?"

"And it was Mr. Nabokov who wrote *Lolita*," whispered June. She seemed proud of me too.

"Russian," muttered Dick. "Communist."

"There's too many of us," I said. "We're destroying Mother Nature."

"Nonsense," said Auntie Pearl. "Earthquake, fires, floods; she's destroying us."

"He must've been on the freeway lately," said Dale's weepy-eyed wife. The doorbell, a muted Big Ben chime, sounded in the distance. Helen rose.

"Actually you're both right," I said, exchanging a knowing look with my darling June, whose honey-colored hair swept forward into her eyes, a strand wisping into the corner of her lush mouth. She had the most delicate skin; you could see down into it through the soft pale texture of its cloud surface. "The planet is overcrowded and all of the smokestacks and automobiles are filling it with gases that shouldn't be breathed. We're destroying her."

"With floods, fires, and earthquakes?" asked Mary Annie. "What happened to the locusts?"

"All dead from pesticides. She's going to starve us, withhold her fruits," I said.

"Sounds like my ex-wife," said uncle poet.

"Excuse me," said a very serious Aunt Helen. "Someone's at the door for you two," she said, pointing to my father and me. We considered each other.

"I don't want to buy any subscriptions or brushes," said dear old Dad.

"I've got enough cookies at home," I said.

"A good American knows how to turn disaster to their advantage," said Pearl. "We'll have dominion over nature soon enough. Atomic power, rayguns, space travel, you'll see. The wonders we have seen in these times."

"Pearlie sounds like Averell Harriman now," said Frankie. "When there's blood in the streets, there's money to be made."

"It's the police at the door, please don't keep them waiting," said Helen, dropping decorum for urgency's sake.

We looked at each other again. We both got up. It stopped the herky-jerk of conversation dead—what must Mary Annie be thinking, I wondered. Or June for that matter. Both seemed indifferent.

"They want us both?" I asked, but my father was already urging me along.

The man slouching in the doorway looked self-important and unsavory. He wore a hat cocked down and a long coat over a shabby suit. He was smoking, holding the cigarette away from his eyes and blinking fiercely. He brightened when he saw my father.

"Joshua, the battle of Jericho," said my father.

"And the walls came a-tumbling down," said the detective. "How kind that you remembered," he said.

"How could I forget?" said Dad, and introduced me to one Lieutenant Josh Boston.

"Negro spirituals?" I asked.

"Oh, your illustrious father and I are something like Army buddies. Though he was already enlisted in the Navy, and we were looking for some AWOL spics. Turned up wetbacks living at the country club, supposedly unbeknownst to Mr. Olympics Avery Brundage, who still owns the place."

"Didn't know you did immigration work," I said, looking at my father.

"The reason I retired from police and went to sea," he said. "Beating up Mexicans was the reason Boston stayed on," he added.

"I'm going to ignore that because today is a day of good news," said the cop. "Your son didn't kill the nurse, I'm happy to report. Her mother-in-law did." He peered at me. "We were looking for you for three days."

"I've been me the whole time. I mean here." I was flustered, and my father leaned into me as reassurance.

"Not at home much," he said. "Must've been here." He looked at the Edgewater house with snapdragons running up its front walls. "The Westin boys did okay. And the son. He also rises. See cops can be literary too."

"You said he wasn't a suspect?" said my father.

Boston ignored him and turned to me. "Your father makes it sound like he was a clean-cut boy—big hero. Back when he ran the Burton Mound neighborhood the word 'beat' had a more specific meaning, huh?"

"I miss our old etymology lectures," my father said. "But please don't let me keep you and the prowler out there from driving away from this house."

"A pleasure," the cop said. "I left messages for the kid all over town. Just want him to know not to worry. Seems like the rash of disappearances might have ended."

"Oh," I said.

"Well, you was the last straw; we couldn't locate you. Then we got word you were still you. Then we found out that Baby Bird left his wife and yapping kid and ran off with some UCSB coed."

"No kidding," I said. "What about Newt?"

"Hah, that's the funny part. We had him the whole time. Picked him up drunk, but he told us his name was Newton Ebriated. Our cops don't really get wordplays. Puns and such. He yowled all day, but we liked his joke so much we forgot about his phone call."

"Thanks," I said. Why did I feel something like disappointment? "Good news. Whole time, you were just looking out for me."

He snickered. "We protect and serve."

Then I remembered Castle Rock. "There's still somebody else."

"Yeah," he said.

"Dooley," I said.

"Him we can't find."

"Francis Xavier, a good man," my father said. "But how did you know to come here?"

"It's called police cooperation. Some of the members of your illustrious family remember where they came from." Dale Flappylips, I thought. He gave a little salute, which neither of us returned.

After he left, my father leaned against the closed door, his nostrils wide as if breathing for the first time in hours. "It's bad about Dooley," he said. "But I have that favor to ask you still," he said, looking fragile.

"Of course, Dad."

"Step into the kitchen and we'll grab a drink while Pearlie's not watching."

I wondered if he hadn't had enough already.

"By the way, congratulations for not murdering any nurses."

"Thanks, I'm trying to avoid both sin and the occasion of sin."

"You keep running into trouble, I have to worry."

"The cops. Out to protect me."

"Sometimes people become lightning rods. Everything happens around them. I'm afraid you're such an anomaly. This will scare the police, and you'll feel more like bad luck than a proper reporter, investigator, whatever … "

I looked at him. "Snake Jake?"

"I don't like that name."

"But you knew him?"

He looked suddenly fierce and took another deep breath. My elementally distant father returned. "I never met him. But something seems wrong in all of this. I'm a little worried for you. I think you should keep your eyes open. Step wide."

"The whole thing was chance," I said. "Then when people started disappearing, I got very curious."

"Seems like you have good instincts. I always think you should trust the things that draw you in."

"I see," I said. "This is like the part in the gangster movies where cops warn our hero away."

"Are you interested in being a hero?"

"No, I'm not like you. I'm leaning more toward Huxley kind of stuff, interviewing the famously interesting among us. He was kind of an eye-opener. There's a chance I might get a job. The *Times*." I don't know who was making me say these words, but I listened to myself to hear what might come next.

"I never told you or anybody in my house what to do growing up, besides the obvious stuff, not taking candy or rides from strangers," said dear Dad. "I have hunches and they're based on the same stuff everybody else uses. Prejudices. Whims. Chance. Old detectives believe in chance. Some people say everything has a meaning, a reason, but that's absurd. Everything has hundreds of meanings. Chance is overdetermined with meaning, and, um, stuff."

"To a life full of meanings," I said, raising the half glass of rum he'd fished out of the hiding place next to the scotch under the sink.

"These favors I want to ask are a bit awkward," he said, not looking me in the eyes.

"Shoot, give, try me."

"I want you to make up with Icaro."

"Say what?" I croaked. "How do you know?"

"Listen, Icaro is an old, well, let's just say he's an old family friend. He's been looking out for us for a very long time."

"What do you mean?" I was two blocks past Incredulous Street now.

"I met him during the war. He worked for me and when I came back, he showed up. I don't know what he does now, but he's a very useful guy. He's tough but he has this sort of artistic side. Brainy but not loath to use his brawn. He's very loyal."

"You sent him after me," I said, anger overcoming the gratitude I ought to have felt. He watches over his son. His troubled son, I realized. "How could you?"

"It's not like that. I asked him in a sort of offhand way to keep an eye on you. I swear it was a casual thing like, 'Don't take any wooden nickels.' He took it more seriously than I meant. Truth told, I'm glad. He almost killed one of the guys who jumped you."

"No, that was me," I said, and then began to wonder. How did my father know about guys the police couldn't find?

"I won't ask for forgiveness. I'm going straight to that cheap emotional ploy all parents use. If you had a son, you'd do the same." He gulped down some rum. "Icaro was hurt by your insinuations. He's probably more hurt that you figured out he was following you." My father was struggling. We both knew the door between us had been jammed half-open for ten years.

"How do I do this?" I asked. "Making up."

He smiled. "Go to Jacques's. Have a chicken à la king. No really. Then ask the waitress to tell the chef if he doesn't know a recipe he shouldn't try to fake it. Make sure she uses those very words. Next thing you know, a big Greek with a cleaver will be marching toward your table."

"Great."

"In a good way, though."

"Okay."

"I'll appreciate this more than you can imagine." He said, and half-turned looking out the window.

"There's something else," I said.

"Yep," he said looking down the street. Held up his hand to signal hesitation. "It's money. Your mother and I need a little more to make the move. The Navy was supposed to take care of me, and well, this was all so sudden."

"Stop, Dad. Please."

"I hate to do it. The pension just has to get straight."

"We've been over this a million times. I wish you could just write a check, whenever, whatever you need. I'll tell Mr. Johnson on Monday, I mean tomorrow. I'm going to give you power of attorney or whatever they call it. This is too hard, just go ahead and take what you need, no, what you want. Whatever you need. I don't touch it."

He sighed. "I'm sorry."

"If you don't stop apologizing I *will* get mad."

He gazed out the window. "This used to be a tomato field not that long ago. I used to play here sometimes, sneak in with my friends. Sometimes the farmer would shoot at us."

"A bit extreme."

"Not in those days. It was almost like the Old West. People living on the coast had come to the edge of it. Everybody here's an immigrant from something; everybody riding into the sunset. After here you get damp. Return to your resting place. I loved the ocean then. Now I'm mad at it."

My father was beginning to frighten me.

"Remember that one summer, down at Carpinteria—grunion

hunting? When you went out into the water that night and I couldn't find you with the flashlight and then those guys from the oil company came around with you in their arms. Big burly guys, called them roughnecks, right?"

The images came back: sea rolling in at night in the moonlight, with scores of people scooping through foam and coming up with nothing. And then the fish arrived on some magical cue, silver on the waves, filling the shallow plane of water with bodies flapping. Hands everywhere grabbing and little pails filling; I was mesmerized and wandered until I saw that nobody was there. I called out, panicked. I started crying and then two men smelling of cigars and beer said, hey, hey, hey, hey. They scooped me up and brought me to my mother, who was shrieking in pain.

"My heart almost stopped. I was glad you talked to strangers. Later your brother, and no one came to save him."

My God, this was the first time he actually mentioned Patrick. I was in shock.

"Make yourself safe."

"How?"

"Icaro works at Jacques's, remember?

"Okay, I'll make friends again."

He grabbed my glass and poured more of the mediocre rum into it. "This is a small place, my son. Icaro's cousins work at the housing tract. They saw you and called him. The job site had one phone. He had to leave the restaurant. Drove over in a borrowed car with his borrowed dog."

"But what about Uncle Dick, maybe he called?"

"Dick. You have to think about Dick. I think you make him nervous. He married into the family. Helen is your friend, maybe. Watch out, and watch out for their daughter. That's the other thing, the last thing."

"Who?" I asked, hearing my voice break.

"Your cousin. You know. June?" He looked at me strangely. I looked out of the window trying to imagine tomato fields, but instead spied a stately fake Tudor and the signs of construction going on down the street, model homes and staked wires flying white rags at the borders.

"Why would anybody want to hurt June?" I asked.

He looked at me. "No, not that way. She's probably more resourceful than any in this family. I just think you should be careful of her.'" He looked at me. "Be careful of her," he said again, as if it were a gigantic effort to tear the words out of his own guts. Now he was making me mad, but I had no way to talk back. My teeth were locked. The kitchen door swung open.

Aunt Helen was behind it. Her head popped through the French portals like a disembodied puppet.

"There you two are. Please come in and stop that old crow from cackling on and on."

"A crow is not a chicken, dear."

"What did the policeman want?"

"Sell us tickets to a ball," said Dad.

"Very funny, now get in here now. That old man can talk, and Pearl is no help."

My father forced a smile. I pointed to the door, with overelaborate flourishes of courtesy. "I'll do my best to do what you ask," I said with sincerity.

He smiled with relief. "That was a nice drink," he said.

"It's hard to believe that a people's history, a shoreline built up over millennia, and the fate of a community can hinge on a rich man's whim about a boat named absurdly after a village in Alaska," boomed out my father's brother Francis as we came through the swinging door. This was just prelude to a rant.

"Pshaw," said Pearl—I don't think I'd ever heard anyone say that in real life before. "You don't even know the name of the boat."

"Ha," said Uncle Frankie. "*Haida*, that's its name. *Haida*. A place where the potlatch was practiced regularly, a ritual stomping of the culture around itself, periodic purification, waves of obliteration that washed away the past—not unlike the people who created your precious harbor, who would rather obliterate the earth. They built it and destroyed the sand flow off the coastline, changed all the beaches. Now they have to dredge out the harbor every year. Nature itself wants to destroy it. Actually, now that I think of it, perhaps this was all very appropriate."

"Oh, Frankie, what have you got against our harbor?" said Dick the obstreperous.

"Castle Rock," I said. "The people who built the harbor obliterated Castle Rock."

"Oh, mercy me," said Pearl. "Here we go."

"The boy's right. There's hope for this generation after all," said Frankie, beaming, knowing we had heard and internalized his legend of legends.

"I don't want to seem stupid," said Mary Annie. "But what's a Castle Rock? Some kind of amusement park?"

"I take it back," muttered Frankie. "About this generation."

"No, dear," said June, who looked flushed. Her hair shining out to its tips and her chest lifting and falling, taking up the rhythm. "It was a huge, beautiful rock that sat out in the ocean. At the end of the cliff, not far from the Plunge, across from Sunseri's." She laughed, looking straight at me. "It had a magical past, there were fairies, a kingdom of them, and a golden-haired boy used to visit them with his mother, though his foolish mother thought they were just going to the beach. The boy knew better. He wanted to join them forever."

"Fairies don't really live forever," said Frankie. "But they live much longer than we do. And they have some magical powers, I believe."

"The boy's father had left the two of them alone," continued my beloved dream.

"June!" said Helen.

"No, she's right to say this," said Frankie, who looked like his eyes might be brimming. "The boy's father just *disappeared*. Swept away by some force of need."

"Maybe it was fairies," laughed Freddy, the only real child among us.

"Something very like," said Helen, disapprovingly.

"Yes, yes," said Frankie, in a quite different tone.

"Then one day," I said, "a very rich man decided he needed a safe place to put his boat."

"We all needed it," said Dick. "It has done us some good."

"Hush, now, Dick," said Pearl, out of character. "Let those who are enchanted enchant."

I picked up the silvery strand. "So he looked upon the harborless seacoast village known as Santa Barbara … "

"At least it was known that way since the Spanish first claimed it away from the affable Indians," said June. "Before that it has an Indian name: Syuhtun. By the way, what does that mean? Did you know Malibu means pounding drums?"

"I thought we had decided on gullible," said Aunt Helen, whose eyes were closed now as if for a séance. "At least the affable Indians were."

"Too cynical. Who's telling this story, Mother?" June asked, her voice tinkling like icicles on pavement.

"Hmm," said Frankie. "And who taught it to you?"

"Anyway," I said, laughing. "Syuhtun means two roads split, heading in different directions, according to dear Dr. Harrington, the linguist Frankie made me meet when I was a kid. He gave me a grinding stone he found in our backyard."

"I was wise to introduce you to other crazy geniuses," said Frankie.

The room ignored him—I pushed on with the impetus of craziness and rant. "And the rich man said, lo, ye heretofore deprived citizens. Let us think of the future. Don't thou thinkest 'twould be merry with a few protected slips for other rich folk like me to disport themselves on barks with silver services and clean white sheets?"

"I think it was tablecloths," June laughed. I looked at her; she winked. Oh, God of Desire, I thought.

"Don't overdo the 'thou' and 'thee' stuff," said my mother, tipping the last drops of wine down her throat.

"And he prevailed on the elders of the village and the landed people to put forth some of their own dough, yet he put out much more of his own, as was fitting. At first they talked of building a channel into a salt marsh on the east end of the town's long dingle, but he said nay" I said, chastised correctly.

"Dingle," said little Lord Frederick.

"'It must be on the west side, and for convenience's sake, it must be matched to the long landing pier,' quoth the rich man. But the hindrance to his plan was a giant promontory rock, and he said he would have no problem if they tore the rock down to make way for his harbor."

"At first the people of the village were opposed," said Frankie. "They liked the rock, which we've already introduced: Castle Rock. The rich man grew petulant. Meanwhile, the boy whose father had left decided to write a poem about the rock and all the magic it contained. It caught the attention of the more callous folk, and for a while it looked like the rich man would not get his way."

"But then nature itself joined forces with the rich man; a terrible earthquake cracked the town and shivered it to pieces. Buildings split in two and sidewalks buckled. But most fearfully, the ancient rock was shattered," I said. "Or so the city elders and the landed people said, and they proclaimed the rock unsafe for visitors. They hung signs about it, warning away the citizenry."

I waited, but Frankie seemed content that I continue. "Now that the rock was doomed all objections to the location of the harbor fell by the wayside, and the city, in the grip of its lust for progress, abandoned the little boy and hundreds and hundreds of little boys and girls stretching back to the time when a more primitive—um, gullible—people lived near the rock. And once the city decided this, the boy made a last pilgrimage up the beach toward it. He saw that the rock was damaged, but failed to understand what was dangerous, and despite the signs, he once more climbed the craggy surface, toehold by footing-place, until he found the cave where the fairies lived. He looked in and only saw dark."

"What do you mean?" said the child at the end of the table. "He saw something else, I remember this story perfectly."

"How could you remember? You weren't even there. Now, hush," said Uncle Francis.

I continued: "He looked for a long time, way past the point where a normal kid would have given up. And then, his eyes got used to the cave's dim light, and he saw the court of the little people in a kind of shabby decline."

"My favorite writer," said June. Her foot lay across mine now.

"The queen had droopy stockings and the king's crown hung low over his brow, as if the power that made him king was running to the ground, draining away. The floor was strewn with copper pieces and the gold was gone. And as the king waved to me sadly, um, waved to him sadly, the little boy gulped and the light faded away."

"And this is how they did it," said Uncle Frankie, speaking from the other realm, where he now was. Everybody had stopped picking at their food for this part. "They got dynamite, lots of it. They went to the base of the rock, which had stood since the before the beginning of human time. And they cordoned off the area around the rock and took the bunches of sticks and they lit the fuses. The violence done was a wave of sound that deafened you to all other sounds for minutes afterwards. They reduced Castle Rock to rubble in a few seconds of overlapping waves. The town split in two—into the golden dream of preserving what nature had bestowed and the corrupt reality of our tiny, undeniable hungerings. The towering thing became a heap, prostrate to the will of a sporty set. And they brought trucks and skip loaders and hauled away the shale of it. The boy was near, even though his mother warned him not to go that day. He was drawn there. Halfway through the blasting, he noticed there was a chip, a piercing splinter in the corner of his eye. He was crying, but when he rubbed it, he saw blood on his fingers along with the needle fragment of Castle Rock. He ran home; his mother, furious, took him to the doctor who sat at the corner of Cota and State Street. And there in the office sat an old man. The boy knew him from reading the newspapers. He was the rich man with the boat. He stared at the man, who gave him a kindly smile and called him sonny. The boy thought, this man has become my father."

Uncle Frankie took a hard turn from his story to the light of his own real memory. "And the old man turned to me and smiled and said, 'Don't worry, he's a good doctor. You won't feel a thing.'"

My father seemed happier than I'd ever seen him. He raised his glass to me, swirled it in a circular wave, and swallowed the wine-dark wine.

Auntie Pearl looked as if she wanted to cry.

Chapter 28

"**D**O YOU KNOW WHAT makes a precious stone precious?" asked Huxley, leaning forward over the tape machine, which shrank down in size when he so large leaned over it. He smiled and looked out from those filmy eyes. "It's not a rhetorical question," he said.

"I never thought about it," I answered. "But I guess it's some sort of Adam Smith proof. Lots of people want them, but there aren't so many around. It's like, let me guess, the conspiracy of silent affirmation that creates the web of illusion we climb around and stick upon." I had begun shivering, then, though it was not cold. Long shudders, almost pleasurable, shook my body.

He considered this for a second. "That's pretty good."

"It was supposed to be a joke," I said, and the Normal Guys let their shoulders drop. Normie number three made the thumb and forefinger okay gesture behind Huxley's back. As the pills waned in power, the brandy and marijuana began usurping them. I felt cocky. I felt admitted into some brotherhood.

"Sorry," Huxley said. "But I was serious."

"I realize."

"I was about to say that precious gems resemble the experience you and I have had with these so-called hallucinogens. They offer a kind of

... objective correlative." He seemed shy for a second. "Did you see the Light?"

I looked around me, cleaning the lenses of my glasses, actively clowning. The boys were with me, taking huge pulls off another bottle and chuckling at Huxley's expense.

"I'm not sure what you mean, but I swear I could hear capital letters in that."

"Maybe I'm blind, but I'm not obtuse," said Huxley, regarding us all. "The Light I refer to is a common experience when people take psychoactive formulas. It's a light of, well, it's like a quest, oh, I guess it does sound funny."

"No. Go ahead, sir," said one of the Normies, withering under Stuurman's overearnest professor gaze. "It's some kind of Platonic thing, right?"

Huxley smiled. He started talking about the *Phaedo*, for Christ's sake, and the world above the world. I began to enjoy myself again. If this was the hard work of the interview, it was in the bag. The world above the world. I believed, though I was too timid to admit it, that I had seen the reality beneath reality, the world beneath the world. This is the dream, the crystallization. The truth was a yawning, beautiful terror.

"There were significant lights in most religions, lights that almost drowned the people who encountered them. Saul on his way to Damascus, Mohammed, St. John of the Cross. The light changed everything in their lives; it set them free in a shower of uncompromising love of God. Well, maybe not free. But even in lesser hallucinatory encounters, people see glowing crystalline shapes. Some see the Light. I haven't."

"Geometric patterns," I said. "I see that. My hands shadowed by following images of my hands too." I looked around, and people were staring, which was awkward. Huxley smiled as if I was the only truth he needed.

"Crystalline," he repeated. "Gemlike. Tell me, Mr. Westin, have you ever been to Notre Dame or Sainte-Chappelle?" He didn't really seem to heed my head nodding. "You know that the world of visions is encoded there. Imagine the feeling a Christian mystic has kneeling on hard stone beneath that dance of lights. We begin to see why precious stones are precious," he said. "They resemble the experiencing of truth, the faceted light."

"Maybe it's the other way around," I murmured. "Maybe the precious stones created the hallucinations. Based on some really simple need for pleasure. Sparkly things."

He didn't hear me. "They represent the direct total awareness from inside of Love as the primary cosmic fact."

"Love," I said, thinking about June and my brother. I loved them, and it didn't seem to help anyone. How did love figure in the vision of nullity I was having at the table? Maybe I love death? Only the restaurant owner looked at me—and then he winked.

Huxley was on a roll. "'And young men glittering and sparkling angels, and maids strange seraphic pieces of life and beauty ... Eternity was manifest in the Light of Day, and something infinite behind everything appeared, which talked with my expectation and moved my desire.'"

"Blake?"

He stared at me. "Thomas Traherne, one hundred years before Blake."

He went on and I was fearful he would never stop. "'So that with much ado I was corrupted; and made to learn the dirty devices of this world. Which I now unlearn and become as it were a little child again, that I may enter into the Kingdom of God.'"

"Speaking of children," I said, launching into a dumb question about his work with the students. He was uncomfortable, shifted in his hard seat, and laughed. Everybody laughed, though I wasn't sure of the joke myself. Then a more or less straight interview took place. I even got him to talk about this idea about population and intelligence genes and the breeding of only one-point-five children, speaking of children. Turns out it was his brother's idea. There were a lot of Huxleys. He proved it with Malthus and math and numbers that rolled off his tongue, though his talk sometimes stopped, and he regarded with long, elegant fingers the grains of salt and rice on the table with otherworldly attention, a Braille of natural signifiers.

The tape ran out as he was mid-sentence, explaining some guy named Maine de Biran and the uses of the world, and we laughed together. We stretched and peed and paid for the tea and said good-byes to the empty café, no ghost light. Then we were at the door and all my worries and the interview were over. People were clapping each other on the back in the now clear night with stars blazing in the dark stillness.

"Are there still some Christmas lights up there on the Riviera, what you call the Riviera?" he asked. A color blue wind flowed through me as I said indeed and shivered with sweet delight, my ears crackling ice.

"That's a folk art," he said, and I was touched. I wasn't sure about Love, but I felt like I loved this gang. "Twinkling lights remind us of the other world. We call them fairy lights, like we used to call movie projectors magic lanterns. There's something touching about Christmas decorations, I think."

At the moment I did, too, even though Christmas was gone. I had entered the outside world, and another long shiver took me. The air in my lungs seemed mentholated, and a rushing sensation rolled up my back. As I relaxed, hallucinations started again in earnest, as if to make up for the time I had repressed them. The fog surrounding the lights made science fiction globes, and I suddenly felt a movement outward toward new associations.

"I'll never forget this night," I said. "Thank you."

"For the interview?"

"No, though that was something I felt I needed in my other life."

"There isn't any other life," said Huxley. "There is this," and he pointed to the sputtering light of the club, which at that moment the tired owner put out.

Chapter 29

"**Y**OU MUSTN'T LISTEN TO them," Pearl was saying, as I tried to pass her in the narrow hallway. "The whole thing is an idiotic coincidence, and the people who tell you otherwise are exploiting your storytelling nature." I was heading toward the bright bathroom with its unendurable smell of Comet or Bab-O or 20 Mule Team Borax. She was returning from a back room where she could make one of her famous phone calls.

"Beg pardon, Auntie?"

"It's not as simple as your uncle, or, I daresay, even your father thinks. The earthquake ruined the rock. The plan was to make the city into one perfect seaside village, like the Spanish Riviera. Losing a big rock helped," she said, but her eyes did not seem convinced, I'd swear.

Before I could ask why, she placed her index finger over my lips, an oddly intimate gesture for Miss Pearl Chase. My heart was beating with an annoying ardor. "There was no conspiracy. It was more like divine intervention or manifest destiny."

"My uncle thinks it was the arbitrary will of a bunch of desiccated wealthy men who in fact believed in manifest destiny."

"Ha," she said. "He's a romantic, even during delusions of persecution—especially then. Listen, dear, there is nothing here to learn. It's all a whirl of events. But that's not so true right now. Come in here with me." She put her hard hand on my forearm and dragged me into the just-visited room with the boy child's model monsters, where my brother, June, and I used to play.

"How long has it been since you've looked around here?" she asked.

"Déjà vu," I answered. "Feels like I just left."

Ignorant of sarcasm, she pushed open one of the newfangled sliding doors to the patio. The weather outside was still dull as a sermon. "This used to be a ranch," she said with mystic nostalgia. Jesus, I thought, everybody's nuts in my family. Then I remembered Auntie Pearl wasn't *in* my family. I wondered: Is it nostalgia if you yearn for a time before you were even born?

"And they grew tomatoes, and my father used to get shot at."

"No, Before that. This was once a ranch given by a royal decree from Spain to some gentleman gone to the colonies. This land belonged to the De la Guerra family, and then to a Yankee who married one of De La Guerra's daughters. Then it was someone else's family and then someone else's and then it was sold and then it was farms, like your father remembers, and then it was subdivided. 'No more can foot feel being shod,'" she whispered, trailing off. "The land is shod."

"Shit, shat, shod. Your father shod a lot of it."

"Where did you get this coarse streak? In college? I always suspected UCLA was breeding vulgarians. Berkeley will always be for free thinkers of poise and restraint." She was smiling. "My point is that the nobility of the land declines as the American grain of getting and spending runs over it. Overruns it."

"Now you're sounding like a Communist," said I, trying to imitate Uncle Dick's splenetic tone. "Besides, Spaniards overran some people too, if I remember my UCLA classes correctly."

"Did you know there was a Presidio in this town before they built the mission? No? Nobody does. Did you know the ironic thing? The mission was always meant to be a temporary structure, standing only until the Indians converted. But the Presidio was to stand forever, protecting the city of God. But it fell first. The political winds blew it over, the Mexicans and then the Americans came. Such is life."

"Is some sort of eternal ironic truth reflected here? The Mission as City of God?"

She narrowed her eyes. "They've found the Presidio."

I winced back in a good attempt at mockery. "What do you mean they found it? It was misplaced?"

"It was an informal excavation," she said, and I thought of that man who found Troy, what was his name? World beneath the world. "A formal one will take place, I hope the end of the year, but they're pretty sure this is it."

"Well, do tell. Where? Over by the Safeway? Behind the Haley Street skating rink?" Schliemann was his name.

"It's near where my offices are," she said. "The foundations of one wall and the chapel are intact, according to an archeologist. It could be rebuilt, like the mission was, another monument to our Spanish past. The big consensus deems this good for tourism too."

"Where, again?" I asked, suspicious. "Somewhere near a spot, oh, say, where the Chinese guy has his corner store? The one he worked since before Roosevelt? Oh, and probably the same place where the rest of the Chinese live. What would you call that part of town?"

"Blighted," she said, turning away from me. "Don't get all revan-chist on me. It's one step up from a slum."

"So you and your friends will knock down these tenements to find a ruin? You know, they have a history too."

"They?" she sniffed.

"The Chinese, an ancient culture. More interesting than a bunch of friars and conquistadors, in my book."

"Gin Chow hated living there. That's why he bought the farm on the Santa Ynez. Before he died," she said sadistically.

"I can't imagine him telling you that."

The air was getting thin in the room. Maybe because of that, I saw my brother's ghost, the way you see things without your eyes. He was proud of me at that moment and pointed to the closet door. I walked over toward it; right now I wanted to show the poem to her, the melancholy waters.

"Jacques Brown had stigmata, by the way," she said. "You know what that is, I assume."

I laughed. "The wounds of Christ, miraculously imprinted on the worthy. Hell, I thought it was fish livers or sharkskin suits that made him dead."

Then she turned to face me. "It's true. A miracle. You can ask his wife. She is going all over town telling people you are going to save her reputation, by the way." Miss Chase winced at some imagined pain I was having.

I looked at her. "How do you hear all this stuff?"

She said, "I'm on the telephone all day long. Wonderful invention. I rarely have to leave my little haven. But I want to tell you one more thing, the real reason we are hiding back here. The Navy Pier is going to revert to the city. They are asking the city to pay a nominal amount for it and the city has no reason to refuse, except the upkeep, which in a harbor is nominal. So who will use it? It's unlikely that the yachtsmen will tie up there, the other harbor pier has ice and is more accessible."

"Maybe vagrants can use it to watch the tides roll away," I suggested.

"Worse," she said. "It will make life ever so much easier for the fishermen to bring in their catch. Next step, they will want the town to build slips inside the breakwater. Dick wants it; he's putting pressure on his cahoots boys. He wants to make a fishing village of that ghastly overcast Mesa property he's building. I'll stop him. I don't want another Monterey. I want you to help me write an editorial about the harbor, Trevor. Stearns Wharf is fine for Mr. Larco's fish business. He can stay at that end of things."

"What do I know about the harbor? Making Uncle Dick's life difficult does seem fun, though." This is his house, where she played.

"Well, for starters, your Jacques Brown adventure. It seems like a foretaste of what will come when that rough set takes over." Roughnecks, I thought, saved my grunion-hunting life. "Imagine, stigmata. He died of natural causes, though he was afflicted with some sort of miraculous manifestation. There will be a story about it in Mr. Storke's paper, this religious phenomenon. Perhaps you should call your Los Angeles editor so the mighty Mr. Chandler does not look scooped. Is that what they call it?"

"You want me to report that Jacques Brown had stigmata?"

Instead of answering, she pointed to a phone at the end of the hall. "That's how it's already being reported. Death by accident. Call it divine intervention if you choose. I'm sure your uncle will not mind a toll charge."

"Does all of this fit together? Navy Pier, presidio, and the manifest destiny of the wounds of Christ?"

"You read too many detective books," she said. "Is it true you got a whole hour with Huxley? What was he like?"

"A prophet of social redemption through the use of certain Hindu chants drawn from Chinese texts and British poets."

"Everybody appreciated your way with words, even as a child," she said. "Are you really writing another novel?"

* * * *

Back in the dining room, the party had become loopy. Aunt Helen was leaning over the stereo console, which was playing Irish folk songs by the Clancy Brothers, and her hand was over the top of her white blouse around her chicken neck, and she warbled in a high, fluting voice something about her hopes to see some Holy Ground or another. My aunt laughing with yet another kind of false nostalgia for a country she visited once with the Lady's Sodality.

Uncle Frankie was snoring in the corner. Dick huddled at the end of the table near a new man on the scene, whose posture declared a still and stiff formality, though I could see his hands shaking on a sherry glass. Coming around on the parallax, I saw that it was a priest.

"Come and meet young Father Virgil," said Dick, snockered. "*He* wants no part of collective conspiracies."

"Who mentioned conspiracies?" I asked.

"Your father says that the policeman wants you to solve this mysterious Jacques Brown murder case." Dick winked wickedly at the priest. "Brown was a fourth degree, you know?"

"I didn't know murder came in four degrees," I said. "I can think of three."

"No, Knight," says Uncle.

"As in Knights of Columbus," said the priest. "By the way, they've done me the honor of asking me to be chaplain. I always thought you had to be Italian."

"Brown is part of the brotherhood," I said, mostly to myself. "They threw him out."

"The Brotherhood of Knights did not throw Jake Snake out," said Dick. "Brown was a brother in good standing, even after Santa Cruz Island."

My mother looked up from a magazine. "Sometimes, Richard, you can be such a pathetic excuse for a man." She left the room.

"I have a feeling I should tell you to apologize to my mother," I said, wondering if my brother had entered the family drama again obliquely. How can you spend a life inside a group of people related by blood and not understand them?

Dick was already telling a pathetic joke about a traveling salesman who always wanted to yodel: *I laid the old lady too*, he crowed. The priest blushed. Uncle Dick was drunker than I thought. I wouldn't have minded punching him. Though I had no idea what was making my mother so hostile.

In the dining room, my father was leaning against the wall at a precarious tilt while my mother sat before him like a supplicant. I decided I didn't want to know. He waved me away. There were no tears in her eyes, and I moved toward the kitchen. Somewhere inside me I felt this order, this generation, was near its end. I was already experiencing this party as a farewell to a golden past.

"Maybe you'll grow up to be different," said a soft voice behind me. It was mind reader Mary Annie. "But not if you date your cousin."

"She's not my cousin and we're not dating," I said, aware of my second betrayal. No cock crowed.

"Prove it," she said.

"I can't do anything tonight," I said "My parents."

"Oh, please," she said. "I'm drunk and tired and particularly tired of older people. I think you're older than me."

"So, you're tired of me?"

"Come over Wednesday at midnight, and I'll show you tired," she said, putting on her fuzzy cashmere. "And walk me to the door like you mean it. I've already said goodnight to everybody. Even to your girlfriend who's not your cousin."

She hooked her arm in mine as we passed through the vestibule, with its school of iron wire fish floating against the walls. She smiled at me. "It's nice to have a family," she said. "Isn't it? What did the policeman really want?"

"To tell me I wasn't a murder suspect anymore."

"How sweet," she said as we both put our hands on the knob at the same time. She squeezed mine. Opening the door she turned and led me onto the front porch. It was misting down rain now. "Don't bother to walk me any further," she said. The door closed behind us and she spun around. She kissed me with her tongue and bit my lip sharply. I've been excited by less, but I felt she could have had me inescapable just by crooking her little finger. "I think you'll remember me," she said, rocking up against me to feel the effect. "Hah. Just like the Arlington Theater when we were young."

I spread my arms wide and shrugged, as if to say I don't know or maybe I don't know, but I did. I remembered a submarine movie and a giant octopus. Mary Annie pulled some kind of folding plastic bonnet out of her raincoat pocket and put it on. "Go back in," she said. "Remember me. Wednesday."

I watched as she ran for her big blue Chrysler, and I could hear the cumbersome door open and close, and I imagined being inside, dry and hearing raindrops, and I could imagine them as she would see them, hitting and pooling and running in tiny tributaries along the glass. I imagined I could hear her turn on the wipers and say my name out loud softly and laugh.

Overheated, I re-entered the overheated room. My father looked bleary. The door blew opened and closed. I walked back through the short vestibule, past the wall fish still swimming away on imaginary tides. The music inside was a silly mambo, and the child was standing on his mother's feet and dancing with her and laughing like *he* was drunk. That seemed like a good idea; I headed into the kitchen to get another rum, but when I got there, Aunt Helen was holding court with Auntie Pearl and June, who apparently was no longer vanquished by her. In fact, most conspiratorially it seemed, they were holding hands.

"Then the man says, 'Do you want a screw for the hinge?' and the wife says, 'No, but I will for the teapot.'" Pearl howled, and I thought that must've been a good joke. June looked up at me and without a trace of irony said, "Thank you for getting her safe to her car. I was worried she would drink too much."

"She seemed fine," I said.

"Oh, I agree. And it was sweet of you to see her out. I'm not so sure she has a big crush on you anymore."

"My Trevor has finally made a conquest other than this old heart?" said Pearl.

"Well, I thought so," said June, winking at me. "We'll just have to see, though I think his heart is made of stone."

She could have seen me out the window at the front door. But there was no sarcasm in her voice. She seemed pleased that I was attentive to Mary Annie.

"I'm gathering my things to go," said June, letting go slowly of Pearl's hand. She looked at me. "I was hoping you would extend your kindness to this poor waif stranded so far from home."

"If I can get this giant boulder within me to roll, I believe the momentum could carry us both home."

"Or at least to the car," she chirped and, whirling away from Pearl, winked with a tender complicity that made my excitable pulse bound up again.

"At least," I said. "I'll go beg my leave from my parents, and our host. Oh, what about Frankie?"

"He'll sleep in the children's room," said Helen, "like he always does. He'll wake up cranky at three in the morning and demand to be driven home, like always. We'll get him a taxi, like always. He won't apologize, like always."

"You won't leave without setting a date with me to write this piece for the newspaper, boy," said Pearl. "You know how persistent I can be, and I'll call you day and night."

"The man who interviewed Aldous Huxley," said my real aunt. I looked at her to hear the rest of the sentence. She just smiled.

"Well then," I said. "Thank you and Uncle for the tripartite steaks and Happy New Year barbecue fun. Pearl, I shall attend your office day after tomorrow just before lunch to see if you would express your gratitude with food."

"I'll bring two brown bags," she said tartly.

Aunt Helen bestowed a dry kiss right on my lips. It occurred to me that Uncle Dick might have a frisky partner awaiting him this evening, if he wasn't about to pass out from vigorous jaw exercises, which he was engaged in with the young, hapless friar, who had wandered in clueless to this tidal wave of chat. A spontaneous thought crossed my brain. "Your wife requests your presence in the laundry room, Uncle Dick. I think she had tea many martoonies." Dick looked annoyed, but what could he say in the presence of an august young cleric.

"Don't know what you missed not marrying, Father," he said, and pushed off from his dining room Danish stick furniture.

"Father Virgin," I said, muffling the last note, thinking myself smug. "I wonder if you knew the Knight who was murdered, or died, or whatever."

"You mean Mr. Brown," said the priest, looking authoritatively bland, like they all learn to do in seminary.

"Precisely," I said. "You're very quick."

"Listen," he said. "Don't patronize me. I can't imagine you have that much worldly wisdom to lord over me, though I thank you for dispatching our windy host."

"There is only one Lord I am aware of, Father. The mighty dollar, and I'm willing to bet the take next Easter Sunday you know more about Jacques Brown than I do."

"I don't think I can take that bet, but even if I could I would likely lose. My conscience forbids idle gossip for profit."

"Is it some sort of privacy of the confessional?" I asked, feeling my stone heart suddenly beat.

"Yeah," he said sarcastically. "Like the Knights are so scrupulous about annual duties in the confessional. Nobody talks to priests about anything criminal that matters, no matter what the movies suggest."

"But what's the big criminal secret? I'll pour you some of the Chivas that Dick keeps for himself."

He smiled. "I think I would've liked you in college," he laughed. "But first I say, get thee behind me. I also want to say I'm skeptical of this stigmata rumor. But you're the newspaperman. Why not come to a K of C meeting, and ask around about Brown yourself. Is it really Chivas? I'd like some."

"I could come?"

"They do recruit new members. I am the chaplain."

"How do you like your Scotch?"

"Neat. Shall we say day after tomorrow afternoon, 4:00 p.m.? You know the place. Say 'swordfish' to get let in."

"Really?"

"Maybe I wouldn't have liked you in college."

I looked at him with renewed interest and flourished out the bottle from Dick's widely known secret shelf beneath the history of philosophy books by the Durants and a condensed version of the Oxford

English Dictionary, bespeaking intellects firmly committed to the Book of the Month Club.

As I put the bottle away, my glorious damsel June stepped into the living room wearing the thin shell-white sweater and carrying a long pink umbrella. I remember the sun coming up over the islands once when my brother and my father and I were deep sea fishing all night long, the phosphorus of the waves in the tips of clouds. I remember the first time I saw snow, I must have been seven or eight and woke at a friend's house uptown and the foothills behind San Roque parish were cloaked with a purity that suggested some idealization of morning light. And now herself. I walked over to June and took her soft hand and for some reason she held mine tight, not even bothering to pretend. I don't think anybody but Father Virgil was witness and he probably didn't register the import. We walked to the door and my ears rang as the blood rushed along the steep narrows of my veins.

I waved backwards jauntily to no one as the door closed. I did enjoy brief encounters with my family. My father, my mother, and the dearly departed among us.

I walked June to the car with wet grass squishing underfoot. I held the door open and held her forearm as she ascended to the big Packard's seat. I had a lap robe in the back and reached behind the seat and put it over her skirt. She was smiling. Home James, she said, and I was entirely happy in that moment of anticipation. Her home, the one with no roommates.

I rolled down the window and felt the rain blow in softly. When I turned to her she smiled. I thought about the past, present, and future, all blowing in the window at the same time. We drove over Carrillo Hill, saw orange groves and the big dairy, rural broken only by the gas stations, which used to be dumpy until Auntie Pearl pulled some strings. I wasn't going to think about my family anymore. June snapped on the perfect radio.

This is this moment, I thought. Her hand reached over to my arm and she slid up close to me as the radio warmed up and started to play the song about the jungle, the mighty jungle where the lion sleeps. I roared softly as she put her hand on my stomach. She giggled. I rolled up the window. The edge of town was hotels and liquor stores. I turned left up De La Vina. "I want you," she whispered in my ear.

The car found its way to her front door. I don't remember driving. "I'll go in," she said. "Pull your car all the way back and I'll let you in by the laundry room."

"Hush my darling, don't fear my darling."

She laughed again. "Don't be dull."

I let the brake go and swung around, the driveway dipped down to a standalone garage that, as I got out in the rain, smelled as if it once held a wood workshop; motor oil like incense and pine. Pearl needs me to write an editorial? I wanted to block out everything distracting me from this now alive joy I've told myself innumerable times I would die to get again. And I was thinking about Pearl? I parked the car. The long driveway had a grass strip growing between pavement rows, an old-fashioned carport. I heard a cock crow, maybe three houses away. This was a neighborhood living on the edge of yesterday.

I walked up the rickety wooden back steps and saw her standing behind the screen door. She was wearing a slip.

I opened the door and she moved into my arms. "I had to get out of those wet clothes. You better too."

"I'll catch my death."

She clucked. "Such morbid talk at a moment like this." I picked her up into my arms and she wrapped her legs around me, throwing me off balance against the washer-wringer. We kissed, and a sound like a sob welled up from her; I broke the kiss and looked at her, with tears in her eyes.

"There, there," I said. "What is it, darling baby?"

"I'm happy, you idiot." She swung her legs down on the floor and dragged me by a bunched up hank of my shirt. "You're stretchin' the material," I said.

She laughed, hah.

I followed her hunched over slightly and there was another laugh on her lips, but tears still flowing. Maybe she's crazy. But so is everyone else in my family. She's not in my family, I thought, admonishing myself.

"You want a drink?" she asked as she pulled me backward through the dim kitchen, night beginning to take the wintry skies.

"Only from thine eyes."

"Try my lips instead."

"And other parts?"

"And other parts."

The bright streetlight entered her room from a high window, passing through a scrim of leaves and rain, like a film of the outdoors projected all around us. I saw it from one eye as we rolled over on her deep, soft bed. She gasped and tore my hand away from her neck and bit my fingers. I wanted to be lost in all of this and managed pretty well considering my stupid, constant self-consciousness. Lust more like hunger ran out through my veins into my extremities, but still I caught myself looking up. City night provided us graceful light and my hunger deepened the more it was satisfied. My self-consciousness slipped away, but I couldn't lose myself. The hunger *was* myself.

Her clothes were almost gone, and she was so beautiful. Her hand clawed down my stomach, electricity arcing between us, and I arched my back and could see her round pale breasts.

The wind started up and it held her moaning in its mouth. She was whispering something that I pretended to understand, but I could not bring myself to hear. I tried hard to pace myself to her, and I did begin to disappear: my arms, my legs, my torso, unspooling themselves away from worldly care, gone. My hand was cupped over the top of her head and I tried very hard not to lose her, to keep her, and I smelled her hair, slightly sour, and she told me I was so strong, so strong, and then it was impossible to stop, and then unnecessary, and then over in a lovely heap. I lay there breathing. She looked at me with surprise, but it seemed as if she was surprised at herself too. She shifted after a long while and kissed me. After another long time, she said, "Now you want a drink?"

"Mmm," I said. "What's with you and the dipsomania?"

"Writer," she said, and pulled the sheet off the bed and trailed it into the kitchen, moaning like a ghost.

When she returned there were two tumblers filled with some red stuff that smelled sweet. She tipped hers toward me in a toast and gathered the sheet around her like a Hindu. Her lips had gone thin.

"Don't worry about it," I said.

"It's just that I want to go. And I already told him I would go. And something else, though I don't expect you to believe me."

"I never said you shouldn't."

"So I'm going to go and I'm going to have fun and he will sleep in his own room and I will be waiting the whole time to see you when I get back. And another thing."

"What, for God's sake?

"People," she said. "People will believe I'm not with you. We'll be safer."

"Goddamn it."

"I want you now, I know it," she said. "I wasn't sure, even last week. I'm glad if you're jealous, though, very glad."

"Oh, and what changed your mind about me?"

"A change in the weather, a change in me. I like the way you told the story about Castle Rock."

"That was this evening."

"Yes."

"What have I done for you lately? You're worried about your family."

"You mean our family, don't you?" She looked at me funny. I could feel something drifting in her.

"Do you want to run away?" I said. "With me? Get out on our own? You won't have to pretend for anyone then. Far away, maybe go to San Francisco. I'm starting to like jazz and poetry. Be beatniks. I mean, are you?"

Her eyes were round. "Am I what?"

"Hip to the connotations of oop-oop-a-do?"

She laughed and came back to me. "I'll make a few noises in your ear."

The next time we went much slower. It was beyond anything I wished for, better even than those three days we lost together in my apartment. Somewhere in there I was concentrating so hard that lights went off behind my eyes. But even so, Huxley talking about love kept crossing my mind. He could be wrong. Love might be just another word, you know, and, therefore a carrier. In my experience it hurts as often as it pleases, and it makes people crazy. As I thought about it while touching her smooth breasts, a wave of love rushed over me, maybe from the vaulted cosmos. Maybe from below, the world beneath the world. Who can say until the wave breaks? What it means to be and to not be at the same time. I stopped and breathed in: the room, her smell.

"I don't know what's wrong with you, but please get back to what you were doing," she said, her hand lying over her mouth and her hair fanned out around her in the tangled sheets. I laughed and began again, and the moment set off a chain reaction.

She fell asleep, balled up and turned away from me, not long later. Everything inside the mind is not love. Huxley was wrong. The rain stopped and there was a sweet silence. Over the window was a small art photograph postcard, a Victorian thing. The kind girls like: a picture of a fairy staring down, her naked peach skin showing through some diaphanous gown, obviously in love with her own image on rippled waters. After sex a man is not always sad. But I took the glass of sweet booze into the next room, which was dark. I brought a blanket off the couch and wrapped myself in it and once again returned to my Noctambulist night.

No matter how hard I tried, the revelations were decaying; only memories now. Home after Huxley, I closed the door behind me and leaned against it after setting the lock. One of the Normal Guys gave me a ride and the phantasms and patterns rushed at me on the road. He asked me if I liked being famous and I said what I always did, that fame was only real when you encountered it, when somebody said you were famous. It didn't stick any longer than an expansive mood. The world was wobbling between madness and joy and I wondered where would the crooked wheel stop, and if it was a wheel at all. Was I wise enough to stay in penetrating bliss or would I fall into my sad mind? The one that plagued me after my novel wasn't enough. The car wheels stopped.

When I entered my apartment I feared that I would see my own ghost there. Alone, I turned on the television—the big box standing upright next to the radio that got me in this mess in the first place—to keep my ghost and me company. I thought it would be fun to watch while high, images wreathed in patterns. But television just stayed black-and-white. I kept flipping channels, sitting below it like an acolyte. Jack Paar was on and then I turned it to CBS and some guy was yelling at his audience. There were a lot of crazy commercials. "Wake Up to Tang." And then Shari Lewis and Lambchop on a rerun Steve Allen, and then back to ABC and there was Huxley talking to some melodramatic guy named Wallace. That was a rerun too. Lost in time and space.

I beheld him enclosed in that television. My big armchair beckoned me. I turned out all the lights except for the television, which hummed softly and filled the room with Aldous, who is and not is in the room with me even after the interview. And then the screen showed an Indian chief in a bull's-eye.

In June's house, where I really was, in the quiet dark, I decided it was happening again, no matter what I did to try to stop it. I felt sad for everything that wouldn't be possible to prevent after the process began. She was going; she would come back, but maybe not to this same me. I thought about the book and how everybody seemed to assume there was another book and that it would sustain me. Is and not is.

Chapter 30

L ET'S PAUSE TO SEE where we have got. Old man and young man, connected back through young man's paternity—alluding to the previous
work, but not bound by it, okay. We can pick up the discussion of
the underwater races, evolution, devolution, and that the two men are
inside the underwater craft and have seen monsters, barracuda, yellowtail, rays, and merpeople … Maybe it's too soon for the end of the
end to come up. Meanwhile they continue moving back and down:

*"Yes," the old man said. "Yes. Yes." He looked out the window, ab-
sorbed by the view below. "In fact, it's all related to the nature of
time, healing all wounds and vice versa. The sorrow of nature and
vice versa. Everything changes in every direction. Being in time—rain
running off the eaves, splashing on the shells of snails. People think
of time as an arrow flying forward into the future, leaving yesterday
behind its stiffened feathers. Others suggest a fall backward, time after
time: a little sparrow, the House of Usher, Roman Empire. Only our
mandates for survival force us to believe we are progressing in and
then out of time, toward a peaceful death, Pearly Gates and Elysian
Fields. Actually, we are falling away from the sun and from the phases
of the moon and from the Golden Ages—time is not a cascade over a
ridge. It is the ridge."*

"That's what you believe?" asked the young man.

He laughed. "I don't believe in much. We are arching and rushing and falling. The mermen and merwomen live in an element called ocean; we live in a moment. Neither oceans nor moments have centers."

"What about the Elayawun? In what element do they live?"

"Behold."

The young man crooked his stiff neck toward a point in the murk at which the ancient man kept pointing. The young man peered into the murk and down to the silted bottom. And then he saw it, the domed palace, the city beneath the waves.

Chapter 31

ONCE LONG AGO IN the Lobero Theatre, Miss Pearl Chase and I attended a talk about the spiritual nature of time. It was one of a series that explored comparative religions, with a heavy emphasis on the next world moving into this one, this interim state. It was mostly boring. Turns out the Lobero has a fascinating ceiling, a kind of beehive arrangement with gold-leaf fleurs-de-lys. It became so tedious, the talk, I got tired of looking at that design. I wanted to get lost in it, but I was there without escape from the droning man. And then he said that some philosophers believe there is no such thing as time.

That perked me up a bit. Think of it, there is no past (gone) or future (unreachable), only that which this speaker said this Protestant philosopher-preacher Tillich called the eternal now.

For days after the Noctambulist, a torment in the skies seemed to pass down to us mortals below. Somewhere in there New Year's must have happened, unobserved by me; you would think I would have heard cars honking, pans clanking, and guns going off, but I'm a little unclear about it. Nothing woke me from my slumbers. Black rags of clouds covered downtown where I walked, splitting open like a veil sometimes to blue, but cold blue. The planet moved into winter. People were muttering when you passed, low in their throats like tormented victims. Occasionally the real world feels like literary foreshadowing.

You want to know, of course, what happened to her. You know, June?

She wouldn't let me out of the house, asking what the neighbors might think if they saw me leaving. I didn't care, because I wanted every second possible. Then there was too much silence late in the afternoon. I said I gotta go. I walked out to my car after a lingering kiss. She followed out the door, apparently unafraid of neighbors now.

It's not the first time in the world that cousins have fallen in love.

"Technically we're not," I said.

She looked at me funny.

The car almost didn't start, and then it did. "Why don't you buy a new car, Trevie?" she asked. "Sometimes you act like you never had a penny."

"Aloha."

"Don't be mean."

"I'm using a salutation that simultaneously infers departure and greeting."

"I'm already back in your arms." Her eyes were rimming with tears again. For all this happiness, she sure cried and from some deep reservoir.

Monday night I brooded. Tuesday I went out to meet Pearl. My car wouldn't start. I walked. Time does not exist.

On my way over to Pearl's office, I saw Storke pull out of his driveway. To my surprise he stopped and rolled down the window, Mr. Santa Barbara.

"You the Westin kid?" he asked, the distinct odor of Old Spice rolling out of his big black car. "Knew your father, it's a shame."

"He's not dead, is he?" I asked. "That would really upset my mother."

He looked me up and down. "I liked your piece on Huxley. Thought provoking, I believe, is the expression."

I forgot. Today it came out. "Thanks," I said. "A considerable compliment considering … "

He interrupted. "Why aren't you writing for me?"

"I thought that my father might be a factor," I said, taken aback. "Didn't you two have a fight?"

"Your father." Now he looked puzzled. "You know, son, you need to learn that other people's histories don't necessarily impinge on yours. That sounded clever, didn't it? Many histories in fact may overlap without consequence."

"Who's talking about history? We were talking about writing."

"One historical fact seems constant. Neither you nor your father seems very respectful. I like that. Come and see me tomorrow, just before lunch."

"I don't see how anything could come of it," I said.

"Hmm. I'll see you quarter to noon." He drove off and I walked the half mile to Auntie Pearl's.

I showed up at her office thinking about time and here I was, right on time and in time, striding up the cement steps to Pearl's place. I thought about that Lobero speech again; it was an okay idea, except for one thing: the people we miss aren't here with us now. So, while we enjoy life without time, they live only in time.

First thing Pearl asked me was to go to this show at the Lobero: *Slings and Arrows*, a satirical review they put on each New Year.

"Apparently I am lampooned in it," she said. "This show."

"The sincerest form of flattery," I said.

Next thing was weird, though. She asked if I remembered the speaker at the Lobero, who said that time did not exist.

"Funny you should mention it," I said. These coincidences were starting to make me nervous. Some were immediately overlapping, like Huxley on TV, which I was pretty sure happened. Like this too. "Why?"

"It reminds me of the presidio. It's now outside of time waiting to be readmitted." Then she said, "By the way, congratulations." She pointed at the *Los Angeles Times* on her coffee table near the stand-up ashtray.

I winced. "I haven't seen it yet. Is it good?"

"Child," she said, and pointed over to the coffee table again. I picked it up, and the moment I began to read, my stomach dropped. "Oh, God."

"What's wrong?"

"Everything. They changed my lead. They took out everything good: the drug experiments and all the mysticism."

"Trevor, what drug experiments? Is this man a scientist like his father or brother or whatever? They're sort of Scopes Trial-types, right? Monkey people? Darwinians? I thought he was a writer. Is he a drunk like that horrid Dylan Thomas who was here?"

"Huxley doesn't drink," I said. I felt betrayed, exposed, naked under the byline.

"Oh, so all he does is inject himself with experiments?" she said sarcastically.

"It's not an injection," I looked at her; she was a little goggle-eyed.

"You," she said slowly, "witnessed this man take drugs. Oh, Trevor."

"Nonsense, Auntie." Though I felt like taking something now. "This is hogwash, they ruined it. I sound like a television host." I was thinking about the Wallace guy, so full of false importance.

"Nonsense yourself. I thought it was masterfully written."

"So did Storke."

"What do you mean? When did you talk to the baboon, I mean, Mr. Santa Barbara?"

"Wait, Pearlie. You're the one said he was covering what matters admirably. I saw him in front of his house today, right near yours. He wants me to work for him."

"Oh, no, Trevor," she said, shaking her head from side to side but somehow turning the gesture into one of consideration. "I doubt I used that adverb. Although I won't deny there's a certain perverse symmetry to it. He chases your father away then hires you. Lovely."

"I never got how he chased dear Dad from the land he loved."

"I'm going to tell you something about your father, and I don't want you to get angry. You know I am very fond of him; that is to say, I always thought what happened was undeserved and cruel … "

Pearl didn't finish because the phone rang. She plucked it up and began to cluck and purr to it in animal voices. Then she turned crisp and assertive. Then her voice plunged to a submissive tone I never had heard before. Maybe she was talking to Mayor Abbott or some minor deity, like Thetis. She had taken the long-corded phone and moved into her absent assistant's chamber, and I was left without companionship. I looked at the article again. I wondered what Huxley or the Normal Guys would think. At the very least, this sold out the spirit of the evening.

I was sitting near her desk, and saw some papers. They were the minutes of a meeting, from some Historical Trust Company or Society of Historical Personification. I thought, if there's no such thing as time, you couldn't really trust history. So Dick was right about the communists, who were wrong. I was still sore about my piece, and I fingered the minutes and under them found some file about Pacific Ocean Park. Under it was something about the presidio unearthing Pearl had mentioned the other night.

While still vociferously engaged, Miss Pearl Chase came into the room, strode up behind my back, snatched the stapled sheath, and slapped my hands. I suppose it *was* rude, me prying into her papers and such. Underneath the Pacific Ocean Park file, on an index card, was the name J. Brown, typewritten out with the word "approval" below it.

Pearl hovered and I got up from my chair. She went clopping around the room in her sensible shoes, agreeing with the caller repeatedly. She turned her back and I was about to reach down for the index card, when there was a knock at the heavy wooden door. Pearl walked over, opened it, and handed the presidio papers out. Then she went back into the other chamber. I picked up the card with "J. Brown approval" on it. I went into her little bathroom, closed and hook-eyed the door, stared at the card searching for invisible ink, I guess, and then looked at my face in the oval mirror above the sink—very 1930s, called Art Deco now. "That's right," Pearl said. I almost jumped because I thought she was in the toilet with me. Turns out I could hear her clearly through a heat duct overhead.

"Brown was supposed to make the report but of course he won't be finishing it. Yes, at Santa Cruz Island, the New Year's gathering."

I listened, and she went back to happy animal sounds. "Yes, and Two Guns will be there." She chuckled, low and mean. "He claims the book makes sense of everything—the past will clarify our mission. I know. I know. But a lot more of them will go missing if we don't do something now. Right out of the harbor they want to run their boats, but I won't have it. I'll blow up the harbor. Two Guns will give them the idea of the city, and they'll take it from there. They'll believe the story from him, not me. Our singing cowboy."

The conversation was like an obscure index to my growing manias.

"The *Haida*," she said, again with the wicked laugh, as if adding a new topic. "I can't talk about that right now. Charlie, I said I can't talk. Go to Mexico if you must. The minutes ought to make you happy. Yes, on their way."

I flushed the toilet, washed my hands nosily, walked out humming, and plopped down in my chair with Brown in my pocket. Pearlie was hunched over, her back to me. There was a silence as she listened to the tiny scratchy voice coming from the black telephone. She said, "Uh" and then "Uh-uh," as in, no. "That's final. Let's meet on the island, in the chapel. Good-bye. I mean it."

I pretended to be engrossed in a report I'd picked up on ocean tides.

"You were saying," she said, hanging up the phone.

"Who was that?" I asked. "At the door."

"A messenger from the future." She smiled.

I stared and she went stony-faced.

"What about my father?" I said.

It took her a second to recall the context, and then she turned her back on me.

"He has no money."

"Auntie Pearl. Let's don't go through this again, it's just frustrating. I can't talk to him about anything that has to do with my money. I'll give him every penny."

"Oh child, you can't give it to him. That would surely kill him. Can you blame him? Neither a borrower nor a lender be; that means something to people from his background. To lose one son and be indebted to another? He's afraid of losing you too."

"He can have the money, I don't use it. Who better deserves a comfortable retirement? After all he's done."

"I can't even imagine retirement," she said.

The time seemed suddenly right to learn something. "It just occurs to me. I have no idea what he's done."

"Well," said Pearlie, looking around for something, which I assumed was the index card. "From the war, I could not tell you. All of those men are close-lipped, to say the least. I think he had some classified role. Here, well, he saved the Fiesta, for one, brought it back after the war and the drought years ended. He made the harbor what it is today and he helped the mayor annex a plot of land ten miles away and make it an airport. He lost one son and saw the other become insanely famous."

And vice versa. "I thought you did all those other things," I said.

"Live and learn, child. I don't actually do anything. I just talk sense into others."

"Then why did he quit the Navy?"

She looked around, and I pulled the card out of my pocket and dropped it on the floor by my feet. "He didn't quit," she said. "The Navy sent him a letter retiring him. The reserve didn't need mid-level officers, even during a Cold War. He still has some official duties, like consulting or something. But his pension is doubtful and he sold the Santa Barbara house, not that real estate in Santa Barbara makes money for anybody. You know, he used to have money before the Depression. By rights, you should be rich."

"I am," I reminded her and then made an elaborate show of reaching down and pulling up the card, handing it. "You lose this?"

She held it in her blue-veined hands, wadded it up, and threw it into the green metal trash can.

I decided to stop being coy. "He wants me to look into this Brown thing," I said, shooting the moon. "He thinks I might draw the lines of coincidence around me into some pattern of meaning. In a timely fashion."

"Tush. I tell you Brown was an accident, and even if it wasn't, he had a lot of people angry for a lot of reasons. Where does your father say you need to look?" The last sentence sounded innocent.

"He has a friend, I made him mad. He wants me to make up and enlist him. Meanwhile, just keep looking."

"That Greek man. He's a sailor, and aren't they all? Tell me, is your father your, how to put this, your inheritor?" It was another innocent-sounding question.

"Of course."

"Maybe you *should* be careful, Trevor."

I was getting angry and I could feel an old irritation. My heart shriveled listening to her.

"Nobody is interested in Mr. Brown except you," she said. "And your father, I guess, for whatever reason. I saw you two come out of the kitchen together at Helen and Dick's; I saw a distinct conspiratorial glow."

"You're mistaken, Auntie. He just asked me to make friends and watch out for my sweet cousin."

She sniffed. "There's an undeniable fading nobility in this family. That girl … "

"My father needs money," I said. I didn't want her to profane June's name. "After all he's done for people."

"Oh, Trevor," she said. "A lot of old money got lost during the crash. And even though this town rolls in it, there isn't much to be made, even now. The Russians had a five-year plan. Maybe we need one—maybe this Kennedy family will bring back the Progressive spirit. When waves of disillusionment hit, some people just wash away."

"That's my father you are talking about."

"So ironic, you left and he just got tired of fighting. Maybe I'll get tired of fighting someday."

"I never fought anybody my whole life."

"What about those horrible men who jumped you? You know Dick has an office up there on the construction site. It's a wonder he didn't come to your rescue, considering your great friendship with his daughter, your cousin."

"She's adopted," I said. "We're not really cousins."

"Ridiculous," she said.

"I remember the party we had like it was last year. 'June is your cousin,' they said. 'Come from the orphanage.'"

"Party," she said. "Maybe that was before my time." She looked distracted, but she also looked like some revelation had occurred.

I felt I had said something wrong; I always did around her. The guilt reminded me of my date at the Knights of Columbus Hall, their big Victorian on Castillo Street. I told her I had to be going.

"Meet me in front of the Lobero at 8:00 p.m." She was already exiting our conversation.

"What about this harbor editorial?" I picked up and skimmed what she had written. It was wooden.

"Oh, that just became moot on the phone. I love telephones, waves on a wire. You know, dear Trevor, sometimes the power of the press is overrated."

I walked out, puzzled, into crisp air. I passed the *News-Press* on Cota Street; inside the open door men in blue overalls with newspaper caps on their heads worked the presses; ink flew everywhere in a fog, stories and voices rolled out like a giant wave. Word viruses cover the earth. That one ghost who clanked around the corner from La Paloma Café was out in the street sitting in a ghost chair, and the big Chevrolets and Fords just rode right through her.

I had three long blocks to walk up State Street and then left on Carrillo toward the west side, past the firehouse with its practice tower, past Radio Square where the big bands used to play, and then left down Castillo. In the middle of the block stood the big sunshine-yellow Victorian that housed the Knights of Columbus. The priest was on the cement path ahead of me with his medieval black robe and funny little Italian hat. Dress up every day in long skirts like queens and pansies. Amen. Little lambs of God eat ivy. A kiddley divey too. Wouldn't you?

"Hurry now, Brother Westin."

"Sure, Father Virgin."

"Don't think I can't hear you. That is considered virtue in my vocation, after all."

"Do marriage problems seem easier to solve? Or do you feel a little less experience might make you better equipped and wiser?"

"I am equipped and didn't exactly become a priest at the age of seven."

"Tell me your war story," I said, feeling vicious.

"It was at the most thrilling front a man has ever encountered. Magdalena Petersen."

"And you were blessed to breach said front?"

"Mmm-hmm. You know, I think it's a sin to happily remember sinning. I think, though it's a matter of theology I'd have to consult my confessor about. Shall we?"

Against my will, I liked this guy.

The door burst open at the top of the varnished wooden stairs, a loud bifurcation of opinion burst out too. A pair of Knights errant stood above us. Smoke came out of their lips in hissing dragon streams, smells of Kool and Chesterfield incensed the air.

"Bastard can take his own boat out, I'm not risking mine again," said the older, whiter, scrub-faced man to the swarthy customer twirling lanyarded keys.

"Hah, what the fug," said the latter man, and made himself small seeing Father Virgil come up the stairs. The other man was mortified. "Oh, Father, forgive us. Such language, Cappie, we ought to be ashamed."

"For your penance deliver unto me more abalone, Red," said the good father. He looked at me. "This is the man who reported on

Jacques Brown's death for the Los Angeles paper."

The men exchanged looks that went blank.

"What's the nature of this heated dispute?" said the priest.

"Why not ask Father to settle the argument?" said Red.

"We need to know if waste is a sin," said Cappie.

Father Virgil looked at both of them. I assumed they meant Onan.

"Depends. What's being wasted?"

"Nature. Sea life. Fish."

"Is this some sort of Larco problem?" asked Virgil, who seemed all of a sudden cool as a cuke again.

"No, it's the oil guys and their shockwaves."

"Father, what he means is, these explosions the oil company's using in the channel."

Father was curious now. Me too. "What are you talking about?"

"Thousands and thousands of dead fish. Every time they set off one of these charges, the whole fishery comes belly-up. Me and Red almost got our engine fouled going through a sea of turbot, sea bass, and what looked to me like red snapper."

"Of course it was snapper, that's all they got out there," said Red, who spat a dry spit.

"I still don't understand," said the padre.

"I think I do," I said. "There's oil out there. All of Summerland Beach used to be derricks. Now, we got platform Hazel out in the water itself. People are bringing oil up from way offshore."

"Fishing's pretty good at Hazel," said Cappie. "That derrick's like a reef, though those got-damn roughnecks are always throwing stuff at us, making waves from their castle above. Got-damn. Oh, pardon."

"Oil company men set off depth charges?" I asked.

"Or something. Then they can read where the oil is with their radar or sonar. And it kills so many fish and they rot on the surface. Hell, I'm afraid of them bombs when they go off."

"Sit down, you're rockin' the boat," said Red.

"Somebody said that's what happened to Snake Jake," said Cappie, scratching his privates with elaborate abandon. It seemed a bit convenient, this.

"Reporter," said Red, "maybe you could write about the fish. I mean, it has to be some kind of scandal, doesn't it?"

"I don't know," I said. "Guess they're killing a lot of fish that you wouldn't be able to catch legally?" I was still after Snake Jake. "Maybe it's a story. Tell me though, you hear anything unofficial about Brown?"

"It's just a waste," said Cappie, ignoring me. "A got-damned waste."

"They're having a meeting inside tonight, you know, Father."

"That's why we're here, Red. By the way, this young man's name is Mr. Trevor Westin."

I smiled and stuck out a hand, which was enfolded by flesh that felt like a lobster claw. "Knew your father," said Red. "He wasn't no Knight."

"No, but he went to Duke, I think," I said.

Nobody laughed. "You even a Catholic?" asked Cappie.

Father Virgil, at this point, said, look at what time it's getting and shoved me through the dusty screen door. Outside it smelled like it might rain. Inside the smell of Pledge and old wet cigarettes took over. We walked by one of those tin urns of coffee that smelled like the intersection of mud and rubber. There were photographs on the wall, though one of them was a negative inside a frame, inexplicably reversed. I thought about ghosts. This building was what, seventy years old? Ancient in these lands and old enough to have gathered to it gusts of spirit, complete social sets, and parties that would ring like echoes up and up in the room. I had a vision of men in heavy woolen clothes, their sleeves rolled up, and that thick alcohol haze that surrounds dumb violence and spontaneous wit. A long way away I could hear shouting accompanied by laughter, a television set turned up to an unbearable volume with Ralph Kramden and Norton on the airwaves, and canned laughter filling the room.

Father Virgil kept walking across the broad, empty room, which had a large table covered with a sheet, a deceased pool table. "This is the banquet room," he said over his shoulder, "though I don't suppose a decent meal has been served here since alcohol was re-legalized. Let's get a drink and let the Brother Knights buy."

"You mean the brotherhood," I said.

"Nobody calls them that," he laughed. "Makes it sound like organized crime, rather than a wife-avoidance association."

A sweep across a threadbare red rug led us through a swinging door and into a long, narrow room. Dim, lit by a small window, though the Knights inside had not turned on lights yet. Shapes arranged themselves in clutches of two or three, seated at card tables or standing near the other bar at the far end. Like a figure from a David or Ingres, a man in a nineteenth-century admiral's hat, with a cape and a long sword, stood in the corner. I wanted to snicker, but a thin apparition had appeared before me.

"Uncle Dick," I said.

"Nephew. What are you doing here?" He seemed to be blinking away the half-light.

"I'm here with Father Virgil to find out if I can find out something. Or maybe I'll join, if they'll have me."

"You're not even a Catholic," he said, breathing hard through his nose.

"Wrong. I attended your alma mater, Catholic High School, baptized at the mission."

"You seen my daughter since the family dinner?" he asked point-blank.

I stared him down. "I asked if she wanted a ride to the airport, but she had a friend, I guess." I looked to him, hoping for some information. He seemed more peeved than usual.

"Airport?"

"She's flying to Hawaii."

He nodded. Virgil winked over my uncle's shoulder and drifted to the table where missals were stacked. "You really want me to bless them?" I heard him say. A thin man with a suit draped about his body leaned toward him and whispered, while giving me the hairy eyeball.

"I'm looking for friends of Jacques Brown," I said to my uncle, but loud enough that the rest of the cadavers could hear.

"I'm his best friend," said an effeminate-looking man sitting at the bar. The others looked at him reprovingly. "I'm his best friend even now that he's dead."

"I want to know if he had stigmata," I said.

The bartender burst into laughter. "I bet Miss Pearl Chase told you that," he said. "And I bet she heard it from Dead-Eye Dick here."

My uncle looked cool, the way somebody inside a joke smirks. "I can't help it, the woman is so goddamned gullible. I once told her that Victorian furniture had skirts so men wouldn't gawk at the legs. She put it in a fugging newsletter."

I looked at my uncle. "What's new at work?" I asked.

"Aw, nothin' much. Supervise a crew of workers, buncha wetbacks up in the Marine Terrace, they call it, three blocks from home. Me and my boys. *Mis amigos.*"

"Those guys are hard workers, and you're always calling 'em beaner and taco bender and such," said the bartender. Everybody stared at him. "The proper term is greaser." A merry chorus of chuckles followed.

"They don't mind," Dick said. "They'll do anything for me. I could probably start my own gang. But speaking of that, it was this man's idea to have Snake Jake killed." He pointed at an elegant shape coming through the swinging door.

"Jacques Brown died for our sins," said the bartender, tilting a highball glass into his mouth and plunking it down on the bare bar.

"Always pointing. Didn't your mother tell you it was impolite?" asked the smooth man whose face I could now make out. I guess I should have known that the Knights of Columbus would have a few Guinea bastards. It was his father, my girlfriend's boyfriend's alleged underworld father, Vince Campagnolo.

"Do you know him?" Uncle Dick asked me. "Let me introduce you to the man who murdered Jacques Brown."

"Jesus, Dick," said the limp-wristed bar fixture.

"I would've murdered him, if I could've got my hands around his thick red neck," said Campagnolo. "Pleasure to meet you," he said, swiveling around on greased ball bearings. "I believe everybody here calls me the Italian Liquor Distribution Businessman behind my back. You may too. But my real name is Vincenzo."

"Pleasure to meet you," I said. "I feel I know you already. Your son and I went to Dolores and Catholic High together."

"He went sometimes. But you still have the advantage of me, I'm sorry to say."

"Excuse my manners," I said. "Trevor Westin. Bet you know my dad."

"Who doesn't?" he said, eyes narrowing, and then the whole face snapped into a rictus of polite geniality. "He was a man who knew the Coast Guard's timetables, at what time they attempted to prevent contraband from coming onto this shore. There aren't enough smart tough guys like him anymore."

"My father, a tough guy?"

"Yeah, he stood up for the plight of the freelance entrepreneur—me. He reinvented Fiesta, and I sold a lot of beer." He was fumbling with a pack of Winstons. From the corner, a shadow moved forward and snapped a lighter into his face. Campagnolo looked annoyed. "Now please remind me how I murdered the late Jacques Brown." He pronounced the surname as if it was a distasteful joke.

"You drummed him out of the brotherhood," said Dick.

I reached for the drink the good padre had fetched for me. It was so sweet I almost spit.

"Mediterranean Stinger," said Father Virgil. "Hi, Vincenzo."

"Father. What do you know about me banishing Brown from a brotherhood?"

"Didn't you get him fired from the state licensing people? That diver thing?"

"Oh yes, I did that. Mr. Westin, I did have Snake Jake decertified as a diver, after he got caught stealing lobsters from my good friend Larco's traps. In fact, I had him beaten up too."

I looked at him, and my throat got thick. "You can do that?"

"Oh yeah," he said. "My boy Salvatore. You know him?"

"Huh, yeah. He beat my brother up once over a girl, when he was six."

"That's my boy," he said. "The other one has the brains."

"But what's this brotherhood?"

"It's a thing, the divers have a thing. You can't go out in the ocean without being certified as of this year. Ironic thing too. Brown learned to dive during the war, probably forgot more than these pencil-necks who do the certifying know."

"Sounds like you liked him," I said.

"I didn't, Mr. Westin. I hated him. But the police know I didn't do it and that's all that matters. Jacques Brown was famous for snooping and blabbing. He only wanted what was in front of him, like a child. The police have decided it was a natural death." He chuckled drily. "Lots of people would have preferred it unnatural."

"What about you?" I said.

"I don't know anything, except my friend Sallie Boniface, who works in the morgue, said Snake Jake was in water a long time before his body turns up at the end of the tourist's jetty. And then there's the wounds of our savior. Which were not a miracle."

"You didn't kill him, then, despite my Uncle Dick's claims."

"Not that I didn't want to. Chief Zanesco tried to make me say I did, but he had to reach me on vacation in San Francisco that very day."

"And you don't know who did?"

"There was a long line and a waiting room. He was making somebody mad five days a week, and on the weekend he bothered his wife, I hear. By the way, she says you did it."

I looked up.

"Just pulling your leg. Looks like it don't stretch too far. I figured out who you were."

"She tried to call me, she wanted a meeting."

"Listen," he said. "You ought to talk to his wife. She can be very amusing. You should ask the fishermen what they think about him and the oil business in the channel. And last, but very much not least, you should know that Jacques Brown had a passion for history—Miss Chase and him."

"And Two Guns," I said.

He laughed. "Yeah, bang-bang, Two Guns. You know they're having a coffee klatch this week out on the island, sort of a tribute to this guy who owned the *Haida*—Fleischmann. He a Jew? I'm going. Your parents too. I'll say hello to my son for you, if you like.

"You'll say hello to your son in Hawaii?"

"Why would you say that?"

"Because that's where he is. Or going."

"No he isn't," he said, looking at me oddly. "But, he is on Santa Cruz Island this week, with this new girl he's going with. I'll see him Sunday and say hello." He laughed. "Not aloha."

My blood was running cold; I barely remember walking out. I looked at Uncle Dick, who avoided my eyes. I saluted the priest, who looked through me. I was gone and she wasn't. I needed to call June; I was afraid to find a phone. If time did not exist, then neither did her short stay in Hawaii.

Chapter 32

On first glance the dark outline suggested towering outcrops of rock at the end of sea bluffs. It was hulking, tremendous, though irregular in form, like the facets and spikes of a crystal growing deep in and from the earth. Windows spread between dark honeycomb girders, an aesthetic gestalt of berserker geometries. Grids stood against ocean pressures. Light radiated out, turning the water from inky black to green. Between the craft and the fat glass sheltering the city beneath the sea swam swarms of living things—sharks, barracuda, yellowtail, and trident-bearing merpeople.

The young man asked how they would enter the dome surrounded by such deep waters. The vehicle answered, rotating with an abrupt swing. As they began to drop toward the base of the crystal structure, a wide stream of bubbles erupted, distorting and obscuring their view into silvery curves, globular cubisms. The merpeople had vanished. From behind the craft came a clanging rasp of metal on metal and a rush of hydraulic release, accompanied by a deep musty smell, like snow clothes hanging from a cabin hook. There was a clack, a locking of metal together, and a gentle thud.

The vehicle was on the ocean floor now, its stern attached to the castle. Above, far away, waved majestic strands of kelp, all one height. Above that, the empty sea whispered. Above that, the young man imagined, the blue sky, crossed by seabirds crowing with metallic shrieks.

He tried to relax against the harness, but his heart was pounding. A locking sensation rocked the vehicle further backward, and there was an abrupt change in air pressure as a door popped open behind them. Because the hammock seats swung with the center of gravity, they were sitting up straight as the vehicle maintained its hard backward angle. The young man realized how ingeniously the craft had been engineered: what appeared to be a fanciful sawtooth design on the wall now became stairs that let the two men out into a damp chamber, lit by gilded shells spaced along the wall.

They heard a metallic shriek, a whistle, a noisy scrape, and hastened their steps. In shadows at the other end of the tunnel stood a towering man with a pointed beard and a patriarchal bearing. He was dressed in light-blue raiment, a vest over jacket over skirt, and wore a black headband that matched the color of his severe beard.

The old man put his two dry-leaf hands on the young man's back. He made an audible greeting as they approached the bearded man, who acknowledged them with a nod and a bow. The three men went into another chamber, more magnificent than the last and lit from below as if the floor were a soft sun. Above them curved an enormous domed tower made of crystals clear and green. Outside, the sea was darker at this depth but light enough to show moving shapes of fish, not the Leviathan but other powerful sea predators.

The young man turned to the Elayawun, whose lips never moved though his words were as audible as sibilant air, like a toy balloon hissing inside the young man's ears. The man "spoke" something brief and profound to them, but the young man instantly forgot the message. No matter how closely he leaned in, the words receded further away.

Chapter 33

WAS ON STATE, REMEMBERING my image of her gone, flying out over the Pacific, and now I knew my image was not true: not flying, lurking here lost in mysteries. I was lost, unfeeling, and before thinking it, I realized I was already about my father's business. But I called June first from a pay phone. And got no answer. Then a voice inside me said, because she is gone. Surprising to think I would be happier if she was off in a tropical paradise with another man, rather than here, alone, not gone.

I walked in to Jacques's, got a table, ordered food, and ate bread smeared with butter and topped with tomato salsa, and leaned familiarly into the waiter with his ridiculous mustache. It wasn't a waitress. My father said it would be. Where is June?

"Please tell the chef if he doesn't know how to make a recipe, he shouldn't fake it." I think I got this whole thing wrong but what the fug do I care?

The man looked at me dubiously, almost sad. Go, I said. I waited for him to scamper off, but he stared at me. I'm blowing it.

"It's a joke. Tell Icaro exactly what I said. He'll thank you."

He looked doubly troubled. "There's nobody named Icaro here," he said. "The chef's name is Aquino, he was in the Navy, he's a flip."

"Tell him the chicken à la king is horrible and he needs a new recipe."

Other men were finishing their three martinis previous to ordering. The few secretaries heading home who passed the place were wrapped in scarves and holding their skirts down and looking red-cheeked and anxious. I was anxious too. On State Street, big Chevys parked at an angle. Out at the end of the street, far away, I had seen whitecaps foaming, the darkness of the blue sea made me shiver. And dark was coming.

I sat staring at the wall until the baffled waiter came over with my second Manhattan. I drank half of it down fast. "I want another," I said. I smiled in a phony way and let the expression drop off my face. "Another Manhattan, please?"

He walked away, stopping at the dark bar. The bartender looked over his shoulder, shrugged huge, and then the waiter went. I suddenly didn't give a shit about fate.

I was moving some salt grains around some pepper pieces when I felt him hovering above me. He had a big knife in his hand and a painful-looking bandage across his forehead. I decided to remain cheerfully aloof.

"That thing any good?" I asked.

"Depends on who's using it."

"If you promise not to use it on me, I'll attempt to apologize." I looked him in the eyes and smiled in my best wistful. "I am an ass. I am sorry. I could use a friend, and my father explained to me how you already are my friend. Or were. Sorry for being an ass."

"A man should never apologize for what he is," said Icaro, laying the broad knife down on a folded linen napkin on the table. It left a pink bloodstain, and one wondered what beast's blood. Maybe a beet, who knows?

"Touché. But the fact is, I *am* apologizing and the decent thing would be for you to either accept it or scornfully refuse."

"The fact is, we both have reasons to regret our past actions," he said. "I knew your father hadn't told you. I just got a lot on my mind besides sneaking around, and I took it out on you. I am often irrational."

"Wow," I said. "Sit down?"

"Not allowed," he said. "But the boss is out in the alley with Cookie the bar girl. That gives me a few minutes. What can I do for you?"

"I want to go out to Santa Cruz Island this week in a sneaky fashion. To snoop. I haven't been out there since my brother and I used to go. Maybe you know how I can work that."

"Friday morning," he said, after a long look. "Marina one at sunrise."

"I'll be there. I'll bring sandwiches."

"Don't bother," he said. "I cook."

After he left, my Manhattan got doubly delicious. I ate the food he sent out and drank another drink. I remembered Mary Annie and forgot June. I was nervous about our date tomorrow at midnight. I shut everything troubling out of my mind.

I had to hustle to remeet Aunt Pearlie. So I hiked, buttoning my troubled shirt up to my troubled neck. At the corner of Canon Perdido and State, I turned between the two banks, and saw the Lobero crowd. For a second, I thought I saw Salvatore, the legitimate businessman's son, who immediately hopped into a big yellow taxi, which U-turned and sped off toward the east side. Impossible. I see what I want to see, I think.

"Trevor!"

I looked up. There was Miss Pearl Chase.

"Would you walk right past me?"

"No, thought I saw an old friend."

"Wasn't that your cousin with that lad in the taxi? Your friend from school, I think. The Italian businessman's son. Cannaletto?"

"Campagnolo?" I asked, my blood gone colder, if that was possible.

"It looked like them. But come on, the help is ringing in the sheaves," she said as the usher with his bell banged noisily against the rising breeze.

"Don't we need tickets?"

She looked at me and laughed. "Pearl's Girls!"

Holding court at the door, Pearlie told me to go on in and grab two seats somewhere on the aisle. As I was about to sit down, I saw the tall, stooped figure of Aldous, hustling. I put my sweater across our seats and began to make my way over, when a hand reached out and grabbed me from the aisle. It was policeman Boston.

"You hear about the writer's kid?"

"I haven't heard anything for a few days. I been laying low." I thought it was funny.

"It's all over the newspaper. That detective writer, Macdonald, I forget his real name—his daughter ran off. That makes it an official epidemic."

"I thought I was in the clear?"

"Let me finish," he said.

"Only Dooley is still missing," I interrupted. "And this girl whoever. Everybody disappears sooner or later, including my girlfriend."

"What?" he asked, perplexed.

"The teachings of Jesus Christ as presented through a mushroom cult," said a voice behind me. I turned, it was Mr. Noctambulist, who was talking to somebody else but chuckled when he saw me.

Huxley walked by me and I said, "Hello." He looked over in a patronizing way. He was followed by Hopper, the actor, and Stuurman, the mystery.

"I loved your piece," said the actor, winking. "Just want you to know, we all did."

"You making fun of me?"

He looked surprised. "No, Aldous loved it. He couldn't believe how much you got into that story."

"He just stared at me a second ago. He didn't even acknowledge me."

"He's blind, remember?"

"I thought they butchered it," I murmured.

Now he started laughing big, rolling belly laughs. "Maybe they did but it read great. You know the story about Graham Greene? He sent a kid to get a newspaper. Kid comes back with the *Los Angeles Times*. Green says, 'I told you get me a newspaper.'"

"I heard that one," said Boston. "What's this stuff about mushrooms?"

"If you'll all take your places," said the disembodied voice from behind the curtain, "we need to get started."

"What about my date?" I murmured, looking around for her.

"Show's starting," he said.

I sat down and Pearl eased in next to me.

She sniffed. "Have you been drinking?"

"Free, white, and twenty-one, dearest. I went to the Knights of Columbus Hall, and I was sipping." I felt the effects of the three Manhattans on top of the Mediterranean Stinger. My stomach gave a gargle.

"Hmmph," she said. "So early."

I bared my teeth. She stuck her tongue out a little. We settled down into the stiff seats with the fleurs-de- lys overhead, in case I got bored. The lights went down and a disembodied voice wished us greetings for the New Year, and now the last word on the old as we stand poised to suffer the slings and arrows of yesteryear.

The curtain parted on a fake, brightly lit garden scene. Gathered there were a bevy of biddies, clearly young male actors in female garb. This was baggy-pants funny. High-pitched quips began to fly about the little garden table, including references to Fiesta Parade horse of-fal filling the famous Street in Spain, Pearl's project. In the corner a string ensemble played "English Country Garden." Then a kicking line dance about architecture, a little number they called "Entering the Pearly Gates," chronicling the hardships of obtaining permits to put in a fire hydrant, since the architectural committee wanted ones made of white stucco and red tile. Herself looked mortified. I told you, it's the sincerest form of flattery, I whispered. She put finger to lips. The jokes meandered off, and Pearlie seemed angrier: the rage of Caliban at not seeing his face in the mirror. I watched the *fleurs-de-lys*. Then lightning struck the valley thrice, and the ladies led out an Avatar of Obstacles, a portmanteau creature. Each woman stroked a different part of the beast, and he, with his rough hooves, began tearing off their clothes and brutally having his way with them. I looked around; everybody was laughing merrily.

"Escape forever into the past," said one of the women as she rubbed the creature's ample haunches. "Live forever!"

"Lo, Death has reared himself a throne!" said all of them in unison, and the creature walked forward, huge but real. His limbs were gar-gantuan and human, waving and waving; his head, that of an elephant with lambent eyes and mottled skin.

"I stand amid the roar," sang the third of the ladies, "of a surf-tormented shore, and I hold within my hand, grains of the golden sand. How few! O God! Can I not save one grain from the pitiless wave? Is all that we see or seem but a dream within a dream?"

Furious laughter and applause broke out. The curtain came down for intermission.

"Is it true, Miss Chase, that you will be bringing the genius behind

Taliesin, Running Water, and the brand- new Montecito home on Hot Spring's road to our city?" asked Douwe Stuurman, hovering over us from the aisle on his way to the bathroom. "The architect Frank Lloyd Wright," he added with a voice that invoked the celestial. Pearl nodded and Stuurman hurried off after chucking me on the shoulder.

"How do you know him?" I said, rubbing my eyes, referring to Stuurman. Pearl ignored the question and then spoke up.

"My girls are bringing the fancy architect, under my auspices. I wasn't enthusiastic, but they hunger for whoever is new. I hear he is a vulgar man."

"I'd interview him," I said.

"Hush," said Pearl. "I'll arrange it. You were snoring like a bull seal."

"We are reflections of some ideal sorrow," I said.

By now Pearl was avoiding eye contact. I was begging to leave. But she wouldn't hear of it. I threatened to snore louder and she was mad but over a barrel. "Like a walrus you sounded. I told you about drinking during the day. Is that the drugged man?" she asked, watching Huxley make his way back to his seat. "His uncle or his grandfather or somebody worked with Darwin. Amazing." She actually looked impressed, though the confusion of names was unlike her.

The lights flashed for act two. I said good-bye and she harrumphed. "Looked nothing like me," Pearl said as she turned to her other neighbor: "The sincerest form of flattery."

I returned to June thoughts on the street. I had to know where she was among those disappeared. I jumped on the first bus that was headed for my place. When I got home, I found an old woman at my door.

"Bet you're that Westin boy, the one that writes for newspapers." The crone's voice spoke from the shadow of an overlarge scarf that covered her head and brow.

I tensed up, imagining some witch sent to kill me, a sea hag. Her voice was familiar, though. She thrust a packet out. I cringed.

"Ooh, a brave one. And you want to help me."

"Help you."

"You don't know who I am, do you? Well, let's just say I want you to travel across the sea. And back in time." She cackled a bit. "But first read these papers, and then raise my husband from the dead. Punish his murderers."

"Yes, ma'am, Mrs. Brown."

She laughed. "I don't know what you're talking about." She left.

I opened the door, let the musty air exhale, and walked into the apartment with the cold eye of the television on me. I opened the sheath and saw the papers, or facsimiles of the papers, that I had seen on Pearl's desk, along with some report about the Undersea Gardens, the thing the studio guy had once pitched me.

I sat down and read. Concerning the discovery and possible reconstruction of the presidio, the historical society, it seemed, had already made its decision. Barely had the thing been found before its tourist potential beckoned. They would rebuild it, reconstructed on lands owned by the Chinese. Eminent domain would be exercised, and the noisome inhabitants, with their questionable parlors and laundering facilities, ejected. The society would rebuild the presidio using the very earth that surrounded it to make its own adobe bricks, probably from the old ones melted back unto the earth. The people of Santa Barbara might consider funding the rebuilding. This rehydrated history could be reconstituted, just like the white Queen of the Missions, destroyed in the fateful waves of the 1925 earthquake. Tourists haunted that replica all summer long in diesel-smelling buses. The whole city could become a reenactment of the conquering conquistadors.

It was all there, written by somebody who might have been

mocking the whole enterprise. I looked through the text, the diagrams, the budget, the plans, and at the end of the last page found the scribe's name: J. Brown, Esq. For Approval.

Just another one of the Brown boys. You see them everywhere nowadays.

Chapter 34

From a proud tower screeches resembling birdsong caught the young man's ear, breaking into shards of sound like refracted lights from faceted stones. He found himself at a wall of glass, his face reflected dark and gaunt, as if drawn by artist's charcoal, and then washed in deepest green tints.

Another face peered back at him. Outside, swimming in a cloud of unknown, the merman stared back—hands flapping in slow motion to maintain a distance from the crystal, his face haggard, wise, and noble.

"They never come so near," said the dignified Elayawun. Indeed, the merpeople had followed the young man with what seemed like concerned devotion from the other side of thick glass since he had first seen them moving through the kelp forest. Now they seemed to be tracking his slow progress inside the dome. "It must be you who draws them."

"How are you speaking to me? Your voice a minute ago was unintelligible."

"That is our tongue. Your father taught us English and how to read without moving our lips. And he left us books."

"My father taught?" the young man asked. He knew that the old man had traveled with his father and now guessed that this was their old

and frequent destination back when so-called fishing trips took them away for whole seasons.

"Language moved from him into us over time. You hear us, but we can only form the outer shapes of your words and know little about their content. Things we picked up by accident. On the other hand, if you learned our true language, it could never deceive you, because it was formed from gestures. Are you quite sure you've never been here before?"

"I didn't even know I was coming today," the young man said, cognizant of the half lie he had told. He remembered sea monsters from childhood dreams of his father's voyages, night journeys filled with creatures swimming with hammerhead sharks, and one recurring dream of a cobblestoned city below his seaside village's Chinatown: a dreamworld where merchants sold odiferous fruits and kept monstrous aquariums. He remembered seeing the sea creatures in those tanks.

"So, it was from your dreams that the merpeople found you," said the Elayawun.

The young man was shocked. "Can you read my thoughts?" he asked. No answer came. "Where are we going?"

"To see a doctor," the Elayawun said. "We want to know if you will be all right here. Are you all right now?"

The young man, whose name was Patrick, decided not to answer as an experiment.

"Good," said the Elayawun. "As for your abiding question: Our evolution took place underwater, so we understand gestures. We read posture, bearing, and the way you breathe with great specificity. We transmit knowledge with subtle but clear movement."

"Where is the old man?" asked Patrick out loud.

"He has gone into the town, the living part of our city. He has friends there. He has served us for many years."

"You mean he works for you?"

"No. I mean serves. We gave him something that he could not earn, that he is grateful for. He does what we ask."

Moving along a corridor outside the city itself, they came to a door. The two entered and found a large chamber with nothing in it but a jar on a table. From above them the dome let down sea light. Another tall figure emerged from behind a hanging tapestry, and was introduced to the young man as a doctor. In his hand this new Elayawun held a long instrument with half-moon-shaped blades.

"What is that?" asked Patrick, fearful.

The doctor covered his ears, unused to the sound of human speech.

"Now," said the first Elayawun, nodding at the doctor who lifted the scalpel toward the young man's bare forearm.

Patrick was horrified. "See here. I didn't come with you to be ... "
He never finished. After the cold touch of the steel on his arm, his red blood moved out into the green light of the room, arcing through the air, and into the jar. "See here," he murmured.

Patrick felt dizzy. He looked around at the room, seeing it for the first time. The walls were seashell-crusted, intricately patterned. Outside in the hallway, through the interior windows, rows of machinery hummed like monks. He looked toward the door and a woman was standing there. Staggeringly beautiful, she nodded at the priest and stood quiet nearby.

"Go with the girl," said the first Elayawun. Patrick felt he needed to obey.

"Go along," the same Elayawun repeated. "There is not much time left."

The doctor put a seaweed poultice on the spot on Patrick's arm where the knife had found blood. The woman, an Elayawun female, was already out the door before Patrick caught up. He asked her name. She said she was called Eve Marie in his tongue.

"Do you want to know mine?" he asked. She held her hand up as if to say she knew. She pronounced it "Pa-da-rake." "Is that right?"

"Close enough."

She said, "But it is wrong for me to speak out loud, and dangerous. It must not happen again."

"Why? What did the priest mean, 'There isn't much time'?"

She seemed confused for a second. "It's just something we say, like you might say, 'Nice weather.'"

"Nonsense," he said.

"Yes," she answered. "Much of conversation is nonsense, about seventy percent. The rest is dangerous."

Patrick did not argue; the linguistic knots made him weary. He looked up and saw a merman looking down at them through the thick glass. The creature had a blank face, like a child watching ants crawl.

"Someone is always watching," she said matter-of-factly. "Do you believe in God?"

"No," he said, not speaking, just thinking.

"People who believe in God, people from dry land, believe that God is always watching, hearing, listening to their thoughts. So everything is a performance, witnessed for eternity. God's job is to just watch."

And judge, he thought. She looked at him.

She brought him to a moving floor. They got on and she held his hand. She laughed without sound at his childish pose. "We must travel into the city," she said aloud. "He was right, there isn't much time. We have business to attend to."

"Don't end sentences with a preposition."

She laughed again.

"Am I funny?" he asked with a smile.

"Too funny for words," she said, using the formless language of her people.

Chapter 35

SLEPT WITH NOISY DREAMS. We had put things right, and she said she loved me and would come back and be mine. At least, I think she said that. All night long, she kept appearing at the door. She said she was going to Hawaii, but there she was on the streets, and his father said no, they never went. So how much erosion of the truth, bad-faith speech, calls everything into question? One rotten apple spoils the whole barrel.

I had that appointment with Storke, speaking of crabbed apples. I languished all morning. I wanted to scream. I wanted to talk to my father, but his phone rang off the wall in Pasadena and in his seedy Echo Park office. I called *her*—she was never home.

My car roared to life, and I picked up the blanket from her seat and threw it in the back. Maybe I should get one of those fancy sports cars, or at least something more reliable. I drove down Santa Barbara Street, and somewhere near Figueroa it died. I coasted the heap into a curb and bade it good-bye. I walked, with plenty of time, my hangover waning, but hungry. There were doughnuts in De La Guerra square, and people I knew, old friends. I told one of them I had a meeting with our former-senator Storke in his wordsmithing place. He said, "The *News-Suppress*."

I crossed the plaza where I so recently had hummed the nothingness and seen the end of my own ego. Now I could not remember how it felt, hallucinating where Fiesta had its epicenter, where the city council sat. The buildings sheltered a world of polite men who got drunk by early evening and then came back to work polite in the morning. Yet it yielded no information, this gentlemanly cabal I tried to absorb through my once-open psychic pores.

I walked in and found Storke's secretary at the bottom of the tower stairs. I gave my name and said I had an appointment. She looked into her book and with a concerned gaze picked up the black phone. She spoke briefly in gauzy tones of respect, showed relief, and gestured me up the sweeping stairs to Storke's office. "I knew your father," she said.

"Me too," I replied, saluting her crisply.

The light shining down seemed a little too celestial. Storke's door was open and I heard a voice speaking in harsh tones, loud and familiar, to the man who had fought with my father over the uses of a hapless harbor, over nothing, really, since the Navy had cashiered him out anyway.

"It doesn't matter what I think," said the voice in the baboon's office.

"Of course it does," Storke said. "You're master of your fate. Far be it from me … "

"If you say 'to interfere,' I'll scream. I would say you have made such a habit of interfering, you don't know how to stop. Anyway, I'm not going to the islands this weekend," said the voice.

"Come on, you know your mother loves to do these things with the whole family. It's Two Guns' coming out party."

"Doesn't he hate that name?"

"Call him that and watch him blush with pleasure. Come on, everybody will be there. Besides, I need you to get between that insufferable Miss Chase and me. She likes you."

"See? It's not about me. It's about what I can do for you."

"I'm your father."

"Amen."

"What does that mean?"

"I think it means something like 'peace,' but that would be a good topic for a holiday editorial. 'The Meaning of Amen: Our Final Word on the Subject.'"

"You see why I need you?" Storke was chuckling. "One day you'll inherit all this, then you'll miss me."

"Can't wait, Pop," he said.

Then the son was standing on the threshold. Turning around abruptly, he winced, catching my eye. "Family stuff, always joyful. Go right in," said Charles Storke, whom I knew. "Maybe he can tell you what to do with your life too."

"He can say anything he wants," I said. "But I do a perfectly good job ruining it my own way."

Charles smiled. I saluted him, too, wondering if he knew my father.

Old man Storke was furious and made no attempt to conceal it. Blustering like a breeze he asked me if there was anything sharper than an adder's tooth?

"The wit and wisdom of Jack Paar?"

He harrumphed. "I don't know what the point of all this is," he said. "The city needs a newspaper, and I have treated it as if it were my family duty. So now my own family turns on me. I've done a few stupid things, but most of them paid off well."

"The lake," I said.

"Goddamn the lake," he said. "Isn't it the prerogative of all free men to take hold of the world and bend it to their wills? Didn't Jesus say something like that? Subjugate the fish and fowl thereof?"

"I remember that he so loveth the world that he gave his son something something … "

"Oh my God," chuckled Storke. "Worse than the devil quoting scripture is the son of an atheist devil quoting." He saw the look in my eye. "Besides, I think he was talking about laying down his son's life. How is your father? Never mind, how about your uncle, the poet. Francis Westin bought Dal Bello's tires, right? Most people called him Francis Dal Bello."

"Even we do now, it's a family joke. He thinks you had no right to change the earth. He thinks the lake was stupid and the harbor even stupider. He thinks Castle Rock should never have been dynamited."

"I think maybe he's right about Castle Rock," said Storke. "The lake is fine, though."

"I didn't expect you to sound almost human."

"You probably think I'm a self-righteous old cuss and maybe I am. You know, this was a horse-and-buggy town when I was a lad."

"Mile through the snow, one-room school?"

He smiled. "Impertinence becomes you. The other day when we spoke on the street, I thought I'd caught you off guard. But you're a full-time son of a bitch. Again no offense to your father, sorry," he said. "But, in fact, it was a one-room school, and most of my class-mates were ranchers. The land is something I fool myself into thinking I understand. If you dam a river and flood a plain, you can grow some-thing to feed the cattle. And then they feed you. This is how it works, Frankie Dal Bello aside. Human history is the process of humanizing the wilderness, and then warring over it."

"Neat," I said.

"But this is not why I sent for you. I don't pretend to understand your father's brother or even his brother-in-law." He eyed me for a reaction. "I try to do right."

"What about? Brown?"

He gazed across his galleys. "I didn't hush up coverage of his untimely whatever it was, you know." He harrumphed again. "I have a good police source, very highly placed, you might say. He insisted that Brown only looked like murder. Brown was a neurotic Catholic. He put nail-holes in his hands to pass himself off as a mystic, Padre Pio stuff. That's what the police said, at first anyway. But now I must admit, I doubt my source. My chief suspect is Miss Pearl Chase."

I ignored it, there was no love lost between Mr. and Miss Santa Barbara. "Was Dooley your source?"

"I don't know him," he said. "You don't listen well, for a man who wants to be a reporter." But the denial sounded unconvincing.

"Well, my source seems to be blaming Miss Pearl Chase, too," I said, returning to my failed Knights of Columbus strategy: blurt wild. "And she thinks it could be cleared up at this big meeting out on Santa Cruz Island. I'm going out there to nose around. If I find something, I could write the story for you."

He looked down at his hands as if forgiving them their sins. "You are your father's son," he said softly. "I was more interested in having you cover the visit of this famous architect, the one with the three names."

"Frank Lloyd Wright. What does he have to do with anything? And with me?"

"Like I said, he's famous. Miss Chase is bringing him here. I think your connection might help you secure a story, something more inside. You did well with Huxley. But the meeting on Santa Cruz is intriguing. Everybody will be there." He thought for a second, pulled out a pipe. "I don't know. I have a feeling we're talking at cross-purposes. You think there is some kind of Hidden Harbor Mystery, don't you, detective's son. Unlock the past. I think the meeting is an opportunity to shape the future."

"So, I'll go and unearth the past and divine the future. And write you a big story set in the present."

"Whoa, Hopalong. I think you could learn something at Santa Cruz, but it's not a whodunit, this thing. And, you are not a police reporter, though you managed to get most everything right in the *Times*. You think I would send you out on an investigative piece? Still, Santa Cruz, you say?" Something on his desk caught his eye, and he lifted a paper to scrutinize. "Do you know Two Guns?"

"Sure," I lied. "But by some strange oversight I wasn't invited."

"It's funny you should mention it, because I'm going this weekend too. I will officially make you my guest, since sonny boy isn't going. People might think you are working for me, though."

"Am I?"

"Yes. You are working on the visitation of Mr. Frank Lloyd Wright, an interview you will convince Miss Chase to provide. It will help her cause. He's an old man you know, maybe a queer or a communist, not that it matters. Maybe a queer, but he's famous, and I would like you to interview him, say five takes. That's 1,200 words."

"And if I see you on Santa Cruz?"

"I would greet you warmly."

"Like a father greets a son?"

He pretended not to hear me, and turned to an edit, forgetting me even before I walked away. But at least I had an assignment and legal entrée to the Two Guns show.

Chapter 36

Patrick and Eve Marie passed through a dark, wet corridor banked with machines. "They are reproducing thought," she whispered. "The winking lights are ideas, the phrases of a syllogism, or the proofs rendered after."

"Thought without pleasure," he said, though he worried about the damp floor under all this technology.

"Thought without pain," said Eve Marie. "And, don't worry, the equipment runs on a different form of power than your electricity. You are safe here."

Outside, the ocean darkened. Night filled the sky and darkness spread down like a poison drug entering lily-pure tissue. She turned her hood up and walked toward an opening on the pathway.

They stopped before a red door.

"Try to prepare yourself for what lies ahead," she said. "Whether or not we made a mistake bringing you here, it's done now and now is all you have."

He was about to say that he had come on his own accord when she opened the door and pulled him through.

He stood in silent wonder. Before them the aquapolis shimmered in radiant light, made more dramatic by their emergence from darkened chambers. First came a painful buzz of illumination, though the light's source was impossible to determine. It pervaded the entire space beneath the dome.

Inside the dome, the architecture felt alien, resembling nothing that is ours. Patrick was transfixed at every turn. Irregular angles created forms that tilted into each other. Doors gaped in oblong shapes. From where they stood, Patrick and Eve Marie could see steel buildings towering in blue shapes, smooth-walled and streamlined as if for flight.

There was bustle of movement that felt timed to some pattern, choreographed. Maybe up close it was chaotic, but their view was all harmonious motion. He found wonder in every quadrant. Oddest of all was the silence, a peaceful bustle.

"Are those flying vehicles?" he asked, looking over at Eve Marie.

Tears filled her eyes.

"What's wrong?" he asked.

"It never dulls," she said. "And I've only been in the outer chambers a few days."

"Has it always been like this?"

"Two millennia ago, by your reckoning, we realized that the past held more meaning for us than any future we might imagine. So we stopped and prevented the vulgarity of constant, senseless change."

"You enshrined nostalgia."

"I suppose. Let's go down."

They descended from the high rim of the dome into the city below over carved rock steps that looked like jade, worn smooth, he guessed, by countless feet. Distracted by the immensity and complex movement of the underwater city, he climbed down, stumbling. Sounds like distant laughter or bickering seagulls reached his ears. They neared the seafloor.

At the edge of a row of buildings, Eve Marie pointed to an arch engraved in English. She made him read it aloud: "Beyond the Castle Rock, the sea was gathering indigo hues. Way out, whitecaps formed, but we knew they meant nothing in the land to which we traveled. Neverknown was its name, and the people there greeted us as we said farewell to vexing winds and waves." Eve Marie made him repeat the words with feeling. She nodded. She looked satisfied, maybe smug.

"Was that a test?" he asked.

"More like a verification," she answered.

"You wanted to know that something literally carved in stone remained the same over a period of time."

"Almost fifty of your years," she said. "I wanted to know if the words changed meaning, if they were still moving. I had another motive. That was your father speaking. I believe it's appropriate to ask how you are feeling now."

Patrick didn't know what to say. Why had she suggested it might have been a mistake to bring him to her world? And why had his father come here? He felt a mounting dread as they moved deep into the city.

When Eve Marie and Patrick broke into a crowded square, Elayawun were everywhere. Glass-and-steel machines, flying cars, floated through air. The sea hissed against glass far away.

"They are staring at me," he said.

"Their curiosity is normal. Imagine if one of them visited your world."

The Elayawun in the square were willowy, tall, and pale with leathery skin that appeared moist. Their wiry hair was slicked back and tied at varying lengths, which he later would learn was fixed according to some complicated combination of factors: sex, official capacity, and age. Patrick never mastered these codes, though. Their eyes were set wide apart and there were vestiges of ears. He didn't find them unattractive; they were humanoid enough and he even felt drawn to Eve Marie.

The Elayawun fell back as the couple moved forward. Roads narrow and wide appeared. The smaller byways seemed to be for walking, the larger were dominated by the glass-and-metal hovering cars. The ground was dotted with gelatinous creatures of dazzling color—slugs the size of Pomeranian dogs. They were pets, Eve Marie told him, bred for amusement.

They soon found themselves at a central complex of huge structures surrounded by high walls. Many more flying vehicles moved around these looming towers. Overhead, beyond the glass, the sea had turned pitch-black as night filled all the worlds. The night glow of the city faded and smaller lights blinked on around them.

As they approached a set of iron gates set in the walls of the central structure, they heard a metallic groan come from inside the gates. Securing wheels turned, and suddenly, a door in the gate opened wide on sighing hinges.

Chapter 37

AT THE TELEPHONE BOOTH on State Street and Cota, I stopped to call the mechanic, what the hell. I had a feeling, second thoughts about my old wreck. The wind blew all around me, and small rain whipped the glass walls of the booth, but a light came on after the door closed and the wind was shut out. Safe against the elements, I thumbed the Yellow Pages hanging there, called, and my mechanic offered to come pick me up in my own car. There was nothing wrong with it, he said.

He said he had walked over after I told him I was going to leave it there, keys in the ignition, for posterity. I didn't remember telling him that and said, you must be psychic. He said, well I went over and it started. No charge, but for everybody's sake, why don't you buy a new car, Trevor? Poor little rich Trevor, I knew he was thinking. He said, my son will bring the fugging car to you. His son and I grew up together on railroad tracks and beach cliffs and in little seashell boats in the harbor. Put him on the line, please? What's up, *huero*? he said. Things do not fall together, I said, cars don't fix themselves. Hell of a thing, he said, to be so pessimistic. Fug you, I wittily replied. He asked where I wanted to go for beers. So of course I said, Tommy's Golden Cock.

Next, I called Mary Annie and she wanted to know why I was calling. About tonight, I said. And she replied, what about it? For one second I felt a kind of stupid relief. I could go home alone and feel sorry for myself, maybe even get drunk. She said, I'm fixing us a nice midnight supper. Bet she never did that for you. We'll see what comes up. What pops up? She laughed in a husky voice. Her bad-girl act was awkward but compelling. I became calm after that.

Outside the booth, the night, in its winter way, slid down fast and felt unnaturally dark, even before John Castano, Esquire, the mechanic's son and my old pal, swept up in my untrusty limo. Sliding over so I could drive, he asked about my cousin, pointedly, like people often do. Went to the islands with the dago kid, I said, hoping to end the rumors then and there, even if it meant summarizing my sorrows. That's what I heard, too, he said. And the air thickened with unfinished business. Unspoken, the topic settled in between us.

We zoomed up the street past State and A's magazine stand and he whistled at some poodle-skirted girl illuminated under a streetlamp; she turned and stuck out a long pink symbol of reconsideration.

"Without fear of contradiction," said Johnny, "I'm saying she wants me. Her body spoke to me."

"In tongues."

On the way up State we picked up little Billie Levy hitchhiking and he told us about some crazy idea for a rock-and-roll song he wanted to write and about a group he wanted to start. He had the last DA I ever saw, and his stupid aggie coat was turned up in the back like James Dean. I was barely listening because at Mission, where they want to put in a traffic light, where the wilderness begins and the rich people's houses end, I swear I saw her in the passenger seat of his pre-war fancy Chrysler that was turning left. We could make out shapes.

"Clunkomtatic transmission," said my car friendly friend, seeing me stare and roll down the window as if that might improve my vision.

"June," I said.

"That's what I thought too," he said. "Looked like the dago kid driving. Maybe they didn't take off yet. For the islands. It's Hawaii we're talking about, right?"

Billie Levy said, they're going to that thing out on those islands. He pointed backward at the ocean and I turned around to gape at him, shaded in the backseat, his face lit from the streetlights. Everybody knows what's going on except me. Channel Islands, he said.

We got to the bar. Billie followed us in through a halo of leftover Christmas lights and ordered a Schlitz like that. I swear Teddy the bartender poured it for him because of the pure swagger of the little fool. He could con the white off a polar bear. Then Ted took a good look at him and started screaming. As Levy ran out the door, Ted lit into us. I said we didn't even know who the fella was. He'll probably wreck this town, if and when he gets old enough.

The twinkling lights behind the bar blurred, and the optical-illusion waterfall in the Hamm's beer sign fell at a ferocious rate. After a half hour of idle chatter I picked the keys up from the bar. Johnny had a girl over near the mission on a little goat farm, near enough to walk. As I was extricating my butt from the wide barstool he asked me if I remembered Vege Mar, the kingdom of the poor who shall inherit the earth? We used to go there and listen to the Mayor of the Hobos weave his vulgar odysseys for any kids who would listen. When's the last time I went?

"The Child's Estate? The hobos are all gone except for the mayor, I think."

He said, laughing, "Soon he'll be gone too." He looked sagely at the bubbles in his golden drink and then tipped it into his mouth.

"What do you mean, gone? Like the 'this too shall pass' gone?"

"They're burning Hobotown down."

"Who's burning down Hobotown?"

"They, you fool: those stupid *gavachos* that own everything and set themselves up as charitable providers. Some foundation owns it. They got the land from Mrs. Child's will, right, which had one immutable condition."

"Keep it a hobo jungle forever."

"But she's been dead a long time. I think three years. They don't want bums living in those cattails, no matter what she said when she left it to them. That's a beautiful piece of land, says the board. They're gonna make it a zoo. Here's the beauty part. They don't have to change nothing, just one article of the English language. It used to be The Child's Estate: now it's A Child's Estate. Hey, my nana's taking us to the Magic Kingdom, you been, nuh?"

"What're you talking about?"

"Disneyland. Happiest place in the world. Foochers, don't you know anything?"

"No, A Child's what?"

"I'm talking about choice develop-able land, sea- view land. They can build another harbor in the bird refuge there, like they originally planned, remember, Gateway to Santa Cruz Island where the Gherini's want to build a resort. Call it Gheriniland, wettest place in the world."

"It's a rich thing to own, an imagination."

"Most of this is in the works, friend. The foundation asked my *tio* to hire some people to clear the land, some landscapers."

He stopped and considered the ring his beer was making on the bar top. "Did you ever see the *Haida*," he asked, dreamily.

"No," I said. "Fleischman's boat, right?"

"I think you better call it a ship, man. I was in the Marines. This is my rifle, this is my gun. This is for shooting; this is for fun."

"It was big."

"Fleischman loved that boat. Anyways it's back. Everybody

thought it sunk in the war, in Greece, or something. But they're all going out there this weekend to see the *Haida*. I hear the legitimate liquor distributor is getting it from his son for his birthday—the son who drives around with your sweet coz. Everybody's going out to Santa Cruz for the party."

"About this I heard whispers . . . You ever hear of some guy named Two Guns?"

"Oh yeah. Andy Devine is my uncle and Broncho Billy's my aunt."

"Never mind. How about Snake Jake?"

"Well I used to know him before he became dearly departed. He was a pain in the ass, but who wants to talk bad about the dead? He worked for your fake *Tia* Pearlie. She's probably the one killed him."

"What?"

"They had a big fight. He thinks she wants to turn this town into a living museum. He always called her the Queen of the City of the Dead. Cute, huh? But she loved him and he loved her and you don't."

"Wow, Mr. Castano. Now you *are* drunk."

"What do you mean? Ask anybody in the harbor. He worked freelance for the oil companies and that infuriated her."

"Worked doing what?"

"He was one of those divers who could weld underwater and make explosions too. Dynamite: the kind of stuff that infuriates fisherman. Helps the oil companies find oil."

"It was a job he had, blowing stuff up?"

"Yeah, part-time underwater demolition. I don't know much about it but radar, sonar, tartar sauce are involved. Blows shit up. Must be kinda fun."

The air was still and we were looking at a mirror under the water of the Hamm's waterfall and then suddenly we were outside.

Again I shouldn't have driven but I did. I walked into the apartment, weaving a bit, and standing by the light of the radio, which was on without sound coming out, I tried to breathe underwater. I was afraid of my television. There was rain outside again. I snapped on the standing lamp with the cone shade that goes up, spreads upwards, splays quavering light, old-style. I had been busy; maybe I didn't mention that. I had the Brown papers spread out on the couch. The presidio, they said, was supposed to be permanent. The mission was meant to wither, once the Indians were with God, Jesus, and the Holy Ghost. The papers I wanted to look at were there, but the room felt odd. I made some coffee in the electric percolator and went to pee a river of beer. I had two hours to kill.

It was over by the typewriter and the pages were askew and it sat on top of them—the note. It sent a chill through me—something dangerous ought to feel cold, but this seemed to leak down through the atmosphere, so I went over to the heater and dialed it up, and it began a rattle and then blew warmth into the room, but I was pinned to the wall and didn't want to cross the room, but I did.

This is the moment, I thought. Revelation is at hand.

Oh Trevor, she said, I told you I wouldn't stay if the place was a mess. Don't you have a landlady who cleans? Shame.

I started sniffing the air—Hypnotique. Jesus, I thought, she was here, but how and why and when? She's supposed to be gone. I sniffed the air and tried to stand in the space that she took when she wrote the note. Then it occurred to me: the pages, *my* pages. She had been reading them. The note had been lying on the manuscript above the passage that described his attraction to a woman not possible to possess.

Oh, Trevor, the note said.

I couldn't breathe or think. I bit my hand and I went to the telephone. It wasn't too late to call but she didn't answer and she didn't have a roommate. Oh Trevor. Then she answered, hello, laughing.

"June. I thought you were gone?"

"I am. I'll call you when I get back."

"I thought you were gone."

"I can't talk now. I'll be back soon."

Then, like it was nothing and it hadn't happened, I was sitting on the couch alone. I smelled the air for the memory of her, flower smells.

And I remembered the snapdragons at her mother's house. The television had a little screen, like a postage stamp in the middle of a big wooden box; we were fascinated. Go watch television, the grown-ups said, because my brother was in the kitchen railing against Eisenhower, some poem he read out loud, he liked poems, the mausoleum in America's heart, he said, holding some magazine from New York in his hand and my father said he didn't know anything about communism and we were putting our careful fingers in everything that came out of the stove and June took mine and licked it. Go watch the television, they said, as I stood mute in the middle of the kitchen staring at her breasts.

To get to the television, you had to cross the courtyard to the family room, a kind of isolated island beyond the garage but walled with windows like an aquarium. We ran outside and she stopped me with her hands on my arm and made me pull off a small branch of the flowers. She said, quietly, my mother can't see us. We ran into the living room and then she made me sit up on the couch. In those days television and radios took forever to warm, and I never knew if they would work, and I was always surprised when they did. She showed me how to snap the snapdragons, giggling, after spreading a light, warm blanket over the two of us. Snap, and she laughed at my wide eyes.

I tried it and it snapped and I went again. "Slow down," she said. "They'll all be gone at once," and then she snapped another right in my ear.

The TV came on loud and surprised us both and she screamed and giggled and moved closer to me. I was under the blanket touching her, leg to leg. I would have never done that a year ago but now my heart was pounding and I felt as if I was riding a bicycle down a hill and happy about the dangerous outcome. The television show was like *You Are There*, but it was called *History's Mysteries* I remember it well. Don't know if they still have it, and she wasn't interested, but I thought a show that interviewed Christopher Columbus riding across an endless blue that could end suddenly was fascinating. An open end of doubt. Only faith kept them sailing forward, faith that the God who made the world flat did not exist.

She was peevish about losing my attention and snapped another and moved toward me and snapped another and I started to push her aside and she said, Oh Trevor what's wrong with you.

"I don't know," I said. I didn't.

She smiled and went to open a last snapdragon but got a weird look in her eyes, and instead of popping, a fat grub, maybe a pupa, crawled out, and she screamed and put her head up to my neck to muffle the sound and then slid her face wet across my face and started kissing me and kissing me and I never wanted the kissing to stop.

It was my first of everything. She didn't wait long to put her tongue in my mouth, and though we kids had joked about French kissing, it wasn't funny now. After what seemed like hours of this, lost in each other, she took my hand and led it to her breast, and if that wasn't wonder enough, she touched me, and she whispered, which was even more exciting. I couldn't make out the words, but that didn't matter, the import was clear.

We heard loud laughter as the whole party of parents moved drunkenly across the courtyard toward us, and we bolted from each other and, thank the God that did not exist, I had the blanket over my lap. And I sat there, knowing I had done something wrong and I had done something right.

Later, she winked at me once and pretended not to say good night, turned sharply away and blew a quick kiss, and left the TV room, and my brother, who had come in, asked me if I wanted to ride home together on the back of his bike. It was a long way: down the Mesa and uptown.

* * * *

I sat in my living room, midway between the television and the radio. Coffee notwithstanding, my limbs felt heavy, like a diver under-water. I remembered that night and how desire seemed to have built a rigid home in me long after the embarrassing erection fell. My brother and I pulled his bike out of a bush and got on where there were side-walks. We pushed off, and the roadway's aggregate of concrete, rocks, and ground-down fossilized sea life slid beneath.

"She's your girlfriend now," he said, over his shoulder. "Not your cousin."

"You were spying on us?" I said, gasping.

"You two were making out in a fishbowl, like you were advertis-ing. It's okay; one of us should get laid. Be careful, though. Families have secret destinies. Did she tell you that she loved you? Did she?"

He was goading me now and I didn't like it. "Girls always want you to say it," he said, always such a wisenheimer for his age.

"She didn't," I said, but when I thought about it, she might as well have. She said, "This can never ever end."

Chapter 38

Three tall Elayawun sentinels stood inside the iron gates that Eve Marie and Patrick had just entered. The men were passing what looked like a small dagger among them. Eve Marie gestured Patrick past the guards. She was wary and attentive until they reached a distant hall where scalloped wall sconces lit the moss green ceiling. She breathed a sigh of relief.

"You need to bathe," Eve Marie said and parted a hanging rug on a wall, which led into a chamber with a pool over which white steam hovered. "Undress over there," she said, pointing to a screen on the other side of the pool.

He walked over, stood behind it, and began removing his clothes. "Will you be watching me?" he asked self-consciously, poking his head around the screen.

Eve Marie slipped off her clothes in one graceful motion and drifted into the warm salt water; he could see that she had breasts and a vagina. He followed her in, no longer hesitant. She made no comment. They sank down into the water, and he felt his body relax. He heard her say, "Oh."

"Oh?"

"This bath may be too strong for you."

"It's not just salt water?"

"No," she answered. "Three minutes ought to do."

Patrick felt light and loose. As he began to drift into a twilight state, Eve Marie grabbed his elbow, and pushed him out of the pool. As she stood up, he saw how ravishing she was. Eve Marie smiled. He was excited. They have smiles, he thought. She turned and spread her arms open. He slid inside them with the effortlessness of a practiced dance. Their lips met. The soft leather of her skin ignited him. She opened her mouth, and her breath was like a flower from the floor of a cold forest. She took his fingers one by one into her mouth, biting and tasting. As she lifted his chin to meet her mouth, she said with a gasp, you are so strong. He heard it deep inside his ears. Their embrace produced a yearning passion in Patrick. Or was it the water in the pool, that strange liquid he craved?

"You mustn't say anything about this," she said aloud. "I couldn't help myself, I needed to try. I read about this. Compose yourself or they will know. Come with me," she laughed out loud, her jubilation a hardened flame. Red and green flashed behind his eyes. Nearby a piece of the chamber wall suddenly fell away, and she laughed again out loud.

"It's true, then," she said.

She said out loud, "This way." There was a sudden noise, a crack. They entered another room, what appeared to be a laboratory.

The doctor entered from a small alcove. He and Eve Marie bent their heads together in silent communication before he pushed her away. She grabbed Patrick's arm and said, "Before we see the others, you have to drink." She looked different now, and sad.

A glass sat on a low table surrounded by comfortable chairs. "You must be thirsty. Here's to making sense of things," she toasted, miming, telepathic.

"Here, here," he answered inside his echoing mind. Patrick drank the salty liquid and changed into a god.

Chapter 39

MY HANDS WERE SWEATING and I tried to stay calm, but as I walked up to the front door, Mary Annie opened it before I knocked. She was smiling. There was a drink in her hand and she offered it to me.

"Did you go out with the boys?" Mary Annie asked, as she kissed my cheek. "Come in and put your feet up. I'll bring the pipe and slippers."

I fell into the role of TV husband. She took me by the arms and sat me down. I put my feet up on a hassock and she took my shoes off, wrinkling her nose and giggling at a hole over my toe. "This little piggy," she laughed.

She walked away and came back with another glass, a bottle, and an old-fashioned spritzer; she sat on the arm of the easy chair. I grabbed her around the waist and held her. She asked if I was going to cry. "I never know what to do when men cry," she said.

"Say, 'There, there.'"

I tried to gently draw her down to me. She said, "I really shouldn't."

But her kisses were so soft and she yielded. She shut my mouth inside hers. She fell from the arm of the chair into my lap and laughed. I straightened up and pulled her close. She opened her eyes long enough to smile, sigh, and I suddenly felt her tongue against mine. It was the sweetest kiss.

"I won't be able to stop," I said.

"I'm not some little girl."

"Like the one in the back row of the Arlington?"

"How sweet, you remember," she said. She took my hand, moved it to her mouth, and kissed it. "I think I lured you there."

"Why didn't it work out?"

"It did, just like I planned it."

"On schedule," I murmured, as she put her hand under my shirt.

"I kissed you during the underwater scene in *20,000 Leagues Under the Sea*."

I looked up, fearful for a moment. It was an omen. She kissed me again. Way later, we had French onion soup and crab Louie with nice champagne. After that, we drifted back to her shadowy bedroom.

Waking up in the middle of the night, I turned and saw her awake next to me, or had she been staring? "You still have some of your clothes on," she murmured. "Are you going to leave?"

I sat up and pulled off my tee and lay down next to her. She smiled. Something, though not everything, passed away from my guarded heart.

"Last week I took a drug that made me have visions," I said.

Her eyes went wide. "What do you mean? Did you see the future?"

"I don't think there's such a thing," I said. "Anyway, the visions were patterns, like that," I said, pointing to the light through lace curtains projected on my side of the bed. "Maybe that's the future."

"Maybe," she said. "Did it scare you?

"Everything scares me," I said.

"Especially me?" she said.

"I think you've been waiting for me, to pounce."

"Grr," she said. "I was the future. Waiting for you here. And she is the past." She kissed me and drew back. "I'm going to pretend you did that with more conviction."

"It will come with time."

She laughed. "Let's do that thing that takes all your conviction."

Later, when I woke up again, her arm clung to me, though she was fast asleep. I got up and walked down the hallway toward June's old bedroom. I stopped in the bathroom on the way there. Inside, words started forming and whispers started hissing from the leaves outside, scraping on the window, through which a wan light of moon and streetlamp passed, making dark shadows. In the rooms of girls, late at night.

Back in the hall, I turned right toward June's room, now an office, hoping Mary Annie wouldn't hear. I opened the door for a second and breathed in the dry rose smell of June, still there. I answered betrayal with betrayal. I closed the door softly, and when I got back to Mary Annie's room, she opened her eyes.

"What's wrong, honey? Can't you sleep?"

"I'm sorry," I said.

"Take me to the beach tomorrow?"

"Anything your heart desires."

"Then you have nothing to feel sorry about."

I joined her and dreamed about a long walk with large waves. Funny thing was, it turned out to be true.

We woke up in the morning, and I was happy. I asked about her neighbors and my Mary Annie laughed. She made scrambled eggs and cut oranges into slices and sent me out in the car for doughnuts. When I got back, her percolator bubbled and then wheezed.

I was happy. She asked me about the drug again. She said she wanted to try it too. She told me that the Noctambulist was cute; all that beatnik crap was cute. She asked me if I liked berets and bongo drums. We both said, "Dig this crazy scene!" and laughed. She told me to take a shower and come for a walk on the beach before I went home.

I was sad. She looked at me and said, "I'm not running away with any rich wop kid. So don't worry. I have been lurking here for you for a long time. Don't forget to clean behind your ears, cute stuff."

The morning sky was filled with drama, some upheaval underway behind the clouds. "I think it *was 20,000 Leagues Under the Sea*," I said as I drove down Cabrillo and turned right toward Butterfly Beach, past the graveyard. "I don't remember any of that movie. I remember looking up and seeing blue. The screen and even the theater were full of blue, like I was drowning."

"Submarine races," she laughed, her hand on my thigh. I remembered the *Nautilus*'s view of wavy lines in an empty distance, an eternity. I almost hit a car that was braking for the stop just before the tracks at the Biltmore.

"Come on dreamboat," she said. "I hope that's me you're thinking about."

The car clunked to a stop at the beach and the doors made a massive groan as we opened them and climbed out. Driving up, I thought there was a peculiar mist hanging beneath the giant palm trees. The mist, which wasn't a fog, thickened as we walked toward the sea verge. That's when we heard the faraway roar.

"Oooh," said my new lover. "Look at that."

Out on the water a wave of frightening dimensions was forming into a crest. It got bigger and bigger until all contexts were lost, and the wave slipped into pure form. And then I noticed two people riding up the side of the wave and the design turned into the reality of a monstrous threat—that old force of nature people discuss with such glib ease. The surfers crashed into each other in weird comic mishap, disappearing over the crest. But something human and flailing reappeared out of the wave top, separating into two discrete black objects. Another wave, not quite as big was coming in behind the monster, which crashed and blew its smoky foam into the sky. This explained the strange mist. Mary Annie was agog. I was too.

"Will they be all right?" she asked.

A beach boy standing there said, "Oh hell yeah. These guys just got back from Hawaii. Waves over there are twice as big and break onto reefs."

"How big was that first wave?"

"Only about fifteen feet, tops."

"Only," I said. "My whole life I never saw the like."

"It's an awesome sight. How's it goin' Westin? Haven't seen you since the hospital."

"Peter Pepitone?"

"Yeah, man." This was scary now. I didn't know him. He looked completely different again.

"Got any good ones?" he asked. "I do. You know how to make a dead baby float?

"How?"

"Take a glass of root beer and add two scoops of dead baby."

"You certainly have cultured friends," said Mary Annie from behind.

"You guys are back together, huh?" said my chameleonic chum. "Hi, we went to school together. Catholic High. You didn't like me back then."

"I didn't like any Catholics," Mary Annie said.

"Wait a minute, you were a Catholic kid."

"I majored in reverse psychology," she said.

I was only half listening. The horizon seemed hunched and irregular. I couldn't put my finger on why and couldn't stop staring. The sea started to withdraw, like a man slowly pulling himself up from a barstool for a fight.

"Jesus Christ," I said.

"What, baby?" she said, and put her hand on my shoulder and squeezed.

"You see it too," I said.

"What about those guys out there?"

Pepitone said, "Oh, those guys."

By then Mary Annie and I were yelling and pointing out and out and out. The whole world was rumbling low and she yelled, "Jesus Christ, let's get out of here."

We ran, but my legs didn't move like they should have, even though I was scrambling, and I turned around and grabbed Mary Annie's hand, and I was happy for a second. Then I looked out at the terrifying blue wall. One surfer had abandoned his board and plunged into the water, the other was riding out his wave. Both were unaware of the monster behind them, rolling with gathering speed and unimaginable force. In an instant, it shot up high and broke with a cascading sound of terror.

We were on the other side of the street running to our car when the water stormed the beach, the steps, the rocks, the sidewalk, the road, and the green lawn around the Biltmore. Mary Annie and I were climbing into the car just as the freezing cold water slid beneath and over it, lifting the car up for a second before pushing it down. I held her close as the wave withdrew. She was screaming and I said it was okay, it will be okay. I heard myself say that.

Then it was very quiet. Pepitone was crumbled over a crushed beach chair. I ran over with Mary Annie's voice ringing. He was all right, but wet. Everything was wet and the lawn had large pools. By that time a crowd of Biltmore spectators was running to us.

"Everything's all right," said Pepitone.

"What about the surfers?" I asked. "Where are they?"

"Yeah," said Pepitone.

Down the beach one of them lay with a small group around him. The other surfer had disappeared. For all I knew, disappeared forever. We stayed for a while, expecting police or newspapers or something, but the crowd eventually just went quiet and disappeared one by one. Mary Annie took me by the arm and said she needed to go home. So did I; my khakis were soaked and it was freezing. But, for a few seconds, I couldn't remember where home was.

Chapter 40

Colors layered down from blue-green to ebony outside. Ocean captures seven-tenths of the globe under its molecular net. (Why do we call it Earth?) The sand at the bottom of the ocean is dry below fifteen feet. Small animals live there: parasites, flukes, and paramecium—a bustling city of creatures found in a teaspoon of sea dirt. The dome rested on bedrock below the sand. Patrick rested after drinking the elixir. Eve Marie stared at him.

"We weren't sure how it would affect you," she said. "The doctor tested your blood but the results were inconclusive."

"Yet you were willing to let me try whatever that was. I'm altered somehow," he said, though the phrase seemed inadequate to describe the transcendent rush he felt. "What did you do to me?"

"We split death away from your body."

"What are you saying?" he asked.

"Nobody can keep you from an accident, but this elixir halts the process of aging and gives you a sharpened range of perceptions. Your senses will be more acute than those of most people born above."

"And I won't die?" he asked. She signaled yes.

Patrick felt the weight of the ancient dread of death lift and the surety of oblivion melt away. It was thrilling, yet it wasn't exactly the peace he had expected. Was it cheating?

"Are you upset?" she asked.

"I'm not sure that's the right word."

"We assumed you would be grateful—overwhelmed with happiness."

"I think I am," he said.

"I don't understand. If you have to think about it, something must be confusing you. I've never had to contemplate the kind of endless end you have faced from the moment you reached what you call the age of reason. The end of everything negates anything you might value."

"I guess that's true," he said. He smiled.

"I want you to rest for a while. I'll show you to an apartment. Sleep, if you can."

He said, in his mind, "Do I need sleep anymore?"

"Of course. But more important, I want you to gather your thoughts and, when you wake, we need to tell you the real reason we brought you here."

"I came here by choice. I could have refused."

She shook her head and gestured him out of the room. She supported him as they walked.

"Think of the immediate advantages, please. You can take as much time as you want to consider anything, look at any object, or pursue any line of thought. You can see everything and know it will not be left behind. Ever. Rest and think. When you're ready, I want you to hear how you can help us, like your friend, the old man, to whom we also gave eternal life. He helped us by bringing you here. I know you will help too after you are rested and hear us out."

"All the time in the world," he said, while outside, the ocean pushed sand slowly, inexorably against the dome.

Chapter 41

SHE WAS TRYING TO wear me down, but I wasn't listening. "I told you I had to leave tomorrow morning."

"Don't go," Mary Annie said for the forty-seventh time. "I don't get why you have to go." She held me tenderly but her eyes were serious. Her brow was pulled together in a bunch. We had been drinking a bit.

I laughed. "It's important I unravel the mysteries of the Godless universe."

"I think that's blasphemous," she laughed. "If I believed in God, I would be very upset." She kissed me on the mouth—that alone should have coaxed me home. "Don't you owe me a little more time? After I saved you from that tidal wave?"

"I owe something to somebody, an explanation, maybe. Who killed Snake Jake Brown? And why do I care? Why does he touch my life at almost every point? My brother used to say the brain had only one purpose, and that one was doomed."

"What purpose?"

"To make sense of things."

"But you can't. It doesn't. Things don't."

"Precisely. It's only crazy people who can."

"Paranoids," she said. "Egotists. Schizophrenics. Too much sense." She looked at me funny.

"Enlightenment. A big fan of enlightenment was my brother. My drowned brother."

She looked up. "Oh, Trev, I'm sorry."

"For what? Did I tell you about the drug?"

"You saw the future."

"No, I saw beneath. I felt as if it made sense of things. Then I lost even *that* crazy feeling."

"What's this got to do with you leaving? You're not going out there to make sense. You want to see her. She might be there."

"I want to see beneath everything," I said. I lifted the bottom of her blouse and exposed the bottom of her white brassiere. She had beautiful breasts. She slapped my hand and then held it to her beautiful breast.

"I want to find out what these guys, the city fathers, are doing out there. They're the ones who run everything. Remember?"

"I remember walnuts and port. I don't think her boyfriend's father runs criminal things anymore, not since Prohibition ended. I think he has a little pull in the harbor."

The line about the boyfriend hurt. It was supposed to. "Well that's the point. The harbor. And there's Storke, and there's the guy who sells popcorn down by the pier."

"Don't laugh, he's sweet."

"So are you, to worry about me."

"I'm going to sit here and worry the whole time," she said, tucking up into an untouchable lump.

"Stop worrying about her at least."

"Listen, mister, I'll worry about whomever I choose." She rolled over and held my face hard in her strong hand. "I heard you walk down the hall to her room last night. I felt you open her door. Empty as it is, it's probably got some ghosts for you." She teared up, which floored me. "I should have never invited you here. I felt, I still feel, what was left of her in you."

I wanted to stay but I got up from the small, soft bed. I was angry at my inability to pretend sorrow or comfort. She was right, there was still something left in that house and in me. Making sense of everything was all I wanted.

"You knew it was a doomed thing. June. She is a doomed thing."

"Nice to have sympathy," I said.

She laughed as she cried. "I didn't say I wasn't sorry. I didn't say 'I told you so' either. That has to count for something."

She got up and ruffled my hair.

"Why with that baboon?" I asked.

"Oh, baby, it was always about him."

"She convinced me otherwise. June was very convincing."

"Spare me the details or don't talk to me about being unsympathetic. I don't think she did it on purpose. Probably one of those unconscious things. You know, Sigmund Freud stuff."

"She's gone forever. She was never here," I said after a silence. "I was never hers."

"Oh come on, don't be so hard on yourself. There was a big problem, an insurmountable problem."

"In the eyes of the world, she's my cousin."

"What other eyes are there?" she said, and after a long pause, "I told you so."

We laughed and wrestled and by now darkness had worked its way into the room. I didn't go right away. But when I left she cried again and I really wasn't used to that.

Chapter 42

Patrick awoke in the domed chamber where Eve Marie had brought him the night before. He looked up through the glass at a pod of whales perhaps eight leagues away and nearer a melodramatic bat-flapping manta, quite common in these waters in early winter. He regarded the blue world so hostile to humanity and remembered there was less need to worry about dangerous elements ever again. Immortality.

He knew he should be overjoyed at that thought, but the idea of not dying was surprisingly abstract. He would not die. How long from now will that matter? How long from now, he mouthed the phrase aloud. Why is time always measured as distance? A far-off event, a short day. Everything could just happen now and consequences would disappear into endless days.

Like most people, he had avoided thoughts of death, created elaborate entertainments to distract himself from it. Death was a blank wall. Now he couldn't get it out of his mind. Suddenly he was face to face with the puff of smoke behind all vanities.

He got out of bed to walk off his nervousness. Last night's bath with Eve Marie had soothed him, but the effects had worn off. He needed to talk to the old man, someone who had been though this all ready. He wanted to ask him about life without end. Where had the old man gone? Patrick lay back down and felt a surge of anger— why had he not been consulted before his plunge into eternity?

Eve Marie entered the room, peeking and tiptoeing. "I'm awake," he said, surprised at strength of his own voice.

"You slept a very long time."

"Nonsense." He stretched and stood up. She touched him. He looked at her lips and wondered what kissing them again would be like. How far would Eve Marie and he go next time? She read his look and said, "Not now, we must go."

She dragged him down hallways; his legs were wobbly. At their destination, she pushed a button and a hatch in a wall sprang open and a wind rich with brine and sea-death smells blew across their faces. An Elayawun officer squeezed through the opening; he was wearing a comical white cap with long black ribbons. Behind him, another officer, stern and with a bumper crop of whiskers on his face, emerged and motioned for them to follow. The two officers led the way.

On the beach back home, the one from which Patrick and the old man had departed, the wind turned colder. Blue sky—blue like a distillation of space into time—passed through the white-tipped waves and merged with deeper blues at the horizon. As Patrick walked through the city that was his new home for eternity, he tried to imagine being back home with the mortals. He looked up at the dome, the sea moving ceaselessly over its surface. Beyond that, the sun wandered in gold patches through the blue like a spotlight on all emptiness.

Chapter 43

WHEN THE HIGHWAY BECAME the freeway across this Golden State, it still wasn't free here, because Pearlie wouldn't let them build an elevated highway, and the water table wouldn't allow them to go low with plows and concrete. Progress bowed to red lights, which also bisected downtown roads heading to the ocean side. I dreamed that night I was in my car waiting for those lights to change, when I saw Uncle Frankie walk up to the car. "Don't go out there," he said, leaning into the window. "The sea is dangerous." Then he turned and disappeared into the night as the light turned green. I got out but couldn't see him; people behind began honking. From my car, a choral dirge on the classical station bloomed, and I got back in and sped off.

In the rearview mirror, though, I saw nothing. The city was gone. I pulled a squealing U-turn and headed back into emptiness. I decided to go to Jimmy's and have a drink, finding it suddenly on an empty road. I pushed open the door and the smells of oil, broccoli, and soy sauce were gone. There was a fugging hot-dog machine on the bar. I was about to ask my friend the bartender what was up when I realized he was a stranger. I looked around the room. The familiar tacky red booths and worn tables were filled with people I didn't know. "Is Sun Lee here?" I asked. "Who's that?" the bartender asked. The room reeled. The usual clump of blue-collar guys telling dirty jokes by the cash register was now a trio of women passing a martini olive on a little silver sword among them. They tittered. One of them winked. It was hideous. I went to my usual booth, where I found some couple making out. The young guy broke off his smeary kiss and asked if I had a problem. "No," I said. Then I said, "Yes. Where is everybody I know?" "I'm here, baby," said one of the three hags. Meanwhile the barkeep, hand firmly on my shoulder, said, "I think it's time you take it outside," and pushed me out onto Canon Perdido. I fell and scraped my hands. A cop was driving by so I ducked into the alley behind the big Art Deco post office. Leaning up against the wall I could finally see that place as it had been: I was standing inside invisible walls of a Spanish presidio built on top of a ransacked village built by a doomed prehistoric people. Underneath my feet were the cannon balls used to subdue and the skulls by them subdone. Soon the place would become a replica of the cruel fortress, recreated as entertainment. "Drunk so early?" said my Uncle Francis, weaving out of the darkness.

"I've been looking for you everywhere. You disappeared."

"Everybody does, Nephew." He laughed.

"Wait. Tell me your poem."

"Toward the sea, its gray sides lean with many a scar and hollowed cave, as if some secret were between its stony heart and Ocean's wave." He stopped and motioned over his shoulder. "Hah. I've got a girlfriend I sometimes see. She was busy." He looked heartbroken for a second, then a wave of happiness washed over him. "But her sister was in."

"Frankie, why did my dad leave the Navy?"

"You know the answer to this."

"Tell me the real reason."

"Don't bother me with history," he said, looking around. "Actually it was you."

Chapter 44

The interview began without fanfare in a vast room. Patrick sat alone at a table facing three Elayawun councilors. They asked Eve Marie if all was in order. She looked distraught but answered yes. The process began.

"What do you want to know?" Patrick asked.

"You were brought here for a number of reasons," said one of the councilors, "some of which are now not clear even to us. For instance, you seem to object to our gift. That's relevant. But first we want to ask you a few simple questions. Then we want to show you something. Then, we hope you can answer a more difficult question. Does that suit you? Are you hungry? Our food and drink are strange to you, no doubt, but they are quite delicious. Your father enjoyed them."

Attendants brought in dishes that looked like seaweed. Patrick picked up a drink and looked at Eve Marie. "Don't worry," she said. "A mild stimulant, like your tea." He wanted to trust her and drank deeply. He hoped it was soothing like the bath. The food was subtle and delicious. He finished and wiped his mouth on scratchy seaweed paper.

"What can you tell us about Castle Rock?" asked the second councilor.

"The old landmark? It's gone. Castle Rock was destroyed to make space for a harbor," Patrick said.

The councilors stared as if they didn't understand.

"A harbor is a construction that creates an artificial bay, a place where boats can tie up, sheltered from elements like wind and waves."

"We know what it is. Why couldn't you build this harbor somewhere else?"

"It was convenient, near town. Humans believe it is our responsibility to improve the world, to use it to our best advantage. The harbor was for shelter."

"It's for pleasure craft," said one councilor, sighing. He told Patrick that sand had recently been building up around the dome. The Elayawun couldn't remove it fast enough. This troubling development began soon after the seawall construction had caused a shift in the coastal profile, which threw off ocean currents. Change made in ever-widening consequences by human agency.

"Who was Hazel?" asked another councilor. "This is a more important question."

"Hazel?"

"Yes, the person memorialized on the large platform that you built."

Patrick realized they meant the oil platform. His father had hated the thing.

"It's a name, maybe the child or wife of the man who owns the company that built it. I never asked. I worked on its design, but I never named it."

"We know, the old man told us all of this. Hazel takes oil out of the deep places of the earth beneath the sea. Right?"

"Yes."

"It causes the seabed to shake and explode."

"Preposterous," said Patrick. "It's taking crude oil from a vast pool.

It will never cause earthquakes or explosions. The geologists are sure of that."

The councilor, visibly upset, conferred with his colleagues in whispers. "Most of us knew you would say that."

"The people who built this dome probably made as many changes to the seafloor as we did building a harbor and an oil rig," Patrick said.

"How dare you," said one of the councilors, who got up to leave the table but stopped to address his colleagues. "I told you, the young people are wrong. He is the problem, not the solution."

"You have young people?" asked Patrick.

"Never mind," said the angry councilor, sitting back down. "We understand there are bombs built to search for oil. Not to drill with but dropped randomly to assist radar exploration of the underseas."

"Is that another question?"

"No. We are finished asking about the world above," said another councilor, trying to be polite and glaring at his angry peer. "Please come help us with another problem."

The three councilors escorted Eve Marie and Patrick into a room with a window that looked out at the sea. The doctor who had examined Patrick when he arrived in the city was also there. On a table, under a white sheet, lay the body of an Elayawun. He was dead.

"How did this happen?" Patrick asked. "I thought you were immortal."

"We brought you here to help us understand that," said the doctor.

Patrick flipped the sheet back and forth. "No sign of trauma," he said, parroting police dramas from movies. He wondered if the Elayawun knew about cinema or television.

"No," said the doctor.

"Then?"

Impatient, the doctor said, "This man was what you would call a scientist. He drowned."

"Here?" Patrick said.

The doctor wandered over to the window and looked out. "Out there, tied to the outside wall with kelp strands, presumably by merpeople. There was a grotesque smile on his face."

No smile now. The flesh on the Elayawun's face looked papery, like an old manuscript. Patrick could see sharp teeth. He shuddered. "You think merpeople did this?"

"Of course not," the doctor said out loud. "They cannot leave off breathing water long enough to grab a person inside the dome. They drown in air." He reverted to his inner voice. "There are caves at the edge of the dome with pools that connect to the ocean. The launching place for the underwater vehicle you came in. He went there often, alone. He worked there."

"How can I help?"

"He killed himself. We want to know why an immortal would consider it. We made you immortal so you could look at the issue from both sides, as it were, and tell us why such a thing might occur."

"Humans do it out of desperation, to obtain peace, to escape troubles and pain."

"Of course, we know that. But to an immortal, well, most problems go away. Mortals have no time to outlive their difficulties."

Patrick couldn't imagine such a state. "I don't think I've had enough time to see from your perspective," he said.

"Let's try another approach," said the doctor. "We want to know why you object to our gift. Perhaps your explanation will supply an answer."

"It sounds strange," said Patrick, "but you didn't really give me immortality as a gift. You took death away from me."

"You imply that death offers consolation, even though Eve Marie says you don't believe in an afterlife."

"Or God," said Patrick. "But I've always identified myself as mortal."

"Indeed," said the councilor who had threatened to leave. "I warned everyone that this stranger offers no insight; he only confuses us more. This will end in tragedy," he said. "Remember. Where we came from is where we are going."

He left the room.

The tall councilor sighed and turned to Patrick. "People here in Leemoo, or, as your father called it, Neverknown, are afraid of you humans."

Patrick stood there at the bottom of the ocean, without words in his head, wondering why eternal life felt like such a burden.

Chapter 45

WHEN I GOT HOME to my empty apartment the night after I had said good-bye to Mary Annie, and before I had the disappearing dream, I was ready to crawl the walls. I had another drink and another drink. Then, I had two more and turned on the radio to hear classical music to slow my mind down. I sat in the chair and stared out of the sooty windows. I could no longer remember the feeling of the drug, but I wanted it back, wanted the indifference to my own mortality back.

I woke up from the dream dry, gaggy, and still nervous. It was eight thirty. The bread truck went by with its long, low whistle. Outside, men were walking with their gunmetal-gray lunchboxes to work, escaping hangover nightmares too. The dream was a virus spreading, I thought. Nutso, right?

The phone rang. Somebody wanted Fred. I said no Fred and the voice sighed in resignation. I turned on the radio and listened to the local historian Walker Tompkins tell Old Santa Barbara stories. One was about a tidal wave that took a ship halfway up Refugio Road. The people on board survived. The TMS in radio station KTMS stood for Thomas M. Storke; those were Storke's waves, broadcast from his tower.

I went out and stole my landlady's newspaper. There was nothing in it about either Jacques Brown dead or June not gone to Hawaii, but there was a piece about the end of the hobo jungle. A letter to the editor wondered where the graceful manners of the past had fled. Suddenly, I became aware of a welling (not hallucinogenic) truth.

It was Uncle Dick.

I was sure of it. He had had me beaten up to keep me from writing about Snake Jake, to buy time so his cronies, maybe even Storke, could plan the presidio, the history amusement park. They could clear the hobo jungle and make it a zoo too. People would come and buy Dick's little ticky-tack houses then. He had Storke on his side, or Storke had him. And Pearlie, that goes without saying. She probably told the thugs I was coming. Wait. I had seen her that day. She called and warned Dick I was coming to the Mesa.

I took a shower and a long time over my toilet, as the English say. My thoughts made more and more sense the more and more I toileted. Dick's culpability was clear. I needed to reconnoiter his home. I needed to gather information. At the same time, I could also find out where his adopted daughter lies, and with whom—a convenient convergence. Then tomorrow, I would go with Icaro and stop the island meeting, or whatever it was, from happening.

After brushing my unkempt hair fifty times, I reached for the phone. I rang up a number and hung up. Then, as an experiment, I did it again. The sounds were identical. But a breeze from behind filled my sails and pushed me forward. I rang the number again.

"Hello," said Helen on the first ring.

"Hi Auntie," I said, gulping. "My mom left a bowl at your place."

"She did? My word, I don't remember it."

"Can I come by this morning? I have to take my car back to the mechanic."

"Oh, Trevor, buy yourself something that works." It chilled me a bit, mother-daughter déjà vu. "But heavens, yes, stop by dear," she said with a carefree air, suspecting nothing. Why should she?

The day was bright, but cold. I went outside and counted my steps to the path then retreated the equal number back to my door, noting glumly that I was not in the exact spot from where I started. I opened the door and went inside to find a corduroy sports coat and put it on over my sweater and long-sleeved shirt with six buttons down the front and one on each sleeve. Some of my shirts have two. I drove three point five miles, humming *"Volare,"* over and over, starting at the part I like each time. *"Nel blu dipinto di blu."* It's something that works, I thought. The blue painted blue. As punishment for my lie, the fugging car ran rough.

Dick's car was not in front of the house when I got there and that made me relax. Aunt Helen met me at the door with flour on her hands, for which she apologized, planting a kiss on my cheek. I walked in the house, the same one June and I exited four days ago. All my pleasures were ahead of me then. The anticipated joy was gone now, as if it had never happened—nothing tasted, smelled, touched, seen, or heard. Five senses and five wounds on our lord Jacques, the stigmatic—Pearlie told me that. Right over there, down the hall.

"I didn't find the bowl, honey," said Helen, with a suspicious note. "Dick tells me you went to a Knight's meeting."

She ushered me into the kitchen and sat me down. Before I could reply, she had an electric percolator of coffee tipping its bitter dregs into a bone-china cup. She fumbled with the Naugahyde-covered box that contained her Salems. She offered me one, which, of course, I refused. I mumbled thanks and pushed a tiny spoon into a china bowl of white sugar. I poured white cream into the murky brew and watched in vain for it to curl up into clouds. An ugly sulphur smell came from the match she held to her filtered smoke, and more clouds went up.

"It's kind of strong, dear," she said, nodding at the coffee. "How are you doing?"

A grocery-store cinnamon roll and a stick of margarine soon joined the concentrated Folgers, and before long I was chattering like a chimpanzee on payday. I told her about my balking research into the death of Jacques Brown. She said she didn't know him, but that Dick did. I hoped she would expand. She drifted into some Sodality of the Virgin Mary intrigue involving flowers that used to grow in the mission cemetery. I was going a little cross-eyed from the story when I blurted out what was on my mind.

"I called June's house, but she wasn't home. Maybe she's the one who has Mom's bowl."

"What?" asked Aunt Helen.

"Do you know where June is?" My right knee was bobbing up and down on its own authority. "I tried to call her and she never answers."

"I think she's just gone out to the islands," she said. "Lord knows, she's a big girl now and doesn't have to tell me anything." Her voice could barely contain the resentment.

"The islands?"

"A camping trip to Santa Cruz with some girlfriends from her school. Well, that's what she told me. I don't think it was such a good idea."

"Auntie, what are you talking about?"

"I'm embarrassed."

I said nothing; the old fool didn't need my prodding. "She's dating that Italian boy, the one whose father owns the liquor business."

"Yeah, so? I knew him at my school. He was all right."

"I think June went out there with him," she said, and looked at me hard. "You're not telling me something."

"I'm not?" I laughed, putting up a non-convincing front.

"You're nervous, Trevor, and don't say it's the coffee. There's talk in this family you know," she said leaning forward. Now, I was uncomfortable.

"What kind of talk, Auntie?" I said, trying to be gay.

"You two were sweet on each other when you were children. Don't, now, Trevor. Everybody noticed. My June used to write your name over and over in the margins of her notebook and then tear out the page and fold in tiny pieces and hide it in her Pee-Chee."

"Didn't hide it that good."

"Well, Trevor. Didn't hide it that well."

My aunt was correcting me like a schoolkid. "I had to look closely at everything she did, Trevor. Especially after you, well, after you … "

"After I what?" I said, looking at my reflection in the smooth, aerodynamic curve of the chrome percolator. I looked flush. I looked suspicious.

She said nothing and went to the sink. "It's not right, Trevor. You know, Dick is awfully upset about it. He's mad at you. And, let's face it, it isn't right."

"I don't understand. Even if what you are saying is true, it's not wrong. I mean it wouldn't be wrong, technically."

She looked at me. "What are you saying?" she asked. "Technically?"

"I'm saying that she's not really my cousin."

"Where did you get an idea like that, child?" she asked, a horrified look in her eyes.

"Is my cousin really my cousin?" I asked. "I mean she's like family. I've known her since she was practically a baby. But it's not real. I mean … "

"What on earth?" she asked. "Are you talking about my June, honey?"

"She's not really my cousin."

"What on earth would make you keep saying that? Trevor, I am beginning to worry about you. Your mother said everything was going well, but … "

"Oh, come on, Aunt Helen. Everybody in this family knows that June was adopted." I was beginning to get angry.

"Is that what you think, Trevor? No. You have it all wrong, honey. Oh, I can't believe you're saying this. Listen, Trevor, dear, tell me again what it is that everybody knows."

"It's embarrassing."

"Go ahead."

"You and Dick couldn't have children, and you adopted June. Hell, I remember when she came home from the orphanage; we had a party. You can't tell me that my parents didn't have a party. I was there."

"Of course you were there, Trevor. Oh, God, I don't know what to say." She looked out the window. "I think I should just tell you the truth, dear."

She was crying now, and I had a terrible hollow feeling. I was about to learn the truth. It was never the good thing that people say it is. "We put June up for adoption in the Catholic orphanage when Dick and I were first married. We were broke, and Dick wouldn't take money from your parents, even though they insisted. It made your father furious. Before his land deals and his job with Schlumberger, Dick was broke and he was proud, a proud man. It was the hardest thing we ever did in our life."

I looked over at her. I felt like I was watching myself listen to her. "You put her in the orphanage?" I said.

"I know. It seems unbelievably cruel now. People did it though, during the Depression lots of parents did it. This was the war time and Dick couldn't go, flat feet, and construction jobs were scarce up here. Maybe you can understand why we don't talk about it." She seemed to be sobbing, her back to me.

Then she turned around, and smiled. It was grotesque. "But it was less than a year. Dick got work and sold that old ranch he owned in

Ojai. And we went to get our June. We had the big party. That's what you remember. I think you were only four. June was never the same girl, but she was our girl. You know what I mean? She was our girl, and she is every bit your cousin."

"*You* put her in the orphanage?"

Chapter 46

Light filtered down through the kelp, wavered like a candle, flickered through clouds of vegetable detritus and small life floating through pulsing waters.

Patrick walked early each day. His laces always came untied halfway through the walk. Why? He went deep into the heart of the city, where he saw abstract statuary he could not decode and undersea gardens that seemed oddly familiar. One day, he found the city's power plant, an ovoid construction that hummed like bass-note bees. Its fuel was a glowing unstable element that emanated waves of heat insulated in a thin compound of iced inorganics layered over lead lodged deep in the center of the egg. Or so the doctor said.

He loved the city's ornate gates and walls of alternating white-and-black rock smooth-cut into brick shapes, the towers with bridges arching between them, made of different stones quarried from moats and covered with brass, tin, and orichalcum. On one of his walks, he found a room behind a partially obstructed entrance. Squeezing through he saw wells and tanks that held merpeople swimming in sea-water. He left quickly.

The councilors wanted him back now. He worried. What more could he tell them? Maybe he should make something up?

Meanwhile Eve Marie had grown distant. Not since their stolen kiss, which seemed dreamlike to him now, had they shared words.

His skin was getting dry again. He felt sure another bath would help. He yearned for its calming effect—his brain was running nervous. One morning after his walk, he asked Eve Marie if they could bathe again.

"Out of the question," she said with her voice, then changed the subject. She asked what he would tell the councilors. "Will you speak of me?" she said.

"Is the bath part of becoming immortal?" he asked.

She nodded but could not look at him. "No," she said, changing her mind. "It's escape for us."

"For you perfect immortals? Was our kiss part of the process or the escape?"

"I wish you would not talk about it out loud."

"Why? Are you ashamed?"

"Worse. Such things are not allowed."

"Love is not allowed."

"The quaintest word. We wonder why you still use it, after all your wars. Your father used it about your mother. And you."

"He spoke of me when he was here?"

Eve Marie shrugged. "Of your birth. Immortality precludes any urge to reproduction. It would overcrowd us."

"Your rulers preclude it. Your desire for me proves that."

"My desire," she repeated with scorn. "It was curiosity, not love."

"When will we completely satisfy your curiosity?" He was trying to be cruel now.

"Why not right now?" she said, calling his bluff.

"Why not," he replied.

She hurried him along a corridor and into her private chamber. There were no portholes or glass walls—the merpeople could not see. She locked the heavy door. This was happening now, he thought. I live here now.

They kissed and the moments blurred out. Skin to skin, belly to belly, it was electrifying. Her skin was stippled but soft, his was easily brought to climax. Afterward, they kissed for ages. Then he realized that living forever could aid a patient man. They dressed to leave.

On their way to the interview, Patrick asked Eve Marie if the Elayawun had children.

"Some people cheat," she answered. "But they are ostracized. It isn't good."

He wanted to know if the two of them could have children, but he left it as a psychic hanging question she could choose to answer. She didn't. Instead, she broke into his thoughts and said, "Listen, I'm pretty sure they plan to kill you today."

Chapter 47

THE OLD CAB HONKED at my apartment. Some brown birds fled up from the icy dew on the crabgrass. I pulled the door shut softly, though I left no one behind. A relic from prewar dinosaur packs that roamed the earth, yellow with black checkers and running boards, the bulky cab made my Packard, useless in the driveway, seem modern. I got in and said, "The harbor." He looked plaintive in the mirror, hoping for more fare and more exotic destinations, but pulled onto the empty streets of the sleeping town.

I got out near the weedy parking lot where ocean smells greet the nose: dead fish and brine of fermenting seaweed, perfume for the traveler. The back of my neck prickled. Heading into the first marina, I saw Icaro's large form bending over a small sailboat, fooling with an outboard motor, mixing oil and gasoline, pulling on a rope to get it going.

"What is this?" I asked. "We can't cross the channel in this dinky thing."

He looked at me with dismay, measuring me against some private standard of heroism.

"It will be perfect," he said. "Long as we get out there before Windy Lane kicks up."

He meant the weather conditions that ruled the channel waters each afternoon, roiling calm seas until dinnertime. Moving aside a gray-green rag, Icaro pointed to the outboard motor—"This is our teeket." He smiled and it was the first time I noticed missing teeth; his accent seemed stronger too.

"Get in," he said. "The rosy fingers of the dawn and all that crap."

I smiled and ran my tongue over the tops of my teeth. Sympathetic. One was rough and hurt sometimes when cold touched it. Immediately Icaro pulled the motor's cord and a percussive banging started deep in its battered heart. A gull flew off the top of the jetty.

He smiled again and said, "We don't have any seatbelts to fasten, but you better put on a fugging life vest if you know what's good for you. I won't laugh." He pointed under the slat of seat.

My feet were already wet from water slopping around inside the hull. I remembered Mary Annie's fragrant body back in her bed not long ago, wishing me to stay. Why was I going? I wondered as we pulled away from the huddle of boats and toward open water. Nobody seemed to notice our passing. This journey begins without witnesses, I thought. How will it end? Nobody else in the world seemed alive.

The seas were calm, with nothing to remind us of the recent rogue waves. Icaro pointed to a fog bank far out on the ocean and grunted. When I asked him if it could be a problem, he gave a more stoic grunt. Strong muscles bulged beneath the striped shirt as he settled into the stern, steering and scowling. "I haven't heard from your father for a long while," said Icaro.

"I don't know where he is either. I tried to call him but the phone just rang." We cleared the breakwater and Stearns Wharf. The open ocean waited. The islands never seemed far away in winter, but I knew it was an illusion and that fifteen miles of sea stretched ahead.

"That must mean your mother is missing too," he said, chewing on the silence before bringing up this chunk of dark.

"Missing?" I said.

"Wouldn't they stay in touch with you, their only son?"

"I'd like to think they would, but you know my dad." I think I was trying to set some kind of trap, but sullen Icaro did not nibble the bait.

Out of the water some two hundred yards away a giant thing flapped. I looked at the spot with fear.

"Devil fish," he said.

"Oh, that's a relief. I thought it was something scary."

"It could've hit the boat easily if it was mad at us."

The sky had an iridescent quality after I looked up from the blue sea. The engine kept us moving forward, and I could see the islands as a huddle of indistinguishable blobs. In about half an hour we would see them apart. An hour later, Santa Cruz would loom over us. I wondered what I was doing here and now; it is always now.

"There iss food onder the seat," said Icaro. "I made red feesh eggs on cream cheese, it wass your father's favorite."

I mulled that, and this new, heavy accent was antagonizing. But I was hungry and the ocean already put the smell of sea life in my nose and a craving inside. The roe tasted lovely, salt in my mouth like the bite of sea air. I found a Hires root beer too.

"Why do *you* think they've gone missing?" I asked.

"Because I had a postcard fraum theym." He chuckled low in his throat. "Your fawthair went to New Mexico. A conference. He wass supposed to call me when he returned, but nowthing so far."

Seasickness is vertigo. The world, which is supposed to be solid, turns into waves, and each wave is relative to the other. I was feeling vertigo. I'd never been seasick before.

"Your father saw this coming," said Icaro, suddenly making with the perfect diction. It occurred to me that he could read my mind. "He said you might want to go out there; he trusted it would happen. Yes,

I see the wonder in your eyes. Listen, I need you to go into the galley and grab me a bottle. There's rye whiskey and ouzo down there. Bring up the rye."

"Whose boat is this?" I asked.

"I'm not sure," said the laconic Greek. "I've had my eye on it for months. I bet it's one of those fugging rich people who use it for trysts."

"What?" I said.

"For fugging somebody else's wife, maybe." He leered at me to transport the import. And I got it.

"The state senator."

He looked at me solemnly. "Your father is right, you are pretty good. Go below. I want a drink."

That was where six-inch Gin Chow made himself known to me. My therapist had told me this was all quite usual—though often such friends tended to disappear approaching the age of reason. From a corner of a cabinet, Gin Chow waved with a chagrined look, as if embarrassed. I wasn't surprised. His appearances have always coincided with some real or imagined need. And right then, I needed guidance. My father, as well as Uncle Dick, might be behind all these mysteries, I thought, and I wondered what that thought even meant. It was as if I was watching and listening to myself, but with great difficulty hearing.

Miniscule Gin Chow jumped onto the table in the galley. He stood next to a box, elaborately carved with fairy-story motifs, on top of which lay a woodsman's knife. Gin Chow gave me a brisk salute and a look that implied he would be available whenever. I saw the bottle of rye, grabbed it, and was heading back when the boat lurched and I almost took a spill.

Coming on deck, I noted a concerned look on Icaro's face, which disappeared when he saw the whiskey. He reached his great paw out and took the bottle.

"Hear you have a new girlfriend," he said.

"Look, my father made me apologize to you because he said you were looking after me. But I'm getting mad again."

"Then it isn't true," he said. "Too bad."

"How do you know these things?"

"Then it is true," he laughed. "You see? This is how a real detective works. He has no need to investigate. He simply knows rhetorical tricks. Besides, it's a small fugging town. People talk."

I was getting angrier, about to take some of the whiskey myself, though I felt that was what Icaro intended. I was playing into some scheme.

"This cozen ees not good for you," he said.

"What? What cousin?"

"The children would be monsters," he said. Melodramatically, as if on cue, the engine sputtered and died. Icaro cursed with the depth and solemnity only a Greek could muster.

"What the hell?" I said.

"Always like this," he said. He yanked and cursed for five minutes. Then the engine started and ran for maybe another fifteen minutes before it sputtered and died for good. By then we were surrounded by deep fog above the plain of water. It was the nothingness. I sat there feeling like a visit below was in order. I felt that all of this was transpiring according to somebody's crap plan that was devised for me.

I went below, where Gin Chow counseled patience but seemed abysmally sad. He said it was too bad about June. I asked him what was. As I came back up, I saw that Icaro had hoisted the sail.

"Eventually we will sail, but not for a while."

"What's keeping us?" I asked through clenched teeth.

He gestured up into the slack, pure-white canvas hanging from a kind of cross. "Wind. You must have wind to sail."

"Can't you fix the engine? Can't we row?"

"You are in a hurry," he said. "Sometime after noon, you will want to not be going so fast."

"Is this a famous philosophical paradox?"

"No, a simple fact. The seas blow hard out in Windy Lane every day after 1:00 p.m."

It seemed iffy to me, predicting weather like that. But I let it go and stretched out on the long bench in the back of the ship. I must have fallen asleep because when I looked up a great deal of the whiskey was gone. Icaro was speaking, maybe to himself, muttering in a slurred voice.

"Tell me about your cozen," he said. "I hear she is a doll, *to kukla mu*," he said. The tone and the booze breath turned my stomach. I got slowly up and stretched my limbs, but lost my balance. Icaro was over in a second grabbing me.

"Leave me alone," I said, wondering how a drunk could be so steady, and I such a clumsy fool.

"Fug you and go below. Another fugging ingrate Westin to deal with. *Ach, mon amu*." He motioned me across the boat, which rode on seas so calm they could have been made of gelatin. I asked again about the motor and he waved me away. I went to the side where he had beckoned. I slumped low, and he swung out on the boom to catch a wind that wasn't there.

"It won't take long," he said. "We're pretty far out."

"Out in Windy Lane," I said.

"Out as far as the big ships travel. You know, the ones that won't be able to see us." He looked a cockeyed glance through the fog toward Santa Cruz, which was floating on the dim horizon like a flattened disk. "What do you hope to learn out there? Some kind of mystery about this man Brown?"

"Don't be coy. You know everything."

Icaro was silent for a second and then smacked his lips. "I knew Brown a long time. Not just his wife. Only, his name back then was Jordan Brown."

"How many names does one man need?"

"Well, who knows? What's in a name? Jordan Brown, sometimes initial J. Brown, maybe J-a-y Brown, but Jake to you, when you knew him. And he would still smell as sweet anyways."

"I didn't know him."

"Right," said Icaro and crossed his eyes like a goof. "If you say so. But when you knew him he was the best Scout on land or sea. Higher than an Eagle Scout. Even then he was like a philosopher, though, fascinated by this Einstein, this especial theory of relativity."

"Special theory of relativity. You can stop playing big dumb Greek whenever you want. It's wearing thin."

He flipped me off and I guess I deserved it. "Order of the Arrow," he said. "That was before the accident, when he got disgraced and kicked out. Later, he went away to school and studied Einstein; he studied *with* Einstein at Princeton, went for long walks with him. And he went crazy trying to write his thesis based on the space-time continuum."

"There's no such thing as time," I murmured.

"Well, it's getting near our magic time," he said, taking out a silver pocket watch chained to his waist.

"I'm going below."

"A very good idea."

I went inside and down. I knew I couldn't hide and that some revelation was at hand. But I wanted to hide. I was afraid of it. But I shook my head hard against the cowardice and stuck it out of the hatch into

the fresh air and saw Icaro at the tiller. "How was Brown disgraced?"
I asked.

He looked surprised, and then thoughtful. "Shit. Maybe you really
do not know. Ask your parents."

"What?"

"Maybe your father never mentioned him to you because he hated
Brown. He got so mad at Miss Chase for hiring him. They fought. I
thought this was the point of your mania."

"My father never hated anybody. And nobody says 'mania.'"

"Hah. He made an exception for Brown. You hate him too if you
think about it. Maybe you forgot to on purpose. Just think back. Brown
was in charge of you boys on Santa Cruz. He gave your brother permission to take the boat. 'Let me row there with Trevor,' Patrick told Jake
Brown. 'Paddle there. I will bring you back a fat abalone for dinner. I
am an expert oarsman.' They fired Brown. They drummed Jake out of
the brotherhood, the Order of the Fugging Arrow, for letting you two
go. He lost your father's son."

"They drummed Jake out of the brotherhood," I repeated. "Not
the Knights of Columbus, not the diving brotherhood. Jesus. Fugging
A. Jake Brown killed my brother. And I'm looking for Jake Brown's
killer."

I was reeling. The seas were surging too.

"What are you talking about, *malaka*? Don't be melodramatic.
Jason Jake said yes to Patrick. I heard it was hard to say no to Patrick.
They almost prosecuted him for it, too, but your father never pushed.
He was numb, like now, emotions gone. Instead, Jake Brown left town.
He went away to school. But he came home after fugging up college.
You should appreciate that. Relativity speaking. His parents bought
him a restaurant, and he gave me a job, and I told your father he was
here. So who cares?"

"Did you kill Snake Jake?" I said and then regretted it.

"Go the fug below. Your father should have let me murder Brown. I offered to." He paused. "Now you think I did it. Well, that's good. I like you to be afraid of me. Go the fug below. The seas are getting rough. I don't want you to go overboard."

I will go below, I thought, and ask Gin Chow to read this man for me. Perhaps Gin Chow could tell me, while he's at it, why *he* didn't tell me about Brown. But when I got there, the tiny sage was a gone, daddy-o, gone. I sat down. The room was moving faster relative to the seas I could see outside. Moving, not still. And I was getting queasier. I was also getting scared. Brown and Icaro and my dad; one dead, one talking without saying anything, and one dead inside. I didn't want to think or feel. I looked around for something to focus on, a book, the funny papers. I pulled out a copy of *Robert's Rules of Order* wedged under the stiff mattress. Some wet dream, I thought. Racy reading: meeting come to order. My brother was old business.

The hour was an hour past noon, and the ocean began to develop rhythmic properties. Seasick, I thought again; out here everything was relative to everything. I stood up and went to the bridge. Icaro was grinning with a nasty undercurrent. Booze.

"What?" He was talking loud like drunks always do. "You think you are doing detective work in Santa Barbara like your famous father? The one lesson he always heeded was the need for silence." His tone changed. "Brown's wife wants to sell you her secrets, by the way."

"How much? Are they worth anything?"

"Ten thousand dollars. I think you have that much easy, right?"

"Even if I did, I can't imagine what secrets she could sell me."

"Nothing. Besides, you need to consider that I already talked to her."

I looked at him and he smiled as a strong wind struck the sail, and we seemed to move instantly over the water, skimming. "Yes. She talked. She told me her story."

"Give," I said. "It'll pass the time. No wonder my father likes you. Hey wait, you knew him when he was a detective?"

"He hates me, and so will you someday," he said and paused. "I shook Brown's wife around a little bit. Does that shock you? I am my own man. Not his or yours."

A cloud passed overhead. The waves were rising. Winds tickled my face. "The secret is a lot more stupid than anyone could guess," he said. "Like always. Truths always ring false to the people looking too hard." He hiccupped and belched and broke wind. The actual wind was here now too, full force.

"You think, go to some party on Santa Cruz and everyone will be there," he said, free of accent. "The leisure class that comes to judge the quick and the dead. And you will find some sordid whiff of scandal or a mystical conspiracy to explain why some mediocre man came to be on the breakwater with Christ's wounds and no blood. Never worry that it might be the repressive state's apparatus grinding away again: another way to distract you from the real and only crime. You'll blame it on some abstraction like lust or greed, call it a sin with your Catholic school sentimentality, and then swim back home with the so-called story that you can pound out on your typewriter in block letters. I'll tell you the truth before we get to the island, but you won't like it, writer. Your truths add up too neatly. Nothing real in the universe does."

Far off there was a hollow boom. "What was that?" I asked, happy for a distraction but worried too. "What did you mean—swim back home?"

"It's the Japanese, back for another crack at Gaviota Beach." He laughed and threw the empty bottle into the drink. "Okay, it's the oil-men blasting the sea bottom to let loose all the petroleum dollars down there. Kills a lot of fish."

"I heard about this. Are we in any danger?" Brown, knocking at my door again.

"Always."

We were in Windy Lane now. The sea was changing, and I was riding on its haunting splendor. The morning calm had given way to a breeze and then to a rolling high sea. We were more than midway to the island, and the sea was at its most treacherous, fanned by winds that swarmed together like a gang of howling lost souls, Paolo and Francesca.

Icaro had lowered one sail and set another. He strutted around, cock of the walk, brought the sail all the way up, and off we flew. His muscles locked themselves in a battle for our survival, yet there was something beautiful in the struggle. First, the winds pushed and drove the boat, as the knots increased. We were going slower than a car crawls, but over the sea it was beyond exhilaration. Once felt, it was like a surrender to the sea and the wind; stop being afraid, I told myself, because surely we would be there in moments, like Hermes skipping on a northeast wind.

The world we were crossing had changed from a flat whale road to a boiling range of peaks and valleys. We moved slowly up crests like pointed hillocks and crashed down, with impossible last-minute upturns. I had no idea what prevented us from submerging. We were going faster and faster, and I was moving in that fine space between thrill and fear. As the waves hove their weight against us, and the little boat coaxed on, I had a vision: I saw myself on the deck, from some clear vantage point above the boat. All action had stopped, and I was looking at a frozen image, like the illustration in an adventure book. For a few minutes I was completely absorbed, looking at the image, locked outside of thought and hushed against its usual babbling. What I was thinking and what I was seeing and what I was doing were all the same thing.

A powerful wave breaking over the boat brought me back to

unfrozen images. We shot up and down the massive crests for fifteen minutes before my heart stopped pounding and I found my legs and a spar to hold. How Icaro knew which way we were heading was a mystery. He screamed at the sea. I looked at him, the wind whistling and keening around his syllables, rubbing the hard edges off his words. He was screaming over the wind that was howling like a banshee come for our souls. "You never thanked me for losing the pachuco's body, friend. For saving you."

"Of course I did, in the hospital. For saving me?"

"From the cops," he said.

"What cops?"

He never turned around; his eyes were on the wave troughs and towers. "The ones who would have charged you with murder. You never said what it felt like to kill that guy. Had to be your first, cherry boy. Maybe you're tougher than your ice-water dad."

I stumbled across the deck. "You're saying that he died?"

"Of course. Why do you think I ran off? I got rid of him good. Me and King." He licked his lips again. "I want that ouzo now."

"I never told you to do that," I said, realizing my hands had taken a life. "Fug. I can't live with this." But I knew that I could.

"What?" He turned around, as if awakening from a dream. His face was rigid. I spun around and almost lost my balance. Far down the channel was a giant ship moving our way.

"Oh no," said Icaro. "He'll never see us."

The ship seemed to be gaining on us faster now. I went down into the cabin, and there was Gin Chow. I sat on the bunk and asked him what to do. He shrugged. I don't know whose fault it is, I said. Me neither, he said.

"What am I supposed to do?"

"Why ask me?" he said. "Let's talk about the nature of time."

"It doesn't exist."

"All things come to those who wait. I feel your brother near."

"Shut up, Gin Chow."

He pulled a thimble out from somewhere and put it on his head and started dancing. "Go away, then."

I stood up and went out on deck. Icaro was still at the tiller. "I need you to relieve me," he said.

"I know nothing about sailing. What about the ship?"

"Don't worry. You don't need a compass; just point the boat at the island. I have to figure out what we will do about the ship. Maybe change course."

A large wave whooshed down on us hard. He looked worried, but handed me the tiller. "Try to make your adjustments slowly and gracefully." As soon as he walked away, my arm jerked, of course. He stumbled and I almost fell off the soggy bench. *"Gamo tis panagia,"* he said. I tried to think gracefully. He disappeared over the cabin to the prow. I had to admit that the island was getting closer. I jerked the rudder, heard a curse, and a wave splashed me straight in the face.

As my eyes cleared, I could see distant green on a hill behind a long pier. It was Santa Cruz. The last time I had been there was with my brother and the Scouts, pushing and shoving and eager to get on land. Patrick couldn't wait to see the cave again. It was all he talked about, to anybody who would listen.

Even though I always try to forget that day, I remember it well. My brother and I are in the little wooden rowboat. He has been there many times before, he tells me. Rowing, heaving at times, he takes us around the island. We row into the sea cave on the turning, outward tide. We never spoke to Brown; my brother just grabbed me and away we ran. We have those chunky, big Boy Scout flashlights the English call torches. The light is narrowing as the evening grows and the tide shrinks. Patrick rows me over to the rock ledge and says, wait here. I don't like the idea. I don't want you to go, I say. I have to show you the sign, he says, the one that no one can interpret.

The inside of the cave is painted with Indian pictographs. They think all of these signs have meanings, but this one has none, he says, handing me the boat's rope to hold. He smiles, stands up, and dives in. He emerges on the far side of the cave and says, mom would kill me if she saw me leave you there holding the boat. The frog, the turtle, the flounder, he points. They each mean something different, according to the Indian guides. Everything points to something else, infects it with meaning. The language is passed from ear to eye. There was a tower surrounded by waves. Nobody knows this, he says.

Say good-bye to mom and dad, he says. I can't hang on in a house like that. It's too silent for me. Remember the tide is turning, so it'll be easy for you to get out. Suddenly, a large wave rolls in and I go up high, near the cave's ceiling. He goes under and he doesn't come back.

After a while I came unfrozen and rowed out of the cave. I thought he would be on the beach not far outside the entrance, just playing, or come popping up beside the boat. We weren't supposed to have been in the cave, so at first I didn't know whether or not to call for help because we would get yelled at.

Then I realized I had forgotten to be a hero. I tried rowing back but the tide was going out. I could dive for him but something told me it was too late. I looked deep into the water and prayed and hoped I would see him in the green, the untransparent green. In my dreams for years afterwards, he came out of the green and asked me: What are you up to, squirt?

You know how you can forget everything in the hustle of getting ready for company? Cooking the meal, making the bed, cleaning up. I needed that kind of distraction right then, and Icaro provided it.

"I have bad news," he said.

"The ship?"

"Well, there is that, although I think we can avoid it if we tack back toward mainland."

"And the bad news?"

"The fog," he said.

Chapter 48

"Why would someone meant to live forever take his own life?" asked the chief councilor. The seven Elayawun who sat around one end of the table turned to Patrick. Outside a wide window in the room a group of merpeople had gathered as if attending a play. Their children wander alone in the sea, Patrick thought, in the quavering light on the seafloor, where rings of light like cells grown spectacularly large envelop them.

"Before we talk, I need to know what your plans are for me," Patrick said, considering Eve Marie's warning.

"What do you mean 'talk'? And what prompts such a question?" asked the chief councilor. "Aren't we taking good care of you?"

The merpeople waved at Patrick, alone at his end of the table. They seem to like me, he thought.

"The old man who brought me here never warned me about any of this. And where is he? He was a friend; I can't imagine him thinking this trial is okay. Why are you subjecting me to all this?"

"Trial? Subjecting you?" said one perturbed councilor. "We saved you."

The chief councilor raised his hand to halt the discussion. "We asked the old man to bring you here and then he left of his own accord to the other world. We brought you here because we hoped you might represent the same strain of wisdom possessed by a person we revered. Your father. He taught us something about humans. But perplexed us too. You know your father loved Homer, left us his works. But we laugh at the part where Odysseus refused Calypso's promises of immortality just to see his wife, son, and home. To die for something so sentimental is ridiculous."

"My father, my father," Patrick said. "Why is he so important?"

"He felt happy and safe here. It wasn't his to lose, he said, so it was perfect. He told us what the other world was doing, how those things might affect us. We offered to keep him here forever and he laughed at us," said the chief councilor.

"Who would turn his back on immortality?" asked one at the table.

"Someone who had thought it through," Patrick said. "Who considered the consequences of remaining still in a changing world. A sublime end might be better than survival. Who knows? Watching change happen without changing might make such a man go crazy."

The councilors fell silent but, Patrick realized, not because of his words. They all stared out the window. Patrick looked, expecting more of his waving fans. But the merfolk were gone. In their place floated the Elayawun doctor. He was dead and smiling, tied up in kelp. The councilors immediately ordered Eve Marie to take Patrick back to his room and confine him there.

On the walk back, a merman, out of breath but laughing, darted past them. He was naked and dripping water. Eve Marie grabbed Patrick with both arms. She made a hissing noise. The merman ran around the corner. Patrick and Eve Marie followed and saw the creature on the ground, being subdued by Elayawun. The authorities told Patrick and Eve Marie to leave at once. Every world offers unique sorrows, Patrick thought. All around him loomed the magnificent city, the heartbreaking castle in the waves.

Chapter 49

CARO GRAPPLED THE TILLER away from me. A massive curtain of fog had advanced toward us as we were being driven forth between land and island. At the same time, the ship coming up the channel loomed larger.

"Jesus," I said.

"The timing is going to be delicate. I think we need to go behind the ship," Icaro said, a steadier tone in his drunken voice. He began sweeping the sailboat away from Santa Cruz and back toward the mainland.

"We're going behind the ship?" I asked. "What about the wake?"

"I haff no idea," said Icaro, "but I would rather that than risk the big fugging thing running over us."

I wasn't so sure, but it was a cinch the ship did not see us. And we had no radio to contact it.

Or did we? I got up and went below. There against the wall was a set I hadn't noticed. I turned it on and an amber light lit.

"Help is on the way," I hollered.

"What are you messing with?" he asked. His voice was menacing.

"I found a radio, maybe we can contact the ship," I yelled.

Icaro began screaming and cursing. I ignored him and played with the radio. I was proud of my pluckishness. I found a large chromium microphone tucked around the back and started talking into it.

"No," bellowed Icaro.

Ignoring his stupidity, I fooled the dial around, saying things I knew from movies. "Mayday. Mayday." Then I added, "This is the … " but realized I didn't know the name of our boat, much less that of the ship bearing down on us.

I popped up on deck to ask Icaro the craft's designation. Livid, he let go of the rudder and pushed past me into the cabin. I could hear him ripping the microphone out of its wall socket. Then, I was slammed onto the deck as the boat rocked hard, as if it had tripped over something in the waves. We were going slower now, away from Santa Cruz with the wind in front of us. In the thickening fog I could barely make out the beaches at Carpinteria and platform Hazel, far off and south. Suddenly the boat dipped and I almost tumbled overboard.

"What the hell," I said as Icaro emerged from the cabin. "You fugging idiot."

"I told you not to use the radio. Listen to me the next time." He went back to the rudder, acting as if nothing had happened.

"Are you crazy? Maybe we could've hailed the ship."

"The argument is over," he said.

No matter how loud I screamed, Icaro sat there like adamantine, though his eyes furrowed sometimes, peering into the haze and looking for the gargantuan craft headed our way. The fog would soon cover us. If we're lucky, I thought, we would pass behind the big ship. But what about its massive, chewing propellers? I went into the cabin and looked at the cord and the radio. I turned the dial through fuzz, crackle, and pop. Sometimes a ghost voice would hover, as if the floating fog were whispering to us. Then the fog voice turned into music.

There was a faint melody. That song everybody was singing about the witch doctor, my friend the witch doctor. It went into your ears and never left—as infectious as disease. The notes soon turned into sea spray and wave hum. I screamed with frustration and wandered back out. I could see the wall of fog poised over us; we were running parallel to it and the ship was invisible on the other side. Icaro pointed into the fog. "This is it," he said. "I have a strong feeling this is it."

"The ship? Where? Will we run into it?"

"No we'll go around. The wake is going to be something, though. I don't think I'm going to make it this time." A terrifying blast of sound came out of the fog bank, and then the ship was on top of us.

"What's its name?" I cried.

"I can't read it."

I saw this magnificent thing come shimmering out of mist, passing silently alongside our boat. Icaro cursed and I looked up in fear. The ship was the most beautiful thing I had ever seen. Blue-gray steel walls curved in a massive wave up to sky. The distances from top to bottom and front to stern were enormous. It towered over every thought possible. Awe is a rare grace, even when it comes as a companion to doom.

"What can we do?" I asked.

"Get ready," said Icaro. He jammed the rudder hard, sending us away at an oblique angle from the passing ship. Our sails collapsed and we rose toward the gray sky in a violent incline. I screamed. We crested the top, then started down into the roiling wake. Water was pouring over us. I lost my grip on the rail and was about to go over just as Icaro grabbed my arm in a hold that left deep blue-black bruises for a week.

The boat went over and we were both thrown into the cold water. Then the sailboat was upright, and I saw Icaro clambering on board. He was breathing and bellowing out farts like a tuba. I laughed at the absurdity of it all. "Here, honey, here," he yelled.

His hand was on my life jacket and he hauled me over to the rail. "Climb in."

"Fug," I said.

"Shut up and start bailing," he said, throwing me a plastic container.

I was cold and wet, but I didn't feel it right away. We were heading somewhere without any visual reference, lost in fog, but alive. As I bailed, I turned to the man who had put me in danger and then saved my life. He looked at me and transmitted a mental message, which had a strange syntax: my father betrayed me, hence maybe my uncle too. I looked at him and he nodded slowly in a weird psychic assent.

"How betrayed?" I said out loud.

"Bail out the cabin," he said.

Down below it was sloshing back and forth. Gin Chow was laughing so hard I could almost hear him.

I poked my head back out. "How do you suggest I bail this?" I asked Icaro, but he was standing still and listening. I tried to ask him again, but he gestured at me; it was a hushing gesture. When I listened, I heard it.

"The ship is coming back," I said.

He turned around and looked at me. "I told you this would be my last day. I'm heading for the island. I don't think it's far. We could swim."

"What are you talking about?"

Sounds rose out of the fog's confusion. Voices raked over the rolling seas. A big motor sputtered. For minutes the noise hung behind in the mist, then began to close in on us.

"*Skata*," said Icaro. A loud voice over the motor sent his eyes rolling.

"Ahoy."

"We have to run," Icaro confided in me.

"Ahoy there sailboat," said a voice. "Are you the one who broadcast Mayday?"

A large white ship came out of the fog bank. "Ahoy sailboat."

"Here," I hollered.

"Shut your fugging mouth," said Icaro.

"What's the sailboat?" said a disembodied voice.

"I can barely make it out. Oh, yeah, the *Chuang Tzu Butterfly*," replied another.

"Gimme a break."

"That's it. Hey doesn't that belong to somebody?"

"It's likely," said a young cadet, now visible on deck. "Hey, you two, now I can see you. Don't you know there's a small craft advisory? You coming from the island?"

"Didn't hear anything about it," said Icaro, who seemed to be hiding his face. "I told you this would be bad," he muttered, more or less to me.

"Christ, that's a boat of note. I know it," said another voice from above.

"Say that fast twenty times," said the other voice, now gone invisible again.

We were drifting away. Icaro opened the sail to catch a wind.

"Ahoy *Butterfly*. Oh Jesus Christ here comes a wake."

"Whee," said the other voice from the Coast Guard cutter, which began to rise in the air as if it were hovering.

"Fugging A," said Icaro. "Let's go." We began to rise then too on a gigantic swell. Icaro turned us at the crest and we began surfing it. We rushed away from the cutter for a short time and then we were close to the island. Another wave caught us coming the other way but Icaro navigated it. For a second I thought I could see Santa Cruz, and then the fog closed back in.

"I'm sorry," Icaro said. "I can't help your father and not you either." He had the ornate box in his hand, the knife too. "I once saw a future where I am the loyal servant of the House of Westin. I will not do dirty work for either of you anymore."

"What is your problem?"

"I'm a fugging alien. The United States takes a dim view of us, no matter all I've done for them."

Aliens. Alien. All I could think of were movie monsters, the giant crab movie, but that wasn't about people from outer space. It was radiation and atom bombs and earth animals grown big. Come to think of it, the beach right across from us looked like a location from the movie. But why were we talking about science fiction? Then I realized what Icaro meant and why he meant the boat to be invisible. "Unregistered?" I called out.

"Go forward and see if you can secure the rope," he said, sounding as if he had resigned himself to something. "I don't think there is an anchor on this boat. Maybe there is. Don't take too long."

I did what he said but didn't really know what I was looking for. The extent of my sailing experience was on little seashell sailboats that the Sea Scouts used. Say that ten times fast, I thought. When I came back, Icaro was gone.

Chapter 50

Patrick was alone now. Eve Marie had stopped coming and he was no longer free to leave his room. There were guards at the door. He was incarcerated, plain and simple. And he wasn't sure why.

The guards told him his next meeting with the councilors was to take place soon. They would summon him early, at sunrise. Grim, he thought. Death row.

And indeed one morning, the guards woke him early from a dream-filled stupor. They brought him before the councilors in the grand room where he had first tasted Elayawun food. Now, after his sea change, he was rarely hungry. He had eaten two or three meals since then, though he no longer trusted his memory.

The councilors ordered the guards to strap Patrick into a chair. They attached wires to his hands and feet.

"Why are you doing this?" he said aloud. A painting, a seascape, fell off the wall. The councilors looked at it nervously; a guard rushed to put it back. "Will this hurt?" Patrick whispered.

"I'm afraid it will," thought one of the councilors to him as he aimed a strange-looking machine at Patrick's head. It looked like a bulging movie camera. "If you move, it will hurt worse," he said.

The councilors and guards left the room. Patrick was alone; all he could think about was the pain to come. "Why?" he said. Somewhere a switch was flipped. Patrick's knuckles felt fire. Pain ran routes inside him until he lost consciousness.

When he came to, the councilors were back and in the middle of a conversation about Castle Rock. Patrick felt reinvigorated, he became chatty and admitted that after the humans blew up the rock and built the harbor, the currents changed and sands were redistributed.

"We were given dominion over the earth," Patrick said, "by our God." The councilors laughed at that, reminding him that he was an athe- ist when it suited him. Patrick said that humans believed they should bend nature to their will.

He asked why the machine hadn't killed him. They told him that it had and, just as they guessed, he had come back.

"You guessed?" he asked.

One of them wanted to know what Patrick's death had been like.

He said he remembered a cavernous room. There was a long table with place settings. He called out but emptiness swallowed his voice. He noticed a doorknob turning and a door opening. After a few sec- onds, paper on a desk moved by itself. In a mirror above the desk, he saw that the room was filled with people about to sit at the table. The next thing he knew he and the councilors were talking about Castle Rock.

"Pah, this one never stops dreaming," said the councilor who always seemed angry. The councilors all agreed it was just a vivid fantasy before he died, somehow preserved in memory, but not a description of mortality's interior. Patrick didn't agree—it felt real, he said. As the councilors talked quietly a door opened and the scientist—the dead scientist—walked in propped by two other Elayawun. His face was wondering and childlike. His lips moved.

"How is this possible?" Patrick asked. "He was dead."

"Do you want to know how we became immortal?" asked a councilor.

"It has a bearing on all of this."

Patrick nodded.

The chief councilor said that long ago a handful of merpeople discovered vast caves at the bottom of the sea filled with pockets of air. Some wandered deep into the caves and gradually, over generations, adapted to breathing oxygen. They found an edible fungus growing there, the source of immortality. They also discovered the glowing element that eventually would provide energy. This is how the Elayawun came to be.

"We fashioned tools," he said, "and built our domed world above the caves. Air-breathers, we no longer swam freely in the ocean, but had to build undersea craft and diving suits in order to harvest food. We also learned to control the merpeople, who feared our technology and gladly accepted small rewards from us. They loved trinkets. After a while, however, they began to refuse both goads and treasures.

"Now, sand gathers around the dome at an alarming rate. That scientist believed humans and their oil drills made this happen. We know we can no longer remove the drifts fast enough, and the merpeople no longer are willing to help. At times, they seem hostile. Some of us, like that smiling scientist, believe Elayawun are doomed to return to the sea and somehow become deathless versions of merpeople, but we would need to breathe water. That's why we study the creatures in those tanks you stumbled on. Yes, we saw you; we followed you everywhere. This scientist was the chief researcher on the project and perhaps our last hope. But now he isn't talking. We can't even hear him think."

"He cannot die," said the doctor. "Like you he came back, but he was gone a much longer time and is not himself. We thought that hearing your story might trigger something in him. He was in the next room listening, but we fear he is more like a hermit crab now, a guest in his own body."

Chapter 51

WAS FRANTIC. AT FIRST, I thought Icaro was in the cabin. When I didn't find him there, I looked under the bunk and, I swear, the foot-wide closets. For some reason, even though I begged him to appear, Gin Chow was gone too. In a crazy moment, I wondered if Gin Chow had abducted Icaro.

Meanwhile the boat had drifted. I went on deck. I was quiet at first, until I realized it was because I was still obeying Icaro's orders. It was obvious now that he had stolen the boat. Hence his wary treatment of our would-be rescuers, the Coast Guard. I began to scream, first for Icaro and then for the cutter, which, if I'm any judge, had given up way too easily.

"Ahoy," I bellowed. My voice was raw. I had taken down the sails, that much I understood. We were now—I was now—in the lee of the island and the winds had died.

The boat swung around and I felt a current. I remembered a Sea Scout commander telling us that the channel's currents moved in every direction and sometimes went dead still. The one that was pulling my boat seemed to be hugging the shore and moving around to the back of the island. A tiny breeze came up; I raised the sails but got confused how to turn them or the boat—it had been years since I had learned that stuff and it wasn't coming back.

I looked into the haze and nothingness, and wondered what was in the cold water. Was Icaro in there? The cold water was grayish blue.

I wanted to see below the gray-blue water. I wanted to see down. I stared and my eyes seemed to unlock themselves, focusing nowhere. My clothes were soaked, but the staring calmed me. Patterns ran through everything, Huxley had said. What pattern was running through my life, which had begun imperceptibly and built to this deep, shivering spasm? The ocean was sloshing me around in the salt and the foam, gently rocking me above her fathoms. The fog passed over, heading to Santa Barbara. I left a message floating on it; help me, I cried out.

The sky was clear now. Clouds crowded white in imperious mounds like brooding islands, though the scalloped shapes darkened where cloud met cloud, and threatened rain and biting winds. The sky, an abstracted blue, and the sun's angle suggested it was getting late. Other scudding clouds lay in the distance, and through the channel I felt freshening winds, not cold but offering little comfort.

The seas were rollicking slowly, and no foam lay on the water. I had no idea where the wind and waves were taking me. I felt like knocking off for the night. I thought about Mary Annie's bed, how much I wanted to be in it.

Then I looked down, deep down, and saw a dark shape like a giant dome, round with crystal outcroppings. It glowed green within, promising warmth and dry spaces. I could make out many small swimmers hovering around the green dome when a small dark object peeled off from the swimmers and wafted up toward me. It got bigger and bigger and slowly changed shape from an oval to something more human. I lowered my face till it almost touched the water.

The shape swirled around until I saw a head with hair. The face was pasty white and the hair looked more like a gray-white bristle

Chapter 52

The interrogations continued once a week. Patrick had lost all sense of how many there had been or how much time—whatever that meant— had passed. Once, when he was en route to the interrogation room, he thought he saw the old man but could no longer remember what his friend's name was. That failure was a kind of death. He also saw a lot of the "dead" Elayawun scientist, who always smiled at Patrick like a happy idiot.

One day he wanted to read about dry land, and asked his guards if there were books. He seemed to remember books left behind by somebody he knew. The councilors got word of his request and sent Patrick some old-fashioned volumes, classics bound in cloth with marbled endpapers, such as the poetry of Poe and the Iliad and Odyssey. There was also what looked to be a handwritten diary among the fancy tomes. He opened it and read something that sparked a low flame:

"The middle of the ocean is an indeterminate spot, like the middle of the universe. It's an issue of perception or perspective. Most blessed are those who lean against cold stone breakwaters and watch the waves form and crash. They see the history of ocean, from wine-dark deep to weed-strangled green at the shore. They revel in the cold stone chilled by its nightlong association with the waves; the daylong sun yet to dry and bake the smooth surfaces. The seawall stands impossibly straight— human, willful—against the jagged lines of advancing tide, against the ragged surge of water, the permanent element of regular vicissitude."

Those were his father's words, Patrick was sure. He then remembered someone who had eaten a limpet from a rock. He could taste the mineral salt of the bite, but could not remember who had been eating the limpet. Maybe he imagined it.

And he missed Eve Marie.

"Do you have friends among our people?" the councilors asked one day. "We have intelligence that there is a movement to liberate you— to drown you and treat you like a martyr and rally the populace away from us. We think they want to discover some nobility in your death, some dignity in your ending. We ask again if you have friends."

Patrick laughed. "Do you?"

They strapped him into the chair and used the machine to kill him once a week, but each time he popped back up like a boxing clown. During his recuperation time in bed, under the sea and alone, he would think only about escape. He would kill the guard at his door and anyone else in his way, then take Eve Marie hostage to prevent any interference and to serve as his guide. His mind had become murky after the interrogations, and she would help him find where the undersea craft lay. It was simple and sound. She would lead him there and leave with him. Then they would look back at the city as they left forever.

Chapter 53

THUS MY DRIFTING LIFE began and lasted for a period of time I can't accurately declare. It might've been days, or hours. I drifted in and out of sleep, I recall, and the light, as I remember it, was dreamlike. There was food too. The sandwiches Icaro had promised were wrapped in a package in the bunk pantry that survived our swamping turn though the sea.

I know the sky got dark, but it also got quite clear and sunny sometimes. Never warm, though. And maybe because the monstrous fog bank kept moving around, I felt in turns present and far away. I kept thinking that I had killed somebody. I didn't feel as if I had; I was caught in a weird dream.

The currents drifted too. At one point, I found myself near platform Hazel, the one way off Carpinteria. Maybe I could have abandoned the sailboat called *Chuang Tzu Butterfly* and swum to Hazel, but I didn't. The fog had rolled in, and I felt far away again.

I heard voices from above and thought about angels. I might have been in shock. I didn't feel much.

"It's called a kingdom and it's divided into four realms."

"Realms. That's a pretty word."

"Well, lands, actually. One pertains to the American past, another to its future. Imagine that, cross the street and you're traveling through time."

"What about the other two?"

"Even more ingenious. One is dedicated to the idea of the exotic journey—into the wilds of reality where primitive life thrives. The other, well, I think you'll laugh at me."

"What? Harder than I am right now?"

"Fair to say. The other land seeks to encapsulate certain literary experiences, mostly from the Victorian age—like J. M. Barrie and Charles Dodgson."

"Show-off."

"Okay, it was a grad-school exam question, Lewis Carroll is Charles Dodgson. There's a river too. Like Ocean, it flows around the four worlds. Everything that appears to float on it, actually runs on a submerged rail that is strictly controlled from below. Nothing is left to accident or chance."

"But what about food. Can you eat and drink?"

"No beer. But the usual stuff, hamburgers, hot dogs."

"No beer. Let them eat smog. Smog on my dog."

"You know what the mystic monk said to the hot dog vendor?"

"Make me one with everything. Jesus. It's like we're married out here. I know every bagatelle you're gonna play. And then you play it."

"Hello," I said from below as the voices started to fade. I wondered if the proper term wasn't "ahoy," like those Coast Guard fellas said.

"What the fug was that?" said one of the voices from above.

"A ghost of a mystic monk. Oh, c'mon. Hey, fug off down there. Stinkin' divers."

"Hey maybe it's that Brown asshole."

"The one that's lost at sea forever?"

"Help!" I said.

"Aw, fug off. Go fug a mermaid."

"That was real funny, Vinnie. You're like Jack Paar sometimes."

Just then an enormous wave lifted the boat and suddenly I was headed right into the platform's spindly struts, but some wrinkle in the fabric of the ocean intervened and I sailed by them and out into the gloom.

Whenever luck like that seemed to smooth out life, I thought about Icaro. I looked for him in the mists and the oily sea. I called out to him from time to time and even wondered if he was holding on to the edge of the boat. Maybe he had made the island, and then again, maybe he had joined the legion of the merely missing He said he had helped me by disposing of a body. One wonders how.

I drifted into a funk. I stared at the surface of the water. What would have made me happy was to get to Santa Cruz, where the truth party was gathering. Icaro and I had set out a day early. Maybe the party was still going on?

My childish knowledge of sailboats served only to keep the boat going in whatever direction the wind was blowing. I cherish a memory of one frightening moment when the wind rose and the sails caught it thirstily and I flew over the long curving swells. It seems stupid now, but I tried hallucinating as if I was on psilocybin again. I closed my eyes and tried to remember the rich feelings and the patterns running through everything. All I could see was the boat heading up a wave, though, at one with the wind and the unwinding sea.

And then, in the midst of my solitude, a giant craft hove to beside me. It appeared without warning, a rope lowered, and men swarmed into my boat and wrapped me in towels and blankets. They swaddled me.

"What the…"

"Don't worry, sir, we have you," said a brawny young man in Navy darks with wide bell bottoms. "The honorable Mr. Hand is secured," he said, his voice like an actor's.

"And the boat," said a voice from the deck of what turned out to be a Navy ship. "We can convey it or scuttle it?"

"Good Lord, what are you saying?" said an authoritative voice. "I tell you it's the senator's boat—his pride and joy."

"I can carry you up the ladder," said the sailor.

"Never mind," I said. "I'm a little shaky, but I can climb."

"Yes, sir, sir."

My heart sunk. Hand was the name of our state senator. Icaro, I realized, had stolen his boat. First his wife, and then his yacht. In cowboy movies they hanged people who stole horses. What do they do out here? When I reached the rope ladder, two pairs of steadying hands helped me across. Hand over hand, I thought, unhand me. "Are you all right sir?" said the grizzled-looking officer as I climbed onto his boat. He was regarding me with something like surprise.

"I'm fine," I said, wanting to disappear.

"Good, sir, good, sir, so lucky we came by when we did. Usually don't stop for anybody—just wire it in to the Coast Guard. Not our usual bailiwick, rescue, sir. Lucky. The old man will want to meet you. But first let's warm you up, all right, sir?"

"Good," I said. "Listen, I'm not alone."

"No, sir, not anymore, sir. We're here with you."

"You don't understand, a man is gone, disappeared, he was on board."

The men on deck stared at each other. "We looked through the boat, sir."

I laughed inappropriately. "I mean, I wasn't alone. The guy sailing the boat. He's gone."

"We have a man overboard, sir?"

"What was this man's name?" asked an officer.

"Icaro," I said.

"Figaro?" said a sailor.

"No, Icaro, like the myth."

The officer looked at me.

"Figaro, Figaro, Figaro," sang a voice off in the mists.

"Shut the fug up, mister," said the officer. "Or I'll put you on report. Call the captain. Stop the ship."

"No, I mean ... no," I said. "It happened hours ago."

"Oh, Christ. Take him below and get him warm. Wait. Does Igaro have a last name?"

All I could think of was Brown, Bruno, Bruin. I had been a Bruin. All I could do was shake my head.

"Take him below."

"I didn't do it," I said. "He just disappeared."

In the cabin, they brought me towels, then blankets, then clean military-issue khakis, white tee shirt, and peacoat. I put dry clothes on and fell back on a cot. The boat was moving at a great speed. Where? I banged on the door, which was locked. I started to worry. I lay down and warmth enveloped me and the feeling of the ship cutting through waters lulled and absorbed me into the deeper sea.

Some time later, the door opened and a rush of air blew in with salt attached to the breeze ends.

"Are you decent, sir?" the officer I'd met on deck said, bending down as he went through the cabin door. "The old man would like to meet you, if you're warmed up enough. We have coffee on the bridge as well, sir. We always have coffee on the bridge."

"Sure," I said. He you-firsted me out the door where a sailor waited.

"Who are you, sir?" said the sailor with surprised features

"Sailor, show some respect for the senator," the officer barked.

I looked around and was about to say something, when the sailor said in a firm voice: "All due respect, sir. This is not the state senator."

"What are you saying?"

"I was wondering why you kept calling me sir," I said.

"Old family friend, the senator, the honorable Hand. This ain't him, sir."

"I guess the old man will really want to see him now," he said.

Once I got up to the bridge, bigger disputes developed. Turned out the USS *Cygnus* was a secret. The watch commander was furious once he discovered they had brought a man posing as a state senator on a secret ship.

"What's the game here?" he asked me.

"There's no game. I needed a ride to Santa Cruz Island. My friend Icaro offered to sail me over. I never asked him where he got the boat."

"Horse pucky," said a tightlipped officer looking over an impressive array of switches and screens and lights. He stood in the middle of a dry, white floor, between rows of humming machines and blinking ice-blue lights.

"That's it there on the bottom of the ocean. A stronghold, built for some purpose," said one of the seamen looking into a scope.

"Will you zip that, sailor?" said the officer. "Get this man out of here. I want him cleared at the island." He didn't look angry anymore. He was engrossed in a screen that showed a line moving across like a wave leaving green residues. Radar, like in the movies. The image looked like a dome.

"Is the state senator here?" said the smooth voice of the captain as he came into the electronically dancing bridge to salutes all around.

"He's not a state senator, sir. The boat seems to have been stolen. This man alleges it was done by a guy named Icaro."

"Oh? The same Icaro we were supposed to interdict? Seems like a funny coincidence. Not exactly a common name like, oh, say, Ishmael or Ahab. What's your name, son?" the captain asked.

I told him.

"The writer? Joe Westin's boy?"

"Yes, sir," I said. "I didn't steal the boat."

"Of course you didn't. By the way, I know your father well."

Chapter 54

One night Eve Marie came to Patrick. He wondered if the guards had let her pass or if she had snuck by them somehow. She smiled, put seaweed poultices on his dry skin, on his hands and feet, which the machine had burned raw. She was soft with him.

He told her he had tried adjusting to immortality, but his efforts seemed pointless—immortality was as unknowable as death. Whether faced with eternal life or oblivion, he still lived only in moments of distracted pleasure.

"But just once more," he said, "I'd like to travel through Leemoo. No guards. Just the two of us."

Her face lit up. "I'll see what I can do."

A few nights later, she came back late, and roused him from sleep. "Hush," she said. "Hush."

"Are you here to take me on a tour?" he asked. She laughed and rolled onto the bed. He took her in his arms. Even though time no longer existed, it stood still ...

Afterward, both of them lay flushed and panting. Laughing, Eve Marie handed Patrick a cloak and said, "Let's go."

The guard that Patrick was prepared to murder was not there. "I took care of the watch for my only lover," said Eve Marie.

They left without incident and entered the city, passing sea slugs in doorways as night vehicles buzzed overhead. Eve Marie took him through a maze of crowded streets filled with shops and eateries, the air full of fragrances. In one place he saw couples clumsily embracing. Dancing? The broadcasting towers were silent.

Patrick felt freedom swirling around him and knew what he had to do. He grabbed Eve Marie by the arm. "I want you to take me to one of the crafts that you use to bring the old man here ... Now."

"Let go," she said.

"You're my ticket out," he said, sounding like a movie gangster.

She jerked away. "Don't you know who I am?" And before she could even yell for help, five patrolling guards appeared in the street. They were on Patrick in an instant. He caught one of them by the throat and throttled him. The guard's neck snapped like a dry tree limb. Patrick rolled the body away, not sure if the Elayawun was dead—would he actually stay dead? The other guards froze. Eve Marie stood horrified.

Patrick bolted. He ran down streets, coming to a large square crowded with more people. Pulling his hooded cloak tight, he slowed his pace to blend in with the moving throng. An alarm sounded.

He picked up his pace, hurrying through a square in which stood a statue of a young human. It looked like his father. He took off into another square where a crowd had gathered and was pointing at him. He was running now. He wanted to get to the dome wall and touch the glass, where he was certain he would get his bearings.

He never made it. There was a pop, like bone coming away from joint. Patrick felt sharp slaps on his neck and chest. Suddenly he was on the ground and couldn't move his limbs. At first the pain wasn't bad, then it was. He noticed tiny red and green pebbles on the ground in front of him. He saw rust and leaf. He went silent as the dome and the ocean and the people slipped away on an ebb tide of fortune.

Chapter 55

THEY ESCORTED ME OFF the bridge and onto the deck. "Just to be on the safe side," the captain had said. I could see the point where neutral sky met gray-slate sea. We were moving at a furious pace and soon reentered one of the gown-folds of the fog bank, billowing and ghost dancing around the channel. I wondered if Gin Chow, the tiny old man, was still on the boat, which we appeared not to be towing. I tried to go below to my cabin but a sailor barred the way.

An officer handed me a paper cup of bitter coffee and asked how long I had been adrift. I shrugged.

"Secret stuff in there," he said. "Don't you remember me from UCLA? But then you were famous, so's you didn't have to talk to us ordinary guys."

"Where's my sailboat?"

"Thought it wasn't yours." He tried to sound cool, but couldn't keep the attitude up for long. "One of the Richie Rich officers is sailing it to Saint Nick's."

"Sure," I said. "Santa Claus. What's the deal with this boat?"

"It's a ship, a SURSS. And not Santa Claus, San Nicolas."

"Sirs, as in, 'Yes sirs'?"

"No, an acronym: S-U-R-S-S: Small Unit Remote Scouting System. It sees underwater. You're not so hot, Mister Boy Genius. You don't know much of anything, do you?"

"Like TV? Like *Sea Hunt*?" I knew enough to know that San Nicolas Island had belonged to the military for decades and was off-limits to civilians.

"No, it's 3D, though, like those movies. Use radar from the ship and have speakers under the water. Shit. I don't know how it works. Special glasses, I guess." He laughed.

"What are you trying to see? Whales? Fish? Underwater cities?"

"Hah, you're funny. No. Submarines."

"What are you talking about? The war's over."

"*Man,* what planet are you from? Russian submarines. Nuclear submarines. As in, we're-all-gonna-die sort of thing."

"I thought the Russians were going to blow up the sun or something."

"That day when the big bomb falls? We'll be out here. The old man will take us away, maybe to Hawaii or Guam. Won't be any bombs there. Blow up the sun, how do you make this stuff up, writer?"

I heard people arguing on the bridge, and the captain came out. He brought me back inside, which started another debate about me. That was when I saw the newspaper clipping taped on the wall. My article about Brown.

"Why is that there?" I asked one of the junior officers, who suggested that my own business would be a more appropriate use of my attention.

"That is my business," I mumbled. "I wrote it."

"What?" he asked, annoyed.

The officer from my school said, hey, yeah, that's his byline.

"Well, we should have an autograph party or something," the junior officer snapped.

"I still want to know why it's there," I said.

"Is it true?" the captain asked.

"Yeah, I wrote it."

"No, son, I mean is it true that Brown is dead?"

"I saw him with my own eyes."

"Those bastards."

"Which bastards, sir? Why is this pinned up here?"

"We were looking for someone who was working for us who was looking for Mr. Brown. We found you, though you apparently lost Mr. Gonzales. Lost and found all around."

"Sir, permission to speak," said the officer who had sent me out on the deck.

"Oh, what is it, Turnsty?"

"With respect, sir. This is all classified information."

"Hear that?" the captain said to me. "Your article is classified, so don't tell yourself about it. That's an order."

"Yes, sir," I said. "Except, I'm a civilian."

"That remains to be proven," said someone, but I lost track of who.

For a few seconds the voices in the room muffled as I looked out at the water. I loved the sea at that moment. I loved the look of it from behind the glass window, and the way the sea smells insisted themselves onto the bridge, coexisting with cigarettes and coffee and male sweat. I closed my eyes for a second. I was almost happy.

"We're coming up on it, sir," said a mechanical voice kazooing through speakers.

"Very well," he said and apologized for leaving me on my own for a few minutes. I asked if I could go outside again. Permission granted.

As I got back on deck, a mighty roar filled the air and I saw a column of fire ascend to the heavens. I almost crapped my pants. It was a rocket taking off. "Wow," I said. "World War III?"

"Hah," said my old new friend, who had escorted me out. "It's the island. Saint Nick. We got rockets, small ones, missiles really."

The ship cut its massive motors and drifted up to a long pier that jutted out from a rockbound harbor. I began to hear pops and buda-buddas, like sounds in a war movie. The missile had gone up from a towering silo nearby, and I could see in the distance a crowd of men dressed in lab coats and camouflage and Navy whites. A few were in suits. Somewhere beyond a high ridge of sand I heard an explosion and felt its percussive sound waves.

"Please put your hands behind your back," said an officer I hadn't seen before, as he walked up without slowing down. I guess I didn't move fast enough, so he grabbed my hands, brought them together, and slapped a pair of handcuffs on my wrists. I felt self-conscious, as if I were watching myself on television. The captain poked his head out and saw me. He clucked his lips and went back inside.

"I'm not going to run away," I said.

"That's for damn sure," said a sailor who was leaning on the rail.

They led me down a gangplank to the pier and nudged me without ceremony over to a row of Quonset huts. They pushed me into one and locked the door.

I sat down on a cot. The canvas smell was reassuring. I tried to lie down. I was tired, but as soon as heavy eyes began to close and warmth set into cold bones, the door burst open and a group of officers came in, apologizing like maniacs. They had brought the officer who had cuffed me with them and made him say he was sorry too.

The cuffs came off and I barely had time to meditate on my ever-changing relationship with fate when they invited me to come to command HQ. On the way, I could still hear battle in the shrouded distance. Men passed us in military uniforms; salutes were exchanged, as were quips. A small group of Hispanic soldiers walked by wearing berets and gaudily decorated fatigues. I looked at one of my escorts.

"Cubans," he said. "They just lost a revolution to commies."

"Why are they here?"

"Dig this," he said, and started whistling a faithful rendition of "Ornithology." He smiled. "Bird lives."

"I doubt it."

"Here we are. The CO wishes to see you," said one of the men. "I must warn you that everything you are about to see is secret."

I immediately imagined an elevator to a sled car, the conveyance gliding smoothly through a tunnel, stopping under the arch of a dome where picture windows showed large sharks and dramatic rays swimming. Instead we entered a metal hut where banks of electronic lights sparkled like Christmas trees in greens, yellows, and reds. I was disappointed yet dazzled and thought of Huxley looking upon the California Riviera's twinkling lights, though this was not folk art. Men in Navy uniforms with headsets sat before the lights. They chattered like robots in a sci-fi film. I wondered what they might be learning and doing.

We walked past this dreamlike chamber into a room full of radar screens. A door at the other end of the room opened to light. I wandered over and saw the island outside.

"Thanks, taxpayers, I think," said my beatnik buddy. "Dig it." Then he straightened. "This is Admiral Daffenblitz," he said as a stooped, elegant man approached.

"And you are?" asked another man standing by with a big brogue. "Oh wait, laddie, that's it. You're the laddie. The one."

"I'm the one, all right," I said. "The seventh son of a seventh son."

"No. The one what wrote the book? The book about the wee explorers, the ocean, that sort of thing. Aren't you?"

"Yes. I'm Trevor Westin," I said.

"Inspired me, it fuggin' did. Ah yeah, your father was out here, mon."

"What? When?"

Behind me I heard an officious throat clearing, and everyone snapped to. "This is the commanding officer, Admiral Daffenblitz," repeated my escort.

The admiral stepped forward. "Never mind that, Crabtree," he said to the officer with the brogue.

"Tell me the truth," Crabtree continued, oblivious. "Are you the author of *Neverknown*?"

"I am as you said it," I said.

The rheumy-eyed admiral looked perplexed. "Welcome to the San Nicolas Naval Base. Where were you going in the sailboat with Mr. Icaro Gonzales?" he asked.

"You know Icaro? Is that his last name?" I was surprised, but the admiral only nodded, settling nothing. "We were trying to get to Santa Cruz Island. Almost there but were blown off course."

"Like Odysseus," he said. "Were you going to Miss Pearl Chase's book signing?"

"Pearlie's having a book signing? I thought it was just a party."

"Big gathering in the chapel at Gherini's ranch," he said. "Everybody who's anybody from the mainland. It's big news out here. You know the place?"

"I camped there years ago with the Sea Scouts." A book signing, I thought. "I am eager to see my Auntie Pearl, though."

"Didn't know you two were family. That's splendid, wonderful. I'll have my man take you to the pier at Prisoner's, or is it Scorpion's. The book signing for Two Guns is tomorrow evening. Please tell your aunt I'm sorry I can't attend. Not a lot of cultural activity on the islands, so we try to be neighborly and military at the same time. And yes, we have been looking for Mr. Gonzales since we first heard rumors he had been seen in Santa Barbara. An associate of your father's, right?"

Icaro, I thought. Two Guns, I thought. Everybody but me knows this guy. But a book signing? I thought it was Friday, or did I? Maybe this was a different party or a different kind of party. Maybe it's some kind of military euphemism. Book signing. And Icaro's last name was Gonzales, is Gonzales. The admiral picked up a phone and began talking in an inaudible voice.

"Okay," he said, switching back to me. "You see what we're doing here? We're on guard for Soviet submarines. They say it's top secret. It's no secret that a Cold War would also be a wet war. Tell Miss Chase how funny I am—she thinks I'm a stuffed uniform. Oh, by the way, I have a spot of bad news. If you can't speak to what I need to know then I need you to be debriefed. And that's before my man can take you to the island. Won't take long. Probably painless." The admiral smiled and turned on his heel. "He can explain Icaro to you, I think."

"Wait a second, please."

He turned around. "Yes?"

"Can you please tell me what Jacques Brown has to do with the SURSS?"

"Probably I can't," he said, no longer smiling. "Maybe in debriefing. I mean, that's what the term means, isn't it?"

"Oh, yes, sir, you're the laddie," Crabtree said to me, after smartly saluting the admiral as we left. "Indeed you are. Do you like *our* version of Neverknown?"

Shouting broke out behind us. Some of the men had gathered around a large radar screen across which three gigantic masses were passing.

"*Niña, Pinta, Santa Maria,*" said a sailor, laughing uproariously. Somebody told him to stow it. Toe the line, said someone else.

My escort and I stopped, and we were watching too.

"They're big," said the guy on my right.

"What are they, whales?" I asked.

"Yeah, daddy-o, dig the whales," my beatnik escort said.

Crabtree whispered in my ear. "It's the beginning of the end," he said. "Soviet newk-ya-lur."

"C'mon," my escort told me. "You didn't see any of that either."

"Or else?"

"Mr. Debrief's not gonna let you off San Nick, no matter what the CO said."

"Is his name Brown?" I asked.

"What a weird-o question, daddy-o. This way, sir."

"Off to see the wizard."

As we left the hut, I wondered about Gin Chow; I would have liked him at the debriefing. I asked daddy-o which wizard we were going to see. He ignored me and chattered like a chipmunk about every twig on the road, and when we got within sight of our destination, he turned down the volume. At the door of a Quonset hut stood another sailor, like a guard but considerably less formal. The beatnik and the doorman, named Ripley, exchanged a weird handshake.

"How did this spooky guy rate San Nick?" asked my escort.

"Spooky stuff. Guy went to Yale, they have this Skin and Bones thing."

"Skull," I said.

"Who, daddy-o?"

"Skull and Bones, sometimes they call it the Brotherhood," I said, but I thought about Icaro, the man overboard, the spy. I thought about my cousin who was like a spy, she was leading a double life in my heart and everywhere else, it just depended on what island you were hopping. The scrub and sandy paths in the distance still echoed gunfire and explosions. My escort and his friend opened the door for me. They looked a little sad.

We entered an office with thick curtains over the windows. The air was heavily scented with Old Golds. I almost gagged.

"We ought to feed our guest," said a disembodied voice out of the darkness. "Get him a ham sand from the commissary."

My two companions skedaddled. I approached a swivel chair in front of a standard-issue desk. I looked beyond it at a mirror hanging on the corrugated wall. There was nobody in the mirror but me.

"Sit down," said the voice.

I obeyed. Looking around for a recording device, I asked the voice if the clear weather might hold. "The fog is departing," he said. "Usually we only get it in summer."

"Bad out here?"

"Worse. This is where fog comes from."

"You know, honey, I never know when you're speaking metaphorically," I said, swinging my legs back and forth in the chair.

He laughed and appeared in front of me, coming up from some sort of trapdoor behind the desk. "Do I bother you?"

"Trevor Westin," I said holding out my hand. "Do I look bothered?"

"Honestly, we know who you are now, but at first we were convinced you were somebody else, a state senator, and that would make two of you."

"Split personality," I said. "They say you're never lonely."

"Now that you mention it, there is some psych stuff in your dossier."

"I have a dossier?"

"You were famous once, remember?"

"You haven't told me your name. Remember?"

"Oh, sorry. Must be the pressure of meeting someone who isn't half the man you think he is—and then is more."

"You know, I would've guessed that happens to you all the time."

"Shit. Not out here. I'm more of a bookworm than a field agent.

Speaking of which, I read your book a long time ago. The admiral wanted me to ask you when you're going to write another one."

"I'm doing it as we speak," I said. The ham sandwich came in the door and I wolfed it—hunger the best relish.

"Look," he said after I was finished. "You don't have to like me. I don't have to like me. But you have to get by me to get off Saint Nick's. You've seen a lot of stuff."

"Including those three Russian subs."

"What subs?"

"The SURSS or whatever it was had big images of big submarines."

He picked up the heavy black phone on his cluttered desk. "Hey. Guy here tells me you have bogeys, big ones. Yeah? Am I not supposed to be notified immediately? Well, tell him he's a pencil-dick. Call me if you see them again."

He looked up. "Thank you. So what brings you here?"

"A stolen boat by the name of *Chuang Tzu Butterfly*. Plus, I'm trying to figure out why everybody is hiding the truth about Jacques Brown. And Icaro Gonzales, who I've been told worked for my father, doing something somewhere."

"Jacques Brown, the diver?"

"Yes. You know him."

"I don't think so. Why?"

"There's newspaper clipping of a story I did for the *Times* pasted up in the *Cygnus* about people finding him dead on the breakwater."

"That's where he ended up? I wondered. Maybe they admire your writing style. I hear you are reluctant to give up Gonzales."

"What are you talking about? I'll give you him if you give me Brown," I said, never once thinking he would tell me anything.

"Oh, okay, yeah, things you wouldn't know yet. There was a boat named the *Eve* or the *Marie* or something like that. The *Eve Marie*.

Engineers from Raytheon were on it, putting out sensors on the ocean bottom for us, quite a ways from here. Something happened. Brown was their diver or pilot or something."

"For an intelligence guy, you don't know much."

"Tell me about it. But they had some kind of accident, currently under investigation, probably by other stupid intelligence guys. Some kind of wave hit them, maybe. They all died. Brown washed away, they said. Disappeared. A swim to Santa Barbara seems a stretch, but that's where he turned up, neat as you please, working for Miss Pearl Chase, professional rectum-wrencher. Sorry, forgot she's your friend. And later they find him dead in the harbor. As for Icaro, he did work for your father, when he was running partisans in and out of Greece during the war. For my people, I guess. Icaro stayed on and got mixed up with the communists or something."

"Why doesn't anybody know this stuff definitively?" I asked.

"The nature of the game, every game, is that we only know our own moves, and that the whole 'definitive' picture, if it ever emerges, is overwhelmed by the people who win making fun of the people who lose. I know that your father was deeply embarrassed when Gonzales first showed up but then seems to have patched things with him. Nobody knows what for or why. Your father was cashiered out of the Navy, but still seemed to do stuff for us. It's confusing. Wait, you were supposed to tell me about Gonzales. I get the feeling that your father is going to make fun of all of us."

I ignored the last part, though it rang true. "Icaro Gonzales disappeared from the ship when the Coast Guard came. He seemed angry. He works at Jacques's in Santa Barbara." Immediately I felt like a low-grade traitor. But this guy wasn't even taking notes. "Good enough?"

The spy raised his hands like a supplicant imploring. "Like I said, it's all under investigation by people who don't want people to know what's going on out here."

"What's going on out here?"

"We're building an underwater city to defend the world from atomic crabs."

"I saw that movie; it was pretty good. Looks like they filmed it out here."

He nodded. "Psych stuff says you've been messing with Huxley, the prophet of Love and Mystical Experience. Put that together with the boat and you have some sort of real poetry going. Plus, you like monster movies. I like those beatnik kids in Santa Monica—they've got good grass. I tried it. Hey, you ever read Ginsberg—'I put my queer shoulder to the wheel.' Huh?"

"Nope. Never. I like Huxley though."

"You know, he's not so far from the truth. Except he's got the wrong conclusions. We're workin' on something out here you might say is parallel to him. I'm doing a lot of experimenting—doors of perception stuff."

"What do you mean?" I was beginning to wonder how he could have seen a dossier on me. I guess it could've been flown in after they found me, but that seemed unlikely. "What kind of experimenting?"

He motioned me closer and opened a little vial, like a prescription bottle, and poured a pile of small pills that looked like saccharin tablets on the desk blotter. There must have been about three hundred of them. "Ever heard of lysergic acid diethylamide?" he asked. I reached over, and grabbed a few of the pills. He didn't say a word; maybe he didn't care. "Perfectly legal. We get it mail order from a company in Switzerland. It kicks butt, psychically speaking. We thought we could use it to do brainwashing," he said. "But it turns out, it's better suited to finding instant enlightenment. Therefore, completely dangerous out there." He motioned vaguely. "Like grass and prophets of love."

The phone rang and he answered it. "They're back, shit. I'm coming over." He got up, smiling and full of life. "The Russians are coming."

"Can I go?" I said. "I mean, leave."

"Oh, hell yes. We'll bunk you overnight on the big boat and then haul you and your sailboat to the islands with a very competent body-guard. And take some of those, why don't you?" He pointed at the little pills; the bottle read Delysid. "Only need to take one for the full dose," he said.

I considered him carefully. "You don't care that I know what happened to Brown?"

"You do? Fill me in, because I don't."

"I work for a newspaper." I swept quite a few of the tiny tablets, maybe fifty, into a pile. He gave me a little manila envelope to put them in—as if he had planned the whole thing. "You aren't concerned."

"Book reviewer, right?" He clucked a few clucks. "Besides, you have a psych file. Makes it awfully easy to discredit witnesses, especially those who claim the U.S. government is building an underwater city off the coast of California. Makes it easy for us to pick you up if we can't make you look ridiculous."

"Then I'll be going. Are these anything like psilocybin?" I asked, shaking the pills in the envelope.

He cocked his index finger and shot me.

Chapter 56

This old man sat on a large boulder in a cave below the dome. The craft he used to travel between the worlds floated nearby in a lagoon. He was holding court before a dozen Elayawun acolytes in hooded vestments huddled together on the sand.

"You hear they cancelled Easter this year?" the old man said.

"Really?" said one of the acolytes.

"Yeah, they found the body."

"What's Easter?" asked another.

A few yards away, lying in the sand, Patrick struggled to sit up. He wondered if this was the place where the sea people had adapted to oxygen. He remembered a theory that human aging resulted from cells exposed to too much air: decrepitude as slow oxygen poisoning.

The acolytes seemed concerned. They kept asking Patrick if he was all right. "Maybe you should take it easy. You were dead not long ago, man," said one. "Is it true you wanted to refuse the gift? You turned your back on eternity?"

"You don't want to be immortal," said another, "and neither do we. We want to burn in a rush of feelings, not simply behold the world forever."

"Listen to this," said the old man: "A guy walks into a bar. The

347

bartender says, 'Hey, that must've hurt.'"

"We want to try love. It makes you do foolish things," a third acolyte said. "The books say so."

"I want to try it too," Patrick said, looking around.

"I hear you had sex with one of us. Remarkable," said the first acolyte.

"You are not really a god, you know," said the old man.

"I never said I was," Patrick answered.

"But you are only the second person in the world to come back," said the old man, whose name was Dooley. "Lazarus and you. Jesus doesn't count. He never came back to a body in the world. Not really."

"I know a doctor who made it back, and a scientist. Besides, I'm not in the world. I'm here now."

"So you say," Dooley said. "The physician healed himself." He pulled out his white flute and began to play "Show Me the Way to Go Home."

Suddenly there was an ominous sound, and the ground trembled beneath them. Surging ocean water lifted the craft high in the lagoon and everybody leaped back as waves rushed onto the sand.

"We've been gone for a considerable time," Dooley said to Patrick. "Much has changed in the city of Neverknown. I want you to take one last glimpse at the city under the sea before we leave forever. Then we'll go to Santa Barbara harbor, fugitives from this dying world." He pointed to stairs that led out of the cave.

The ground shook again, harder than before.

"Don't make waves," Patrick said. The old man laughed; he loved those kinds of jokes.

"Why is the calendar so sad?" asked Dooley, as they hurried to the stairs.

"Why?" said one of the acolytes, following.

"Because its days are numbered."

Up the two men climbed. They heard crashing sounds, keening, then a scream. When they reached the entrance to the cave, Dooley tried to hold Patrick back and said, "This is bad."

Destruction was everywhere. A long, slow temblor moved under the city, raising dust and shrieks. Above them, seawater was pouring down from cracks in the dome.

"This is worse than I thought," said Dooley. "Let's leave now."

"Not without Eve Marie." Patrick ran headlong into the crumbling city.

Dooley shrugged, turned, and went back down the treacherous steps.

Stunned Elayawun surged around him, not knowing where to go or what to do. The ground shook several more times and water mixed with blood ran in the streets. Patrick found the building where Eve Marie first made love to him, ducked in the main entrance, and ran to her door. He pushed it open, and she was there, sitting on the edge of her bed as if waiting. Water covered the floor.

As he came toward her, she opened and closed her eyes, winked, took his hand and gently bit his fingers. "Hello," she said aloud. "You survived."

"Some people from a cave saved me."

"We knew someone must have carried you off when we couldn't find your body. Did you hear about the end of Leemoo? It has an end, apparently. Some people think life is possible in those caves. We could start all over."

"What happened?" he asked.

He sat on the edge of the bed. She threw her arms around him and pulled him down. She laughed out loud, and it sounded eerie.

"It began in the bedroom when I spoke, using your words," she said, smiling too wide and talking too fast. "I shattered the silence, the pure dream. Once I met you, I could not stop talking out loud. The dome broke because I preferred the crude music of your tongue to our silences."

She stopped and looked at the wet floor. "Do you know the real name of this city?" Eve Marie asked. "Since you love me, I'll tell it. Not Leemoo, not Neverknown. Its real name is Swaxil. A secret, unspoken word because it was the name of the dry-land village the sea people came from. That place is gone and we don't say its name. The Elayawun wanted to remember only the times they choose. So they forbade it. I said Swaxil over and over to hear its sound, and the dome began to crack. It wasn't the sand outside; it was me."

"No. Hush. I'm so sorry for what the humans did," Patrick said. "It wasn't you. It was the sand and the earthquakes, and the oilmen's bombs. It was my people's fault."

"Because you love me you say these things," she whispered, gripping him tight. "You do love me. I think you do. Though I can't read your mind anymore."

"Come with me to the transport. The old man is waiting there. You can survive. You can live in my world."

"I thought you wanted to die."

"No. I wanted to feel time again," he said.

"Sit here. We can watch the destruction progress over time. Sit here with me and watch. And I'll sit with you and wait for everything but love to end."

Chapter 57

THE FOG LIFTED AND the sea was magnificent. I shuddered at the sublime light as I stood on the bow. The night had passed in a cot in a hut and fathoms-deep sleep after the secret agent or whatever had given me his offhand clearance. The admiral's "man," a sandy-haired, Ivy-League-quarterback-looking guy fetched me in the morning, walked me through an empty sailor's mess for a spartan breakfast, and then down to a pier where, to my surprise, the *Chuang Tzu* was tied and ready. Someone had swabbed her down, straightened her tackle and fixed the radio. The admiral's adjutant had filled the tank and the motor snarled. "Looks like Mr. Gonzales was not careful," he said. "Stupid. He ran out of gas and paid for that."

After my surreal security clearance, the admiral insisted I be granted a detour to Pearl's book party at Santa Cruz, and then the Navy would return both the boat and me to the mainland after sundown so the *Chuang Tzu* could slip into its S.B. harbor berth like nothing had happened. An officer waiting on the pier expressed concern that I stay on schedule. The less said about top-secret stuff, or Icaro, the better, he added. He didn't seem worried, though.

The naval officers were still interested in finding Icaro for their own reasons. But I wasn't thinking about him, now that someone else, the government as it turned out, was watching over me. Still, I wondered at my sudden acquisition of indifference.

I stopped thinking about the man who attacked me on the Mesa too. You know, the one I allegedly killed. The soul of the man was gone, I said out loud, and felt nothing but the empty wind. Death looks gigantically down.

And so does the sunlight. The day spread itself overhead like an enormous stained-glass dome, faceted with colors. My heart soared as we shoved off from San Nicolas en route to the meeting on that other island, named for the tree upon which the Messiah, in whom I did not believe, had died. Brown had Christ's wounds too. I had a bunch of pills in my pocket and one down the hatch.

The sea was calm and I could see my own city far across the blue. In two hours we would reach Santa Cruz, where the truth would be revealed to me. Until then, we had dolphins. They burst up blue from the water like emotions. As they played and raced alongside, I was filled with the blessing of grace and, as before, transported out of my body. I was floating well above the mast, looking down at the ship, the sea, and the dolphins.

The admiral's man never made a sound. He left me alone in my pure joy. I was free forever now. I could make sense of things that would never go back to bad. The moment I had experienced in college on the beach in Santa Monica was a piffle compared to this diorama of refracted connections shining all around me.

All the time Santa Cruz was getting bigger. I had a bottle of rum that the admiral had given me. I drank one large swig and fell into the next reverie.

One by one they left me. So many of the people I had known. Sometimes I experienced their leaving as a loss, hopeless and sad for a long time, but often it was a relief. Sitting there skimming the bright sea, I realized that, in the end, it was always a relief. The ties of family and friendship became long strands that pulled you under. To change, the heart needed its freedom.

On the ocean, a pall of smoke hung in the distance. It was familiar and horrifying at the same time: Maybe the island chain harbored a volcano. Perhaps a ghost *Haida* was spewing a combination of soot and residual spirits from its smokestack. Maybe it was the mushroom cloud you read about and fear so much, or the hobo jungle burning, setting its mayor free.

I was shivering with delight now. I looked across the water to the beach we were approaching. Sprigs of weed, red and green, grew there. An indelible shadow lay across the sand, cast by light reflected from the many deaths that had happened there, that happen everywhere.

Wait. I remembered, with a shiver, it was Thursday. Incinerator day. When had I last seen that? Two weeks ago? How could you tell anymore in a world without time? But, hey, long live king coincidence. The smoke always accompanies the vision.

We cut the engine, coasted in, and tied up to the pier at Scorpion Bay. It was late afternoon. As I stood up, everything around me seemed strange. I got off, bid good-bye to the officer, and promised to return by sundown. The sound I made walking down the pier was ominous and cosmic. I felt eyes on my back as I started up the dirt road that wound toward the ancient ranch where the book signing was to be held.

The island had been full of Indians not so long ago. Two villages near the pier. My uncle said that Harrington had said the Indians had been there for ten thousand years. I tried to imagine the generations: five every century, times ten times ten. Five hundred generations on this rock. Say, a thousand people at a time? Fifty-thousand-thousand Indians lay beneath my feet. Where are the bones, the indestructible teeth, and the ghosts of emotions let loose, giving birth and taking death?

No ghosts presented themselves, only island blue jays. They were bold, swooping in closer than mainland birds and unleashing their scoldings. You must walk faster, I told myself. I came to the ford of a meandering creek. I knelt down and smelled some sage. I remembered my brother. Here the earth puts forth creeping bushes, tangled ivy, and the roots of trees with poisonous red berries, the cycles and the seasons distilled into the present. Whatever happened to New Year's? Really, how did I miss it tied up in foolish activities? Come to think of it, why was my mailbox no longer full of magazines? Did I let all my subscriptions die? Where did I get my news nowadays? No wonder I never knew the date. There is no such thing as *Time*. Then I remembered. It was Saturday.

Hah, I yelled, then heard a car coming and it made me nervous. I didn't want to be captured again. The sound was coming from the heart of the island, over a small ridge where the dirt road ran. I decided to hide, but there were only bushes, the leafy fingers of the emanating patterns.

They will take me, I thought. I quickly ripped a pile of ivy out of the earth, draped it over me, and sat stock-still. The noise was getting louder, and soon a jeep appeared from around the ridge—the one split by the road. It goes both ways, I thought: hither and yon, forward and back, into the future and out of the past. The jeep roared by me. For a long time I remained part of the scenery, covered with ants, inhaled by the land around me, absorbed. A blue jay swept toward me; overhead I heard the screeching of a red-tailed hawk. I stood up. Slowly, I inched forward with my obscuring cover as a cape.

It was a long road to travel. My eyes were sore. My throat felt thick. My mind bent everything toward it.

I had been walking forever when I saw the people, so many, from the top of the ridge. The ranch house below had dirty white walls—possibly adobe. The roof was red tile. Smoke curled from an outdoor oven surrounded by long tables, probably the ranch hands' mess. I heard a horse nicker and whinny behind a small chapel, in front of which I saw people walking in a circle like silent marionettes, kicking up dust. Not wanting to be seen, I pulled the ivy around my shoulders. Then the doors to the chapel opened, and the people went inside.

They were all there, I imagined: Baby Bird Bennett, whatshis-name the policeman, the nurse from the hospital, Brown, the old man from the craft, Jimmy Stewart and Midge, poor, sad Midge from the Hitchcock movie, Vincent Price, my brother, my parents, June and her boyfriend. They walked into the chapel with a staggering forward motion and no expression on their faces.

I stumbled down the hill and through the empty yard to the open chapel doors. I pretended that the ivy wrapped around my shoulders was seaweed. It made me see-throughable.

A placard near the door read: Meet the Author of *Yesterdays*. The people were sitting in the chapel's pews with their backs to me, except for Pearl. She was standing before them in front of the altar, like a high priestess. I entered quietly, casting a shadow over the center aisle. I slid into the empty back pew. I could feel Pearl's eyes on me, but I was still invisible. The ivy slid around me onto the old worn bench.

The chapel looked Spanish-grant old. But it felt new, as if the smoke of candles had dusted the walls but not yet infused them with ashes. Maybe time was not real, I thought, yet it undeniably left side effects. Now they were rising, the ten thousand—well, maybe a hundred—crowded into this fake temple of worship. My fake aunt now seemed like Medusa. Her eye sockets were hollow like a skull. She was death. In the ornate monstrance on the altar, where the Eucharist should have been, I saw a glowing gate of hell.

A cloud outside passed by and sunlight leaked into the room. I yawned. A man whom Pearl had been introducing ad infinitum came forward, stood behind a pulpit next to the altar, and began to speak. He wrote *Yesterdays*. He told a story from it about a group of Spanish-born boys during the American occupation of Santa Barbara who, as a joke, stole a cannon, rolled it over to the salt flats on the east side of town, and sank it in the deep mud. The angry American soldiers demanded either the cannon be returned or a fine be paid for its loss. Unable to unearth the lost cannon, the plucky Spanish residents held a fiesta raising enough money to by the gringos a new cannon. The Americans, no longer worried that the stolen cannon presaged the beginning of an uprising, were happy and free again to pursue manifest destiny. The chapel crowd nodded and murmured approval.

Then the man in the pulpit told a story I had never heard before. It was about a Chumash woman who lived on San Nicolas Island—where I had just been. My being tingled, the story was meant for me. Catholic priests, fearing a raid on their village by ruthless Russian trappers, had convinced the ancient inhabitants to leave the island. A girl jumped from the boat to save her little brother who had been left behind.

Only the two of them remained to eke out an existence on San Nicholas; the brother would die a few years later, torn apart by wild dogs. The girl lived on alone, surviving on berries and shellfish for seventeen years; her only companions were birds and small foxes. Until one day, a fishing boat spotted her, now a woman, and took her back to Mission Santa Barbara. Her language was incomprehensible to the other Indians there. When the padres tried to teach her to speak their tongue, she died within two weeks. Death by language.

I started laughing and even though people turned around, I couldn't stop laughing. This was it. I tromped outside where ranch hands were eating. They laughed at my ivy getup and I laughed with them. I turned around in the midst of one sharp gale and there she was.

I started to stagger away and she stopped me. She was terse, this

June. "What are you doing here? Who are you looking for?"

"Brown," I said. "You know."

"He's dead Trevor," she said, eyeing me carefully.

"I know that. I do. I just think somebody out here can help me find out why."

"It was in the paper. It was an accident."

"You don't have to believe newspapers. I know because I write for a big one, and they change stories to suit their bosses. I bet one of these big cheeses out here knows what really happened."

"You're the only mystery in this whole story, Trevor, sweet man."

Maybe she wasn't mad at me—but I don't know why she was there and I couldn't figure out how to ask. Some detective.

"Did you really read my book? I mean my manuscript, with me not there?" I said, remembering the note by the typewriter. "And why was the ocean so full of smoke?"

"Hush, honey, it was wrong."

"What?"

She looked around to see who was looking, listening. We were alone.

"They made love."

I was baffled at this newfound Victorian squeamishness. "Yeah? So?"

"Like we do. I don't want the world to know what we do." She was clouding up. "I'm not happy."

"What have *you* got to be not happy about?" I asked. My stomach was knotting.

"Oh, Trevor, honey," she said.

"Don't honey me." I said. "You're supposed to be in Hawaii."

"Oh," she answered. "The islands. That's why you said aloha. Imagine that. It's like an *I Love Lucy* plot. Everything based on misunderstanding. It's like everything. This is 'the islands' and you are here too."

I was dumbfounded. Maybe that was right. At any rate, I liked the sparks forming on my fingertips, like icicles.

"You were willing to let me go that far away with him, after all that happened the last time we met?" she asked, her eyes narrowing. "Anyway, I figure at this point you wouldn't care. Word is, you're dating my old roommate, already." People started to come out of the church. She took me by the hand and pulled me away. "Not that I mind, Trevor. I was going to come see you for the last time, anyway."

"What?"

"It has to end, Trevor, honey. And I guess this is it."

I laughed, out of control. "Why?"

"Why?" she asked. "Because you are why. You went to see my mother, and she told my father. And he hit the roof. He almost hit me. Listen, Trevor. Maybe you have a lot of money and can take care of yourself, but I have nothing. I have what my parents give me, and this job, this stupid political job. Pearl hates me … " She trailed off and we sat down on a rough wooden bench near the chapel.

"This thing we had," she said.

"Had?"

"It has to end here." She said it out loud in front of the people who walked by. "It has to end."

What was I supposed to do? The world was flapping around me. I felt like laughing—this was not happening, or, if it was, why did I feel such relief mixed with pain? Why were the tears on my cheeks so pleasurable? "This is a hell of an awkward time," was all I could manage.

"Would there ever be a better time? Remember, you brought this on. And, in a way, I'm doing it to protect you too."

"Protect me from whom?"

"Our parents, for one," she said. "Did I not just say my father went through the roof? He told me the next time wouldn't be just a beating." Now she was whispering and we were alone.

"He beat you?" I said.

"He wasn't talking about me. And he said that your father's friend couldn't help you, either. I don't know what he was talking about. Do you? Oh, stop crying Trevor, please. Mary Annie wouldn't like it. I don't like it."

I was shaking now. I saw people in the distance—I felt their presence more than saw them. But I'm alone, I thought.

"I know what they are both capable of, dear heart," June said. "When they want something done, they have little compunction ... "

"What do you mean?"

"They were famous tough guys, our fathers, before the war. They were all for keeping the Negroes and the Mexicans on the east side and quiet. It was their job, their beat, so to speak. The street called Indio Muerto? People there say it ought to be Westin Street."

"Oh come on," I said. "My father was not like that ... "

Although at that point, I wasn't so sure.

"People are coming, Trevor. Here," she said, handing me a handkerchief with a little starfish embroidered in its corner. "Blow," she said.

"I'm not a child."

June looked at me. She blurted her fondest regrets as another crowd gathered within eyeshot. When they walked away, she went back to the old June. "Our parents are here. Don't let them see you, looking like this," she said, flicking at my coat of ivy. "We're all going out on the *Haida*; jeeps are coming to get us. Don't come with us, please." She looked away.

June looked back at me. "Parents and children," she said. "It has to be over, what we have. Agreed?"

I had no answer for what she was asking and knew no answer would do. "Good-bye," I said, suddenly noble, thinking of my ride home on the waiting sailboat. "The *Haida*, really?"

"Well," she laughed a little. "It's actually the *Haida IV*. The original was scrapped a long time ago."

"He bought it for his dad."

She sighed. "He thinks it is history."

"Which he?"

"Which history? See there, you've stopped crying. Let's go inside and wash your face and get rid of this stuff that's covering you. Why are your pupils so large, Trevor?"

The ranch house was real adobe, not faked-up like the chapel in the courtyard. Inside, the house was cool, in a way that implied subterranean depths. It held onto haunting smells—straw, cooking oil, old leather—the way a miser holds pennies in a weathered purse, lovingly tight. The halos around all the objects were firm. Sounds shifted back and forth, and a thrill of energy passed down my spine and back up again. I washed my face, pulled off the ivy, and joy passed into me. Maybe it came from the walls. I thought about the woman on an island waking every day to the new light, alone, free from any west or east, with time enough to take it all in. I asked June about the man who had told the story.

"Tompkins," she said. "Colorful old cowboy writer who's found himself some history. What is his nickname? Shotgun?"

"Two Guns," I said, getting it. Suddenly, the story of the woman who lived alone for seventeen years was shining in the core of my mind. I was happy to discover there *was* a fugging core to my mind. June had broken my heart, but I was never happier. Would I ever see her again, I asked? She said, maybe, we'll see. I almost hoped not. She asked how I would get back home.

"The United States Government protects me."

Outside, we ran into Storke, who was seeking "the amenities," as my mother used to say. I was free of my parents too. Storke looked confused, seeing me with June. I told him I wanted to do a profile of the writer I had just heard in the chapel. "That Two Guns sure makes the past come to life, doesn't he?" he asked. "History better than fiction. Tell me something. Did either of you see all the smoke on the ocean today? My father told me there were dormant volcanoes at the Rincon and in Miss Chase's Hope Ranch. Wonder if I could get a reporter on that?" He looked at me.

"Nice to see you again, sir," I said.

"Good-bye, son," he said.

Chapter 58

"No. We belong together. Come with me," said Patrick to Eve Marie as the water in the room continued to rise. Past pleading now, he stood in front of her and said, "I can protect you. I can't live without you."

Something stirred in Eve Marie. "You know what it would be like for me in your world?" she asked. "Of course you do. You must. I would live there as you have here."

He started to protest and she put her long fingers on his lips. "Imagine the doctors wanting to examine me. And what would they assume about us. I would seem freakish, and you worse for loving me," she said. "That's why you came after me."

Love, he thought. Not so long ago she called it a quaint idea. Now it seemed an obsession with her.

Another crash outside and more water surged over the threshold. Eve Marie turned her back to Patrick, and stared at the wall. He didn't know what to do. He couldn't physically pick her up and carry her; he was too weak. That left only one alternative: stay here and die with her and for her. If he could die; if she could die. The Elayawun machine that killed him was one thing, but how would he die here? Crushed or drowned or maybe electrocuted. He didn't know.

Then, in a vision, he saw himself escaping, leaving the city in the craft, surviving. Dooley, he thought. The castle in the waves soon would be nothing, dead forever.

Outside the room, a much larger sheet of gray water swelled and pushed the door off its hinges. In that moment Patrick made up his mind. Eve Marie gasped—she could read him again. He touched her and said he would do anything she wanted except die when survival was at hand. She stood up and said, "I was wrong. It was only a word."

He took a step back and turned from his Elayawun lover. And then he was gone.

Cold water splashed up as he ran. He moved fast. Above him he saw the dome's girders displaced and dangling at strange and ominous angles. There was chaos in the streets. The ocean poured down through cracks and pushed him on. He thought about her parting words. Had she said she loved him? Maybe she couldn't, he thought. Maybe the Elayawun can't.

Patrick reached the cave entrance stumbling as the ground shook in rolling waves again and another wall of water bloomed salty and cold nearby. He took one last look as he darted into the cave and stumbled down the stairs. Hurt, stunned, and barely breathing, he crossed the debris-strewn strand and saw the craft bobbing in the lagoon. Dooley stood in the open hatch, motioning Patrick to hurry on board. He was wrestling with the hatch and his hands were bleeding.

"Where are the acolytes?" Patrick said. Dooley was struggling to stand and fell to one knee. Patrick rushed to help him and noticed a lot of blood on the floor.

"They were pleased to think life was almost over and left the cave to experience it," said Dooley. "Hurry, we have to get out of here."

Rocks began to fall into the water as the hatch, uncooperative at first, snapped shut over them and the two men swung into their seats. With headlights glowing the craft took off on its own, rushing through a long tunnel crusted with life and festooned with treasures washed though the salt veins of the earth. They could see round-bellied ingots, right-angled bars, and wire-wrapped pipes. A sudden lurch from behind pushed them forward. Dooley stood up and then fell. Patrick tried to help him into his chair but the old man waved him away.

"How did it happen?" asked Patrick. "Was it the sand?"

"Some say it was you who brought Leemoo down," said Dooley. "A riot broke out after you were killed. Your body disappeared. The merpeople disappeared too and some thought they were helping you, or vice versa. Maybe it was sabotage. Did you do it?"

Dooley, out of breath, continued. "Officially, the council claimed it was the weight of shifting sands along with a seismic disturbance. Thus it had nothing to do with either you or the merpeople."

Dooley coughed, hard. The craft caromed off the cave's wall and his head hit the control panel. He passed out as the ship burst from the tunnel, crossing first through black liquid—oil perhaps, or sewage— and then into the dark blue of the open sea. Cold radiated into the coach and the craft began spinning wildly as Patrick attempted to take control. Below him, he could see the dome's orange and yellow glow and then a blast of red as it crumbled.

The light exploded up and then went out. If there were voices now he could not hear them—he waited for psychic signals from Eve Marie but they never came. A swirling current sucked the craft forward and then backward. Dooley hit his head again and moaned. The console was blinking like madness as they sailed away from the ruins of the ancient city.

Patrick wanted to turn back. He wanted to feel something beyond mere relief at his escape, but there was nothing. He found what looked like a steering rudder, but he couldn't get the craft under control. Up they went and down; through the willowy edges of the kelp forest and soon they arrived at the bottom of the sea.

Dooley woke and sat up straight, a trickle of blood had formed at the corner of his mouth. "I don't think I will make it," he said as he looked out at the kelp. "It can grow ten inches a day and has bulbs filled with gas the plant itself produces," he said. "I wonder if Charles Darwin knew that. It is the science of wonder." Then Dooley passed into dreams again.

Outside, on the seafloor, Patrick could see living stars. They were golden and sickly white and radar orange. He watched them move the same way he watched clouds flow. Stop and the world swims around you, he thought. Time moves to the still man's advantage.

He saw abalone, thousands, red and black. There were lobsters and spiny urchins. He gazed at rocks encrusted with life, horned, wavering, and tipped with poisons too infinitesimal to wound humans but deadly to small fry and spawn. The shadows spun as the light danced down. It reminded him of early Mass when sunlight first found the colored rose glass of Our Lady of Sorrows. He wondered if the moon was ever visible down here.

The ship rose where sharks, barracuda, and rays swam. Nearer the surface sea lions and the few otters left after hundreds of years of pelt hunts played. Between the kelp sheets, he saw something move, a flash of white flesh. Swordfish. They looked nothing like Elayawun, not even merpeople. He wondered at his father's naming of the race that now wandered without a home. His memory was tangling now like the kelp.

The craft took off again. Patrick hoped it was heading toward the coast. They passed over a vast canyon, and then the craft traveled across a stretch of what felt like shallower waters without plant life, only white sand below. In the distance, an underwater tower reached high, rising in concentric circles, sunlight corkscrewing down towards the spire, a small volcano from which leaked black oil.

The current moved the craft towards the tower, the proud tower crowned with a shaft of light. Near the top of the rock, Patrick's eyes caught reflected light from a bed full of flowers, though the blooms were precious stones. On a branch of lapis sat red agate and yellow chrysolite surrounded by white carnelian, amethyst, and yellow serpentine bright as an imaginary summer. He saw his face reflected back a thousand times in the edges and bevels of the stones. He thought about love and what was lost.

As the craft moved away from the garden of precious stones, Dooley groaned out of his slumber and saw the expression on Patrick's face. "What did you see?" the old man asked.

Patrick told him about the branch of stones.

"Aha, a vision: not the pure light of the void but the intensification of light refracted through a prism. They were right, you know."

"Who?"

"The Elayawun." He coughed. "You killed them. Your need of constant change killed them." Dooley slumped as the lights on the console died.

They drifted into another kelp forest and then into an immense clearing. From far away, Patrick saw the Leviathan. Like a sunfish hanging walleyed and still: a monster. It wasn't a whale, though blues and even killers frequented this channel. As it grew closer Patrick saw a red star on its side. The sun was wan and wintry above, filtering down all these leagues. The sailors inside could not see him, and he had no radio. They might crash into him. Yet the submarine was the most beautiful thing he had ever seen. Blue-gray steel walls curved up. The distances from top to bottom and front to stern were enormous. Awe, he realized, even when it comes close to doom, is a type of grace. Patrick was in love with the blind and death-bearing ship. Everything he knew was a shadow burned onto a fly-apart wall.

The craft bobbed away from the sub like a Japanese globe and drifted toward the city made of time. Just outside the winter harbor it broke the surface. The hatch popped open and Dooley struggled to stand straight, but slipped. Water came rushing in, and the old man floated out and disappeared. Patrick followed him out, water sponging his clothes as he dove down and down after Dooley. But he was gone. Exhausted, Patrick surfaced and dog-paddled toward the rocks. A wave picked him up, smashed him into the seawall, and covered him with seaweed.

The lights of Leemoo were gone, the lights on the craft's console had gone out as it sank under the weight of the water it had taken on, and Patrick could feel himself going too. This time, he knew, he could never come back. Only echoes were left, the wakes we create with words. Though the sea was full of graceful life, the cold stone was better. Here, chilled by its nightlong association with the waves and the daylong sun yet to dry and bake its smooth surfaces, was the wall that stands impossibly straight against the jagged lines of advancing tides: willful, human, against ragged surges of that cold element of constant vicissitude.

People came later with a sail, and wrapped it around him. A man with a giant Brownie took pictures. Death looks gigantically down.

Chapter 59

STUBBED MY TOE ON the table leaping up from the armchair. Samuel Johnson, I thought. I refute him thus, I thought, reality is real. I spent the night in a chair again, the boob tube still on, an image of an Indian in a circle like the crosshairs of a rifle's scope, electronic hum, and then ring, ring, ring, the phone again.

It was my photographer from the newspaper. "You all set for today?" he asked. "For Frank Lloyd Wright?"

"Today," I said. The Indian on the screen turned into Howdy Doody time. Princess Summerfall Winterspring.

"Are you watching television?" he asked. "A kiddie show? You got kids?"

"The famed architect will tour until 1:00 p.m. and then address the crowd. After he speaks, I get an interview." I was reading from my notes.

"He has a foul mouth somebody told me," said the lensman. "Where's the interview?"

"Maybe inside the El Paseo, the world-famous Street in Spain."

"Corner of fake and phony avenues," said Mr. Cynic.

The famous architect would talk to me; the famous Miss Pearl Chase, who had built the famous fake phony street, had promised. I got a letter to that effect from her office, when I came back from the island outing minus one cousin lover.

I would walk down Santa Barbara to De La Guerra where the famous architect would give a speech after he toured the remodeled downtown, red-tile and white-stucco wonderland. The phone rang again.

"Hi, honey," she said.

"Aren't we forward," I said.

"Get used to it. When did you get back? Did you see her?" asked Mary Annie.

"I'm not sure."

"What happened to the frog's legs? I distinctly heard you offer so long ago."

I was happy to hear that. It sounded fun. I was on my own, after all.

"Well?" she asked.

"I gotta go interview the man with three names. The master builder. Are you going?"

"Of course, but that's not till two or something, daddy-o. A girl has to have lunch."

"Breakfast for me," I said.

"Must be nice," she said. "Meet me at Las Ondas Café."

"I've never been there."

"It's on Castillo next to the Knights of Columbus."

"What's wrong with the Copper Coffee Pot?" I asked.

"Even though they have no frogs legs, it's CCP in an hour."

"I'll treat."

"Of course you will."

Coming out of my apartment and walking, I thought about buying a little house. Maybe by the beach, over in the Burton Mound neighborhood, near Sunseri's and the harbor and the ocean breezes, near the miniature golf course, and the pony rides and the guy who parks his pinwheel-festooned truck to sell hot dogs on the weekend. And then I will become a writer like I promised myself so many years ago. I will walk on the beach daily; leave footprints in sand.

The road I live on tumbles down from the Old Mission like a concrete stream, pouring from a tourist source where the Indians are buried, to the lanes of commerce below. Every Sunday, big yellow buses roll up to this once-cloistered environs and Bermuda-short squads debouch on the long, wide porch near the terraced stairs. Below, a rose garden blooms even in winter in this unnatural land. Above all arch the white clouds, though it never rains and when it does we always call it a storm. There was never much water here, and we dream of rain constantly. Everywhere else, people dream of our weather—oh, the dullness of paradise.

The Mission Hill stones in winter's magnifying air stand out brightly each from the next. Nothing actually touches, say physicists. You could see the town was changing, anyone could. But into what? Maybe the old guard would die off clean. Ford wagons and Chevrolet coupes replaced streetcars, which rolled over surreys not that long ago. Maybe we were becoming Los Angeles, more famous now for smog than jeweled movie-star dreams. Maybe our Fiesta pretensions will forestall the sprawl for a spell, or maybe Uncle Dick will build tract homes until all the cities touch. Nothing actually touches.

Past Our Lady of Sorrows I thought about another book. Forget June and this *Neverknownagain*. I felt happily nerve-wracked thinking about the new idea. Revving. The CIA guy's drugs got me closer to the feeling I had lost on Santa Monica Beach, the rapture. More little pills were in my desk drawer, maybe forty-nine raptures left.

Our Lady of Sorrows' doors stood open and parishioners were rolling out happier than when they went in: *ite, missa est*. Thanks be. The end really comes.

I walked down to State & A and looked at magazines. The five-and-ten store across from the museum smelled like popcorn. I don't think I had ever been in there. You could see nice round fountain chairs, a drugstore lunching place. Imagination fills in the rest. Past the State Theater, a block to the Copper Coffee Pot, where the old began to congregate. The couples: tall, silvered men leaning over their shuffling wives always too richly perfumed. This was their town. The tourists came and went in waves, momentarily important. But the old, they remained and made every block both dignified and unnavigable if, for some crazy reason, you needed to move around in a hurry.

I waited at the light with four cigarettes surrounding me. The wind came down past the Carrillo Hotel, from whence these aged issued forth on doddering leather steps.

At an outdoor CCP table was the smartest couple I knew, the Stiffenbaums, Audrie and Peter. He was a psychologist with a matted Van Gogh beard. I stopped to visit. "Did you watch Jack Paar last night, darling," said Audrie in her Gabor-sister voice. "He's such a card, really."

"Paar's not too bad," seconded Peter. "Aldous was on talking about working in Hollywood, for Disney."

"Did he mention me?" I asked. They said, no, why? So much for fame you win writing words.

"Talked about magic mushrooms, Simple Simon, or whatever. On American television. And this other thing, the speech he's giving at this joint called UC Santa Barbara. Ever heard of it?"

"I think Pearlie invented it," I said.

"Miss Pearl Chase," he said, "and hark the angels sing. What was that book about drugs he wrote?"

"*The Doors of Perception*," someone near said. I turned around and there was Mary Annie. I reached out my hand, drew her in, and introduced the Stiffenbaums. They were charmed and they were charming, but everybody could see something was troubling her. She paused and pooh-poohed their concerns.

"Just hurried over here, a little winded," she said. I knew it wasn't true.

"Not Simple Simon, psilocybin," said Audrie. "He claimed that the drug was being studied to induce schizophrenia, which was preposterous, and Paar laughed like he agreed."

"Why is it so silly—it's surely not normal to hallucinate. I would take it as a pretty convincing omen of my own incipient madness," I said, joking about my own nutso life with all available private ironies.

"Everybody's crazy. I think Freud says that somewhere," said Peter.

"Oh my God, Sigmund's ubiquitous," replied his wife.

"And that, children, was our Daily Vocabulary Builder. Do you know the difference between a neurotic, a psychotic, and a psychiatrist?" the doc asked. "Maybe you've heard this one, but let me tell it."

"You must," wife replied.

"A neurotic builds castles in the clouds. A psychotic lives in them."

"And you dear? Renowned shrink?" asked proud Audrie.

"The psychiatrist collects the rent," said Mary Annie inducing widespread waves of groan.

"You have heard it."

"I blocked it out. Whatyoucall, repressed it," she said, my sharp lass.

There was nowhere else to ride this merriment so I begged us off and inside to get coffee and push trays past the same gray sausages and buttercup-yellow scrambled eggs. Inside, more of the aged were rocking to patterns that ran through the atmosphere. We got coffee from the big brass samovar, the copper coffee pot. Or whatever it really was.

"Nice people," she said. "Was he your ..." she stumbled over the word.

"No. My psychoanalyst lives up San Marcos Pass in the valley somewhere. He's very famous. There's no need to be embarrassed. I'm not. I had a breakdown in college; I always blame it on the hoopla around my book. Probably I would've been on Jack Paar if he had had a show back then. It was a lot of pressure for a boy."

She looked away.

"What is it?"

"Oh, Trevor, something awful happened just now."

I knew it.

"I was walking down State Street and I got to the Woolworth's."

"I was just there," I said.

"I saw the mayor coming out the door. He looked right at me, I swear, and then his eyes started to roll up and he made a funny noise … "

"A funny noise?"

"And then he just staggered forward. At first I thought it was some kind of joke, but he fell toward me, and I almost caught him."

"He fainted."

"I don't think so. Somebody who knew mouth-to-mouth took over. I waited a few, but then I felt beside the point."

Just then Audrie and Peter came in the door. "Did you hear the news?"

Mary Annie held my hand in a peculiar way that made me shut up while the people all around me were exclaiming the surprising fact out loud. Some just shook their heads offering the banalities of mystification and denial. I can't believe it, they said.

"It's true," said Barney, this young *News-Suppress* reporter I knew, who had just walked in. "I was there." He said hello to me and looked hard at Mary Annie. "The Mayor's dead. She was there too." Someone asked why he wasn't covering it. "I called the desk. They've got someone from the city desk on it. I'm here to interview the great architect. The one with three names: Shadrach Meshach Abednego. What are you doing?" he asked me.

"Same as you," I said. But I couldn't remember why I was even working for Storke. My thoughts skidded back to death. Mary Annie was tight-lipped. "How come you guys didn't cover Snake Jake?" I asked.

"It was declared an accident. We had a photographer out there, you know."

It felt good—this question at that moment: "So why didn't somebody write about it? Accidents are news too."

"The holes were not bullet holes. And there were no bullets. That's what the police said. It might've been fish. Probably those news guys were too stretched thin." He was scrambling for plausibility. Why?

"I've got an exclusive with Frank Lloyd Wright," I said. "After he gives a speech, I'm going to have Miss Pearl Chase conduct me over to some cozy little bar for a talk."

"How nice for you."

"You could follow and I could pass him off to you. Best man wins."

"Shit," he said. Mary Annie was looking a little disturbed, not impatient but as if she had more important things to think about than this moronic journalism dribble. "All right," said Barney. "I'll tell you why the smokescreen around Brown. Between us and never repeat: Storke doesn't like the kinds of stories that leave people low."

"Oh come on, what about the mother who had her son's wife, that nurse, killed?" It was a lurid tale splashed across the front page two days ago. That nurse was Marie.

"Everybody loves that gruesome stuff. I mean stories that don't have much sense to them: bad luck and misfortune. Storke cherry-picks, anyway; some he has to cover, but he doesn't like to smudge this city up, this city he built."

"So much for integrity," said Mary Annie.

"They call it the *News-Suppress*," Barney said. "You know that."

"So," I said, "it's not like it didn't happen."

"No, it isn't. We just ignored it."

Brown, the mayor—I wondered if death would go away if we just stopped talking about it. Of course, nobody did talk about it, really.

"You gonna pass him off to me?" asked Barney. "Storke said you wanted to work for us. The city desk gave me the assignment; who assigned you?"

I grunted something and took Mary Annie by the arm away from Barney. She was looking green around the gills; though once we made the chill air outside she turned to me and latched on with both arms.

"Do you believe in heaven?" she asked.

"Of course not," I said. "But this is supposed to be paradise."

State Street had been empty below the Coffee Pot and the stores were closed for Sunday, but now it was beginning to stir to life the closer we got to Miss Chase's El Paseo folderol.

"All of these people believe in eternal bliss," she said.

"They have to or they would go crazy. Like I did."

"Oh come on, it's the one fact everybody has to face, death, and not everybody's crazy. Not like you. The one real trauma is realizing you will die; the rest of our life shocks are only echoes of it."

I laughed. She didn't.

"I think about the mayor now, but he can't think of me. I was the last person he saw for all eternity and that was probably puzzling. But he doesn't think anymore. And he'll never figure it out."

"Some people would say he's beyond all that."

Now she laughed. "Think about it, and then you can't. You try to imagine a state in which being beyond your own life makes sense.

It's nothing, but even then you think about yourself thinking nothing. Nothing ever existed from your nothing point of view. I spent the last five minutes while you were talking to that beady-eyed kid trying to think about not being able to think. It's not sleep if there isn't any dream, not to mention any morning."

"What about the parts of the dreams we have that we forget? Last night's dream you already forgot."

Mary Annie tilted her head. "What did you mean just now when you said people would go crazy like you did? Are you saying that the sure knowledge of dying was what caused your breakdown?"

"The part of the dream you try to remember but the phone rings and you never get back to it. Lost. Maybe some crucial bit of self-understanding, some clue. Dead. Like a whole life gone forever. That's what death is all about, I realized."

"You worried about that when you were fourteen?"

"Yeah. Later too. I had a conversation with Clifton Fadiman after he interviewed me in New York. End of the tour, under gray skies. He liked me. He had a cousin who was a math prodigy. He liked children's books too. *Neverknown* was a daydream about immortality, he said, and he admired that, even if it was hopeless. He was afraid to die, the famous intellectual."

"That drove you crazy?" said Mary Annie.

"Thinking about it at college where I was a nobody again, after my fame was gone. Maybe crazy's too strong a word. I wanted to know that what I did would matter. But I was already over. We're already dead, if our lives go nowhere."

She looked at me. "It's a sure bet the mayor's dead."

We heard music coming from El Paseo. A big crowd was there so I showed my ratty press card from the *Times* and the seas parted. I got up behind the big grandstand acoss from the little one where the guest of honor himself was seated. I saw Pearl Chase and, in the center of my vision, I saw her. I saw my cousin. More beautiful than ever, she had her ear inclined to an old man who, I suddenly realized, was the architect. Her head came up laughing. Her hair fell back, her arm rested softly on his, but her eyes caught mine and my fate was obvious and undeniable. She smiled. I felt my face redden.

"Told you she would be here," said Mary Annie, looking around. I walked up to an older man standing in the way of ingress. He started to gruffly push me back.

"I'm here from the newspaper," I said. "The *Times*. I mean the *News-Press*." He looked confused, and I was too but one of Pearl's Girls smiled, held up a halting hand, and went off to report it to Miss Dibbs herself. Then primly returned.

"I knew your father," my new friend said, adding that Miss Chase was on her way. I nodded.

Pearl came over, and hissed like a goose. "I'll take care of you, but you have to take care of me."

"What does that mean exactly?"

She outlined the plan in between "The Stars and Stripes Forever," a mariachi band, and a girls' chorus from Our Lady of Sorrows. Bunting flapped above the timid old, the cranky children, and their starchy mothers: the nearly deads and the newlyweds. Another fog rolled up from the harbor, I could see it piling over the *News-Press* office.

"He'll talk to you after his speech, we'll run him over to the restaurant where the reporters go to drink," she said. I relayed the message to Barney who wandered by in the muffling crowd, but he didn't seem at all interested. I never saw the photographer. Barney was staring at June. She swept her honey hair back behind her ear and she let out a sharp peal of laughter, somewhat angelic and a bit deranged, still talking to Wright. He was blushing, the old artificer, and who could blame him? He had June at his ear. And then she turned, looked me full in the eyes, and blew a kiss. The architect turned around with some difficulty to see who the lucky man was. She pointed me out and he waved. He'll like me now.

"Who is that?" asked Barney.

I let him hang and sidled up to the edge of a bleacher, a little higher than my waist, and I pulled Mary Annie up. She squealed. Apparently she had lost the sorrows of a few minutes back. Either the town had not learned about the mayor, or they were already over him. The old gatekeeping goat kept looking at me, confusing youth with chicanery. Santa Barbarians were at his gate. I saw the doctor from the hospital, and even Huxley and Stuurman, I thought. I saw Father Virgil with Monsignor Twobaduddy of Dolores, Our Lady of Sorrows. The architect sat alone now, shooing off anyone who approached him.

The speechifying began after a wordy invocation from the pastor of Trinity Church, the rock edifice where Rock Hudson had married a couple of romantic moons or years ago. Miss Chase spoke of the many people who saw the future of Santa Barbara firmly founded in this vision of Golden Past. At length she introduced the architect, who looked disgusted, Pearls before swine. And after long waves of applause, he got up with his stabbing cane, took the podium, coughed, and looked around. "Congratulations," he said and paused for effect. "You've managed to preserve a form of architecture that never existed."

He then turned around and walked away. The crowd applauded for a second or two and Miss Chase said, "Well I never." And we looked at each other, Mary Annie and me. I asked her if she'd dine with me later at the Talk of the Town. She said sure, if snails were involved. I said fish eggs, too.

"I better follow him," I said. "Meet me in the plaza in about an hour."

There he was, I could see him. And there was someone else, unexpected, trailing seaweed. The crowd parted right and left. He gestured, I would see him later too. And Pearl. I started walking into the hallway at the Paseo Restaurant, which was decked out in a marine theme, as an underwater city. Perfectly round mirrors, suggesting bubbles, dotted the hallway giving back my image following the crone who would set me up in conversation. I was positive the interview with Wright wasn't happening, but I knew there was much to talk about with Pearl.

She turned around in the darkened light and looked ghastly. "Walk this way," she said, suddenly veering right and crossing two courtyards, pulling me down an alley of adobe behind the crowds. "My other office," she said. Before the door, she turned to me and said, "You should go back to your underwater city, Trevor. I mean writing it."

I looked at her. "I already have."

"Oh, excellent," she said, pushing open the door into a truly historical hacienda house, the De La Guerra adobe, cobwebbed, musty, and piled with what looked like civic records. The walls of her part of the building were covered with corkboard pinned with documents. "Just think," she said. "They want to divide this old historical shell into tourist shops. This white elephant will do somebody good."

Pearl looked around; her teeth in the half-light looked long and sharpened. "How far along are you? The sequel."

"First draft: good. I destroyed the city, forever."

"Oh, no, no, no. Don't you understand how much attention that book brought us? People putting around the harbor looking for, what was the name of the city?"

"Neverknown."

"A fourteen-year-old boy finds a passage to an underwater city. And with his Yankee ingenuity preserves the inhabitants against their enemies, the communistic, unfeeling sea creatures."

"People. Sea people. I had no idea what my story was about," I said, though I had always realized some people thought they knew. "I always thought my book was about Patrick."

She ignored this. Meanwhile she searched the dimly lit room, knocked on the lavatory door, and seemed flustered that nobody was there. "Stay here," she said. "Wright's an old man and probably wandering. I'll return. I shall return."

Fat chance, I thought. The old architect dropped his pants outside and now, if he had any sense, he'd be cruising through Ventura on his way back to Hollywood or wherever architects commingle. I got bored quick. I looked on the corkboard, and stuck there was some kind of prospectus concerning the goddamned Undersea Gardens I had been asked to underwrite long ago. Now the dream was real, or about to be. The amusement consisted of two chambers, one floating, one sunk on the ocean floor. The floating chamber was tied to a dock and had all kinds of marine décor. Between the two was a winding stair, encased in waterproof something. The submerged room below had picture windows that look onto the seafloor.

I went over to Pearl's desk and sat down on the rolly chair and slid back and forth. I put my hands flat and there was dust, thick. It didn't add up. I saw the stack of mail on the desk and all of it was addressed to Jacques Brown. Shit. I picked up a letter, some kind of bill and what you call junk mail. I picked up another, advertising *Boys' Life,* a Scout magazine.

Pearl came back in and I threw down the letters. She was fuming. "He's gone, disappeared, can you imagine? After all the trouble my girls went through to get him here. I knew this would be a disaster. So much for your interview."

"In a way, I really don't care. But I can't imagine how you could imagine it otherwise. He fled. He's from the real world. We must seem simple to him. Speaking of which: What is this building?"

"This musty place." She was lost in blinkered dreams.

"Yeah, well, I can't help but notice the digs are not up to your usual. Whose office is this?" I said handing her the envelopes. "Or was this."

Her answer was pat enough to seem rehearsed. "You must understand, Trevor, child. It was horribly stupid bad luck that you were out on the breakwater that night." She picked up some of the letters and held them with surprising tenderness. "He would be forgotten by now."

"Just so I know: The people who know about me knowing about Jacques Brown aren't interested in killing me?"

"What a thing to say."

"In other words, you're not interested in killing me."

"Nonsense," she started rambling. "By the way, the *News-Press* got it right, Trevor. It was an accident. We just didn't want attention drawn. He was doing underwater electric welding work, quietly, getting the older moorings ready, the harbor ready, for its wonderful eye on the world beneath our world." She pointed to the drawings. The fugging Undersea Gardens.

"Wait. You're saying Brown's death was an accident. And that's all you are covering up, either because you have no permission for this project, or because you wanted to wait and surprise everybody? Well? Which is it?"

"Both," she said drily.

"Pearl's gift to delight the people and keep the smelly fishermen away."

"I won't have another Monterey here."

"And the wounds of Jesus?"

"The electric arc ran through his limbs and burned the holes. I think. I'm going to call it Neverknown by the way, this sea garden."

"I'll sue you if you try."

"Bother. I said I would take care of you and I will. You're right. I didn't ever think Mr. Frank Lloyd Wright would show. I wanted you to see things apart from the crowd, to hear me out. You caught on. You impressed the other people who don't want attention either. Not just me: other investors—your uncle for instance. But you were too connected to just brush away. Beating you up didn't work. Again, your uncle, but that seemed personal, his daughter or something. I don't know, I'm sure. I wasn't for that; I suggested keeping you silent by rewarding your Westin ambition. So I pulled one big string with Storke to get you a job.

"And now here's what I propose. No, insist. You shut up and leave Brown alone. And you don't mention the presidio, ever. In return, you get your job with Storke. He's hopping mad, but he'll do it. Also, we will forget the mad scene out on the island. Your mother wants you back in the hospital, you know. They were there at the book signing. I protected them. I already have kept them from committing you."

"You protected them? They're the ones I fear. Uncle Frankie said my father was afraid he could contract my schizophrenia, somehow backwards. But Frankie was wrong. It's my money my father wants to inherit backwards. If I'm just crazy they won't get it. If I die, then fine."

"When did you talk to Frankie, child? He's been in the hospital since the barbecue."

I looked at her and squared my shoulders. It was a dream I remembered, the dream about seeing Frankie in the alley outside Jimmy's. I was lost at the bottom of my own ocean.

"I want a new life," I said. "I don't care about your stupid presidio, either. You can make the whole town a colonial mausoleum. What do I care?"

"You were such a disappointment to us," she said.

"I'm sorry. Nothing is this important. It's all better forgotten."

"Maybe," she said, her cold heart on display. Then some automaton voice kicked in: "No. It's better to keep the past alive, the values and the beauty. It's how we go on together. I was taught all of that is important—transcendent." She picked up her purse. Snapped it open and looked into the darkness there. She snapped it shut. "It really was just an accident. Brown, who I liked very much, died a random death."

But it wasn't enough; my whole mind told me so. It wasn't enough to find absurdity at the end of an absurd quest.

"I have to leave," said Miss Pearl. "But go see Storke on Monday like you own the place." She breathed in, held for three seconds, exhaled, and left.

June was there in her place.

In the darkness she stood. Maybe the rooms were dark. I was flabbergasted but she looked annoyed.

"Where is she?" she asked, a bit icy considering the circumstances. The darkness helped her obscure cause.

"She just walked out. You must have seen her swinging her purse like a weapon."

"Not Pearl. Her. I knew it would be her you latched onto. I knew I couldn't trust either of you."

"What are you talking about? Refresh my memory, please. You broke up with me."

"Don't be tiny, Trevor. You were never small before." I thought about Gin Chow and wondered if I would ever see him again, any size.

"She always asked about you. Did you wait an hour or was it even before? Oh, I don't want to know. Maybe it's all for the best."

"You broke up with me," I murmured, now more out of my depth than ever, leaning back against Jacques Brown's workbench.

"It was a show, you knew that. And you were great."

"What?"

"You played the part perfectly and now no one suspects—at least no one suspects me. And that's enough. We needed to let everyone know, it was over for all time. My parents. The opportunity couldn't have been better. Still, I almost wish you hadn't gone out there. Especially drunk or whatever you were. But you were great."

"At what? The breakup was a show?"

"Satisfied about Mr. Brown now? I told you he didn't matter."

"His death," I said, grasping for an anchor in reality. "It was all a stupid accident. I don't want to believe it."

"You can't believe it because you are a writer," she said. "Anyway, it's all for the better. Nobody can know about this, honey. Us. We can't change, I know that. But we can't survive in the open either. Even you know that. It's not just my father. We've been careless. What would happen? I want to have children someday. And we can't."

"You mean, you'll have children with mister liquor distributor?"

"God, I don't know. With someone. There's a lot of time. Don't smirk at me, Trevor. What did I tell you about us?"

"This can never end." I thought about time and seeing the future. "You will get married, maybe to the rich Italian. And she's in love with me. Mary Annie is."

"Of course she is. Writer. Rich boy. You're very handsome too. By the way, I found a place we can go," she said. "It's on the ocean in Big Sur; and there are hot springs."

"You would meet me there?" I asked.

"Already made reservations. Next Wednesday."

"There's lots of time. No need to rush things."

"Listen to you, all patience." Then the kiss I didn't expect and it lasted forever. I thought about snapdragons so long ago.

"I have to go now," I said.

"Don't keep Mary Annie waiting. I do wish it wasn't her, but I'll have to learn to live in the new world brave. By the way, she told me about the pills. Can you bring whatever it is you took? I want to try one. To see the future. Isn't that what you told her? This way it will work out for us. Maybe someday the world will change and all these prejudices will melt away. We can shake off our parents and this pretense. But I need you now, and soon."

I nodded. She swayed away, and I picked up some of Brown's papers to use as a calling card in the unknown future. I was surprised the girls had shared pillow talk— the pills, Delysid. By this point, I supposed anything was possible. I wondered if the world my parents lived through could just disappear. And then our world next.

I stumbled into the plaza and there was Mary Annie. She and I would soon be eating in the most beautiful restaurant, awaiting us with linen, silver, and finger bowls: last links to that fading world. I would celebrate my new job. I'd order crow and toast my departed soul.

We ran into the beatnik boy Van Cortlandt, or maybe it was Petey Pepitone. He said, "What's up, daddy-o. Haven't seen you so long, I thought you were splitsville."

I said, no, I went to the islands for a time but now I've returned.

"Back from the dead," he said.

"Never gonna happen," I answered.

"You solved your mystery?" he asked.

I nodded. The official explanation I told him was called the Undersea Gardens. And he agreed that was stupid because it added up too well and it wasn't amazing. It made me feel let down, like after the psilocybin had worn off—I wanted to keep it all alive but couldn't.

Van Cortlandt and I talked and decided, laughing, that the underwater accident just didn't hold water. We tried this instead: The killer rowed up in a boat, rope trailing the corpse, tied through hand and feet holes in case the Coast Guard came and he could cut the load and his losses. The body would sink to the channel floor to roll around with holdfasts and urchins and the plentiful abalones. But then we thought, maybe the men on platform Hazel had found Mr. Brown, a diver for divers' pleasure; his body tangled in fishnet under their rig. Or perhaps the Knights had needed to get rid of Brown's corpse; his stigmatized body a temple of the Lord cast from their den of iniquities. Or maybe Brown was my brother, preserved all those years by cold currents. It was he who sang folk songs through my radio: turn, turn from the wind and the waves. Or, last, the sea people had hit on the genius plan of dropping his body on the mainland, because, they reasoned, the police wouldn't have a clue and the newspaper, well known for swallowing controversies whole, would whitewash the incident. The Elayawun slung his body onto the rocks and pierced his side and fog billowed.

"Some good theories. Maybe not the last one," said Van Cortlandt.

"Who is that?" asked Mary Annie, hushing us, pointing deep into the plaza.

There he was in the middle of the plaza, still dripping seawater.

"You can see him too?" I asked.

"Of course. Go talk to him. He wants you to."

I wandered over to Dooley, cold as the deep seas and seaweed-draped. He said Gin Chow was gone but his new name would be Jack Powers who ran the Hounds Gang. He laughed. Chinatown is doomed; he knew the presidio plan and had already told the Tongs about the city fathers who would condemn the neighborhood and close the temples and the joss houses and the little store where the man took a bite out of quarters that you handed him. Someday a loud family would become stupidly famous. Miss Pearl Chase would tear down this land,